A KIS

MIDNIGHT

Forbidden SERIES

Book One

Annotated

MELODY ANNE

Printed and published in the United States of America.

Published by Falling Star Publications

Editing by Karen Lawson and Janet Hitchcock

DEDICATION

This is dedicated to my Aunt Janet. I lost her this year, making my heart bleed. This world is much smaller with her gone. I look forward to seeing her again on the other side of the veil.

NOTE FROM THE AUTHOR

I originally wrote the Forbidden Series early in my career. I've changed a lot in the years I've been writing and coming back to some of my earlier work . . . I find I **despise** some of it. Soooooo, in saying this, I'm reworking a few series I did long ago, tearing them apart, ripping them up, changing them, and rewriting them, using the things I love, and throwing out the garbage I don't know what I was thinking when I wrote it.

This is one of those series. It was originally a part of my Forbidden Series, and I love the heroine, but don't like the circumstances I put her in . . . and really hate how the hero treated her. So I threw most of it out, kept a few of my favorite parts, and made this new series. I hope you love it because I sure do now. This is much more fitting to who I am now and how I see my heroines. When I began my writing career, I needed a man to come in and save me. I no longer need a savior; I need a partner, which is exactly what I've found with my husband, Mike. He's the kindest, strongest, most romantic man I know, and he's inspiring me to be a better person. I hope you notice the changes in my writing and I hope you love the new material. This book has been one of my favorite rewrites ever!

With Love,
Melody Anne

Books by Melody Anne

FIRST SERIES
He Saw me First
She Saw me First
At First Sight

THE ANDERSONS
Wins the Game
The Dance
The Fall
The Proposal
The Blackmail
The Runaway
The Final Stand
The Unexpected Treasure
The Hidden Treasure
The Holiday Treasure
The Priceless Treasure
The Ultimate Treasure

ANDERSON BILLIONAIRES
Finn
Noah
Brandon
Hudson
Crew

HORIZONS OF CHARLIE
Diamond
Sapphire
Opal
Emerald

THE TITANS
The Tycoon's Revenge
The Tycoon's Vacation
The Tycoon's Vacation
The Tycoon's Proposal
The Tycoon's Secret
The Lost Tycoon
Rescue Me

TRUTH IN LIES
One Too Many
Two Secrets Kept
Three Out
Four Seconds Gone
Five Goodbye's

SURRENDER SERIES
Surrender
Seduced
Scorched
Saved

UNDERCOVER BILLIONAIRES
Kian
Arden
Owen
Declan

ANDERSON HEIRS
Sweet Noel
Jacob's Challenge
Jasmine's Homecoming

HEROES SERIES

Safe in his Arms
Baby it's Cold Outside
Her Unexpected Hero
Who I am with you
Her Hometown Hero

Following Her
Her Forever Hero
Her Found Hero

ANDERSON SPECIAL OPS

Shadows
Rising
Barriers
Shattered
Reborn

TAKEN BY THE TRILLIONAIRE

Xander — Ruth Cardello
Bryan — J.S. Scott
Chris — Melody Anne
Virgin for the Trillionaire — Ruth Cardello
Virgin for the Prince — J.S. Scott
Virgin to Conquer — Melody Anne

BILLIONAIRE AVIATORS

Turbulent Intentions
Turbulent Desires
Turbulent Waters
Turbulent Intrigue

Forbidden Series

A Kiss at Midnight
Kiss Me at Dawn

Prologue

Blake

MY BREATHING CATCHES, watching Jewel from the corner of my eye as she takes her sweet time stripping her clothes away . . . her body a thing of beauty. Will I ever want any other woman again? I suspect the answer to be a flat *no*.

"Lean your seat back," I tell her, my voice strained. She has so much power over me and I'm not sure how to get it back . . . I'm not sure I want it back.

Jewel searches for the controller on the side of her seat, and then slowly, surely, it moves, and her body stretches out for my eyes to feast upon. Setting the plane on autopilot as we drift high in the sky over empty fields, I turn and take my fill of her beauty.

She has so much power over me and I'm not sure how to get it back. . . . I'm not sure I want it back.

I run my hands down her smooth skin, pausing to feel the peaks of her nipples jut against my palm, making my groin throb. Trailing down the slight indent of her stomach, I slide my fingers slowly along the slick folds of her core, nearly losing control when I feel how hot, wet, and ready she is.

When I slip two fingers inside her, the echo of her groan fills the small cabin. Her scent is driving me mad. I need her now, but the last thing I want is for this to go quickly. Hell, if we crash, at least I'll die one very happy man.

Reluctantly withdrawing my hand, I yank off my shirt, tossing it somewhere in the backseat, then unbuckle my seat belt and begin undoing my jeans. I look over and take pride in the knowledge that Jewel is watching me take off my clothes, her eyes hungry.

Sliding my seat back as far as it will go, I take a moment to catch my breath. "Take me in your mouth." My voice doesn't come out nearly as strong as I want it to, but I'm past the point of no return.

Sex with this woman is an experience I'll have difficulty finding again. Though untutored, she seems to know instinctively what to do. I grip myself and squeeze to tame the pulsing when she sits up, her hair drifting over her shoulders and playing hide and seek with her breasts.

Jewel leans over, and her ass rises in the air as her head descends. I throw my head back when her hot mouth circles the tip of my arousal. She sucks hard, making me lurch upward on my seat.

I grip her ass with one hand while holding the back of her neck with the other as she slowly moves up and down. I hold back my cries of pleasure as things grow intense for me and I come close to ending this indulgence much too soon.

"Enough," I say after she licks my entire length, then sucks my tip again, groaning in pleasure at the task . . . her lips vibrating against my sensitive flesh. She loves this, loves bringing me pleasure as much as I love doing the same for her.

She slowly lets me go, turning her head, her cheeks flushed as she looks up at me, her eyes shining, her nipples brushing my thighs. She's the most beautiful creature I've ever seen. I grasp her hips, pull her over me, and sit her on my lap with her back to me.

"We can't do this — the plane will crash," she gasps, though her stomach shakes beneath my hand and her head falls back, passion in her voice.

"It's on autopilot, and there's not another plane for miles," I assure her, not that I'll let anything stop me right now. If I have to do an emergency landing in a cornfield to finish, I'll damn well do it. I've never before made love while flying, and that's all I can think of right now.

Unable to wait a minute longer, I lift her, then push her inch by delicious inch onto my erection, filling her. When I don't move for several long moments, she begins to grind her hips seductively against me, her body quivering with the need for release.

"Wait!" I order. I need a moment to regain control.

She falls still as I slide my hands up her stomach and clasp her breasts, kneading her sweet flesh before pinching her nipples and making her cry out again.

When she begins once more to move up and down, I don't even think about stopping. Her slick heat coats me, so I hold her tight as pressure builds low in my stomach.

Leaning forward, I suck the smooth skin of her neck, then run my tongue along her shoulder, delighting in her taste, in the way her skin feels against my lips and tongue. "You make me lose my mind," I whisper in her ear, and a shudder rushes through her as I grasp her hips and set the pace for our movements, guiding her now instead of following her lead.

With our rhythm in perfect sync, I run a hand up her stomach and take hold of one of her breasts, squeezing the flesh, rubbing her nipple, arousing me even more. My other hand finds the slick bump that will take her over the edge.

I rub her, making her pant while she continues her dance on me, and then I lose all sense of time as wild sensation rushes through me. Our bodies glisten with a fine layer of sweat, and I keep tormenting and delighting two of her crucial pleasure points while sucking on the honeyed skin of her neck.

"Blake!" she cries out, and the taut grip of her core convulses around me with exquisite tightness. I thrust deep inside her and groan loudly as I let go, my release washing through me, blurring my vision and making me lightheaded . . . and then the alarm goes off as we begin to plunge toward the earth.

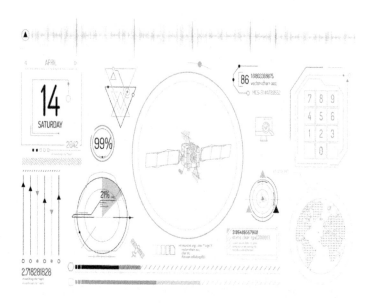

Chapter Review

Three Months Earlier

Jewel

MY HANDS ARE TREMBLING, and my body is hot as I stand in a courtroom desperately trying not to shake before the judge while wearing my thrift-store suit and fighting tears as I hear my brother sobbing behind me, his child advocate holding him back. I want to grab him and run from this room.

"I'm sorry, Ms. Weston, but you haven't shown the courts anything we've asked for."

"I realize I don't have a full-time job yet," I say, unable to keep from glancing nervously back at Justin,

14

"but I was working part-time until last week, and the temp agency promised more work, so within three months I'm certain I'll have enough saved to put down a deposit on a new apartment. I already spoke to the manager of a complex over on West Street, and he guaranteed me a place."

"And where will you and your brother stay until then? How will you feed him? How will you get him medical insurance?" the judge asks in a level voice.

"I'm staying in a studio, but I can make him a private space until I can get a bigger apartment." I can't lie about where I am as they do wellness checks. "There are people living in tents on the streets. I at least have a roof over my head."

My brother has been through so much already. When he was little, our father ran off with another woman, and then, four short months ago, we lost our mother. He's only ten. This is so unfair to him. In addition to all of this trauma, he's been ripped from his childhood home right after losing his mother and thrust into the unpredictable world of foster care.

"I'm truly sorry, Ms. Weston. I want to reunite you with your brother. I think the two of you need each other," Judge Malone says. "Which is why I won't close this case, and why I won't release him for adoption."

A spark of hope wells up inside me. But the judge speaks again, and his next words aren't quite as encouraging. "However, if your circumstances haven't changed by your next hearing, which comes in three months, I'll be left with no other choice but to provide a more stable environment for your brother. He's been through enough, and the longer he's in the system, the less likely he'll return to you. He deserves to have a home, one where he can find comfort in routine, safety, and stability."

"I can take care of him. My mother wanted that for him — for us. She wanted us to stay together. The cancer was sudden, unexpected, and we lost everything, *absolutely* everything, but I can take care of my brother, I swear. Please, just let us be together while we work to put the pieces back together." I hate that I'm begging, but for Justin I'll do whatever it takes.

The sad expression on the judge's face tells me before his words that I won't be walking from the courtroom with Justin — not today, at least.

"This case will be adjourned for three months." With that, Judge Malone hits his gavel and rises before the bailiff can say a word. However the judge doesn't leave the room immediately. He first turns toward me with concern in his eyes. "I know you love Justin — I have no doubt of that," he says and then sighs. "Sometimes, the best thing we can do for someone we love is to let them go so they can have a better life than one we might be able to give them."

Sometimes, the best thing we can do for someone we love is to let them go so they can have a better life than one we might be able to give them

He leaves me shaking so badly that I'm barely able to remain on my feet. But I look resolutely into the sweet blue eyes of my brother and pray I can keep my composure long enough to reassure him that we will indeed be together again. I go through agony each time I have to let him go.

"Jewel? Can we go home now?"

Oh, how his innocent words rip through my very soul.

"Ah, Bubby, soon. I have to do a few more things to prove to the judge that I can take care of you," I reply, disappointment thick in my voice as I walk up to him and bend down to be at eye level. The advocate lets him go and he falls into my arms.

"But why can't we go home? I miss you every day. Ms. Penny doesn't read to me like you do, and she makes me eat peas. I *hate* peas. You promised we'd be back together again. You promised it would be now." His tears soak through my thin suit jacket, and his small frame shakes with each heartbreaking sob.

"Oh, Justin, I promise I *will* get you back. I'll do anything and everything for us to be together again. I love you to the moon and the stars. I love you more than any other person on this planet."

"I love you too, Sissy. Please don't make me go back to that house. She yells at me when I cry for you, and she makes me eat gross food. I don't like it there."

"Ah, baby, it won't be much longer, and I'll come see you every single Saturday, okay? And then after twelve Saturdays we won't have to be apart anymore."

"Twelve Saturdays?" His eyes widen with hope.

Thank goodness he doesn't understand that means three months.

"Yes, only twelve more Saturdays. And after that last Saturday, I'll pick you up and you'll never have to go back to another strange house again." I'll keep this promise to my brother no matter what it takes . . . no matter what I have to do.

"You swear?"

I'm heartbroken at his question. How can any boy be so distrustful at such a young age? My brother should be playing with action figures and Legos, not worrying about where he'll sleep at night, or whether he'll be with a mean foster parent or a nice one, or if his sister loves him.

"I swear." Or I'll die trying, I silently add.

"I love you, Sissy," he sobs as the advocate shifts on her feet, letting us both know our time is up.

"I love you too, Justin."

His sobs grow into screams as the advocate removes him from my arms and pulls him from the courtroom. As soon as the door shuts, my mask of strength comes crashing down and I collapse into the closest chair.

When the court security officer tells me I have to leave the room, I stand and walk zombie-like into the cold white marble hallways of the courthouse. After making my way slowly to the restroom, I splash my face with water and don't even recognize the eyes of my own reflection.

When our mother died, I didn't have time to grieve, because from the day of the funeral I've been fighting to get my brother back from the state and the people who took him away from a loving sister. My brother and I lost everything in the last few months of our mother's life. But we simply can't lose each other.

Once I exit the courthouse, I wander the streets of Seattle until it turns dark, and then I slump against a dirty brick wall, too tired to go a single step farther. Anguish fills me every single day. My mother had been my best friend, my rescuer, my only person to lean on and love in a world full of people who don't care about me.

Closing my eyes, I think of that phone call, my mother's strong voice, for once, sounding defeated.

"I need you to come home and take care of Justin. I have cancer, and I only have two months left."

The pain of those words still sits heavy in my chest, just as they will for the rest of my life. Of course I went home immediately, and I've never regretted that decision. Bills piled up, money ran out, and Justin and I lost it all. Our home. Our security. Our mother. And now . . . we've lost each other. I want to give up, and if I was the only one I had to think about, I'm afraid that's what I'd do.

I don't have any energy left to go on. Wanting to stop feeling for at least a few hours, I rise and move through the streets back to my tiny apartment in a crappy part of town. I gather myself together and finally arrive, then throw myself on the floor because I don't have a bed. I need sleep. For a few short hours I can dream, and with luck my dreams will be filled with images far more pleasant than the reality my life has now become.

For a few short hours
I can dream, and with
luck my dreams will be filled
with images far more
pleasant than the reality
my life has now
become.

Chapter Review

Blake

L OOKING OUT MY WINDOW, I take a deep breath. This meeting isn't going the way I was hoping it would. What's wrong with people that they think a man's worth is measured in his family? My brothers and I have been successful for a very long time, and we don't need women on our arms or children in our homes to make us trustworthy. Apparently, this guy doesn't feel the same.

I turn around and face Stanley Sheppard, CEO of Sheppard Malls, the largest conglomerate of high-end malls that are quickly expanding all over the United States and Canada. These malls cater to the wealthy, and I want a modified version to be built within the newest and largest housing division I've ever created . . . well, that we've ever created. My brothers and I are equal partners.

This newest development covers two square miles and will be its own contained community. Those living in this development won't have to leave for any of their needs to be met. This mall is the cherry on the top of a big fat whipped cream pile. I'm not giving up, and my expression doesn't show a morsel of the conflict I'm feeling as I face him.

"Stanley, I'm glad you've come in to talk about this," I tell him.

He's wearing a smirk, not giving away what he's thinking. All of us in the business world wear the same expression. It's never wise to give away what we're thinking, not when millions, and sometimes billions, of dollars are involved.

"I'd really like to be business partners, Blake, but I have reservations," Stanley says. My expression doesn't change.

"Astor Corp has been incredibly successful for ten years, Stanley. I don't need to sell our product anymore. I'd love to partner with you on this project as it will add several hundred million to both of our bank accounts, which is never a bad thing. I also understand if it doesn't work out. There are times when it's better to walk away."

I'm not calling this man's bluff. I mean these words. I never play chicken. I'm all in or I'm out. I'm not ready to walk away from working with this man as it's something that fits perfectly with my vision . . . but I won't beg him to be partners. I don't beg anyone.

"Our corporation hasn't done too badly," Stanley says, making me laugh.

"We both know there isn't a venture out there with your name on it that isn't a success," I tell him.

He finally smiles and lets out a chuckle. "Okay, I'll admit the same goes for you and your brothers."

"I guess we're all just that damn good," I say.

At first glance the two of us might come off as smug and self-satisfied, and we might look at multimillion-dollar investments the same way an average person looks at depositing twenty dollars into their savings account, but that's because we're shrewd and our self-assessments are based on solid fact, not ego. We know how to make money, and we know we'll always keep making more.

Only a select few rule the world. When I was a young boy, my parents' lives ended right before my eyes; I decided right then I'd never be vulnerable again. I've kept that promise. I'll never be one of the weak, never be easy prey in a world packed with predators. No one will ever sneak up on me and catch me unaware.

I'll never be one of the weak, never be easy prey in a world packed with predators.

"Let's have a drink, and you can fill me in on what you've been doing with this project," Stanley says.

"That sounds a lot better than sitting in this office," I say. Some of the best deals are made in a bar with good whiskey and a cigar. The two of us move toward the conference room doors of Astor Corp.

I've never been a man who likes to leave things left unsaid. We have one elephant in the room so we might as well get it out of the way.

"Why is it so important to you that your business partners be married?" I ask as we walk. I've known this man a very long time, and he's certainly changed over the years.

He chuckles. "I love how direct you are, Blake." He pauses for a minute, and I let him gather his thoughts. "Happily married men have more to lose, put more value in their work and the outcomes, and use compassion where others might cut corners. I was an asshole before I married, and I'm not proud of some of the decisions I made. I tend to work with others who have been humbled by marriage and families now that I know the power of a healthy relationship."

I laugh. "A woman doesn't make us into a new person," I assure him.

"I disagree. I know for a fact that my wife has changed my life and made me a better man."

"Oh, please, *please*, for the love of all that's holy, do not continue speaking like some cheesy romance-book hero," I say, horrified to hear these words coming from a man who was once one of the most ruthless bachelors I ever met. "I remember the days when you thought no woman was true, no woman could ever be trusted. Marriage may have ruined you. There's a term for it, you know . . ."

"There was a time, Blake, when I would've thrown you up against a wall for thinking I was the slightest bit weak."

"Ha! You would've tried," I say. Neither of us are remotely upset by this exchange. It's all friendly banter . . . though it still might end this deal before it has a chance to begin.

Stanley smiles and speaks reflectively. "I came to realize that the anger I'd held for so long was pointless. I also realized having one woman to love doesn't end my life or my freedom. It makes everything better. Becky is full of surprises and delights that I'll never get tired of exploring. I know you'll scoff at such talk, but what she does for me is indescribable."

"Yeah, whatever, Stanley — and thanks for *not* describing it. I happen to be a big fan of variety. After a few weeks, anything gets old, and women are no exception. I grow bored with them — always! Besides, though I know it's not politically correct to say this, face it: women are weak, pathetic creatures, and they always have an agenda."

Stanley knows of the horror that my brothers and I suffered when our mother's little game she'd been playing hadn't ended the way she'd wanted it to end. The woman who was supposed to protect and cherish her children hardened my heart, and though I'm letting my resentment toward one woman carry over to all of the females in the world, it's understandable. Hell, Stanley did the same for a very long time, and he wasn't a dick because of trauma, but just because he wanted to be. Stanley changed . . . I will not.

"Not every woman is like your mother, Blake. You'll see that someday." Before I can say anything, Stanley continues. "Who are you seeing now?"

We arrive in the lobby of my building and quickly move forward, stepping out onto a busy Seattle sidewalk. We're heading toward a favorite bar of mine.

"No one at the moment. I haven't had time — all of these deals to be closed. You know the drill. I've had to do a lot of the work on my own with my brother Byron being off in Greece for the past year, and my other brother, Tyler, gone for two years. Now that they're home, I may take some vacation time of my own."

"Now that's a joke. Men like us don't do vacations," Stanley says. "Why were both of your brothers away?"

"Byron was working on his own project in Greece while still working with me on deals for the home front."

"It's good to branch out on your own, Blake. I'd like to hear more about this from him. I personally love spending time in Greece. It's a beautiful country."

"Yeah, and Tyler was simply gone for two years — we don't know where, and we didn't hear from him the entire time. I was about to send out the Marines, but he finally came home."

"Now that sounds like a story," Stanley says.

Before I'm able to give Stanley details, we're interrupted.

"Stanley. Blake. How are you?"

I turn to see Mathew Greenfield, a man who's helped me through more than one bad time in my life. He's a business partner, but more than that, he's been there when I've needed to choose which road I'm going to take in life.

Luckily, I've taken a more positive path than the one he originally thought I would. Mathew has given me the support and praise I needed to change my life for the better — no easy feat under the circumstances. Mathew also knows all of my dark secrets, and he's someone I can not only count on, but fully trust.

"It's good to see you, my friend," I say.

"It's been a long time," Stanley tells Mathew.

"Too long," Mathew replies.

"Join us for a drink," I say. "We're deliberating a possible new business venture."

Mathew throws me a smile. "I have a few minutes. Why don't you tell me about it?"

The three of us walk into the bar and proceed to the back, where I have a table on standby at this same time every day in case I need to conduct business away from the office. A waitress quietly sets down menus and disappears.

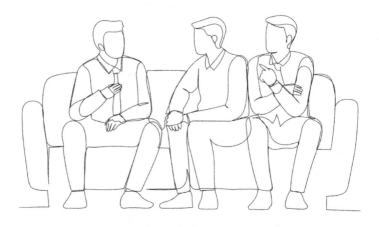

Once the topic of business is out of the way, the conversation turns back to my lack of a love life. This doesn't make me a happy camper, especially since the last people on earth I'd want to discuss this with are teaming up on me.

"We all need to take time to have our itches scratched," Mathew says with a knowing look.

"I have no trouble getting my needs met," I tell him.

"Do you use professionals?" he boldly asks.

I laugh. "Never have and never will," I quickly reply, disgusted at the thought.

"Don't knock it till you try it. I went to this place a friend of mine runs and she has high-class girls who can escort us to functions, or ease the ache over a few days," Mathew says.

Stanley looks at him in horror.

"You have to pay a female to be with you?" Stanley asks, making Mathew laugh.

"We *all* pay women. At least through a service, we know how much we're paying," he says, not offended at either Stanley's or my scorn over the subject.

"I've never had trouble getting my needs met, and anyway . . ." I say before getting interrupted as the waitress drops off our appetizers and drinks. I don't get to complete the words as Mathew jumps right back in to speaking.

"Sometimes a man is just too damn busy. It might be worth your time to seek a professional service."

"Sorry, but there's no way in hell I'm going to a place like that," I tell him. I'd say this even if Stanley wasn't sitting here.

"Just trying to help. A happy man is much more fun to hang with," Mathew says. "After my last divorce I decided I'd never marry again. And yes, Stanley, I understand that some people have great marriages, but I've been married four times now, and all I got out of each of those marriages was a lighter bank account and some gray hairs — hell, not even a T-shirt. A monumental waste of time and money."

"Blake, ignore this crap," Stanley says. "We've both been assholes for long enough and we don't need escort services or to treat good women like whores."

"Believe me, I'm not interested." I pick up my drink and take a long swallow.

Mathew isn't even a little bit annoyed at our reaction. "Fine. Fine. But I know you, Blake. You'll think about it."

The subject changes, and no further mention is made of needs being met. Still, though the night finishes on a good note, I'm restless by the time I arrive home. I might not want to go to an escort service, but I do have an itch that needs to be satisfied. The question is, what am I going to do about it? And how firm will Stanley be about at least one out of the three of us brothers being in a committed relationship?

I don't like being backed into a corner, but I want this mall in our community. The question is: do I want it enough to jump through hoops? Do I want it enough to let a woman into my life? Maybe. It could be temporary. I smile. It could even be . . . pleasant . . . for a short while.

Chapter Review

Jewel

T HE SMELL OF BACON ISN'T scenting the air. A fresh cup of coffee isn't brewing. And there are certainly no birds chirping when I wake up. It's another typical morning of darkness in a depressing city, and the ability to keep my head held high is becoming more and more difficult. It would be so easy to give up, to move back to Florida. I can't do this to Justin though. None of this is his fault, and what kind of person would it make me to give up on him? A terrible person. I won't do it.

No. I'm better than that. For brief moment I want to give up; I decide it's all too much to endure . . . but the moment is already over . . . just as every other time I quit ends before I can blink. I have three months. As much as I want to break down and cry, as much as I want to curse the powers above for taking my mother, for interrupting my life, and for ruining me, I can't.

If I give up, Justin won't have anyone fighting for him. And my mother's final words had been a plea for me to take care of my little brother. My mother had closed her eyes for the last time after I promised never to allow our family to break apart.

Mom had found peace in a world that had turned against her, a world that seemed no longer to care about any of us. As much as I want to take back the promise I gave her, I know I can't. Today will be the day I find a new job, save every single dime I make, and then get a place with furniture, in a neighborhood with a good school.

Today I'll start the life I promised my mother that Justin and I would live. True, it's overwhelming — all the more so because everything had started out well for me for such a long time . . . only to crash and burn. I'm twenty-four, graduated from college two years ago, then landed a wonderful job with a firm in Miami, Florida where the execs told me I was a rising star. My life was supposed to be easy from that point on. It isn't turning out to be so easy after all.

Maybe Justin and I can go back to the Sunshine State once he's securely mine. I won't be able to go back to the company I walked away from. They didn't understand me leaving to come home and take care of my mother and little brother. As soon as I walked out their door, they forgot all about me. Like many out there, many who'll stand in line to take my place, none of them will let something as insignificant as family come between them and their careers.

I'm too different from the sharks of the finance and business world. Family will always come first for me, and right now the only family I have left is Justin. I won't fail him. I climb from bed and head into my claustrophobic bathroom that has a broken door.

My image in the mirror horrifies me. My hair looks as if a crew of hyperactive mice have made a nest and settled in overnight, tangling it and leaving it filled with filth. Streaks of dirt run down my sunken cheeks, and my clothes will surely have to be tossed.

Still, none of this is going to stand in my way — not today. I take a very short shower in lukewarm water, my hair feeling terrible with the dollar store shampoo. But I'm clean. I climb out, brush my hair as best as I can, and put on minimal makeup. My stomach rumbles, reminding me I haven't eaten in twenty-four hours. I'm losing far too much weight, but I can't waste money on food. I take what I can get from local food kitchens in the city, and I'm dang lucky I haven't gotten food poisoning so far.

No matter. I'll have plenty of food for both my brother and me when I secure a new place. It won't be fast food or cheap crap. Our mother was an excellent cook, and I truly loved standing next to her in front of our gas stove, taking in all she was doing.

Right now it doesn't matter how good of a cook I am, since I don't have time or a stove to prepare a meal on. Even if I have to give up sleep, I'll soon have everything my brother and I need to live a decent life. I'm a soldier, and today I won't stop until I have at least one job, hopefully two. I'll work seven days a week, twenty hours a day if that's what it takes.

I need new clothes, so I head to a local shelter I found a couple of weeks ago. I walk through the doors and sign in on the visitors' sheet. It isn't long before I manage to find a small bite to eat, and then find a halfway decent outfit from the communal clothing closet.

Next I sit down and begin flipping through the classified section of the newspaper. I'm not taking no for an answer today when it comes to a job. I'm going to walk in with confidence and force them to see what an asset I'll be to any business lucky enough to have me come through their doors. No more refusals.

Overqualified.

Position already filled.

Come back once you have more experience.

Over and over, at each place, I've been refused employment. What good is my degree if I can't use it? I can't get a job as a secretary, because I'm overqualified; can't get a job in an advertising agency, because I left the one I'd had after only two years. No one cares that I left because my mother had been terminally ill.

These heartless bastards seem to deem helping my mom as an unfortunate weakness on my part, a sad sign of unreliability. If I've walked out on a job once, I can easily do it again. The truth is that I will if I have to. I don't regret sitting with my mother, don't regret those last precious moments we shared, and I don't regret getting to be a family for just a while longer.

But now I have to find a job to help save my little brother, and it feels like the weight of the world rests on my shoulders. I promised Justin I'd do whatever it takes to get him back, to bring him home with me — wherever home will end up being. If I can't keep this promise, I'm nothing.

I give myself a pep talk as I head out of the shelter. I found an entry level secretarial position at one of the larger corporations in town and I'm going to get the job. In a company like this one they're going to take one look at my clothes and know I'm out of my league, but if I conduct myself with confidence, they won't be able to refuse me . . . I won't allow them to turn me down.

It takes nearly an hour to arrive and I gaze up at the beautiful building, stop and double-check the address. It's the right place. I take a deep breath, firm my shoulders, hold my head high, then walk through the tall double doors.

It's beautiful: marble floors, huge glass windows, gorgeous artwork, fake plants, and expensive furniture placed perfectly around the vast lobby. I'm intimidated, that's for sure, but I refuse to show it.

I confidently step up to the huge reception desk where three women are sitting, headphones connected, smiles on their perfectly made-up faces, in clothes that probably cost more than the rent on my tiny studio apartment. It's okay, someday, there will be other women looking at me, being envious of me, just as I am of these women. This *will* happen because I'm motivated, not content to be nothing.

"I'm here to drop off my résumé. I'd like to speak with personnel," I say when one woman asks if she can help.

"Do you have an interview?" she asks.

I panic for a moment. Should I lie? No, that would be foolish. I paste on my most confident smile.

"No, but I'm the perfect fit for this job so I'd appreciate it if you could find a place on the schedule for me. I'll wait all day if I need to," I tell her.

She gives me a bemused smile, then looks on her computer. "I think Ms. Beaumont will like you," she says. "There's an opening in two hours. We do have a café around the corner and down the stairs if you'd like to wait down there. Here's our Wi-Fi info. Good luck," the woman says as she hands me a card.

"Thank you so much." I turn and walk away, keeping my composure until I find a bathroom. Once inside I jump up and down like a kid on Christmas morning. I'm going to get this job. There's no doubt about it. Confidence. All it takes is confidence.

I sit in the café for an hour and a half, drinking the free coffee they offer. I have a bit too much and become jittery, but at least alert. I make my way upstairs and, at exactly two hours, the receptionist sends me to the elevators where I travel to the twentieth floor.

I've had plenty of time for my nerves to calm. I'm immediately led into an office . . . and a striking younger

39

woman with beautiful blue eyes walks in. She doesn't say a word as I stand to greet her, simply sweeps her gaze over my body before meeting my eyes.

Whatever this woman is looking for, I think I've come up short. I don't let it shake me as I look at her. She's wearing at least five-inch heels, doubtless an intimidation tactic. It's working to a degree, though nothing really matters except getting the job. I won't be intimidated. I'm going to paste a smile on my face and make this woman *need* to hire me, no matter what the job entails. There's no way I'll suffer the disappointment of seeing another door close in my face.

"I'm Jewel Weston, and I'm going to impress you with how hard I work." My voice comes out strong, determined, positive.

"Thank you for coming." She doesn't even greet me. Ugh, this isn't going the way I want it to, but I assure myself it will get better.

There's nothing in the woman's words or voice to indicate whether she's interested or not in me working here. Maybe she's bored with what she does for a living. She could at least introduce herself, so I don't have to think of her as *the woman*. But, hell, I'll call the lady anything she wants to be called as long as she provides a much-needed paycheck.

"What can you bring to us, Jewel?"

We're in a small room with a table and two chairs. The woman doesn't gesture for me to sit, so I stand awkwardly in front of her.

"I finished college in four years, getting a business degree with honors," I reply without hesitation. "I'm bright, always eager, and willing to learn, which I do quickly."

"That's a must," the woman says with a cryptic smile.

"Well, then, you have your newest employee, and there's no need to look further," I tell her with a raised chin.

"Hmm. We'll see."

The woman gathers papers from a file in the corner of the room and then sits down at one end of the table, still not offering me a chair. Should I sit? Is this some sort of test? The walls are bare, with nothing on them to focus on, making me even less comfortable, but I'm determined not to look nervous.

"Where did you attend school?" The woman isn't even looking up as she asks this question.

"I went to UC Berkeley on a full scholarship," I say, quite proud of this.

"Very impressive. So you're smart." The frown between the woman's eyes suggests she isn't particularly pleased about this. Does she think I'm competition?

"I've always worked hard to be at the top of my class, which is why I can excel at any job." I have to close my lips to keep from saying more. Some potential employers want a lot of talking, and some don't. I have the feeling in this case, the less I say, the better.

"Please have a seat, Jewel."

The tone of her voice indicates she *is* pleased I haven't sat before I've been asked. Good. I'm doing something right in this freaky interview.

"Thank you," I say. "Might I have your name?" I'm through waiting for the woman to introduce herself.

"I apologize. I should've told you already," she replies with a slight laugh that doesn't reach her eyes. "McKenzie Beaumont. I'm the personal manager for Blake Astor and oversee the staff."

"It's nice to meet you, Ms. Beaumont."

For the next hour, Ms. Beaumont asks all sorts of questions I've never been asked before in an interview, but the longer we sit in the small, stark room, the happier I become. If she isn't seriously considering me, she wouldn't want to sit here wasting her time . . . right?

"Do you have family, Jewel?"

This question makes me pause. Should I lie? What if the woman thinks my personal life is too much of a hindrance and then doesn't give me the job? With a pang in my heart, I speak. "My mother passed away a couple of months ago. I have no family left." It feels like acid traveling up my throat as I deny the existence of my brother to this woman, but I seem to have no choice. There's no reason for my potential employer to know about Justin. My personal life is just that, mine.

"And friends? Do you have close friends?" What a strange question to be asked. On this subject I can easily speak the truth.

"No. I moved back home about four months ago to take care of her before she died. I had to leave everyone behind in Florida where I was working. I haven't had time yet to make new friends. I'm not a really social person, anyway. I much prefer to do my job and relax alone at home."

This is somewhat true. Sure, I enjoyed going to happy hour with my friends back in Florida, but my idea of a perfect weekend is sitting in front of a fireplace in the winter with a glass of inexpensive wine in one hand and a good book in the other. I don't need an exciting social life. I've been teased about this my entire life, and it doesn't bother me.

"Would you like to hear more about the position, Jewel?"

The intensity in Ms. Beaumont's eyes makes me feel suddenly tempted to turn around and bolt from the room. I don't have the foggiest idea what this woman will say next, and I'm not sure I want to know.

"Yes, of course. I'm willing to learn any job, and I guarantee I'll do it well."

"We put all new employees on a yearlong probationary period to make sure they're a good fit for the company. While, if you're hired, you'll have a job title, it's essential that our staff learn other jobs in the company as well to fill in when and where needed. We offer full medical, cost of living adjustments, a fair salary, and the company owns several apartment complexes which we offer discounted living for all staff members. I like your résumé, Jewel. I think you're green, but I see some good things here. I'll have to check to make sure everything's correct, but I can safely tell you I think you'll get the job. We need someone to begin immediately. If you accept, I'd like to see you in here tomorrow. As long as the résumé checks out, you'll make it past the first week. If it doesn't, you'll be immediately dismissed. We don't leave positions open for long as the Astor brothers don't like empty offices."

"Thank you, Ms. Beaumont, I won't disappoint you," I tell her, trying to keep my tone respectful and not shout for joy.

"Report to the front desk at seven tomorrow morning and you'll be taken to HR. I hope this works out," Ms. Beaumont says as she stands. I quickly jump to my feet too excited to keep sitting, and glad the interview is over. I'm awed I got the position. Everything on my résumé is a hundred percent correct so there's no chance I'll be let go.

Ms. Beaumont walks me to the front desk on the twentieth floor, says goodbye, and disappears. I make it all of the way outside and around the corner before I let out a happy cry that has several heads turning my way.

I got the job. Ms. Beaumont was an intimidating woman, and I still got the job. "I'm coming to get you, Justin. You'll be released to me at the next court hearing. Everything will be fine now."

I don't care if people think I'm crazy. I'm happier than I've been in months, and from here on out it's only going to get better and better. The sun is shining once again. This office building is a bit scary, but I don't care. My life is finally on the right path again, and I only see sunshine in my future.

Chapter Review

Chapter Four

Blake

"HELLO, MR. ASTOR. You're here early today," McKenzie says as she greets me with a smile. She's one damn good office manager and sees everything. Even knowing this, I still like to do my own walk-throughs in the building. I'm not predictable though, and I take different routes at different times.

"Good morning, McKenzie. Anything new to report?"

She begins talking and I give a critical look around as I move through the huge building. A boss who doesn't walk each space of his own business is an owner who will fail. I know the people who work in my mailroom all the way up to those who sit on the top floor. I'm filled with pride as I move through this building my brothers and I have lovingly built.

The building is done in varying shades of beige, red, and blue, and it sports expensive crystal chandeliers, unique furniture, and tasteful plants. Elegantly dressed men and women sit and chat with potential clients and co-workers, their voices low, their conversations muted.

I recognize a congressman in the corner with a talented young architect and I smile. Our services aren't cheap, and we're known for being the best . . . as it should be.

I'm careful who I hire. I don't want office politics. That means I want someone serious, who loves working hard, and who has drive. I've gone through three secretaries in five years because two have moved up in the company. A person can start at any level in my business and rise to the top . . . or close to the top as my brothers and I will never step down from our positions.

I look around and nod before we move to the elevators and go to another floor. Even after many years, I find it amusing how people stand at attention when I come into a room. I'm well aware I'm one of the elite in society. That, of course, means my ass is kissed on a regular basis, which annoys me. I prefer honesty. Then again, my brothers and I are cynical because of all we've been through. That's okay. It's all part of the world we live in and created for ourselves.

The three of us learned from our mother at a young age to trust no one, not even those we should be able to trust above all others, and that depressing lesson actually helped us. If we don't wear our hearts on our sleeves, and don't allow anyone even remotely close to the recesses of our hearts, we don't risk ever being traumatized again. This is the world we've created. It's a good world.

If we don't wear our hearts on our sleeves, and don't allow anyone even remotely close to the recesses of our hearts, we don't risk ever being traumatized again.

Our greatest strength — our fraternal bond is paramount with us — it's also a weakness. If an enemy wants to get to one of us, he or she can do it through one of our siblings. We'd kill for each other, and we'd go to the ends of the earth, though we've never spoken about that. We try not to think about it.

We all have reasons for doing what we do, reasons that we, at least, consider valid. The world might not deem what I do as right, but my brothers and I survive each new day by guarding ourselves. Our mother did this to us . . . she and our pathetic excuse for a father.

The woman who gave birth to us had been cheating on our father, her husband, and that's what had led to their deaths. My father had been a weak man, and it's something that I'm determined never to be. I'm not the sort of man a woman brings home to her parents. And I have no regrets about this.

McKenzie and I walk into the development department where about twenty people are busy working, but I stop in my tracks as I spot a new employee sitting at a desk, concentrating on the computer in front of her. I can't turn away as I take in the mussed dark tresses traveling down her back that she's obviously run her fingers through a thousand times and the ill-fitted suit she's wearing that's showing a hint of tempting cleavage . . . just enough to have my mouth going a little dry.

The woman turns in her seat, causing her modest skirt to pull up, giving me a glimpse of her tanned thighs that are certainly toned and tantalizing and just the right shape for my hands to wander across. I've never been this drawn to a woman at first glance. She might be the first woman in a very long time to inspire a small trace of lust in me. Small? Hell, what I'm feeling as I stare at this woman is anything but small.

I tune out McKenzie as I wait for this new employee to turn, to look up, and to see me. What will happen when our eyes connect? Maybe I'll feel nothing . . . then I can be done with these strange hormones invading me. The worst part of this invasion is that this is my sanctuary, my offices, the place my brothers and I built with our own hands. I don't get thrown off in this building . . . not ever . . . not until spotting this damn woman.

Finally, after what feels like forever, her eyes lift . . . and the room disappears. I take an involuntary step backward, the power of our connection so intense it literally makes me stumble. Never in my life have I looked at a woman with such intensity. Never before have I been filled with such a flood of desire for a woman . . . especially without a single word being spoken between us. Right in this moment I'll do almost anything to possess this stranger. This thought should stop me cold . . . but I'm not running.

"What's her name?" I ask.

"Who?" McKenzie asks, breaking off in the middle of whatever sentence she was saying, looking out at the room, finally realizing I'm not listening to her. I don't bother saying who as it's more than clear who I'm staring at. The woman looks a bit in shock before she turns away, hiding from this intensity between us.

"Um . . . her name is Jewel. She's been here less than a week. She seems to be doing well, but she's still in her trial phase," McKenzie says. "I see some raw talent and good traits, but we need to investigate her further."

My brothers and I are sticklers when it comes to our employees. We need to trust our staff so they go through an intense trial period. If their background checks come back badly, they're out. They have to sign many papers to even begin. We build billion-dollar complexes, and use a lot of other people's money. We need staff we don't have to keep an eye on to be handling the business.

"Jewel," I whisper. I start walking toward her before I realize I'm moving. McKenzie doesn't seem to know what to do as this hasn't happened before.

Jewel looks up again as if she can sense me coming. The woman next to her looks up and smiles at me. It takes all I have to nod at her. I have eyes for only one woman right now.

"Hello, Mr. Astor. We didn't know you were coming down today," the other woman says. I believe her name's Lisa.

"We're simply doing a walk through, Lisa," McKenzie says when I say nothing. "How are things going?"

This is why McKenzie's in the position she is. She's good at her job and the employees like her. I'm too intense. I'm well aware of this, but I'm okay with it.

"How are you enjoying working here?" I ask, gazing at Jewel, who seems uncomfortable with the full force of my attention on her.

"It's a great place to work," she says, her soft voice husky, a bit unsure, her fingers clenching as they rest in her lap. It's clear she's aware I'm an owner since Lisa said my last name. She just isn't clear why I'm speaking to her. Hell, I don't know why I am. It's almost like it's happening against my will.

"Blake Astor," I say, holding out my hand.

Her fingers tremble as she lifts her own hand . . . and then her fingers are clasped in mine and sparks shoot between us in the most delicious way as her cheeks turn pink. The raw innocence behind her blue depths has to be fake . . . doesn't it? Who cares? I want this woman. I need this woman. Everything within me is telling me to possess her, and to do it right now. Because I want to do just that . . . I let her go, then turn and walk away without saying another word.

I leave the floor, quickly telling McKenzie I have things to do. I march to my office and shut the door. What in the hell is wrong with me? A smirk curves my lips upward. A woman. That's what's wrong with me. It's *always* a woman who takes down the strongest of men. Maybe I'm not as strong as I believe. Maybe I'm just as weak as my father.

This thought fills me with fury. No! I'll have her fired. I reach for my phone, intending to call McKenzie to tell her to dismiss this latest employee . . . but I can't make myself dial. After a full minute I slam the receiver back in place.

"Dammit!"

I jump from my seat and move to the window to gaze at the Seattle skyline. I have a feeling that things are about to get messy in my life . . . and there's nothing I'm going to be able to do to stop it.

Things are about to get messy in my life . . . and there's nothing I'm going to be able to do to stop it.

Chapter Review

Chapter Five

Jewel

MY ARMS STRETCH ABOVE my head as I try to focus on the clock sitting on top of a book next to my makeshift bed on the floor in this crummy apartment. The blurriness starts to come into focus, and I see it's six in the morning. I smile, oddly enough not wanting to throw the clock against the wall for the first time in a long while as I wake up early. I'm not a morning person on the best of days.

Things are better now, though. I *love* my job. I've been there for a month and my first paycheck was the most beautiful thing I've ever seen. Astor Corp pays their employees well, and I won't do a single thing to mess up my job. I love it far too much.

I dance my way into my tiny bathroom and get ready with purpose. I'm going to be reunited with my brother . . . soon. Once that happens the two of us will run to the farthest reaches of the planet if we have to . . . though I love this job and don't want to leave. Still, nothing and no one will ever separate us again.

I'm not willing to spend much money, but I did make a trip to the local Goodwill and got some decent office attire. I stayed in darker shades and similar items so it won't be so clear to everyone that I'm wearing the same things over and over again. I get dressed, then stand in front of the rusty mirror and smile, something I've done much of in the past several months.

It doesn't take long to rush out the front door, then take the morning bus to work. I don't even mind the forty-minute commute. I'm reading a great thriller by James Patterson and the ride flies by in a blur. There's a spot at work where we can trade books. There's always something new so I have one and a spare at all times now. Who needs a crappy TV when there are millions of books to read? Not me.

I arrive at the office thirty minutes early and get to my desk. I'd rather be early than risk being late. The bus is too unpredictable to take any chances. I'm well aware I'll be on trial for my first year at this company, and I have to keep this job to ensure getting custody of my brother.

"Jewel, can we chat for a few minutes?"

I look up to find Ms. Beaumont gazing down at me, concern on her face. My stomach clenches.

"Is everything okay?" I ask.

"I'm not sure. Come with me to my office," she says, her tone not giving anything away. I feel my minimal breakfast bar wanting to come back up as I follow her to her office. I can't think of a single thing

I've done wrong, but what if I unwittingly screwed up? I can't lose this job. I'm not above begging.

We reach her office and I see a file sitting on her desk. I'm trembling as I take the seat across from her. I can't wait for her to ask me to sit. I'm too scared right now and there's no chance my knees are going to hold me up.

"What's wrong, Ms. Beaumont?" I ask, begging her to not prolong this torture.

"Do you have a little brother?" she asks. I feel the color drain from my face as I look down, tears filling my eyes. I'm not sure how, but she found out.

"I do. I'm sorry I lied about that, but I *had* to get this job. He's a great kid. He won't affect my work performance at all. I swear," I tell her, my voice shaky.

"He's currently in foster care," she says. It's not a question. A tear falls and I wipe it away with frustration. "Tell me what's happening with this," she demands. I can't even think of holding back now.

"My mother had cancer that took her fast. We lost all of our money and our family home. They took my brother into foster care, saying I wasn't fit to be his guardian. I live in a tiny studio apartment right now, but I can afford to get a bigger place with my next paycheck, and with a stable job they'll give me custody. Justin's ten years old and he'll be in school. I can care for him *and* work here. I've already looked into after-school programs so if I need to work overtime, he has a place to go. I swear it won't affect my work." I spit all of this out as fast as I can. I finally look up. McKenzie's gazing back at me with sympathy.

"I understand why you felt the need to keep this from me. We ask about family because we want to know our employees. You didn't know this though. Your brother's information came back in your background check." She pauses as she pulls out a card. She doesn't hand it over.

A good job fills us with pride, but a family fills us with hope

"Jewel, I believe family is the most important thing in our lives. A good job fills us with pride, but a family fills us with hope. Never feel you have to explain your love for your brother. I think it's wonderful you love him so much and are fighting for him. I told you during the interview that the company has apartments. We normally don't offer these units to employees until the trial period is over, but a two-bedroom unit just became available. I'm offering it to you. I also know a very good attorney I'm happy to refer you to if you'd like to speak to him about your case."

I'm in shock as I gaze at this woman I thought was so hard when I first met her. She's not that way at all. She's certainly strong and determined, but she has a real heart too. I give her a grateful smile.

"I'd love to take the apartment and to meet the attorney," I tell her.

"Good, call him and see if you can get in this week."

"It will have to be on my lunch break."

"If you need an extra hour let me know," she tells me. "I'll have the apartment lease sent to your desk this afternoon. Just fill it out and send it to HR. They'll take the rent right from your paycheck. I think you'll love the building. It's not too far from work so you'll save some commute time. The building also offers a swimming pool and gym that both you and your brother can enjoy."

"Are you sure I can afford it?" I ask, realizing I haven't talked cost yet.

She chuckles. "Yes, you can. Like I told you, we offer a discounted price. We like to keep our employees happy so they stay with the company for a very long time," she says as she stands.

The meeting is over. I walk away from her in a daze. I call the attorney's office before my shift officially begins in five minutes. Luck of all luck, he has a brief opening during my lunch hour today.

I sit back with a smile, knowing today is going to be a great day. I'll walk into that lawyer's office, exuding confidence. It will all work out. The attorney will tell me exactly what I want to hear . . . I'm sure of it.

A few hours later I'm sitting upright in a stiff leather chair and listening to the attorney speak . . . feeling far less confident as the man takes a quick glance through the few legal documents I have with me to show him.

"The court asked for a visible change in your circumstances, Ms. Weston, a sign of stability. You don't have a positive employment history, though you've now had a good job for one month, but are still on a trial position with that company. You still don't have a proper residence, and you are young."

"How can the courts possibly think it will be better for my brother to be raised by strangers who don't care about him?"

"It's not a matter of who will love your brother more. It's very black and white, and they don't want to see this boy bounced around for years until he ends up as yet another lost child in the juvenile-justice system."

I don't like this man, not one little bit. McKenzie said he was good, but all I can see is a cold-hearted person who isn't saying a single thing I want to hear.

"I disagree with you, Mr. Sharp. My brother's much better off with a sister who loves him and who will do whatever it takes to ensure his safety."

"I've been doing my job for a very long time, Ms. Weston, and I won't take on a case I'm sure to lose. I took this meeting as a favor to McKenzie, but I'm telling you right now that this is a losing case." The way he says the words isn't exactly cruel, but still they cut me to the bone.

My stomach sinks as I look into his eyes, which are now almost sympathetic. That is all I need — pity. I'd feel better if he simply sported a sneer, because the expression he's wearing tells me I don't have a chance in hell of winning this case on my own.

"You're sure there's nothing I can do, Mr. Sharp?"

I don't want to hear the attorney's next words, but I brace myself for them anyway.

"I'm sorry, Ms. Weston, but at this point you don't have a winning cause. If your life doesn't undergo drastic change, there's no reason for you to even try to reopen this case. Sadly, that means that your brother could very easily be swallowed up by the system."

Once again, I hear the depressing pity.

"What do you mean by *drastic*?" There's nothing I won't do at this point to get my brother.

"This is strictly off the record, but the courts want to see stability. They want to see two-parent households, and they want to know that the household will remain intact and welcoming to the child. No more disruptions. You need a home, you need security, and you need a lot more than you're showing right now."

I'm horrified but I fully understand what he's telling me. I'd be on solid ground if I could tell the courts I'm a happily married woman who can provide a stable home for my brother. They don't see a newly employed twenty-four-year-old who can barely pay for a small apartment as suitable to raise her ten-year-old brother. They don't care that I graduated from a top-notch school at the top of my class and left a great job to take care of my ailing mother. All they care about is where I am right now.

This is the twenty-first century, and yet some things are so damn outdated it would be laughable if I wasn't so close to tears. I have to fight back maniacal laughter as I nearly reach the point of hysteria. My hope is slipping away, and it might be scratching the surface of utter misery.

I can't comprehend a world without my brother in it. As much as it hurts, isn't his happiness far more important than my own? Of course it is. What if I step back and he manages to find a family who will love him for the rest of his life? Wouldn't that be better for him? Even this thought brings me to my knees. They might love him, but I'm his blood, and we need each other. We're happier together, both of us. I'm not being selfish wanting him with me, I'm being a loving sibling.

"I can't give him the home he needs, can I?" I ask Mr. Sharp. Even though this man doesn't know me, sometimes it takes a stranger to tell a person the truth in a way they can actually hear.

"That's not what I'm saying, Ms. Weston. I don't know you. But from the look in your eyes, I can see that you love your brother very much. Love, unfortunately, isn't always the answer, and love certainly doesn't put food on the table or offer a roof over your head."

Love, unfortunately, isn't always the answer, and love certainly doesn't put food on the table or offer a roof over your head

"Ah, but love can turn mountains into molehills," I reply with more than a trace of sarcasm.

"In theory," he says with the slightest of smiles.

"What would you advise me to do next?"

The attorney pauses for so long, I figure he's giving up on talking to me. I'm sure he wants nothing more than for me to leave his office. But at least he hasn't led me on and taken my money. He finally leans forward and looks me in the eyes.

"If you can't lose him, do *whatever* it takes."

And those are the words I carry with me as I walk out of his office. No, he won't represent me, and I have no doubt that, no matter how many attorneys I visit, my situation won't improve. I'm now left with a simple choice: give up or fight. What am I going to do? I make my way back to work. At least I can control this part of my life.

I won't drown in my own defeat. I turn the corner and McKenzie steps out, blocking me from moving forward.

"Hello, Jewel. How did the visit go?"

"I appreciate that you helped me find him."

"You seem upset. It must not have gone well." McKenzie says it as if she knew all along that the meeting wouldn't go well. Then why had she put me through that? Because she knows I'll fight to the end, that's why. I might have to hit rock bottom before I can dig myself back out again.

"I'm fine," I tell Ms. Beaumont.

"I don't believe you, Jewel, but I won't pry. I understand. Besides, I value my privacy too much to invade someone else's. Just know I'm here if you need to talk."

"I'm grateful for that," I reply.

She pats me on the shoulder then lets me pass. I go to my desk. What will I do next? *Anything*. That's what

I'll do next. I'll do anything it takes . . . no matter what that might be.

Chapter Review

Chapter Six

Blake

THE VIEW FROM MY office is almost indescribable. My brothers and I managed to eke out a perfect piece of paradise in the middle of a city that's certainly gone downhill through the last several years. We love it here though and aren't willing to give up on Seattle . . . not unless we absolutely have no other choice.

We gaze out at Mt. Rainier as the sun drops behind the horizon, painting the sky in oranges, purples, and every color in between, each of us holding a crystal glass in our hand, amber liquid sitting on ice. We're kicked back in our chairs, and far enough away from the busy traffic that's always rolling through the streets below; we almost feel alone in a world that never stops moving.

"I want that mall to be the center of our project," Tyler says.

"We could build our own, not using Sheppard Malls, then we'd get to keep all of the profits for ourselves," Byron points out.

I sigh. "You know all of us are stubborn once we settle on something we want. We're done staying local. This project, when it's finished, will take us nationwide. We'll have other states begging us to build in their area. We need to stay with Sheppard Malls so we can take this all through the country, and even into Canada, maybe beyond. We'll have a waiting list that stretches for miles. We can change the entire industry and how it's done with this one project, especially with the patents that have just been approved," I tell them.

"Okay, then who's going to be the sacrificial lamb and find a wife?" Byron asks. The funny thing about his words is that he's deadly serious. If this is what has to be done to get what we want, he'll find a way to make it happen. For some reason the words make me laugh.

"I don't think one of us has to *actually* get married. He just wants to see that we can commit to a woman for more than a night," I say after a long moment.

"I don't like some man, even a business partner, telling me what I have to do in my personal life," Tyler says.

I again laugh. "Yeah, I don't do too well with that either. But he's not exactly *telling* us we have to be committed, he's just made it more than clear that he prefers working with men in . . . um . . . healthy relationships," I say.

"I heard the Palazzos and Corisis are feeling him out, thinking of something too damn similar to our idea for me to be comfortable," Tyler says, frustration clearly evident in his tone.

"We got to this first. Our plans aren't out there for anyone to get their hands on," Byron says, looking horrified at the thought that someone might have a spy in our company. "With the Copyrights and patents there's nothing they can do . . . right?"

"They don't know about our project, they only know we've met with him, and it's making their wheels spin. We've been planning this for two solid years and managed to keep it away from the world. We knew we'd have to move fast once we got the patents, once we were ready to break ground," I tell my brothers.

"So, what do we do?" Tyler asks.

I drain my glass, then go to my built-in bar, and refill. I bring the bottle back with me, knowing my brothers will want more of their own. We don't often drink, but when we do, we do it with purpose. I sit and sip on my drink, not allowing myself to drain it this time.

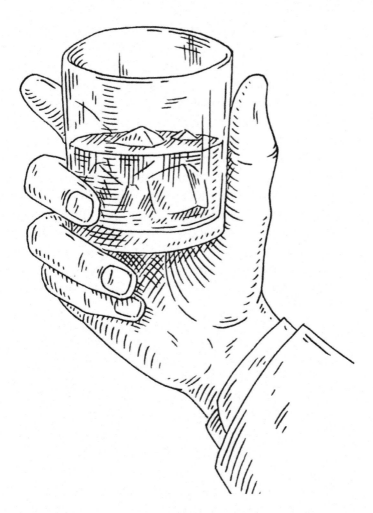

"We prove he needs to partner with us. The money doesn't seem to matter to him. Hell, all of us are richer than we need to be. It has to be about pride in having something new, in having a project that blows the rest of the world out of the water, and makes it impossible for anyone to catch up to us for at least the next century," I say.

"Then I'll ask again, who in the hell is going to get married so this guy will do business with us?" Byron asks.

I run my fingers through my hair as I look at my brothers. I then close my eyes, and a vision of Jewel flashes before my closed lids. I haven't gone near the woman since that first glance that shook me up over a month earlier. I've proven to myself I'm in control of my own body, and certainly in control of my actions.

The craziest part of all of this though is that I've looked at her one too many times through our security system. There are cameras all over this building, and I hate that I caved and followed her as she walked through the halls just to sate my desire to see her. I must be showing something in my face or body language because both of my brothers sit up a little straighter as they focus on me.

"What aren't you telling us?" Tyler demands.

"I'm not even close to agreeing to marriage . . . however, there's a woman I've been intrigued by for over a month now. I might be willing to come up with a mutually agreeable contract with her that could convince Stanley I'm in a committed relationship." I hate the words as soon as they come out of my mouth.

"Who?" Tyler and Byron demand in unison.

"Just an employee," I say, not wanting to give out her name. They'll immediately search for her in the company data. For some reason I don't want them to see her. It's not like I've put a claim on her. If one of them wants to take my place . . . that should be fine. Right? If so, then I'm not sure why the idea fills me with rage.

"Come on, spill," Tyler demands.

I sigh. "She's new, been working here a bit over a month. I find her . . . very attractive," I concede.

"Have you spoken to her . . . or possibly . . . done something more?" Byron asks. This is highly unusual.

None of us have ever dated . . . or done *anything* with one of our employees, not in all of the years we've owned this company. It's not a policy, just a standard we've always lived by . . . until this woman shows up and knocks me off-kilter. Even then I've managed to restrain myself.

"No, we've only spoken a few words one time. I've stayed away ever since," I say.

"Then how do you know she'd be interested?" Tyler asks.

Byron laughs. "Hell, Ty, you aren't so foolish as to believe *any* woman could *possibly* turn away our brother's attention if he focused all of his charm on her, are you?"

I roll my eyes. "Shut up, Byron." His words are filled with too much sarcasm to be a compliment. "If I went after her, there's no way she'd turn me down." They chuckle at my words, but I have no doubt I could have her if I want.

"This could work," Tyler says. "Stanley's a family man. If we want to lock this in, he needs to see we're more than forever bachelors. Put this woman on your arm, have her play along. Pay her a lot, screw her brains out, then find her new employment once the contract is signed." He shrugs as if this is no big deal.

I flinch the slightest bit at his words. It's not that I disagree with his line of thinking, it just sounds so damn cold as he says the words aloud. I shake my head after a minute. Are we really this cold, this removed from the real world? Maybe.

"At least tell us her name," Byron demands.

They aren't going to leave me alone about this. "Jewel," I finally say. Just the sound of her name on my lips feels right. I've done nothing to curb the power of the crush I feel toward this woman. This isn't good.

"I'm not doing this. The man can do business with us based on our merit, not on our damn sex lives. He's either in or he's out . . . period."

Tyler and Byron look at me, much less conviction in their gazes.

"What's wrong with a hot woman on your arm . . . and in your bed?" Tyler asks. "If it helps seal a deal, there's nothing wrong with it."

"I'm not screwing someone to get a job," I insist.

"You wouldn't be screwing her to get a job. You'd have her on your arm to push us over the edge of the other guys. The screwing would be an added bonus," Bryon says with his trademark grin that draws the ladies to him.

"This is ridiculous and stupid for us to even be thinking about," I say as I stand, moving to the window and looking out at the rapidly darkening sky.

"We've done worse to get what we want," Tyler points out.

I don't bother to reply. I've made myself clear about how I feel on this. The thing is, it doesn't sound horrible to ask her to be mine . . . for a short time. It's wrong to do it because someone's trying to make me. I can't do this . . . can I?

My brothers keep talking, but I'm no longer listening. I'm lost in my own thoughts. I'm torn. On one hand I want to make this happen . . . on the other . . . I won't be told what to do. It's a damn good thing I have no idea that we're currently being overheard . . . by the last person I'd want to hear this conversation. We might all be going to hell together.

Chapter Review

Jewel

I T'S BEEN A WEEK SINCE I walked past Blake's office . . . and heard the conversation he was having with his brothers. No, I wasn't spying. I'd been told to drop something off with his secretary who wasn't at her desk. Then I heard talking. The door was open and there were three sets of incredibly deep, mesmerizing voices speaking. What girl would turn away? Apparently not this one. I moved forward and listened in for a moment, guilt eating away at me for spying.

I then walked away in shock, at first offended he'd been speaking about me as if I was nothing more than a piece of meat that could be his if he wanted to take a bite. But then . . . well then, it had me thinking. I've got a problem I can't seem to solve on my own. What if we can make a deal together? What if we can do something that will be mutually beneficial?

Blake's brother had told him to give me money, use my body, and then find me a new job. I do need more funds, but more than that right now, I need to have a man on my arm, show the courts I can provide a stable family for my brother. It's frustrating and ridiculous, but I vowed to do anything to get Justin back. That's exactly what I'm willing to do.

At first the thought of sex with the man horrified me. I've had some time to think about it though. I'm twenty-four years old . . . and he's hot. If I'm going to experiment, he's the man to do it with. I'm not sure how I feel about all of this, but I'd be a liar if I said I wasn't attracted to him. I don't like the thought of being a whore, but my brother needs me. It's just sex. It happens every single day all around the world. I can do this . . . and I don't think it will be a hardship when it comes to such a gorgeous man.

I *can* do this. I've been telling myself this for the past week. I've now recruited an old friend to help me. I take in a deep breath and walk forward into her salon. If I'm going to seduce Blake Astor, I'm dang well going to need help. He might've made comments to his brothers about me, but he hasn't made a move on me since that meeting. It's time for me to make the first move. I know he stays late on Fridays in the offices where he can be alone, something I've discovered he likes a lot. It's now or never. My friend Amy greets me, then takes me to a back room.

"We're going to turn you into a dream," she promises.

I let out a breath. "I'm scared."

"You don't have to do this."

"Yes, I do."

I've told her everything. We used to be friends when I was in high school. We lost contact over the years, but when I called her, she was more than happy to reconnect. It doesn't do me any good to hide away. I need friends. I need people in my life. I need Amy.

She doesn't say anything more as we begin. She starts by cutting and highlighting my hair, then doing my makeup to perfection. It takes hours, but that's okay. Blake will be at the office all night. If he's not there when I get back, I guess the fates have spoken and this isn't the route I'm supposed to take.

By the time Amy shows me the clothes, I'm a mess, my nerves jumping. Amy smiles as she turns me to look in the mirror. I don't recognize myself in the short dress that hugs my curves and highlights my body. This is what I wanted. I need Blake to want me, to lust after me.

I'm putting myself up for sale, hoping he'll bite. I'm turning myself into an empty shell, and it's best for me to keep emotion out of this. My gaze meets Amy's in the mirror.

I'm putting myself up for sale, hoping he'll bite

"You look incredible, Jewel," she whispers, her voice sounding both sad and awed.

I nod at her, too choked up to speak, then turn back to the mirror. I'm staring at a stranger as I meet my own gaze. My long, dark hair has been shortened. Expertly applied makeup conceals the circles beneath my eyes, and bright red lipstick matches my dress to perfection. My legs are on full display, one of my best assets if I had to pick. Amy agrees.

Justin.

I think of my brother as panic flows through me. I'm doing all of this for Justin. I need to bring him home, and I'll do whatever it takes to do just that. The only thing that matters in my life is my little brother. My body is nothing more than a tool, and I look good, so this tool should be perfect.

"It's not too late to back out," Amy says, seeming worried.

"This has to be done, Amy. I'm fine . . . just scared," I admit.

"You have so many options," Amy says. "It might feel like you don't, but there are other ways."

I shake my head. "Nothing's working. Every day Justin stays in those heartless homes is another day I lose my brother. I don't want him broken, don't want the trauma to be so great he'll never be able to be fixed. I can do this. What's a body, anyway? It's just flesh and blood. I can seduce a man to get what I want. Women have been doing it for many years."

"*You* haven't been doing it," Amy says.

"There's no difference in falling in love and giving your body, or in using what you've been given to get what matters most. I can do this."

Amy doesn't argue anymore. She turns away, and I'm glad. I don't need for her to talk me out of this. I'm afraid I'll back out if she argues too much. I can't do that to Justin. Heck, Blake might reject me anyway. This might all be for nothing.

From the moment I made the decision to do this, I knew my world would never be the same again. I've managed to suppress my fears though. My brother matters more than I do right now. I'll do anything and everything to have him with me. This is the reason I'm here, basically selling myself to the highest bidder.

"If you aren't going to change your mind, you'd better get going," Amy says.

I smile. "Let's do this." I don't recognize my own voice. It's determined but void of emotion. I'm taking myself to another place so I can do what needs to be done.

I turn from the mirror and follow Amy out the back room and into a waiting car that will take me to the office building. I have a coat over my skimpy dress, but I still don't want to ride public transportation with what I'm currently wearing.

I arrive at the office building, nod to the guards on duty, then make my way to the top floor. It's dark and eerily quiet. I stop in the bathroom, my nerves trying to get the better of me. I curse myself. *Shape up, Jewel!* This is simply another day in my life, a day I'll soon forget. My body is just a tool to use. It's not sacred . . . it's not important . . . and it's not special. All that's important is for me to get my brother. He has a lifetime ahead of him, and all of that can be shattered in an instant if the wrong hands get hold of him while he's in state custody.

I need to look at this as a job, an acting job. This is a role I'm playing. I'll do my best to think of myself as a character in a film, being the woman Blake was speaking about to his brothers . . . a seductress.

At the end of our time together, the director will yell cut, and I'll slip out the back door.

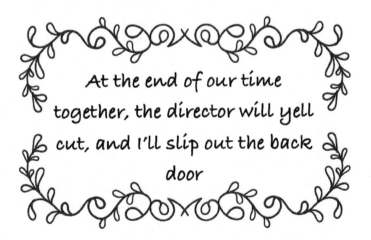

At the end of our time together, the director will yell cut, and I'll slip out the back door

I walk with confidence down the hall and see Blake's door open, his light on. No one else is on this floor, a very good thing. If there was another soul here, I'm sure I'd lose my bravado. I move forward and boldly slip through his door. His head whips up as he stares at me, my coat still covering my body, but my hair and makeup done to perfection showing him something is different about this midnight visit.

"Jewel?" he asks, his tone confused and questioning.

I don't hesitate, finding my strength. "I heard you talking last week. You need a woman . . . and I need money . . . and a fake boyfriend."

He looks shocked for a brief moment before he covers up the look, leaving a smirk resting on his lips. He leans back in his chair as if he's intrigued. So far, so good. He hasn't told me to leave the room.

"I like an honest woman. What do you need money for?"

"That's none of your business," I tell him, not rudely, just matter-of-factly.

"It's not my business, but you're willing to use your body to get money?" he questions.

"Yes," I tell him. There's no point in playing the blushing virgin now. I've made him an offer and if I shrink at this point, the entire game is over before it's ever begun.

"What makes you think I want you?" he asks, and I can't help but flinch as I've been wondering this same thing. Why would a man like Blake Astor, who can literally have any single woman he wants, ever desire me? He wouldn't. But he told his brothers he wanted me. That's what has me in this room right now.

"As I said, I was passing your office last week and I heard you speaking to your brothers. I decided to let you know I'm available." There's a slight tremble in my voice, but not enough for him to notice.

"You're taking a big risk in losing your job right now," he warns.

My stomach hurts with how hard it's rolling. "I've hit rock bottom. I have no choice but to take risks at this point," I say.

He grins, but it's not a happy, friendly smile. No, this is the look of a predator . . . a predator who's hungry. A shiver rushes through me.

"What will you do to prove how much you want this?" he asks. He kicks back the slightest bit as he leans back in his chair, his toned legs spread, his posture seemingly relaxed. This man owns his piece of the world and if I stand a chance at winning this game, I have to act like I belong here.

When Blake Astor had held my gaze over a month ago, I'd felt like I was in the middle of a hurricane. He touched my fingers and I hadn't been able to breathe. Maintaining my composure around him will be difficult, but I have too much to lose not to do this. I either play this game . . . or my brother is lost forever. I *can* do this.

Mustering all of the confidence I can, I begin sauntering toward Blake. My body language makes it seem like I want him, and nothing more. I undo the buttons of my jacket, and let it fall from my shoulders as I move toward him, a little thrilled at his sharp intake of breath as his eyes rake me over from head to toe.

I might not have the greatest body in the world, but it's pretty dang good . . . thanks to excellent genetics. Fear lurks beneath my skin, but much to my surprise there are also stirrings of excitement . . . something I don't want to analyze when the stakes are so damn high.

I stop in front of Blake, only a couple of feet between us. I've never done this before and I'm not quite sure what I'm supposed to do next. I can't show my indecision to him, but I really don't know what to do next.

"Are you happy being here, Jewel?" Blake asks, not moving to touch me.

What a strange question for him to ask. No, I'm not happy to be here, I'm forced to be here. But it's not him forcing me, it's my own decisions that have brought me to this place in life.

"I'm pleased to be here," I finally say, the lie easily rolling off my tongue. I've never been good at lying and I don't like how easy it is for me to do right now.

His lips turn up in a sardonic smile as I do my best to keep looking him in the eyes. I can't tell what he's thinking, though I'm sure my own face is an open book no matter how hard I'm trying to hide what I'm feeling from him.

"No. You aren't thrilled to be here, but give it some time and I guarantee you'll be begging me to not let you go."

I want to put a dent in the man's ego, but that's not what I'm here to do. My job is to make him feel good, to make him desire me.

"I assure you there's nowhere else I'd rather be, and though I'm sure it will be a disappointment for me when our time ends, I have no doubt we'll go our separate ways when we're finished getting what we want from each other."

He laughs. "Did you memorize that speech from a learner's manual?" He tilts his head as if trying to read me, trying to solve a puzzle and not quite sure how.

"Of course not, Mr. Astor. I find you *very* attractive and I'm sure you're not an easy man to walk away from."

"Then prove to me that you're happy to be here, that you want to be mine," he says, his voice calm, almost mocking. "Prove to me we can have an . . . arrangement together." This is it. This is what I'm here for. I either go all in now, or I run . . . which way am I going to go?

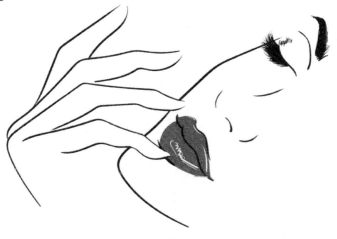

Chapter Review

Jewel

THERE'S NO DOUBT BLAKE is testing me. If he doesn't like what I do next, he might send me packing. Not only will this little game be over, but I'll most likely lose my job on top of it. I've made a calculated risk . . . and I dang well better follow through or I'm screwed . . . and not in a good way.

There's a small part of me that wants him to reject me. If I don't manage to sell my body and save my brother, it won't be because I didn't try, but because I was rejected. As soon as this thought flits through my mind, guilt eats away at me. Justin needs me and I *will* be here for him . . . even if it makes me hate myself.

Justin will never have to know what I've done to get him back . . . and I'll have to forgive myself for my sins.

I'll have to forgive myself for my sins

"How do you want me to prove myself?" I hope I'm making my voice sufficiently sexy.

He grins, looking utterly relaxed in his chair. "Be creative."

Hesitating only another second, I step forward and lean down, allowing my breasts to brush lightly against the smooth material of his suit jacket. The small contact makes my nipples harden and my breath hitch. Maybe I won't have to do much acting with this man, because he creates sensations in my untouched body that are unlike anything I've ever felt before.

When he doesn't show the slightest sign that he approves of my attempt to be seductive, I lean in closer and run my slender fingers up the sleeves of his jacket and embrace his neck. I lean against him and kiss his jaw, then trail my lips across his firm chin and down the side of his neck.

Am I having any effect at all on this seemingly untouchable man? I trace the side of his neck with my forefinger to test his pulse. It's beating rapidly. Yes! He isn't as cool and collected as he's making himself appear. This gives me the strength to continue, though I'm far from a seductress and have no clue what to do next. I'll have to listen to what my body tells me to do.

I don't get the chance to do that.

Blake stands as his hands snake around me, and he pulls me tightly to him, then reaches into my neatly coiffed hair, quickly loosening my locks so they fall over my shoulders. Grasping a handful of my hair, he forces my head back, leaving me far too exposed, my neck a succulent dish for him to feast upon.

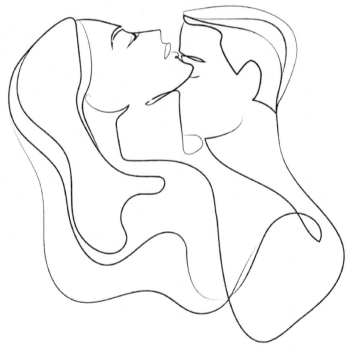

This is fast . . . almost too much, too soon. I want to pull away . . . but know that I can't. This is going to happen no matter what, so isn't it better that he takes whatever he wants instead of me trying to figure out what to give him?

Without a word, he leans forward and his lips crush mine, punishing me for something I'm not aware I've done. He doesn't ask for permission to invade my mouth; he simply thrusts his tongue forward, diving between my gasping lips, while one hand moves down my back and grabs my derrière.

As quickly as he begins the kiss, he pulls back, and once my lids flutter open, I gaze at the fire in his eyes.

"You make me want to do things I shouldn't," he growls before turning us and leaning me backward over his desk.

He pushes his hand up my side and scorches my skin as he slowly moves over the mound of my breast and squeezes. The feel of his palm against my covered nipple undoes me. I'm barely conscious that we're in his office with the door open. But my desire is too great to care. He leans down and takes my lips once more.

Sensation washes through me, forgetting where we are. When he moves his hand to the hem of my skirt and begins raising it, I'm in the throes of a desperate internal struggle. There are security guards here. I really don't want to be caught in this position with the boss. I should've shut the dang door. This is what I want, though. This is what I came here for. I can't think, dammit.

It's impossible to reason with his masculine scent surrounding me, making my stomach clench as need claws through me. This is something new . . . something I've never felt before. I wasn't planning on feeling so much attraction when I started on this mission.

I need to take control of the situation. I was the stronger one, and somehow he's managed to take over. No more. I step away from him, give him what I hope is a seductive smile, then move back so he has a clear view of me.

"Do we have a deal?" I huskily ask.

"I'm not sure yet," he says, not showing any emotion in his beautiful silver eyes.

"Then let's make you surer," I tell him. Holding the fear back, I begin undoing the buttons on the side of my dress. The air is warm in his office and I remind myself I'm playing a role here.

I shrug off the dress, leaving me standing in nothing but my skimpy bra and panties, the dim lighting of the room accentuating my body as I gaze at him with my head held high and my shoulders back. I dare him to turn me away. He won't get anything unless we have a deal.

It's not too big of a deal, because all relationships are this way. Some people demand items, and some people want emotional payments, but *everyone* is looking for something when they pick a partner. I'm looking for a person to assure the courts my brother will be fine with me. If only they knew. It'd all be a joke, the whole system is screwed up.

"Do you want to see more?" I ask, making my lips turn up in a slight smile.

"Yes," he says.

"Then do we have a deal?"

He gazes at me with what appears to be respect showing in his eyes. The emotion flashes by so quickly I might be imagining it.

"What's my part in all of this?" he asks.

"I give you whatever you want while you finish your business deal . . . and you appear in court with me . . . once," I tell him.

His eyes narrow. "Court?" he asks. "For what?"

"That doesn't matter right now. It's not illegal. *Apparently* our justice system is still rigged, and a woman isn't good enough without a man in a sexist judge's eyes," I spit out. I have to rein it in before I go off on a tangent.

"You have me intrigued," he says.

"I don't care if you're intrigued. I want to know if we have a deal."

I'm standing before him in red lace that isn't leaving much to the imagination. I won't go any further with this unless I have his word. A man like Blake doesn't lie. If he tells me we have a deal, it's set. There's still a small part of me that wants him to turn me down. The larger part, the piece of me that has to help my brother needs him to say yes. I ignore the part that knows I'll enjoy my time with him.

"We have a deal," he huskily whispers. I feel a mixture of euphoria and fear. This is what I want. He doesn't move. If I don't finish this little game, the deal will be off. I need to be braver than I've ever been before.

I reach in front of me and unclip my bra, letting it glide open before I slowly slide it down my arms, then let it float to the floor below. I can't stop a blush from burning my cheeks as the air touches my nipples and they harden, his gaze narrowing as he clenches his fingers, not as much in control as he wants me to believe.

"Beautiful," he huskily whispers, and this one little word gives me courage to continue.

I can't hesitate any longer so without further delay, I hook my thumbs in the elastic of my panties and draw them down my legs, then kick them out of the way, leaving me standing before him in nothing but a garter and red heels. I slowly spin, then face him again and give a hint of a smile.

My stomach is shaking as I begin walking toward him, leaving my pile of clothes behind. Am I about to lose my virginity on a desk in my boss's office? It's so damn cliché, but I'd be lying if I said I wasn't turned on. This is so out of my league, but I'm loving it because of this simple fact . . . even if I'm doing all of this because I've been forced into it.

I move up to Blake and gently run my fingers down his arm. I'm really unsure of what to do next. I've never been a seductress. I needed to watch a few movies to figure out this much. How pathetic is that? He's clearly turned on though, so I'm doing something right.

He reaches for me, touching my throat, then slowly moving his finger down between my breasts and circling across my trembling stomach. He stops and splays his hand over my flesh, making my already hot body even warmer, making me shake before him.

"Very beautiful," he says almost reverently. His touch alone is making it difficult to stand upright because my knees are shaking, and I feel like fire is licking through my veins. I take in a deep breath then run my fingers from his arm to his chest. I feel a shiver beneath his clothes.

I move downward, and my fingers skim over his pants where his hardness pulses beneath the material. I'm hot and breathless. He wants me . . . and I want him too. I wasn't expecting to feel this need. I expected this to be a chore . . . not a pleasure.

I run my fingers over his hardness, then squeeze through the pants, satisfaction filling me as he sucks in a breath of air. This is what power feels like . . . this is control. No one will ever own him, but in this moment he's mine to do with as I want. This gives me confidence, gives me courage.

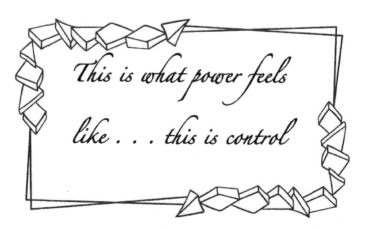

This is what power feels like . . . this is control

I'm shaking as I kneel before him and reach for the button of his pants, then slowly slide his zipper down. He tenses beneath my touch as I open his pants, finding silk underwear beneath. I should hate this, should despise this man, but I don't.

I'm surprised to feel pleasure building inside me as I free him from the confines of his silk briefs . . . and oh my. A surge of panic washes through me as I gaze at his solid length, slowly cupping him in the palm of my hand. He's hard, thick, and long, and I'm not sure how we're going to fit together. I squeeze his thick flesh and am rewarded by a low groan rumbling from his throat. I want to make this man come. I like that he's shaking beneath my touch.

Knowing I'm causing him to tremble gives me the confidence to continue. I slide my palm over the slick tip of his shaft, using his own lubrication as I glide my hand up and down his length. His breathing quickens, and I begin moving faster, knowing it won't take long for me to learn how to make him explode.

He's breathing heavily as I stroke him and lean forward, taking a couple of inches of his thick shaft into the warm recesses of my mouth. I suck him as I stroke, his pleasure surrounding us as he moans. I take him deeper, feeling him pulse on my tongue . . . and then warmth fills my mouth as he groans loudly and shakes beneath my touch. I gentle my sucking as I lick the head of him, tasting every last drop of his pleasure.

Finally I pull back, then look up at the man I've pleasured, the first man I've ever done this with. There's a visible sheen of sweat on his forehead as he gazes down at me, shock and desire still sparking in his unusual silver eyes.

He finally reaches down and pulls me to his body, my legs shaky as he presses me against him. Neither of us has spoken. I'm not sure what comes next. He leans down and kisses me for a brief moment. Then he pulls away and moves to the pile of my clothes and grabs my long coat.

He holds it out and I shakily move toward him. He places the coat on me, then begins buttoning it . . . all without saying a single word. He grabs my discarded clothes, shoves them into his computer bag, and moves to the door of his office. I'm staring at him, unsure of what to do next.

"Let's go," he says.

I don't ask where. I made the offer to him, and now I'm his. I'll soon find out what comes next by following him from the office, feeling incredibly self-conscious, knowing I have nothing on beneath this coat. I feel like the guards can tell I'm naked beneath my coat as we pass by them. They stay professional . . . and I start to wonder if this is a terrible idea. I don't need office gossip to chase me out of this building.

We move to the garage, he holds open the passenger door of his vehicle, and I slip inside. He climbs into the other side and begins driving. I'm not sure where we're going . . . but I'll soon find out. I started this . . . but there's no doubt he's going to be the one to take over . . . and the saddest part of all is . . . I think I like it.

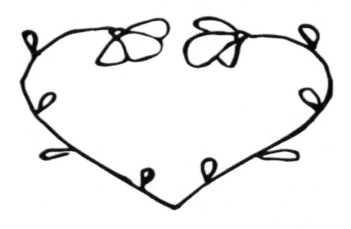

Chapter Review

Blake

I'M NOT SURE WHAT I'M doing. This isn't something I normally think, let alone say aloud. The only thing I do know right now is that I've desired this woman for over a month, and here she is, showing up at my door, offering me a deal I can't refuse. I shouldn't be this hasty, but it's too late for that now.

We're in my car, driving to my apartment complex. I could stop this . . . but I won't. I can tell myself this is nothing more than a business transaction . . . but I have a feeling I'm wrong about this as well. I desire this woman far more than I want to make a deal with Stanley Sheppard.

We pull into the underground parking garage at the huge apartment complex.

"You're taking me home?" she asks, looking and sounding confused.

I smile at her. "We live in the same building, Jewel," I say, dropping this bombshell and seeing her eyes widen in shock.

"I . . . uh . . . I didn't realize you lived here," she tells me.

"There was no reason for you to know," I say. She flinches. I turn off the vehicle and let out a sigh. I'm not sure what I'm doing here, but I don't need to be an ass. This isn't easy for me. I don't trust women. I like a warm body beneath me, but I don't trust a woman to be true, to be honest, to be a partner. I far prefer a business deal, which is what Jewel and I have here.

I do show respect to my business partners. I certainly don't bow to anyone I work with, but I like mutual respect. I don't need to make snide comments to Jewel, and I don't have to scare her.

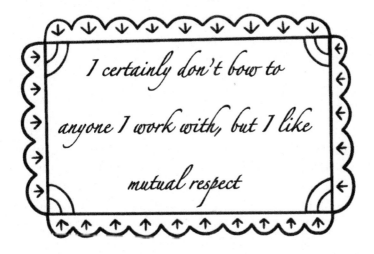

I certainly don't bow to anyone I work with, but I like mutual respect

"Of course not," she says. I feel a little better at the defiance in her tone. She might be instigating this, but she has her reasons. I'm not sure what they are . . . but I'll find out.

I might be able to disguise my emotions like a professional poker player, but if I'm honest, I'm shaken up. I'm far from a newcomer to sexual pleasure — in fact I've pretty much seen it all — but still, when Jewel performed her striptease I had to force myself not to reach out to her, not to beg her to be mine. It was very difficult to stay calm.

I nearly lost all control when she lowered herself to the floor and her sweet, plump lips closed around my dick. I . . . don't . . . lose . . . control . . . not ever. I'm *always* in total command of my emotions. I need to be more careful so I don't slip up again.

Knowing I have to be careful, even though I've just had a mind-blowing orgasm, I want more. I *need* to feel myself sinking deep within her heat, to feel her body cradling mine. I love sex in many different ways and positions, love how for a few glorious moments the only thing on my mind is pleasure — no stress, no worries, no thoughts of yesterday or tomorrow. This is a haven for me in a world that has been less than kind.

I also love the buildup to sex. I love the way it feels to caress a woman's body, to taste every inch of her skin, to hear her sounds as she's pleasured. I love the different shapes of the partners I've been with, the different sounds they make.

Still, in thinking about all of this, there's something different about the woman walking beside me to my penthouse. I want so much more with her, which is totally unacceptable. We can have a mutually beneficial arrangement, but I can't crave her this much and still keep my sanity. I won't stay with one woman . . . not after what I saw with my mother.

I close my eyes and am assailed by the sound of my mother screaming in pain. A shudder rushes through me as I snap my eyes open, then shake my head and force out the eerie note of my mother's dying cry.

It's been twenty-five years, and the anniversary of her and my father's death is quickly approaching. I'm aware of what this means . . . this entire week will be hell. It doesn't matter how much I think I've hardened myself . . . *nothing* helps. I've heard people say that time heals all wounds . . . but they lie.

people say that time heals all wounds . . . but they lie.

Time does nothing but haunt me. The only thing that helps: I've learned to numb myself from the pain as a means of self-protection. I also know I can only run on adrenaline for so long before instinct grows exhausting and can't save me anymore. I've discovered that sex *can* ease the pain. Lots and lots of sex with *many* different women of all shapes, sizes, and colors can make me forget the pain of my childhood.

There are times I refuse to have my needs met, just to prove to myself I can go without it. I can't give power of my emotions over to women. One thing that's sure in this life — *all* women are like my mother. They need to gain something, and in the end, they'll try to take it all from their latest victim.

I'm incredibly good at reading people. It's how my brothers and I have gotten to where we are in life. I know who I should go into business with . . . and who I shouldn't. I also know who I should have sex with and who I shouldn't. If I were a smarter man I'd send Jewel packing . . . apparently I'm not above thinking with my dick. I can't send her away though . . . not yet.

I look at Jewel as we walk through the entrance into my living room. She's taking it all in, her eyes wide. I try to see my place through her eyes. Yes, it's large, *very* large, but it's not ridiculously opulent. I need a lot of space without tons of furniture, and I can't stand knickknacks.

The only semblance of an emotional connection in the entire room is a framed photo of my brothers and me that's hanging on the wall. Tyler brought it over while I was away, and the pest hung it up without permission. I vowed to take it down, but it's still in the exact same place two years later. The picture shows me laughing with my brothers, giving the appearance that there's a softer side of me not many get to see.

"What happens now?" Jewel asks. "I've never made a deal like this before and I'm unsure of what to do."

The vulnerability in her voice wounds me. What in the hell are we doing here? Is this innocence she's portraying real or is it an act? Am I going to hell for agreeing to this? The women I'm normally with know the score. We're happy to scratch each other's itches

100

and then be on our way. Something about this makes me feel like a villain.

I should stop . . . but I won't. I can't. I don't want to admit how much I'm drawn to Jewel, but I can't pull back. Before I realize I'm moving, I turn and pull her into my arms. Her eyes go wide as she stares at me for a solid two seconds. Then I bend and take her lips, desperate for another taste of her.

I'm shaken once more by the power of our connection, by the current of electricity shooting straight to my groin, and the erratic beating of my heart. My mind goes blank, and I push harder, trying to drive these feelings away. I can handle lust, but I can't accept loss of control.

I pull her tightly against me as I plunder her mouth, greedily swallowing the groans she can't hold back. Our passion grows hotter. I slide my hand down her back, then find the edge of her coat and move my fingers along her naked skin. She whimpers as her lips slide beneath mine.

I curve my hand against her butt and pull her leg up as I move us backward, pressing her against the wall. I groan against her lips as I slide my fingers between her thighs, nearly coming undone with how wet she is for me. She might think she's sacrificing herself by being with me . . . but she's as turned on as I am and wants this as much as I do. This is no sacrifice, this is passion that can't be stopped.

There's no doubt I can have her right here and now; I can take us both to heaven again and again. My loss of control scares me, though. I need to think . . . and I can't do it when she's in my arms. Reluctantly, I pull away from her, taking one step, then another, and another. It's more difficult than it should be to walk away from her.

"Head home for the night. I'll set up a doctor appointment for you for tomorrow to get tested and make sure you're on birth control. I'll give you a copy of mine so you can be sure I'm clean as well. I don't like condoms," I tell her.

> This is no sacrifice, this is passion that can't be stopped.

Her cheeks turn red at these words, and I'm unsure what to think about this. She acts so innocent one second and then like a seductress the next. This is a topic lovers should talk about without embarrassment.

"Okay," she says, her voice quiet.

"We'll talk about what's next after that," I tell her. I move to the front door, and she follows. She seems . . . relieved, which I don't like. She shouldn't be happy to leave my side. I want to push her against the wall again and remind her of how good it feels to be in my arms . . . but I don't.

I open the door and she walks out without another word. I quickly make a phone call, and within minutes I have her appointment scheduled. It's good being me. Even at midnight people answer when I place a call.

I send her a message, letting her know the place and time. I could go with her, but I don't trust myself enough yet. I have to gain control over my damn body. I won't see her for the rest of the weekend. By Monday I'll be back to myself. I'll have her sign a contract that will protect both of us. If I look at this as nothing more than a business transaction, I'll be fine.

I move up my stairs to my bedroom, shed my clothes, and climb into a very hot shower, the spray pouring over my head as steam surrounds me. My dick is pulsing no matter how much I try to qualm my desire. I'm always able to turn it off. But the more I try not to think about Jewel's lips around me, the harder I get. Her lips, red and wet, going up and down my length is the hottest thing I've ever seen.

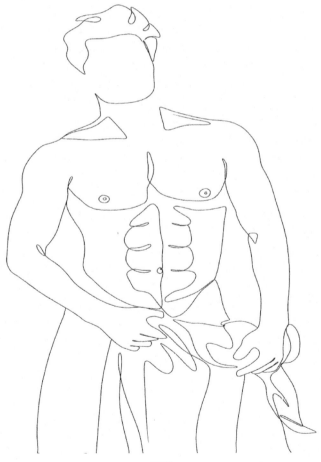

I give up trying to fight what I'm feeling as my fingers slide around my thick shaft. I groan as I lean my head against the shower wall and my hand begins moving back and forth while hot water cascades over me.

My eyes are closed; I picture my fingers sliding into her slick folds and my dick pulses in my hand as I pump it faster back and forth, a groan slipping from my lips. I could be buried inside her right now, but instead I'm stroking myself, remembering how good it felt to have her mouth on me, how good it felt to feel her tight folds squeezing my fingers.

I groan as an unsatisfying orgasm rips through me, my body shaking. The last of my release drains from my body, and I let the hot water fall over me for a few more minutes. I splay my hands on the wall, then throw my head back and let out a yell, frustration ripping through me. What in the hell is going on? Why is this woman overpowering me? This doesn't happen to me!

I step from the shower and throw a towel around my hips as I storm out of the bathroom and fling myself onto my bed, not caring that I'm still wet. It will take a while to get to sleep, but I force a smile to my lips as I assure myself that when I wake up I'll be under control again. Jewel simply surprised me tonight.

This thought makes me feel better. I don't like altering my routine. That's all this is. She took me by surprise. When I wake up in the morning, the world will be right again. I smile as I say this again and again . . . until I finally fall asleep. The world will be right as soon as I wake.

Chapter Review

Chapter Ten

Jewel

I FEEL LIKE I HAVE SAND in my eyes. Each time I open them, they hurt, so I squeeze them shut again. I didn't get much sleep over the weekend, but it's Monday and time to go to work, something I'm not looking forward to for the first time since I started my amazing job.

When I realize I can't waste any more time, I slowly lift my eyelids. I'm on my side facing a rumpled comforter, proving I was restless the night before. It still takes me a few seconds to remember I'm in a new place in a very comfortable bed. I'm no longer sleeping on the floor. My mood lightens in seconds. I run to the bathroom, then rush to the kitchen to my easy-to-use coffee pot. Heaven. Pure heaven. I load coffee in it, hit the start button, then turn around to see a blue piece of paper sitting next to a box on the counter.

My smile fades as I glance at it. I look over at my door and see the deadbolt is still secure. I didn't drink the night before so I know I didn't put this here, and it wasn't sitting on the counter when I went to bed. There's only one person it can be from . . . Blake . . . and clearly he has a key to my apartment. Of course he does . . . it's his building. I haven't thought about that until now. I could complain, but then our agreement would be over. So far, I haven't seen him since he agreed to a mock relationship. It's going pretty dang well.

I did have my doctor appointment on Saturday, and that went fine. I was expecting him to come to my apartment that night, but he didn't. I have mixed feelings about all of this, confusion over how attracted I am to him.

I signed on for this though, so I need to see what's on the note . . . and what's in the box. I open the note and read through it . . . twice, my cheeks flaming as I turn to look at the box in horror. What have I gotten myself into?

If you truly want to be mine, prove it. I like to play games. I want you to be thinking of me all day long. I want to play with you when I can't be at your side. Use the device in the box. There are instructions for what to do. Keep it inserted all day. If you want out of the agreement we've made, just write no and have this note delivered to my office. You won't lose your job. We'll both simply go our separate ways. The decision is yours.

Blake.

I look at the box again as my eyes narrow. He wants to play games? Okay, I'll play games. I've always liked games because I tend to win. I gingerly pick up the box and gaze at it for a long moment. It's now or never. I lift the lid and see a bullet-shaped device sitting on silky fabric. It's quite small, and I'm not sure what the point of it is. I pull it from the box and look at the device in confusion.

Reading the instructions, my cheeks heat at what I'm supposed to do. No one's watching me so why in the world am I embarrassed? Probably because he's going to know it's inside of me. There are cameras all over the office building and he's going to see me and . . . and what? It doesn't matter. It's not as if my co-workers are going to know about this.

I pick up the bullet thing and the tube of lubricant, then move to the bathroom. I set the items on the counter and take a nice long shower. When I'm done, I decide it's time. I follow the instructions on the box and insert the bullet inside of me. I move around and am aware the foreign object is in me, but it's not uncomfortable. I *really* don't know what the purpose of this is.

I walk to the bedroom and get dressed. It's time to leave for work. I leave my bedroom and as I'm moving down the hall, the foreign object shifts within me. It's fine, though. I'm sure I won't notice it . . . until the thing starts buzzing. My body heats up, and arousal flows through my system. What in the heck?

I try to keep moving, but have to stop and lean against the wall as my breathing grows heavy and my nipples harden. The feeling grows more and more intense. Okay, maybe I do like this stupid little device. How is it doing this? What is happening?

Just when I don't think I can take it for another second the toy stops vibrating. I slowly move back into the kitchen and slump against the counter. Is this thing on a timer? How in the world will I get through work if it does this every hour, or more? Should I call in sick? No! I'll have to learn to deal with it.

I grab my purse and exit the apartment building, praying I can get to work without the bullet going off again. I get onto the bus and am tense as I make my way down the street. My new apartment is close to work so I jump off without any further problems. Once I'm inside the huge Astor Corp building, I let out a relieved breath. Okay, this isn't so bad.

I hop into the elevator, several people are around me . . . and the thing goes off again. I let out a gasp that makes several heads turn my way. I bite my lower lip and thank the heavens above this toy is silent, or that my body is at least cushioning any sound it might be making.

"Are you okay, Jewel?" a woman asks.

I give her a grimace and nod. She doesn't look convinced. "Cramps," I mutter. She nods in understanding as she finally looks away. I'm mortified.

The elevator doors open, and I rush down the hallway, my breathing growing heavier as my body tightens. Staring at the floor, I move as fast as I can, needing to find a private place. I make it to one of the solo restrooms, and rush inside, quickly closing and locking the door behind me.

I lean against the door as the vibrating inside me turns up a notch. I let out a moan I can't stop as I sink to the floor, my body on fire. And then I explode as fire shoots through me, leaving my nipples hard and a fine layer of sweat over my skin. I'm panting as the vibration finally stops. I sit right where I am for several moments, trying to get my breathing under control.

Orgasms are beautiful things, and, like potato chips — no person can have just one

My phone dings. I ignore it. It dings again. I still ignore it. Then it goes off for a third time and I reach for my purse and shakily pull it out. I can't open my eyes to gaze at the messages as I sag against the door. As inconvenient as this toy is, I'm no longer complaining because I decide right now that orgasms are beautiful things, and, like potato chips — no person can have just one.

When my breathing is under control, I stand on shaky legs. I'm officially late to my desk now, but my co-worker will let the boss know I'm having cramps. I'd much rather my team think it's my lady time than I'm having spontaneous orgasms. That's too much to bear.

I look at my phone and can't help but smile.

Blake: *Enjoying yourself?*

Blake: *You found the one spot in the building I can't watch you. That's not playing fair.*

Blake: *Get ready for a very erotic day.*

Oh, holy hell. This is only the beginning. If I were alone, I'd love this little game. The fact that I'm going to be around my co-workers doesn't make it such a joy. I hope I get through the day in one piece. We'll have to wait and see what happens next because I can't hide in the bathroom any longer . . .

Chapter Review

Jewel

B Y THREE IN THE AFTERNOON I'm exhausted. I barely made it through lunch, having my co-worker hand me a couple of Pamprins that had me turning bright red. I had no choice but to take them, because I certainly wasn't going to tell her I wasn't *actually* on my period, but I'd just been having orgasms all day, including while waiting for my salad to arrive. With my flushed cheeks and the glean of sweat I've carried all day, it's obvious something's going on. I might have to kill Blake . . . when I quit smiling.

It's embarrassing as hell, but it also feels so damn good that I can't be all that upset about it.

"Delivery," a young woman says before she drops off an envelope on my desk and then rushes off. No one pays attention to me as I lift it. I open the flap and find a note and a key inside.

Wait at my place. I'll be home by six. That's all the note says. There's no signature, nothing that will let anyone know who this is from. As I'm reading it, the toy buzzes again and I look up at the wall where I know there's a camera . . . and plead for mercy.

The buzzing stops when I nod my head yes, letting him know I've gotten the note, and I'll be at his place. How much of the day has Blake spent watching me? I can't imagine he's gotten much done.

When I leave my co-workers and walk home, I'm more than grateful that Blake seems to be busy and the toy doesn't go off. I have time to go to my apartment first, where I strip out of my clothes that are sticky from how much I've sweated today. I take a nice long shower, then put on cotton sweats and a loose tee. I grab some ice cream then make my way to his penthouse.

Without him in it, I have a chance to look around. I don't want to snoop. I value my privacy too much to invade someone else's, and I'm sure a man like Blake has cameras . . . but that doesn't stop me. Curiosity killed the cat, dang it.

After checking it out, I move to the couch and curl up, playing with my new phone. I can see how these dang devices become so addictive. I was too busy in college to play on a phone, so I didn't pay for an iPhone. This is the first I've had one, and I vow to be careful to not get hooked on screen time.

"How was your day?"

I jump at the sound of Blake's voice. He's in front of me, moving closer. I didn't hear him come in. The large man can move like a damn ninja. The first word that comes to mind as he asks this, is *exhausting*. My day has been outright exhausting. Thanks to this contraption, which is still obediently sitting inside of my incredibly tender core, I've had more orgasms than I knew was possible . . . and I'm wrecked.

I've had more orgasms than I knew was possible . . . and I'm wrecked.

I don't tell him I snooped around in his place. I didn't find anything . . . like nothing at all. Blake doesn't seem to have anything personal to his name. There aren't any photos except for the one of him and his brothers that's hanging on the wall. Nothing. Zip. Nada.

It might be wrong to snoop, but I agreed to be with him for who knows how long. I'm curious about who he is. What if he has a dark side? It's too late to think about that now. I'm in this for the long haul.

As I looked around I didn't go into his office. There are some places sacred to a person, and an office is one of them. That doesn't mean I'm not curious of the hidden gems that might be inside his closed door. Isn't an office where all of our deepest secrets are stored?

I shake myself out of my head and realize he asked me a question. What was it? Oh yeah, he wants to know how my day has been. I'm certainly not going to admit how much his little toy impacted me all day. Even if he threatens to pour fire ants on me, I won't confess how much he controlled my body.

As I look at him I realize that he most likely knows, if the smug look on his face is anything to go by. Maybe the man truly was glued to his computer screen all day, watching me in the office as I nearly collapsed almost everywhere I moved in his building.

"My day was normal," I tell him. I feel some heat in my neck as I try to keep my face from turning red. I've never been good at lying, especially on the spot. I might be able to come up with a tall tale if I have enough time to plan it, but on the spot I'm going to give myself away fast.

He gazes at me for several long moments with his penetrating eyes, making me break out in a sweat. I desire this man . . . and I hate myself for feeling this way. Wanting Blake seriously undercuts my inner claims of self-sacrifice and makes me feel vaguely dirty about seducing him. Ugh, why does life have to be so complicated?

"I'll let you lie to me for now," he says with a knowing smile. "But I did watch you for most of the day, and I'm very aware that your body has been in a constant state of arousal from the moment you inserted that toy. I'm sure you're currently dripping wet and ready for me to plunge deep inside of your delicious heat." He places his hands on the back of the couch and leans in, letting his warm, sweet breath wash over my face. "And, Jewel," he adds, making me barely able to back hold a gasp, "I'm going to fuck you hard tonight."

He moves away, removes his hand-tailored jacket, and drops it carelessly on the arm of a chair. His white fitted shirt showcases every muscle in his back as he unconsciously flexes his arms. Next, he removes his cuff links and is rolling up his sleeves when he turns back around to find me staring at him. There's no chance I can look away. The man is absolutely beautiful.

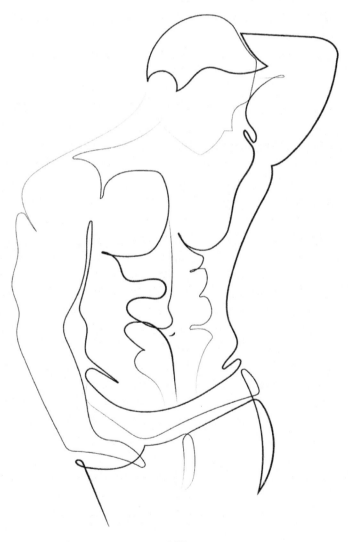

I can't move, can't breathe . . . and certainly can't speak. This man has nearly made me reach another orgasm with just his words and the caress of his breath on my mouth. I pray I'll be able to survive my time with him, because right now I'm not sure that will be possible.

"I got you a gift if you want to wear it," he tells me as he saunters closer, a bag in his hand that he'd previously left on the chair.

I take the bag from him without saying a word. I want to be horrified that we seem to be moving forward . . . but I'm not . . . I'm excited. Maybe if we get the sex portion over with, I won't be so nervous about it. I ascend his stairs with grace, inwardly cursing at my body as new moisture flows in my lower regions and my nipples harden. Of course this is how I've been most of the day, but with Blake so close to me now, the sensation grows even stronger.

I reach the bathroom and empty the contents of the bag on the counter . . . and let out an embarrassing groan. If I put this contraption on, there will be nothing hidden from Blake. Of course he's already seen me in my birthday suit, so wearing some lace and silk shouldn't mortify me. I started this game as a seductress, and I can't chicken out when we're close to the edge of the plane and about to jump.

I take my time discarding my clothes then slip into the garter and tiny skirt that barely skims the bottom of my behind. It takes a couple of tries to get the bustier on, the tiny thing pushing my breasts up, my hard nipples clearly on display through the black lace. I take a long look at myself in the mirror.

My skin's flushed, my eyes bright with the pleasure I've been given all day, and the thrill of this moment. My body's trembling, and this outfit is doing nothing to hide my arousal. I'm going to enjoy this next step with Blake, even if I don't want to admit it to myself, and certainly not to him.

I give myself another full minute, then leave the bathroom and move to the top of the stairs, trying to act as if I know what I'm doing, as if I'm walking right out of his dreams and straight into his arms.

I'm halfway down the stairs when I hear the doorbell ring. Feeling trapped at the sudden intrusion, I pause, not knowing if I should rush back up the stairs or slink down and try to hide. There's no way I'm making an appearance in these scraps of material if someone is stepping inside. There's no way he'd let someone in, is there?

As quietly as possible I retreat back up the stairs. I reach the top as my vibrator turns on, making me bend over as I pant, biting my lip to keep a groan from escaping. I try to fight the sensation, but there's no stopping it, and I whimper as a powerful orgasm rips through me, leaving me in a puddle at the top of the staircase, praying no one walks to the bottom and looks up, seeing more of me than I care to show.

It's only about thirty more seconds before Blake appears at the bottom of the stairs, a satisfied smile on his lips as he gazes up at me, clearly knowing what happened.

"Come down, Jewel," he huskily whispers as he begins unbuttoning his shirt.

Holy hell! His chest is something dreams are made of. No mere mortal should possess such looks, poise, and money. He has it all, and it isn't fair to the people he wields power over.

"Give me a moment," I say. I don't think I can walk just yet.

"I'm ready for you." His tone is sexy, making my skin heat more than it already has as he makes a show of letting his shirt land at the foot of the staircase. It takes another few seconds before I'm able to grip the banister and pull myself to my feet, even as my thighs tremble and I weaken.

Taking the steps slowly, I attempt to blunt the impact of the toy rubbing against my swollen walls. I force myself to focus on the walk, not the pleasure and pain still coursing through me. This is going to be a very long and exhausting night if he keeps playing with me like this.

I near the bottom of the stairs and he smiles at me, a predators smile, a victors smile. He knows he's in control . . . and the worst part is that his power turns me on even more.

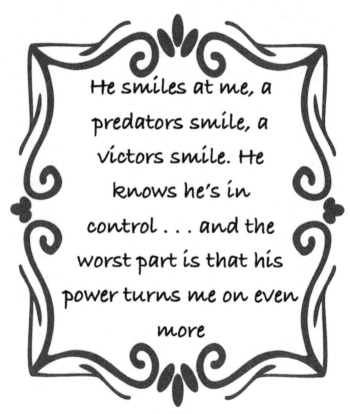

He smiles at me, a predators smile, a victors smile. He knows he's in control . . . and the worst part is that his power turns me on even more

"Sit down," he says. I pause not understanding. I still have a few stairs to go.

"Is someone in the house?" I ask as I gladly sink down on the steps. My legs aren't going to hold me up much longer.

"No. That was our dinner being delivered," he says.

Relief washes through me. He's standing before me, gazing at me like *I'm* his dinner. His eyes are glinting, filled with desire, passion that's aimed directly at me.

"Open your legs." The deep growl in his voice tells me more than anything else that he's close to the edge as he stands only a few feet from me.

I lean my head back, unwilling to make eye contact when I'm in such a vulnerable position. I do as he says, spreading my legs for him to see all I have to offer. I brace my heels and wonder what I look like in this pose.

A groan of honest appreciation from him brings an extra surge of moisture to me, and I hope like hell I'm not dripping onto his polished wooden staircase.

"Damn, you're glorious," he whispers reverently.

Okay, so *that* isn't exactly humiliating. With my eyes closed, and trying my best to act the seductress, I don't hear him move, but suddenly his finger rubs from the top of my core, along my swollen clit, down my slick folds and back up again.

"Push your hips forward, and grab the railing," he whispers huskily, and I can't do anything other than comply.

When the heat of his breath brushes against my swollen clit, my body clenches with need. At the first swipe of his tongue against the bit of pulsing flesh, I jump.

"Stay still," he says, pulling his mouth away.

This makes me want to scream. A low rumble sounds from deep in my throat, and for the next few seconds all I feel is his warm breath against my swollen flesh, teasing my sensitive pleasure point almost intolerably.

I want to beg him to go back to doing what he was doing with his tongue, but I can't. This isn't about my needs. He needs to be the one in control. He needs to have me do his bidding.

So with all of the willpower I possess, I wait in silence for what he'll do next. When his lips circle my clit again, I don't even try to contain my moan. While sucking the little mound into his mouth, he simultaneously pushes a finger inside me, moving it around the toy resting there, a cry of pleasure escapes from my lungs as I convulse against the hard stairs. When I finally come down from my high, I slowly raise my head, and find his silver gaze burning into me.

"Damn, you're responsive," he says with a shudder as he gets up and sits next to me, putting his face only inches from mine. I want his lips, want to feel him pressed against me. How can I possibly want or need anything more after all he's put me through today? I don't know, but I do suspect the games are only beginning.

He leans forward and gently clamps his teeth down on my bottom lip and sucks, sending a whole new level of desire through my small frame. Just as confusingly as this sexual play date has begun, he ends it by casually leaning back . . . and then standing.

What's next? Should I get up, hold out my hands to him, beg him to take me to bed? No. I need to wait . . . and wait . . . and wait.

"Time for dinner."

With these words, he leaves me panting on the stairs. I want to yank out the device and demand he stop toying with me. I do none of that. Instead, I struggle up on unsteady legs and follow him into the dining room.

A table is set with candles already lit and soft music playing in the background. Why the seduction scene? I'm already a guaranteed lay. And yet he holds out a chair for me.

But when I sit down, he leans over me and asks, "Ready for round two?"

Hot damn!

I don't know how, but I do know that I'm more than ready.

Chapter Review

Chapter Twelve

Blake

WHILE PUSHING JEWEL'S chair in, I brush my fingers across her shoulders, and desire shoots through me. I reluctantly pull away and sit, but immediately move my seat close to her. I *need* to have her sitting beside me, need to feel the softness of her skin against my fingers. How in the hell is this woman becoming such an obsession for me? This is a business deal and nothing more . . . right?

The buildup, the anticipation, the hunger of playing these games with her — this is the best I've felt in a very long time. I need to see how far I can push her, how far I can push myself. I've never had so much enjoyment with the preliminaries of sex. I've never waited for so long to possess a woman . . . until this one. Sure, the buildup always has its charms, but if Jewel was anyone else, I'd have bedded her the night she offered herself to me . . . and already be tiring of her.

This woman has me thinking twice, though. The way she holds herself, the burning in her eyes, the confusion. She's a mystery, and I can't stand mysteries involving women — why waste the time solving them when so many out there are easy to read? It's different with Jewel though, because I *need* to know her . . . and even more confusing I *want* to learn her story. On the other hand, I want to get as far away from her as possible, but I can't make myself do that.

Jewel responds so well to me. And though I can see she wants to ignore me, wants to turn off her emotions and pretend this means nothing — if she did that she'd be smart — whenever I touch her, she goes up in flames. Her body's a canvas for me to paint, and paint it I will. She intrigues me, makes me think that no amount of time will be nearly enough.

Her body's a canvas for me to paint, and paint it I will

When our affair comes to an end, I swear to myself I'll never think of her again. She's one more woman in a long line of women. It doesn't matter that another man will eventually touch her, do the sorts of things to her that I'm about to do.

Then why am I having these thoughts if I don't give a damn?

Crap! I don't need my own brain to argue with me. Tonight is about sex, it's about pleasure, it's about taking from Jewel what I want, and giving her only what I want to give.

What makes it so frustrating, though, is that I want to give her so much. Yes, I've pleasured her because I want to, but I've gotten even more joy from her orgasms than she's received. That's what this woman, this stranger, does to me.

She makes me feel alive and excited. She makes me forget about my past. She makes me think of only her. I'll have to do better at keeping the walls I've built around me intact, because if I'm not careful, she'll have a hold on me, and that isn't acceptable.

Jewel looks at me as if she can read my mind. I don't like feeling as if I'm being analyzed so I turn my gaze away from her. I serve us both dinner and she takes a bite, then sets down her fork. It feels like she's seeing straight into my soul. I shift in my seat, frustrated that in my turmoil I'm hard for her, as I've been all day. When I'm finally sheathed in her, it will feel like coming home.

"What are you thinking about that has this brooding look on your face?" she asks, shocking me at her boldness. This woman is full of surprises. She doesn't seem to have an issue speaking about whatever's on her mind.

"I'm thinking I'm not sure I'll be able to finish this meal with how much I want you," I honestly tell her. I add a smirk to the end of my words just so she's aware she doesn't hold power over me. I might want her body, but that doesn't mean I'm her slave.

She slowly lifts her fork and takes two more bites without saying a word as my gut grows tighter. I want to shake her, want to demand she submit to me. I almost smile at the thought. Would I want her this much if she was subservient? I bet I wouldn't look twice at her. Her strength and stubbornness turn me on more than her body does . . . even if it equally frustrates me. I'm very used to women doing anything and everything to please me.

Finally Jewel sets down her fork, then gives me a sexy smile as she rises. She moves closer, her body on full display with the tiny lace and satin barely covering her. I scoot back in my seat, not knowing what she'll do next. My arousal is screaming now.

She straddles my thighs and sits across my lap, and it takes all I have not to groan at how good it feels to have her right here where I've wanted her all day.

"You want me?" she asks with false innocence in her voice. I know this game she's playing, and I still can't resist.

"Oh yes," I say as she stretches her legs wider, her breasts now perfectly level with my face, her hard nipples straining against the thin layer of lace I want to rip off of her.

I slowly trail my hands along the outside of her thighs, over her hips, and along the alluring indent of her waist, then run them over the fullness of her beautiful breasts. The passion shining in her eyes is more than enough thanks for my attention.

"How much?" she seductively asks.

I try to harden myself. I try to push down my desire. She's the one smirking at me now. She knows she has all of the power. I'm not used to having such a loss of control. I want to stop it . . . but I can't.

"Be careful playing games, Jewel. If you awaken the beast, you might not like what happens."

Be careful playing games, Jewel. If you awaken the beast, you might not like what happens.

Her smile grows. "Maybe that's *exactly* what I want." Her sexy purr has me nearly begging her to be mine forever.

Before I can do or say anything, she climbs from my lap, moving away a few feet, then begins to dance, taking my breath away. She starts slowly, her hips swaying as her feet stay firmly planted. After a moment, her eyes close and she lifts her hands above her head, her upper body swaying as her knees dip and she lowers herself to the floor. She lifts back up, moves to me, turns, then rests her fine ass on my thighs for only an instant . . . a tiny moment that has me going from rock hard to complete steel.

She pulls away, turns again, presses her hand briefly against my chest for balance, and lets go, nearly making me protest until she turns again, showing me her delicious ass as she undulates before me, her sweet curves screaming at me, almost ordering me to take her.

When she bends forward, sticking her sweet ass high in the air while spreading her legs and swinging her hips again, I involuntarily rise from my seat. This goes beyond need, now to utter obsession. I have to take her this very minute. I step toward her, then realize what I'm doing. A shudder passes through me as I bite my lip to keep from calling out to her. I sit back down and grip the bottom of my chair to hold myself in place. I need to see how far she'll take this . . . *need* to see how this dance will end.

Standing up, she turns her head and looks at me, desire a blinding light in her eyes, her expression one of both arousal and innocence, confusing me. She's not innocent. She's the reason we're here. She's the reason we made this deal. She knows exactly who she is and what she's doing. This innocence is an act . . . and she's *very* good at it. None of this matters, though, because I still crave her. She turns away from me, breaking my control once again.

With her back still toward me, she lifts her hands . . . and I hold my breath as she loosens her bustier and lets it fall to the floor. My arousal throbs painfully.

She turns toward me, her small hands holding her breasts, giving me a show of peekaboo as the luscious mounds sway while her hips seductively swing. I can't take it another moment.

"Come here," I growl. Her eyes sparkle as she takes a couple of small steps toward me before she stops.

"Closer." She gives me a satisfied smirk as if she believes the power is all in her hands. I'm going to prove her wrong.

She's shaking as she steps flush against my body, her breasts inches from my mouth but still covered by her hands. Nearly shaking too, I grip her hands and pull them away. I barely stop a moan from escaping as I take in the sight of her hardened nipples. I *need* a taste.

"I'm going to take you long and slow, and all through the night. I'm going to pleasure us both for so long we won't be able to walk tomorrow. Always remember that your pleasure is *mine*. I own it."

Always remember that your pleasure is mine. I own it.

Her gasp of arousal is my reward. As I pull her onto my lap, I'm done playing. I want her . . . and I'm going to take her . . . even if it might take both of us straight to hell. The destination is worth the journey to get there.

Chapter Review

Chapter Thirteen

Jewel

I'M ON THE VERGE OF ANOTHER orgasm. Blake greedily takes my lips while he runs his hands down my back and pulls me against his thick arousal. My dance moves made the little vibrating toy inside me keep shifting, and I'm dripping with desire as I sit on his lap.

His kiss takes my breath away and makes me ache. Yes, I'm doing this because I've been pushed into it by the circumstances of my life, but it's turning out to be a pleasure . . . not a hardship. If I'm going to give up my virginity, this man is a good person to lose it to.

He makes me burn, want him with nothing but a look from his smoldering eyes. He's cynical and brooding, but he's also passionate and strong, and I can't pretend I don't want to bring this song and dance we've been doing to its foregone conclusion.

His mouth leaves mine, allowing me to take in a much-needed breath — not that it stays for long in my lungs. He moves to my breasts, and as he sucks one pebbled nipple before nipping it gently, I try to gulp in oxygen, but can't.

When he shifts to my other side and licks the sensitive bud as he grinds against my swollen core, I quit trying to hold back my consuming pleasure. My muscles tense, and I cry out from the pure bliss of release. I quiver in his arms as he sucks harder on my nipple, beautifully drawing out my orgasm. When it's over, I sag forward against his chest, too weak to move. I could easily fall asleep.

"We aren't done, Jewel," he whispers, his breath fanning across my neck.

"I . . . I . . . can't do more." I can barely get the words out I'm so exhausted.

"Oh, Jewel, you can . . . and you *will*. You've been pleasured all day — I've watched you come over and over again. Now it's my turn. Now *you* get to please *me*."

It seems impossible, but the deep timbre of his voice awakens my body once more. There's no way I'll survive this. A normal human being surely has to have a cap on how much physical pleasure he or she can receive in a single day.

"Please, Blake, please . . ."

"What are you begging for, Jewel?"

His hand drifts up and down my back, almost tenderly, as he asks this question, and his lips tantalizingly graze my neck.

"I ... I don't know. I ... I don't think I can do anything more. It's too much, all of it's too much." I hope he'll have some kindness within him.

"Let's see if I can change your mind."

He moves me to sit sideways on his lap, one of his arms cradling me as I rest my head against his chest. Then he stands, slowly and smoothly, with me in his arms. I don't have the energy to protest — not that I would.

He carries me through the penthouse, up the stairs, and into his room. He lays me on the bed, and I barely manage to open my eyes and look at him towering above me. But when he begins removing his clothes my stomach tightens, and I direct my gaze down.

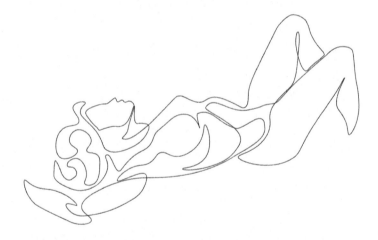

In seconds I'm seeing his long, thick, smooth shaft, hard and ready to plunge inside me. His size makes fear and desire battle within me. I'm glad he had me insert the toy. My initial thought about it — that it might help stretch me — had been silly and naïve, because the toy is nothing compared to him. But it certainly makes me wet, makes my folds more eager to hold him.

The tip of his shaft gleams with his desire, making me wetter than I've been all day. Yes, I'm tired, and I feel as if I can't go on . . . but oh, how I want him, want to feel what it's like to be taken by Blake.

"Are you ready for me, Jewel? Are you excited to quit coming on your own? If you thought you felt good with your previous orgasms, they won't hold a candle to what I'm going to give you." He sits on the bed caressing my thighs as he spreads my legs wide open.

"I . . . I'm afraid." I'm mortified to admit this.

He stops touching me as his gaze turns suspicious. "Why are you afraid?"

I tense, not willing to tell him the truth. "You're . . . um . . . large . . ." This is certainly the truth, if not quite the *whole* truth. He is indeed large.

He laughs as he resumes caressing me. "You've obviously been with pathetic men before me."

I refuse to respond to this statement. I couldn't speak even if I wanted to, because he quickly leans over me and runs his tongue along my stomach before moving down and kissing my thighs. Spreading my legs as far as he can, Blake again finds my pulsing clit and sucks and licks while his fingers slowly slide inside me. He grabs the toy and begins pulling it out.

I shake with ecstasy mixed with a shot of pain as the toy moves inside my heat. Then I feel the foreign object exit. I want to squeeze my thighs shut in relief. I've discovered that pleasure is a good thing, but a woman can only take so much before she can no longer move.

"Ah, Jewel, you're so wet, so hot, so ready for me," Blake growls before swiping his tongue up and down my folds.

"Yes, oh yes," I gasp as my head twists on the pillow. I'm ready for him, ready for *all* of him. My trepidation is quickly evaporating, and I'm no longer worried about pain, because at this moment I fear it will be more painful *not* to have him inside me.

He moves back up my swollen body before covering me with his bulk. It takes only seconds for him to be in the right position, his face lined with mine, his arousal pressing against my heat.

"Open your eyes, Jewel. I want to see what you're feeling when I'm buried deep inside you."

"No." It's the first time I've outright refused him. But I don't want him to see my expression, don't want to share this intimacy with him. It's too much. This is supposed to be clinical. This is a contract . . . and I can now admit, it's pleasurable. But there's nothing about this that's romantic. I can't look him in the eyes because I fear that will truly make me his.

"Open your eyes, Jewel — now!" he commands, the head of his desire pressing against me.

Oh my, it feels good. His thick, hot shaft is so much better than the cold, lifeless toy that was inside of me all day.

"Nooooo," I groan as I lift my hips, hoping to push him into entering me, hoping he'll lose control before he can get me to open my eyes.

"Now, Jewel. Open them now!" He leans down and bites my lower lip, sending a burst of pain through me, causing my eyes to pop open in surprise.

He smiles as he gets what he wants, and before I can even think about closing my eyes again, he drives his hips forward, filling me with one powerful thrust.

A cry of pain shoots from my mouth as my body tenses. This is nothing like what I've been expecting, and I want to back away, want to push him from me. It's too much, *way* too much. It hurts, it's foreign, it's too much.

"What in the hell?" Blake freezes, his eyes wide as he gazes down at me. Mixed emotions pass through his eyes — confusion, anger, surprise, desire . . .

"Speak now, and speak fast, Jewel."

I can't do this. I was wrong. Yes, desire has been overtaking me for days, has had my body burning, and making me think I wanted this. But I can't do it. It's too much — too intimate, too consuming, too much!

I turn my head so I won't grow weak and look at him. I'm barely holding my tears at bay, and I want to escape. Struggling will be useless, so I lie beneath him, his body still connected with mine in the most intimate way possible.

"Talk to me now," he says, his voice filled with shock.

"I . . . I can't," I say, my lip beginning to tremble.

"This is wrong. It has to be wrong." He almost sounds as if he's begging for this not to be true.

"No. No." I'm panicking now.

"How can you still be a virgin? You're twenty-four years old." I say nothing. "It's not possible."

I can't take his shock and mortification anymore. "Obviously it's possible. Are you going to finish this or let me leave?" I'm almost surprised by my words, but I can't continue speaking while he remains inside my body.

The pain has stopped, and now the fullness of him, the pressure against my inner core, is making me feel pangs of arousal again. I don't want to be aroused, don't want to desire him.

When he shifts and his chest brushes against me, my nipples throb, and he suddenly seems to notice as I wriggle beneath him, trying to make the desire go away.

He withdraws a few inches from me, then easily slides back in, my slick heat beckoning him. He stops once more.

"Do you really want to stop?" he asks, the question seeming to be ripped from him. He's given the choice back to me. Thirty seconds ago I would've said yes, I want to stop. I look up at him, panic rising in me again . . . but this time it's because I no longer want him to pull away. I assure myself it's only because of my brother, because I have to follow this through. It certainly can't be about desire.

"No, we have a deal," I finally say after what feels like a lifetime of silence between us as he rests within my body, his hardness pressing against all of my walls. He looks at me for a long moment. His eyes then narrow as he shifts, the movement giving me pleasure. I hate how much this man makes me burn.

He still doesn't move. "This is still a business deal, Jewel. You being a virgin doesn't change anything. Don't get attached to me and think it will last forever," he warns. He still looks stunned, but he seems to recover. I decide to help him get over his guilt at me being a virgin. I smirk.

"I expect the same from you. I want your money. You want my body. I think we understand each other just fine."

A flash of rage consumes Blake at my words. Though he's made it abundantly clear that he believes all women are out to get whatever they can, what I just said seems to be a slap in his face. I don't understand him most of the time.

"I'll make you forget all about money," he snaps. He grips the back of my neck less than gently, then surges within me, making me cry out in pleasure. No more pain is anywhere to be found. I try to hold on to my defiance. I look him in the eyes as my body burns and I attempt another smirk.

"It's not possible. I only want your money." When his mouth crashes against mine, I'm well aware our battle of wills is ending . . . and he's the clear victor.

"Virgin or not, money or not, you want me, Jewel," he growls. "And you're now officially mine." He begins slowly moving in and out of me, making my core burn, making my body tremble beneath him, and making me climb toward another release, this one low in my stomach, building stronger and stronger . . . so much stronger than anything I've felt all day.

"I hate you for this," I gasp.

"I don't care," he coolly replies. He stops all words with a kiss that steals my breath along with all thoughts of defiance.

He moves faster, his steel rubbing me in every pleasurable way possible, his lips caressing mine while consuming my cries. The faster he moves, the higher my pleasure grows. When his body tenses and he groans, I know we're nearing the end.

"I'm going to come, Jewel. I'm going to shoot deep inside of you. Come with me," he demands, his voice breathy but confident. Grabbing my hair, he holds me in place and takes my lips with an urgency that inflames me.

A passionate scream rips from me as he slams against my core, burying himself deep, setting my release free, and making my body convulse with an overload of sensation. He was right. The sexual pleasure I felt during the day is nothing compared to what I'm feeling now.

He shouts in ecstasy as he shakes within me, as his thick desire pulses powerfully against my walls. His release goes on for an eternity, and then he collapses against me, his body molding me to the bed. Too spent to move, I shut my eyes. It's all too much, and there's no possible way I can keep going. Sleep provides sweet relief. Sleep is my sanctuary. I give into it and fall into darkness with Blake still buried deep in me. I don't realize yet that I'm in too deep now to get out easily . . . don't realize I truly am his . . .

I don't realize yet that I'm in too deep now to get out easily . . . don't realize I truly am his . . .

Chapter Review

Blake

JEWEL RELAXES NEXT to me, and it takes me a few more seconds before I find the strength to carefully pull myself from her, then shift to my side. I gaze at this woman peacefully asleep beside me. Part of me wants to shake her, to wake her up, and demand she explain herself.

She was a virgin! How in the hell hadn't she told me this important information? I cringe as distrust runs through me. What's her game? What does she have to gain by keeping this from me? Is it a trap? I pause for a moment to self-analyze.

Would I have believed her had she told me? I'm not sure . . . I think I wouldn't have, that it wasn't possible.

144

I want to think of her as nothing more than another female wanting to get whatever she can from me. I want to believe we're equally using each other. We are, aren't we? I'm so damn confused. I've never been in this type of situation before. All of the women I've been with have known the score.

Sure, these women might've wanted to turn it into something more, but they knew from the start that any sex was temporary. I thought Jewel knew this as well. Was I wrong?

We have an arrangement that's mutually beneficial to both of us. Even if she was a virgin, it doesn't matter, does it? No! This doesn't change anything. She's still selling herself to me. She came into my office, stripped down, and offered a deal I couldn't refuse.

I run my fingers through my hair as I flip over onto my back. I want to be hard here. I want this not to matter . . . but it does. Why is she doing this? Why is she selling herself to the highest bidder? Everything within me screams there's more to this story than she's sharing. I shake my head. *Stop this!*

I might be her first lover . . . but I won't be her last. This thought doesn't sit well with me. Jewel has this strange innocence in her eyes that fills me with guilt when I look at her for too long. An odd eagerness to please rests within her. I crack a small smile. She also possesses a stubbornness that shows the world she'll never be owned. When our time ends I have no doubt she'll be hunted . . . wanted . . . and taken.

It won't take long for some man to break her . . . to erase the optimism I faintly see in her that's trying to break free from whatever's sent her into this situation. I won't be the man to take that hope from her. Dammit! I can't think of her like this I can't grow attached to her. We have an arrangement, and at the end of our time together it *will* be over. I remind myself she's already lied to me . . . and she's *certainly* played games from the very first moment our eyes connected.

She possesses a stubbornness that shows the world she'll never be owned

I stay where I am for a few more minutes, finding it difficult to pull away. I force myself to climb from the bed. As she feels the loss of my body she whimpers in her sleep and reaches out as if seeking me . . . and my stomach tightens. I want to crawl back into bed beside her.

No! I won't do that. I won't allow her to have power over me.

I lean over and carefully cover her sleeping body. She turns and snuggles into the pillow I was using. A small smile plays across her lips as she sighs and falls into a deeper sleep. I walk from the room, then march across the hall and use the guest bathroom. I stand beneath the shower spray for a very long time, hoping the water will wash her from my system.

It doesn't work.

I'm restless when I climb out and pace around my home until, nearly an hour later, I'm wearing only a towel, standing next to my bed watching her sleep. She looks so young, so innocent with her lips turned up in the barest of smiles, her breathing deep and even.

"I'm only doing this because I want you near me when I get the urge to take you. It's all about convenience." I say these words aloud, though only in a whisper. I'm lying to myself. I crawl into the bed, lying next to her. I let out a curse as I reach for her, then pull her sleeping body against me. Unfortunately I enjoy how it feels to have her head rest trustingly against my chest as I lie on my back.

No woman has slept in my bed. Not ever. I've never allowed something so intimate. Yet as she snuggles against me, her smile growing a little bigger, I recognize the first stirrings of peace I've felt in a very long time — maybe ever.

Refusing to analyze this because I know that if I do I won't be able to let this situation continue, I pull her tighter against me. I nearly come undone when she wiggles closer, seeming to need the comfort of my touch to quell whatever demons reside inside her.

My body hardens and I consider flipping her onto her back and waking her up by plunging deep inside her. That's why I'm sharing her bed, isn't it? Of course it is. I should do this without a second thought, but I don't move.

Instead, I continue to hold her, involuntarily caressing her back. Tomorrow I'll be myself again. This out-of-character behavior has to be from the shock of discovering her innocence. That's all it is. It can't be that I actually *care* about this woman. I've never cared about any woman . . . and I don't plan to develop feelings for her.

Certainly, I'm only holding back from having sex again tonight because she was a virgin, and I realize she's sore. I don't want to make it worse. I need to give her a few hours to heal so she can be a better lover for the rest of our time together.

I'm well aware I'm lying to myself, but it makes me feel better. I'm going to lie here for hours without rest. There's too much on my mind. I turn, pulling her just a tad closer and close my eyes . . . and sleep claims me before I know it.

Chapter Review

Chapter Fifteen

Blake

H OW IN THE HELL DID I end up with a virgin?"
I'm ranting as I pace back and forth in my
brother's living room. I throw back a burning
shot of scotch before moving to the window to view the
picturesque boats gliding effortlessly across the busy
inlet.

"I think it's funny as hell. You're the only guy I
know who has a woman step into your office, do a
striptease, demand you make a deal . . . and ends up
with the most innocent girl in Seattle. Whatever gets
your rocks off, I guess," Tyler says as he lazily leans
back on his sofa.

"Shut up! I don't even know why I accepted this ridiculous deal, but I did, and she's now in my apartment building and constantly on my mind. Now I have to figure out what in the hell to do."

"Did you at least have a good time with her?" Tyler asks.

I turn and cross my arms over the back of the chair to face my brother. "The sex was unlike anything I've ever known, and though she has one hell of a temper, she intrigues me unlike any other. Her attitude is what I seem to like the most in some twisted way. Of course, if she were a complete doormat, what fun would that be?"

"If it's just about sex, who cares what she is or isn't?"

"Yeah, but a virgin? I want nothing to do with that."

"Well, she isn't a virgin anymore."

That makes me stop. I haven't thought about that, which is crazy. "I guess you're right. What good would it do to end the deal? It's not like she didn't know what she was getting into. *She* came to *me*, not the other way around. You know, though, she's not getting a hell of a lot of money out of this. That might mean she's either naïve to what she could get, or she's simply in over her head."

"Maybe she just wants you on her arm like she said," Tyler says.

I shake my head. "I don't know what it is," I admit.

"You always take what you want, so maybe you're made for each other," Tyler says with a chuckle.

"Go to hell, Tyler. You and I both know we aren't ever going to settle down for good, and when we're with women, we sure as hell want them to know what they're doing in the sack, because that's pretty much the only place we waste time with them."

"So you aren't happy with her? Send her away."

"I didn't say I wasn't happy with her. I said I don't want the responsibility of a damn virgin." I'm getting more frustrated by the second.

"Okay, but it's too late now, so either suck it up and finish your deal or send her packing, but whichever you choose, please quit acting like a love-struck fool."

"You're a freaking pain in the ass!" I thunder.

"Yeah, I've heard that about fifty thousand times since I was a child," Tyler says with another chuckle, but the mirth fades from his expression and he suddenly looks solemn.

I don't want the conversation to turn. I know where it's heading, and it terrifies me. Not much strikes me with fear these days, but the topic we're about to embark on is the one thing that can bring me to my knees.

"Sunday is the day," Tyler says quietly.

"I know. But we have to think of other things. It's been twenty-five years, Tyler. Don't you think we've allowed that woman to punish us for long enough?" I ask dryly.

"It's easier for you to hide it, to push it from your mind, but I also know you'd never have considered something like this if it weren't the twenty-fifth anniversary of their death."

"Yes, I know. This is a tough year, but we need to get over it. We've suffered long enough, and that sadistic bitch can rot in hell for all of eternity for all I care."

"I don't disagree with you, but are we going to do anything to mark the date? The nightmares have come back, and I can't . . . I . . ." Tyler trails off as a shudder passes through him.

"I haven't had nightmares for years. I've been waiting for them to return, but nothing has happened so far. What does Byron want to do?"

"He said he wants to do absolutely nothing, that he doesn't ever think about them."

"He's full of crap. We'll go to their graves. We're going to let this go once and for all," I fiercely tell him.

"How? Yes, you can say that, but years of therapy didn't come close to erasing it, Blake. We watched our parents get murdered right in front of us," Tyler says, his voice rising.

"And that happened because our mother was such a selfish bitch that she didn't care if our father's death traumatized us, her own freaking children. Her game backfired and we had to pay the price!"

I can't talk about that time in my life, that long night twenty-five years ago, without overwhelming anger.

But I won't take out my rage on Tyler. We did that to each other for years. It's over.

"Byron will come. We'll let this go and never speak of it again."

Tyler's eyes narrow. "Is that an order?"

"Come on, Tyler! You know it's not that way with us. You're just itching to fight. Our sanity — yours, mine, and Byron's — depends on us getting past this."

"If you're letting it go so well, then explain this woman in your bed."

"I don't know what in the hell is going on with Jewel. Call it temporary weakness, but that weakness just ended. I'll use her for sex and then ship her away after this is over."

"We'll see," Tyler says with a smirk that makes me want to crush my brother against a wall with a bulldozer.

"Look. I don't need this woman for anything more than sex. So what if she hasn't been with another man before me? I don't give a damn. She'll certainly be with a lot of men after, a lot of men who will probably offer more than I ever will."

"That's probably the only truth you've spoken about her . . . and yourself," Tyler says. He sounds as if he doesn't have a care in the world.

"Thanks for all of the helpful words of advice, little brother," I snap.

Tyler's grin widens. "You know I'll be here for you anytime you need to be kicked off your pedestal."

I don't bother responding. I don't know why I came to Tyler, why I felt the need to share, but it seems that whenever we brothers have a problem, we always end up on each other's doorsteps. It will be this way for life.

I leave Tyler's house, get into my car, and make my way to the office building. Work is good. It's what I need. I won't think about my parents, won't think about Jewel Weston, won't think about any of it. I clear my mind and focus on numbers.

It's what I've done in the past, and it always works . . . so why in the hell isn't it working now?

Chapter Review

Chapter Sixteen

Jewel

THE SMELL OF MUSK AND spice drifts pleasantly across the pillow and into my sleep-fogged brain. I inhale, wondering where I've smelled this before. Then my eyes fly open, and I twist my head to look around, my body stiffening until I realize I'm alone.

The night before comes flooding back to me, and my face flushes as I remember the incredibly erotic night. It had been out-of-this-world amazing, but I'm not supposed to feel this way. I'm supposed to be doing this for one reason, and that reason isn't for myself.

Still, I can't keep my eyes from closing in soft remembrance as I think back over our time together.

After falling asleep, or, more accurately, passing out, the world went blissfully dark. Sometime in the night, I woke to find Blake's head buried between my sore thighs and it hadn't taken him long to send me spiraling into another beautiful orgasm.

When he moved up the bed and brushed my lips with his incredibly hard arousal, I didn't hesitate to open to him. I took his velvet skin into my mouth and sucked until he released his pleasure onto my greedy tongue.

We didn't speak, didn't acknowledge the power of our connection. He simply pulled me back into his arms and I once again fell blissfully asleep. Now, as I sit up in bed, I wonder what's happening. This time with Blake Astor is a constant up and down, and yet I'm not close to being miserable. Is it because he keeps throwing me off balance?

Today is Saturday so no work, but I'm not sure where Blake is. I sort of like having his huge apartment to myself. He could be downstairs, but I don't hear a sound so maybe he's gone.

I smile as I get up, then walk into his bathroom and gasp at the large sunken tub and glass-enclosed shower big enough for six people. My mouth waters at the thought of using either one, but I don't think I should. Granted, he brought me into his bedroom, but I'm not sure if he'll want me to leave now. I shouldn't take advantage of the super-fancy facilities here . . . should I?

Grabbing a thick robe I find hanging on the wall, I wrap my petite body in it and return to his bedroom. I crack the door open and look both ways. No one had been in his apartment the day before, but that doesn't mean there won't be someone today, and I *really* don't want to meet anyone for the first time while doing the walk of shame from Blake's bedroom in his bathrobe.

The coast is clear, so I sneak down the hall and make my way downstairs. It doesn't take long for me to figure out I'm alone. I need a shower. I find a guest bedroom with a nice shower . . . not as nice as his, but still better than the one in my apartment.

Dropping the robe, I climb into the shower and stand beneath the hot spray for several minutes without moving, the water and heat a welcome relief to my stiff muscles. My body was put through a workout the night before, using muscles I hadn't known existed. I have a feeling I'll be sore for days.

Once I feel better, I turn off the shower and put the robe back on. I need to find my clothes and do the walk of shame back to my apartment. I move back downstairs . . . and that's when I notice a bag on the counter.

Maybe if I don't open it, I can pretend ignorance. I'm sure it has another skimpy outfit inside that won't be at all comfortable. I can't find my dang clothes though. Is he playing a game with me? I have no clue.

A buzzing sounds, and I turn to see my phone plugged in on the counter. I move over and see several messages showing on the screen. I start a cup of coffee then move over and pick it up.

I hope you slept well. Make sure you get plenty of rest this afternoon because tonight will be . . . aerobic.

I want you to take a long soak in the tub in my room. I've had special bath salts delivered that will help ease your soreness. Spend at least an hour in the hot water.

I left a bag for you. Enjoy.

I'll be home around four. Stay at my place. I want to see you as soon as I walk in the door.

Before I can decide which message to respond to first, another one pops up on my screen. This one makes me smile and then frown.

Good morning, Jewel. You did well last night. I'm quite pleased with our arrangement.

Blake seems to have awakened something inside me, and I don't know if I'll be able to turn it off, a terrifying thought, because this is *absolutely* temporary. I can't get attached to this man. I can't forget why I'm here.

And still, even though Blake isn't Mr. Perfect and he's demanding, he also doesn't seem to be the type to do sick things to me. Does it really matter, though? Haven't I vowed to do anything and everything for my brother?

I pray I won't be forced into choosing between my brother and my self-worth. Because if I'm ever treated in a demeaning way, it might not matter whether I save my brother or not, because I'll be lost forever.

You have to be awake by now . . .

I smile at this newest message. Even though a part of me fears what this arrangement will do to me, I'm also excited to tease Blake, seeing how far I can push him. I text him back.

You're impatient, Mr. Astor. I was simply trying to decide what to answer first.

I don't like waiting.

Then you'll surely be disappointed often.

Not knowing why I'm doing it, I add a bit of salt to my comment by adding an emoji of a face with its tongue sticking out. I'm a whole lot braver when I'm communicating with Blake by text. He isn't quite so intimidating.

You need a good spanking. You're not jumping when I say jump.

You need a good spanking. You're not jumping when I say jump.

This makes me smile. We never had any agreement that I had to do *exactly* what he says. This arrangement is mutually beneficial.

You didn't tell me how high.

Instead of striking fear into me, his threat gives me a shiver of excitement. I don't really know him, and have no idea what he's capable of, but if he really wanted to hurt me, wouldn't he have shown that by now? I haven't seen anything in his place that looks menacing, and I've spent some time here wandering, so I surely would've turned something up by now.

You're pushing me, Jewel . . .

Maybe you need to be pushed. Maybe too many people kiss your ass and that makes you a grumpy man.

When there's no response, I wonder if I've taken things too far. Although texting a message makes me feel brave, I don't want him to cut our arrangement, don't want to lose him at my side as I show the courts I'm fit to take care of my brother. I can walk away once Justin is securely in my home.

Go take your bath, Jewel. I'll show you later what happens when someone displeases me.

This time I don't reply. Pacing worriedly from the living room to the kitchen and back again, I chew on my thumbnail. Is he serious?

I see there's no response, Jewel. Maybe you're figuring out that if you challenge me . . . you will lose.

Relief floods through me at this message. He isn't telling me to leave. He isn't screaming at me with exclamation marks. Why I feel the need to challenge him I don't know, but as much as I'm trying to suppress my personality to get through our time together, I can't kill my defiance. That's a part of who I am.

I was raised by a strong, beautiful, brilliant mother, and I respect myself. I don't always make the best choices, but can't that be said about everyone? I'm a good person and deserve to be treated with respect, even if I offered my body to a stranger.

I don't always make the best choices, but can't that be said about everyone?

With an extra sway in my hips, I turn and move toward the stairs. I'm doing it because *I* want to use his bathtub, not because *he* wants me to. Let him think he's won some imaginary skirmish in our battle of wills. I take the bag and my phone but don't look inside the bag until I'm in the bathroom.

Of course the bag contains more lingerie, in a style that will show *everything* to him . . . and makes me feel like the prostitute I'm acting as. Angry tears spring to my eyes, but I refuse to acknowledge them. I put the bag down and move to the tub and start the water.

I let the robe fall to the floor, then pull my hair into a bun. At least he thinks of everything, having far more vanity products here than I own. My phone buzzes, but I ignore it. Instead I move to the tub and pour bath salts into the hot water . . . just as he commanded earlier.

My phone buzzes again. I don't acknowledge it. He told me to take a bath and that's exactly what I'm doing.

The phone goes off a couple of more times, and with a frustrated breath, I finally go to it with the intention of turning it off. However, I quickly check the messages first. This man is going to drive me insane.

Do you like your garments? I personally picked them.

Don't ignore your phone. I've already told you I don't like that.

Dammit, Jewel, quit being difficult. Do you want this to end? I'm more than willing to find a woman who's more . . . cooperative.

This one makes my stomach clench, but I can't show him fear, can't give him that power. He thinks I'm nothing more than a slut, and I sort of have to agree with him there, but I can't let go of my pride. I do need to keep him happy, though.

You drive me crazy!

Are you in the tub?

I gaze at the device as I stand in his bathroom and grin. He might eventually break me, but he hasn't yet, and I won't go down without a fight.

I'm currently naked, hot, and wet. Think about that, Mr. Astor.

As soon as I hit send, I turn off my phone, then step into the tub. If he wants to think of me as nothing more than his own personal slut, I'll act like one. I know who I am, and he won't change how I feel about myself. The water is hot and smells heavenly. I slide down deep and let out a sigh. I may never leave this beautiful thing.

I wish I could hate this man, but as arrogant and demanding as he is I'm anticipating him coming home . . . looking forward to what will happen next. He's woken something in me . . . and I don't think it will ever be shut off again. Bring it on, Blake, because this is only beginning.

Chapter Review

Chapter Seventeen

Blake

I LOOSEN MY TIE. I know better than to play games with a woman, to allow her to get to me, to consume me, to think of nothing but her. I've seen what that does to other men, yet here I am doing the same damn thing as so many of the other fools who've come before me. I'm well aware of what Jewel's doing. She's trying to gain back some of the control she thinks I've taken away.

Instead of being frustrated with her, instead of wanting to punish her, to send her away, I'm more excited than I was when I first met her. The damn woman makes me crazy . . . and I seem to like it.

She's pushing me just enough to turn me on, to make me want to leave my office and rush home to show her who's in charge. I'll take great pleasure in doing just that . . . but not on her timeline . . . on mine.

Right now though, I have to force myself to remain seated. I refuse to rush home, because that *is* giving her power, and I'm unwilling to do that. This exciting battle of wills will continue, and I'll sit right here, dammit.

As much as I tell myself I have to focus on anything other than Jewel, I can't think of anything but her in crystal clear water, her skin soft and silky, her body deep in the tub, her breasts gently swaying as she moves.

I lean back, close my eyes, and imagine her squirting soap into her hands, rubbing them together, then starting at her neck and slowly moving her hands down the sweet curve of her breasts.

I dive deeper, picturing her massaging her nipples with her thumb and forefinger, letting her head lean back against the rim of the tub. My arousal painfully pulses as my fantasy continues.

I can see her lips parting, a moan escaping her sweet red lips. A groan escapes me as I fight cardiac arrest, but I still don't stop. I see her hands traveling down the luscious line of her stomach, moving between her spread legs . . . then sliding along her hot, sleek folds as she pants in excitement.

My body pulses and I jump from my chair, unable to take another second of this. I don't give a damn if she has the power to drag me back home. I need her. She's mine . . . and I'm going to take what's been offered to me.

The offices are empty as it's the weekend, so I practically run from the building as I fly down the stairs, too impatient to wait for an elevator. I reach my car and peel from the parking garage, squealing my tires before entering the busy road. I need to get home.

The drive is a blur and I'm shocked when I manage to park my car without hitting another vehicle. I don't question it as I jump out and dash for my private elevator. Impatiently I tap my foot while the stupid box takes an obscene amount of time to reach my penthouse apartment.

I only slow down once I'm inside the apartment. I take a deep breath and tell myself I'm in control, I can turn around and walk back out if I choose to. I almost roll my eyes at myself. If that were the case, why do my feet keep moving forward, and why am I now bounding up the stairs?

My bathroom door is cracked open, and I hear a sigh that makes my already hard body throb painfully. After stripping naked, I take another breath and fling the door open. It bangs against the wall, and my reward is seeing Jewel's eyes widen.

She sits up in shock. "What are you doing here?"

"I needed to see you after your taunts," I say as I stride forward, my arousal proudly jutting out.

"I . . . uh . . ."

"Don't know what to say now that I'm standing here, Jewel? Did you really think you could play games with me and not see them through?"

I step into the tub before she can answer, and pull her onto my lap, my body thanking me when her skin comes into contact with mine. She gasps as I clasp my mouth around her nipple and suck hard.

"Well, I happen to love the games," I tell her before switching sides, making a low moan tumble from her throat. "And I'm taking you now." I grab her, and pull her down, giving a rumble of pleasure as I fill her tight heat.

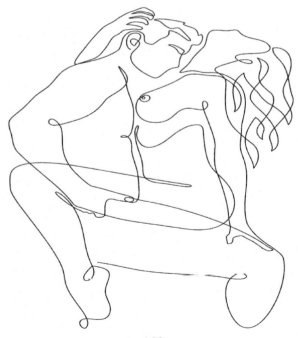

"Damn, you feel good," I groan as I begin lifting her up and down.

I don't let her speak as I keep up the primitive rhythm. I grab the back of her neck and my lips claim hers. The sweet taste of her mouth and the feel of her inner walls gripping me tightly are quickly making me lose any vestige of control.

Finally, with a growl, I force my hips up almost violently while pulling her down, and then I explode inside her. Her cries echo off the bathroom walls as she simultaneously finds her pleasure.

I hold her for several moments, and then reluctantly let her go. She looks confused as I climb from the tub. I'm being an asshole. I'm well aware of it, but I can't seem to stop. I don't like that she was able to call me home without actually calling me. I couldn't stay away no matter how much I tried . . . because she's an obsession I can't quit.

"I'm going back to work."

"Okay," she says, not seeming fazed by my words. This angers me. It makes me want to march right back to the tub and demand some real emotion from her — makes me want her to beg me to stay. What in the hell is wrong with me?

I force myself to walk away from the bathroom without another word. My emotions are turbulent as I dress and then leave my bedroom. I'm grateful she waits to emerge until I'm finished. This woman caused me to leave work in the middle of the day and has made me want and do things I've never wanted before.

Maybe I *should* end this agreement — job paid in full. That would be much safer for my sanity. But even as I ride down to the parking garage, I know that isn't going to happen.

170

I'm not nearly finished with Jewel Weston. A few more days with her will surely do the trick . . . right? Then I will use her on my arm without needing her. Ignoring the pang this idea causes, I focus on anything but her. Instead of driving back to my office, I head to the work site of a large apartment complex our company is building.

What I need right now is a hammer and nails so I can pound out my frustration on inanimate objects. I sure as hell hope I don't run into either of my brothers, because there's no way I can explain my black mood or the chaos now ruling my thoughts. I need to be alone . . . and I need to gain control over my life. It will happen . . . one nail at a time.

Chapter Review

Jewel

BLAKE LEAVES AND I feel A mixture of relief and sadness. This is stupid. I'm well aware I'm naïve when it comes to the ways of the world. I'm even unaware when it comes to human nature. This doesn't make me stupid; I just haven't been corrupted yet. This might all change soon. I'm waking up quickly.

I need to get through this arrangement with Blake without making waves. Apparently, my instincts when it comes to my own survival are off. Consequences happen when I poke the bear . . . and I seem to enjoy doing it over and over again.

Then again, I know my own worth, and being this submissive woman Blake seems to want me to be will break me if I don't stand up for myself. I don't want to change, don't want to break. If I don't hold on to my pride, I won't make a good caregiver for my brother . . . and he's the reason I'm doing this.

I sigh, pushing these thoughts away. No matter how many times I go over this, the answers won't come to me. I need to get ahold of myself, and in the end it will work out. I go downstairs, not wanting to be in his luxury apartment anymore. As I open the front door, I stop in my tracks when I see a large man holding a key, ready to insert it in the lock.

"You must be Jewel," the man says, and I back up a step. My eyes narrow as I take a good look at his face. I *know* this face. I've seen it a dozen times as I pass the picture on Blake's wall. It's one of his brothers I haven't met in the office yet. Though Blake is tall, his brother has a few inches on him. I'm not sure which brother this is.

"Tyler Astor," he says, holding out his hand when I stand in the doorway for too long, leaving an awkward silence between us.

Finding my voice, I accept the hand that's hanging in midair, waiting for my decision. "Jewel Weston."

"So, you're the girl scrambling my brother's brain this week," he says with laughter after releasing my hand.

"I wouldn't say I'm *scrambling* his brain. He's a tough egg to crack," I say, being careful. This *is* Blake's brother, after all.

"Ah, Jewel, you're most certainly scrambling his brain," Tyler tells me before pulling me out the door and firmly shutting it behind us. "Where are you off to?"

"I'm not sure; I needed to get outside."

"Good. We'll have lunch. I'm starving," he says, placing my arm around his. I'm not sure this is such a good idea.

"I was only planning on a quick stroll," I tell him. Blake might not like me hanging out with his brother, especially when our relationship isn't real. What has he told his brothers? Do they believe we're in a real relationship? Or do they think I'm a slut who's gone after their brother for greedy reasons? If I knew what Tyler's been told, I wouldn't be so uncomfortable.

"Nonsense. Everyone needs to eat, and I refuse to do it alone. You can fill me in on what you're doing to drive my brother crazy . . . so I can do the same." He doesn't give me an out. Are all of the Astor men this bossy? With their looks, money, and confidence, they have reasons to be.

Outside, Tyler's still holding on to me and pulling me along. Once again, my options are limited — I have the choice of following him or falling on my face if I stop and he doesn't.

175

"Are all three of you overbearing and used to getting your way?"

Tyler keeps walking, but he laughs and throws me a smile. "Pretty much. What would you like to eat?" He isn't even a little offended by my question.

"I'm easy," I say before wincing. Yeah, I'm pretty damn easy. At least now I am. Talk about a depressing thought.

"All righty. Sushi it is," he says as he approaches a shiny black sports car and opens the passenger door.

"Perfect." Raw fish doesn't exactly float my boat, but some company won't be so bad. I like my co-workers, but we haven't gotten close enough to hang out together after work. Hopefully that will come with more time . . . that is if they don't find out I'm sleeping with the boss. Then all of them will hate me.

Once I'm settled into my seat, Tyler rushes to the driver's side, hops in, revs the engine, and pulls into traffic.

"So, is Blake treating you well?"

I don't know how to answer. Has Blake sent his brother to quiz me? Is Tyler going to report all of my answers? I have to be very careful with whatever I say and remember this is Blake's brother. His loyalty is to his sibling, not some girl who won't be around long enough to get to know. I can't stand pretending though, so I need to put the truth on the table.

"I can't complain." I pause for a moment giving myself courage. "You know this isn't a real relationship, right?"

"Don't fool yourself. Anytime a man and woman are together, it's a relationship, babe." He turns and winks at me, nearly giving me a heart attack as the car swerves a bit across the centerline.

Don't fool yourself.

Anytime a man and woman are together, it's a relationship, babe.

"Well, I'll only be with him for a little while."

"I'm not so sure about that," he says with a secret smile that seems to say he knows a lot more than I do. I wish he'd fill me in on what he knows.

When we stop at a small restaurant, my door unexpectedly opens. An attendant in uniform holds out a hand to assist me. Then Tyler comes around, takes my arm after tipping the attendant, and leads me inside.

"I've been craving fresh crab rolls," he says as he leads me to the sushi bar and holds out a chair for me before sitting himself.

I'm soon relaxing as we're served, and Tyler begins filling me in on old stories from the workplace, from a time when both he and Blake were more hands-on in their business.

"Yeah, I totally thought I was a badass. Our electrician was nowhere to be found, and the lights were off, so I thought, how hard can it be to hook two wires together? We needed light. I was up on the lift and, thinking the power was cut, grabbed the wrong wire. It sent me right down on my ass and scared the hell out of me. I don't frighten easily, but I walked from the building and went and laid down in the back of my truck for the next hour, thanking anyone up above who was listening that the electric jolt hadn't stopped my heart."

"That's horrible," I gasp. "Why didn't you go to the doctor?"

"Because I didn't get hurt. Yeah, my heart was beating erratically for a little while, but I was fine. You can't run to the doctor for every little thing." He shrugs and pops a roll into his mouth like nearly getting electrocuted was no big deal.

"When it comes to electricity, I wouldn't mess around."

"Ha! Blake's done worse. He was on the job site and his finger got caught in the door. Blood was pouring out, and all of a sudden he went white, passed out, and smacked his head. Then, when he came to, he wrapped his finger in tape and finished the day. It was two days later when the finger wouldn't stop throbbing that he finally agreed to go to the doctor. Not only was it infected, but he'd broken it in two places and needed to have surgery because it had already begun to heal wrong."

"I don't think that's brave, Tyler. It's foolish."

He laughs again. "I dare you to tell *him* that."

"You have an infectious laugh," I say, unable not to join him. "And no way I'm telling him."

"You're all talk, aren't you?" he says.

"Pretty much. I do what I need to survive. I might snap back a few times at your brother, but I know when to push something . . . and when to take cover." This makes Tyler laugh again. It's really impossible not to join in his merriment.

Too soon, it's time to go, and he leads me back out to his car.

"Thank you for lunch, Tyler. I enjoyed visiting with you. I should get back now, though." I hesitate to think about what Blake might be thinking. I didn't take my cell phone, so he might be furious if he's trying to get ahold of me.

"You're a buzzkill, Jewel, but I suppose I'll take you back so my brother doesn't think I'm trying to steal his woman."

I don't correct him. Why bother repeating I'm not his brother's woman? Whatever I am, it will be over in before it even begins. A speaker in the car rings. I hear Blake's voice. What bad timing for him to call Tyler. I stay quiet.

"I need you to get over to Bill's house," Blake tells Tyler. "The stubborn fool sent our crew away. He said he won't accept charity."

"What do you mean? I thought it was taken care of," Tyler replies with a frown.

"Yeah. So did I. But when the roofing crew showed up, Bill came out and threatened to have the cops haul them off for trespassing. Tim called me and asked what he should do. I told him to head out, that I'd talk to Bill. I got here thirty minutes ago, and he said there's no way he'll allow me to pay for a new roof." Blake's frustrated sigh comes through loud and clear over the speakers.

"Damned old man. There's no way that roof will last another winter. What are we gonna do?" Tyler asks as he turns onto the freeway.

I'm not familiar with this area, but it seems like we aren't moving toward the apartment complex. Has Tyler forgotten I'm in the car? I don't want to say something and have Blake hear me, so I just fidget in my seat.

"It looks like we're roofing the place. He won't let us pay for it, but he'll sure as hell let us climb up there and do it ourselves," Blake says, a smile clearly in his tone.

"Yeah, I can see that. What I can't see is you up there with your pristine white shirt, holding a hammer," Tyler jokes.

"Whatever. I don't see you up on any roofs anymore either," Blake fires back.

"Point taken. Let's see if we still know how. I'm ten minutes out. See ya in a few." Tyler pushes a button, and the call disconnects.

I sit in silence a moment longer to make sure Blake's really gone before I speak. "Um, Tyler, you took a wrong turn."

"Nope. Change of plans. We have to go roof a house." He turns off the freeway and heads down a city street.

"I . . . um . . . can't roof a building. Maybe you should drop me off first," I say, growing more and more nervous as he continues in the same direction.

"No can do. We've already lost half the day."

"I can't go there!" I'm more insistent this time.

"Look, Jewel. Bill was my grandfather's best friend and has always been good to me and my brothers. He's also been the most stubborn old coot I've ever met in my life. He won't let us pay for anything for him, won't accept what he deems as charity, but his roof needs fixing. The only way we're going to get it done is by doing it ourselves. And it's supposed to rain in a few days, so we have to haul ass. You'll be fine. You can visit with Bill while we work."

Tyler's tone seems so reasonable, but Blake's going to flip out when he sees me pull up with his brother. He might be furious I had lunch with him, maybe even angry enough to end our deal. It's not like we have an

180

official contract. None of this matters, though. I realize arguing with Tyler is pointless. The Astor men don't take no for an answer.

We pull up to a small home surrounded by at least two acres of land, and as Blake walks toward the car, my heart thunders. His eyes lock on me in the passenger seat; his silver glare sears right through me, making me wish I was any other place in the world.

"Smile, Jewel," Tyler tells me. "It looks like my brother's going to growl." He opens his door and says hello.

When Blake doesn't reply to Tyler, but instead comes immediately to my side of the car and rips open the door, I'm seriously considering diving across the seat and out through the driver's side door, then making a run for it.

"What in the hell are you doing here?"

Words won't come. He suddenly takes my arm and practically drags me from the car. This is bad — really, *really* bad. I've never seen him angry before, and right now he's *angry*. Does he think I'm fooling around with his brother? If he does, he's a real asshole. I might've introduced myself by stripping, but that's not who I am.

I don't know what will happen next . . . but it's beyond my control.

Chapter Review

Blake

AS I BOX JEWEL IN against the side of my brother's car, I can't remember ever being this angry. Fury rolls off of me in waves, and I want to punish her, punish Tyler, punish anyone who dares to even look at her. What in the hell is wrong with me? Why am I this upset over Jewel being with my brother? It makes no logical sense.

"What are you doing with my brother? Are you two messing around?" I demand, my voice way too harsh. I can't stop myself, knowing I'm overreacting. I move in a little closer to her, my breath hitting her face as I speak too loudly.

There's a hint of fear in her eyes that should stop me cold. I sober up, realizing I'm out of control. I open my

mouth to speak and feel a sharp pain in my shoulder as a
hand pinches down, spinning me around. Before I can
respond, a fist lands on my jaw, sending me flying
backward against the car right next to Jewel, whose eyes
are wide. She immediately steps away, obviously as
confused as I am about what's happening.

"What the hell?" I snap. I'm about to kick someone's
ass. I clear my vision; my brother Tyler stands before me,
fury blazing from his eyes as he stares me down. Tyler is
my easy-going brother. I've never seen this sort of look in
his gaze before.

"What was that for?" I ask, lifting my hand to rub my jaw now that I don't feel a need to pummel someone.

Tyler takes a step closer, and I wonder if my brother and I are about to get into the first brawl of our lives. "You're an asshole on the best of days, Blake, but you're currently walking a very fine line of insulting both Jewel and me. What is wrong with you?"

"I just . . . she offered herself to me. I don't want her doing the same with you," I say. I immediately know it's the wrong thing to say as Tyler makes another fist. This time, though, I'm ready and sidestep the hit. His anger confuses me. I don't want to fight my brother.

"What in the hell has you this worked up, Tyler?"

"I like this woman, and like how you've been acting since you've been with her. She does a fantastic job in the offices, and I wanted to meet her. I stopped at your house and practically dragged her out with me for lunch. We were returning when I got your call. She's done nothing wrong, and you're treating her worse than you'd treat a stranger. If you're going to be this big of a dick, you should stay the hell away from her. I'll step in for a fake arrangement to please Stanley."

"Like hell you will," I thunder, immediately pissed off again. He opens his mouth to speak when we're interrupted.

"Um, do I need to run interference?" Both of us turn to see Byron looking back and forth between us with a brotherly smirk on his face.

"Stay out of this, Byron. I'm about to kick Blake's ass!"

"I'd love to see the two of you go at it," Byron tells us. "But Bill's standing in the doorway looking at you like you've both lost your minds. I might have to agree with him."

"I certainly think *Tyler* has lost his mind. He slugged me," I say, keeping a wary eye on my brother, unsure if he'll attempt another punch.

"I'm sure you deserved it," Byron replies. "Now, if you two girls can kiss and make up, we can get this show on the road. We're already getting a late start." He stops speaking when he finally notices Jewel standing about ten feet away, looking in horror at the three of us. "Ah! *Now* I see what's going on. It's always a woman . . ."

"I didn't do anything," Jewel says, surprising us. "I basically got kidnapped and taken to lunch." She turns to Tyler. "Not that it didn't turn out to be a very nice lunch. Then Blake calls, and I'm dragged here against my will, and the next thing I know punches are thrown. If you want to act like Neanderthals, be my guest, but I want no part of it." She folds her arms across her chest.

Byron blinks. "Sooo, you're here with Tyler?" He looks confused.

"No, she's with me," I snap. "Tyler decided he needed to *bond* with her."

"Ah, a love triangle, a recipe for disaster," Byron says in a bored voice.

"It's not a damn love triangle," Tyler snarls. "I can talk to a woman without the need to push her against a wall and rip off her clothes."

"All righty, then. Can we get to work now?" Byron asks, knowing that keeping up this topic will lead to fists flying again.

"Yes!" both Tyler and I exclaim.

"And what about me?" Jewel asks. We all turn in her direction.

"You can sit down and be quiet," I tell her, immediately regretting my word choice. Damn, I truly am being an asshole.

To my surprise, her eyes narrow, and she storms up to me, shoves her finger into my chest, and, after taking a deep breath, unleashes her wrath.

"I can put up with a lot, Blake Astor, and I've been doing that over the past few days, but I am *not* going to have you talk to me like this in front of people. I'm human, and I deserve at least a *modicum* of respect. It wasn't *my choice* to come here, but now that I'm here, I won't just sit around and wait. If you're going to work, I can do something too."

No woman has ever snapped at me like this or demanded my respect. I've never felt such an urge to give in and do exactly what she's asking of me.

"No. It's dangerous," I say, and then thinking the subject is closed, I turn away.

"Then I'll find something to do on my own." She leaves me and walks over to Bill. "Hi. I'm Jewel. What can I do to help you?"

I stand right where I am for several heartbeats as I watch Bill put out his hand, clasp hers, and give the first smile I've seen on the old man's face in years.

"Bill Berkshire. It's a pleasure to meet you, young lady. How about we start with a glass of iced tea, and then we'll find some work?"

"That sounds lovely." Jewel walks with Bill inside the house after casting a final, contemptuous glance back at all three of us. My brothers and I are left standing with our jaws hanging.

"Well, brother, that's a woman you might not want to lose," Byron says before moving over to the work truck. He puts on a tool belt. After a moment, I shake my head and follow him. It's going to be a long day, and yes, I'll be having a talk with Jewel about her place in my life, but right now I don't have the time.

Taking off my expensive suit jacket, I roll up the sleeves of my white shirt before thinking twice and yanking it off, leaving me bare-chested. I'm not dressed for this type of work, and in fact, rarely swing a hammer these days. I only do it when I need to work out some aggression.

I've already fiddled around one of the worksites this week in hopes of dealing with my frustration, but this job will cause a hell of a lot more sweat than what I did the day before. I should curse the old man, but I won't.

The thought of getting some alone time with Jewel later keeps me going as I climb up on Bill's roof during the hottest part of the day and start ripping off the ridge cap. Oh yes, I'll be the last one standing later tonight. We'll see how defiant Jewel is when I'm finished with her. This thought immediately takes away my frown . . . and I even begin whistling. Ignoring my brothers' looks sent my way, I work faster. I'm more than ready to get home . . . where Jewel and I can have a nice . . . long . . . chat . . . preferably one without words.

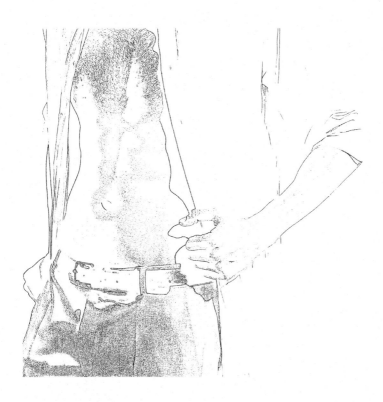

Chapter Review

Jewel

W HAT ARE YOU DOING with a cad like Blake?"
I stop sipping my glass of sweet iced tea and
laugh. "I don't know, Bill, but I can tell you
it's worth it. Because if I wasn't with him, I would've
never met you. For that matter, what are *you* doing with a
cad like Blake?" Bill laughs at my evil grin.

"I've known Blake since the day he was born," Bill
says, and his smile begins to disappear. "His father was a
good man, but his mama beat the good right out of him. It
broke the heart of my best friend, Blake's granddaddy. I
was glad he passed on before he saw the final chapter of
their story play out."

"What do you mean?" I know I shouldn't pry into Blake's life, but it's like watching a movie that you can't turn off because you *have* to know how it ends.

"I don't think I should talk about that dark time," Bill says with a shake of his head.

"Of course not. I'm sorry. I didn't mean to pry." But of course, I do — I'm dying to know everything. I hope Bill doesn't tell Blake about me digging for information.

"You aren't doing anything wrong, sweetie. It's a really sad story," Bill says as he gets up to refill our glasses. When he returns and hands me a glass of tea, he looks at me intently. "Do you care about Blake?"

I'm so shocked by the question, I don't know what to do. Since this man is obviously attached to Blake, I can't tell him I'm only here because I need Blake to pretend to be my boyfriend. At the same time, I don't want to say a whole bunch of mushy stuff either. It would be a lie.

"You don't have to say anything, darling," Bill tells me after the silence stretches on. "I can see I put you up against a wall here."

Still, I have to say something. "I'm sorry, Bill. I just . . . it's . . . Well, we've only been together for a few days, and the situation is . . . well . . . it's complicated."

Bill's penetrating eyes bore into mine, making me squirm in my seat.

"I understand, darling. When I was younger, people didn't play all of these games they play today. If a boy liked a girl, or a girl liked a boy, they told each other. If it looked like it was going well, there was no need to draw the whole dating process out. Heck, you often know on a first date if the girl looks like she'll be the one. I married my Vivian three months after we met, because I knew there'd never be another girl for me."

"What happened?"

"The good Lord took her four years ago. I still think of her every single day, and I can't wait until I get to be with her again."

"I'm sure she's waiting for you right at the gates."

"Not quite yet, darling. My Vivian was always too busy to wait around for anyone. But when it's time, she'll be there to meet me."

"If I may ask, how did she die?"

"In her sleep, so there was no pain. It was simply her time to go home. I was real angry about it for a while, but I finally accepted that someone up there knows more than I do, and being angry all of the time doesn't do any good."

"You're a wise man, Bill. I'm glad I got to meet you." I reach out and take his hand, smoothing his wrinkly skin with my thumb.

"I'm glad I got to meet you too, darling. You remind me of my sweet Vivian. She was always so calm and loved everyone, but if you fired her up, she'd have no problem taking the hide right off of you," he says with a chuckle.

"I don't normally lose my temper, but . . ." I don't know how to complete this sentence.

"Don't give up on Blake. He's been through some dark times in his life. His mama wasn't fit to be a mother, and it was her fault that she and the boys' daddy died. To top that off, the three boys watched it happen," Bill says with a sad sigh.

"Wait! They *watched* their parents die? Was it a car wreck?"

"No. If only it were that easy. Blake may one day open up to you about it. If he does, take the time to listen. I want you to understand that he's dealt with hard times since he was real young. Sometimes his bark is pretty bad, but that boy has a heart of gold. He's buried it deep for a very long time."

"He's lucky to have you in his life."

"Of course he is, little missy. I'm a great man." Bill smiles, and the talk of sadness is over.

After the two of us visit a while longer, Bill falls asleep in his recliner without giving me any tasks to do. I cover him with a blanket then go outside and see the three brothers on the roof. They're working quickly, and shingles are flying over the side of the house.

A huge dumpster's in the driveway, one that wasn't there when I went inside with Bill an hour earlier. I walk over to the work truck — *Astor Construction* stenciled on the door — and find a pair of gloves in the back.

Over the next few hours, I pick up roofing from the ground and throw it in the dumpster. By the time the sun is getting low in the sky, I'm completely exhausted, but the yard is mostly cleared of debris, and I feel pretty good about myself.

"You don't listen too well, do you?"

I turn to find Blake behind me. He wipes his forehead with a rag before looking me in the eyes.

"No," I tell him. "It's always been a fault of mine."

"We'll see if I can help you change your ways," he says with more than a hint of anticipation in his smile.

"You don't have time."

"I invent time. Especially for those who need punishing." He throws the rag down and puts his shirt back on, leaving it unbuttoned. "Let's run back to the apartment and shower. We need to get a move on because I want to do something tonight." He takes my hand, leads me to his work truck, and practically thrusts me inside.

"Where's your car?" I can't picture Blake as a truck guy.

"I had my employee take it back when he delivered the truck. We needed tools."

"Oh, makes sense," I say, at a loss of what to say next. Everyone keeps throwing me new curves, and it's overwhelming my brain to catch up.

He doesn't say goodbye to his brothers; he just starts the truck and drives into traffic. After a few minutes, my curiosity overrides my need to be quiet.

"Where are we going?"

"That's a surprise," he replies. The eager gleam shining in his eyes makes his face look so much more handsome — not that he's a slouch in that department, even in his worst mood.

I've already argued with him far more than I should've today, so I'll bite my tongue for the remainder of the night. An hour later, I'm seriously regretting my choice not to argue.

Chapter Review

Jewel

MY HEARTBEAT THRASHES in my ears as I look at the tiny plane before me. I immediately flash into fight-or-flight mode — except that *flight* is the last thing I want right now. I want to know which way to *run*.

"Do you honestly think I'm getting into this thing?"

"Yes. Why wouldn't you?"

"Because it's a death trap on small wheels!" My face is ashen with fear, and I begin to pace, trying to think of a way out of this. I can't do this, no possible way. What good will I be to my brother if I die of a terror-induced heart attack or from landing in a fiery heap on the runway of Blake's private airstrip?

"Don't be ridiculous. I've been flying for years without even a minor mishap. My mechanics certify the plane, and it's inspected before and after each flight. If the smallest thing is wrong, the problem's immediately fixed."

"I'm not going." It isn't the first I've outright refused this man, but it's the first time I'm certain I won't change my mind. I don't know if I'm panicked more at the thought of flying or at the thought of his reaction to my refusal. But he can't make me go up in this thing. My brother won't want me to.

"You can do this, Jewel. There's nothing to fear."

"Please don't make me do this. I can do anything else you ask — just not this."

He's silent for a full minute before his expression changes. It isn't anger or frustration on his face; it's patience, something I haven't seen from him before.

"Come sit inside," he tells me, holding out his hand.

"No, please," I say in a tear-choked voice.

"We won't go anywhere until you're ready. I simply want you to sit in the plane, feel it, see that it's not so frightening."

I eye him with suspicion. Is this a trick? He hasn't lied to me so far, hasn't told me anything, and then taken it back. Can I trust him?

I barely manage to give him my hand before I'm propelled forward and climbing onto the small front seat. It's at least a full minute before I let out my breath, and that's only because he's left the door beside me wide open. He goes around the front of the plane and climbs in beside me, his thigh touching mine as he gets situated.

"See? It's not so bad," he says, his voice soothing.

"It's not bad because we aren't going anywhere," I choke out.

"Why don't you ask some questions? I'll tell you whatever you'd like to know."

How can I ask questions when my throat's completely closed? Since he's silent, I look around the plane, gazing at all of the dials, knobs, and screens, not knowing what any of them mean.

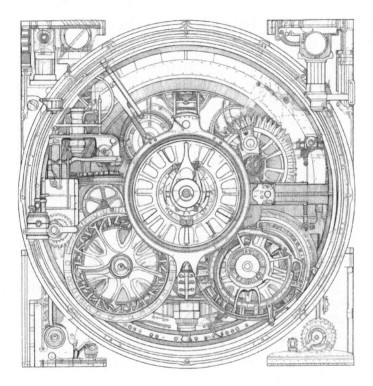

"There are so many buttons, so many different functions for you to perform. What if something fails? Or if the screens go out? Or if the wheels fall off? Heck, what if a wing pops off?" I don't give him time to answer anything before I blurt out the next question.

He waits until I stop, sending a blinding smile my way.

"I can almost guarantee you that the wings and wheels won't pop off. They're on pretty damn tight."

"Almost? You said *almost*." Of course I've latched onto the one worrisome word.

"I wouldn't risk my life for a cheap thrill. I know this plane better than I know my car. I guarantee I'll take you up in the sky and safely land you back on solid ground. I also guarantee you'll be in heaven while we're up there."

"You *can't* guarantee that."

"Yes, I can, Jewel. I'm confident in my ability to control this plane, just like I control my life — and, for that matter, your orgasms. Even if the engine stalls, I can safely land."

My breathing grows more frantic because I know I'm going up in this plane. The door is going to close, and we're going to speed down the runway, and then lift into the sky. There will be no more talking.

Blake climbs from the plane and walks to my side. "Trust me," he says before leaning in and coming within inches of my lips — not that I really notice . . . for the first time ever.

My seat belt locks, and the door closes. I should say no, jump from the plane, give up on the entire thing that's happening between us, but I can't even breathe, let alone speak. He's soon back in the pilot seat and saying words I can't comprehend.

"clear prop . . ."

"pressure good . . ."

"cleared for takeoff . . ."

And then we're moving. The small Cirrus emerges from Blake's personal hangar and sits at the end of his runway while the engine revs, gaining power. My eyes are wet with worry, my vision blurred. We start forward, the small plane quickly picking up speed.

As the plane lifts off and rapidly rises up, up, up in the sky, I hold my breath, sure my face is turning blue.

I know we're going to come down in a fiery blaze of glory. Where will this leave Justin?

As we climb higher, a gust of wind shakes the plane, and my hand shoots out and grips Blake's thigh. My throat closes again, and I'm unable to think. A cry for help? Not possible. Who can help anyway? There's no 911 number for the sky. Maybe he can try a Mayday call over the radio, but what good will that do?

Then the most amazing thing happens. After making a large arc, Blake levels the plane and faces it toward the setting sun. The sky is filled with color, and his softly spoken words register in my brain.

"Look at that. Just take a deep breath and look."

I can't tear my gaze away from the view. I know we're barreling through the evening air, but it feels like we're barely moving. The only sound I hear is his whispered words through my headset, and the only thing I see is the brilliant reds and oranges lighting the horizon.

"It's spectacular," I say, jumping when I hear my own words echo back in my ears.

We're both too awed to say anything else as we zoom along and watch the sunset, then we're in a pitch-black sky, flying over fields and small cities. Blake reaches down and adjusts the lights on the dashboard, the glow outlining his handsome face.

His eyes are shining as he looks intently forward, his lips turned up in an almost secret smile, a smile that tells me he's happy, he's where he belongs. He loves this. My fear evaporates because I realize I'm safe. I trust his word, trust him to protect me . . . and this fills me with an entirely new fear.

"I've always loved to fly," he says, "from the very first moment I sat left seat and took the controls of the airplane for the first time — I was twenty-one and taking lessons. But my favorite time of all is night.

Everything after the sun sets feels different. It's like the rest of the world disappears, and I'm finally free. Free from chaos, from noise, from work, from anger — I'm free from it all. I'm up here, and my worries disappear for an hour or two — or five — that I decide to stay in the sky."

I realize I'm safe. I trust his word, trust him to protect me

"I wouldn't think a guy like you, a guy who holds the world in the palm of his hands, would have a single worry you need to forget about," I reply, my voice quiet, not wanting to shatter this moment. Right after saying it, my conversation with Bill pops into my head, making me regret my words.

"I don't," he says a bit harshly, but then I hear his sigh through the headset. "Sorry, Jewel. I . . . it's just that I *have* to be perfect. I have to do everything right. That's what's expected, that's who I am."

I turn and look out the window, fighting tears. "I don't expect anything from you, Blake. I know when our time is up, you'll be gone, and I'll move on to whatever comes next. But thank you for helping me beat my fears, and thank you for sharing this with me."

He turns toward me, his eyes gleaming as our gazes connect. "You're a dangerous woman, Jewel. You make me think things, feel things, and do things I can't and don't want to do."

You make me think things, feel things, and do things I can't and don't want to do

His words seep in, and deep sadness washes over me. This man is holding in a past full of pain. But I'm nothing to him, and I don't need to know his secrets. We only have a short time together. And in our time, I can't fall for him.

When shutters fall over his eyes, I almost feel relief. I can't afford to become acquainted with Blake's vulnerable side, or to start to care about him. I have to remember this. If I forget, I risk being burned so badly, I'll never be able to heal.

Blake does something with the controls, then, to my horror, takes his hands off the wheel and turns to me, reaching out a hand.

"You need to hold the wheel," I tell him in absolute terror.

He chuckles. "It's on autopilot. We're fine. Come here." There's both coercion and demand in his tone.

My stomach tightens as I shake my head. He laughs again and crooks his finger. I again shake my head. He doesn't give up as he reaches over and undoes my seatbelt, leaving my heart thundering.

"You're fine, Jewel, come here," he tells me.

He could grab me and pull me to him, but he wants me to come of my own free will. I'm filled with a mixture of fear and desire. The fear is enhancing my desire for some sick and twisted reason.

He waits . . . and I finally scoot over, not too far, but close enough for him to reach out and put his arm around me. He pulls me close, then kisses me, knocking the breath right out of me again. I shouldn't desire him, but I do, and there's nothing I can do to stop it.

He kisses me long and hard. Before I realize what's happening, he pulls me onto his lap and he's taking off my clothes. And then he's sliding into me and I'm forgetting all about fear as I climb far higher than this plane can take us. I'm lost as we come together, our panting fogging the windows . . . and I don't even notice.

We explode at the same time, gasping for breath as the plane continues to soar in the sky. I lean against him, then let out a cry as pain shoots through my knee.

"Ouch!"

Blake looks startled and dazed from his own pleasure. "What's wrong?"

"My knee hit the dash."

I'm limp against him, utterly exhausted, my voice weak. He's sagging against the seat as he tries to recover.

"You'll live," he says with a chuckle, fully relaxed.

"I don't think I'm afraid of flying anymore," I finally say, and that's when everything goes wrong.

A loud sound goes off, making me jump. "What is that?"

"The stall horn. We're no longer on autopilot. You must've hit the switch when you bumped your knee." The plane suddenly takes a dip to the side before it begins heading straight down, and then starts slowly spinning, sending terror through me as Blake holds on tight.

I let out a gasp as Blake quickly sets me in my seat once the plane is upright for a brief moment. "Seat belt," he calls as he clicks his into place and reaches for controls that I believe he said are called rudders. We're up high, but still falling fast.

I struggle with my belt, clicking it into place as we spiral toward earth, making Blake struggle to get the plane back under control. I'm panicking, which he seems to notice while he fights the plane. He starts speaking, letting me know what he's doing.

"I'm reducing the power back to idle and pushing the rudder control in the opposite direction from the spin." His voice is soothing. "Now I'm applying forward pressure on the controls to break the stall." I'm focused on his voice, not the motion of the plane. "Stall is broken. We're now holding the rudder nose down."

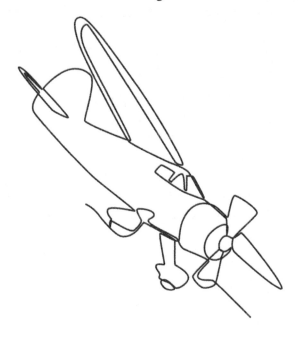

Within seconds he has the plane back under control. I don't think I've taken in a full breath since this began. It seems to have taken forever, but it probably all occurred in less than a minute. He lets out a sigh, and much to my shock, a chuckle.

"I've practiced this several times while in pilot school, but I've never gotten to experience it in real life."

"I wish you hadn't experienced it right now," I tell him.

He looks over and I notice a sheen on his face. He's sweating, and I don't think it has to do with the sex we just had. It's all about the fact we nearly died. He chuckles, boggling my brain.

"If you wouldn't have been in here with me, I would've enjoyed that. It's different when another life is in my hands though."

"You might be crazier than I ever imagined," I tell him. I'm still frozen in my seat. "I'd say mixing sex and flying isn't the smartest decision in your life."

"Nope, that was worth it," he tells me. He then smiles. "You might want to get dressed before we land," he offers. I was so scared I forgot I'm nearly naked. He just has to put himself back in his pants and he's fine. I'm a wreck.

"I'm not sure I can move to get dressed," I tell him, my voice barely more than a whisper.

"We're fine, Jewel. Spins happen. Pilots are trained for them," he says, not seeming shaken up at all by our near disaster.

"Well, I'm not trained for it," I say, my voice growing stronger.

"Give it some time," he says with a chuckle.

I finally look away from him as I try to get my clothes on with the seatbelt in place. I'm not willing to take it off for even a second. Nope. Been there, done that. Not happening again. I get somewhat dressed as sadness washes through me.

We don't have enough time for me to get used to this. We most likely won't have enough time together for me to fly with him again. I'm okay with the not flying part . . . I'm not okay with this ending so fast. I'm not thrilled about it, but I'm getting used to being with Blake. I want to shout out a Mayday, but it might already be too late.

Chapter Review

Chapter Twenty-Two

Jewel

I WAKE IN THE MORNING with Blake's hands rubbing along my naked back. Undoubtedly I'll never be in a real relationship with him, and I'd be wise to keep him at a distance. Even knowing this, I'm well aware that a piece of me will always belong to him. This frightens me.

"Tell me, Jewel, why are you doing this? You haven't told me why you need someone at court with you. It's clear you're not stupid, and many normal men would want to be in a relationship with you. Knowing this, you clearly don't seem the sort of woman to sell your body."

"We've discussed this before; I need someone standing at my side in court."

"Why do you need someone at court? Did you kill someone? Did you shoplift? What's so important that you're willing to do something you don't want to do?"

"You wouldn't believe me, Blake. Let's just say I want to keep my personal life separate from this transaction."

"If you have nothing to hide, tell me. It doesn't have to make things personal.

I take a breath, fighting whether or not to share this with him. I want to tell him about Justin, to have someone understand, and for some reason, I want Blake to know I'm *not* a scarlet woman. But at the same time, I fear falling for him. Sharing this with him might make me more vulnerable. That would be foolish.

"Maybe I like to screw hot men," I say as cavalierly and crudely as possible. His arms tense around me, telling me he doesn't like my answer.

"I don't buy that, Jewel. You were a virgin. Women don't wake up one day and decide to sell themselves. There has to be something behind this. Is there really a reason? Were you hoping to hook yourself a billionaire?" He asks this question as if the answer must be a yes. This ignites my wrath. Why does he need to go for the jugular, to say the meanest thing he can think of?

"Does it give you pleasure to be this cruel? Maybe we're more alike than either of us wants to admit. Maybe I do want to hook a billionaire. Maybe I'll indeed do that," I say.

Blake fastens on my question. "Yes, it usually pleases me to be an ass. That way people know where they stand. They don't have expectations of me."

The slight vulnerability in his tone makes me want to open up a bit more. I reflect on my conversation with Bill, and the pain Blake and his brothers suffered. I desperately want to know his story, but today isn't going to be the day I learn what happened to him in his past. I most likely will never find out how his parents died. So I decide to tell him nothing.

"Well, since we're only together for a short time, Blake, you don't have to worry about my intentions. We'll go our separate ways and never have to bother each other again."

He isn't the devil I initially thought he was, but he's far from a saint. I don't know exactly who or what he is. His company doesn't repulse me, and the sex is beyond anything I could've imagined sex to be.

Still, sex isn't enough. It's wonderful in the moment, but when it's over, emptiness swamps me, even while lying in his arms, because it isn't where I'm supposed to be, and I know he'll have another woman lying with him before the bedsheets grow cold.

"I hate repeating myself, Jewel . . . but I will. *Tell me why you're doing this.*"

"You don't give up, do you?"

"No. You should know this by now."

My time with him will be miserable if I keep fighting him at every turn in the road. I'm doing this for a noble reason, aren't I? It scares me that I'm doing this more for myself than for my brother. It's not a hardship being with Blake. I'll walk away from him once I have my brother, but it will haunt me. That means I'm still doing this for Justin . . . doesn't it? I can't keep fighting this man every step of the way. I give a long sigh.

"I have a brother . . . a ten-year-old brother."

He pauses as if taken aback by my words. Whatever he expected, it certainly wasn't this. I hold my breath as I wait for him to comment.

"He must be proud of his big sister," he says, his words dripping with sarcasm.

"If he ever found out, I'd . . . I can't imagine what I'd do. But I had no other choice. I have to do what I'm doing. There isn't another option, another way. I fought this battle for months since our mother died . . . and the attorney told me I have to have a stable home with a man in it to have a real shot at getting him. It's an obnoxiously outdated notion. He's my brother, and he belongs with me. So I need you to go to court with me, and say we're in a healthy, stable relationship. I'll get my brother, then we can go our separate ways." I trail off when I see his body language growing increasingly tense. He isn't my friend. He doesn't want to hear my story. This is more than obvious. I'm a fool to think I can trust him.

He surprises me, though, when he speaks again. "No other option?"

Maybe he *does* care, if only the slightest. After all, he isn't a man who lacks all emotion. And it's clear how much he cares about his own brothers, so why can't he understand my love for Justin?

"He's in foster care, and I need money, a stable home, and apparently a man so the judge will let me keep him."

"What proof do you have?"

"About what?" I ask, utterly confused.

"That this story is true."

"Proof?" What is this man talking about?

"Do you have court papers?"

"No," I say slowly. I haven't kept any of the court papers. I lost a lot of stuff when I was forced to leave my mother's home, and then when I moved to this apartment building they must've been thrown out. The papers aren't what matters. I know exactly what the judge wants from me.

"So, you have this story about a brother, and you need a husband?" he says, a mocking smile on his lips.

"I didn't say I need a *husband*. I said I need someone standing at my side in court, acting as my partner," I clarify.

"I've heard these sorts of sob stories before, Jewel. This sounds like every story a million women have come up with to snag my brothers and me to get what they want."

"But it's not a—"

He shakes his head. "I'm an incredibly wealthy man. You want a piece of it. I'm not even blaming you for it. My mother was the same. The thing is, though, I'm not affected by lies, and I don't hand out cash so you or anyone else can get a fix, or whatever it is that's driving a person."

"Why in the world did you ask what this is about if you aren't going to believe me?" I say, fighting the urge to cry.

"I guess I'm a fool because I was almost taken in by the innocence in your eyes. You're incredibly good at appearing as the girl next door — like a lost puppy who needs to be taken care of. I guarantee that I can't be fooled," he says.

"I'm so glad you have me figured out, Mr. Astor," I tell him, my body stiff. I'm sure he doesn't appreciate this, doesn't like being mocked.

He quickly flips me onto my back and covers my body, staring down at my face, refusing to release my eyes as he makes it abundantly clear which of us is in charge.

"Let's agree not to play games anymore," he growls. I feel his desire. He might think I'm a liar and out for what I can get, but he still desires me.

"Don't worry. I won't even think of telling you anything again." How I hate my traitorous body for responding to him.

213

"I'm not worried, Jewel," he assures me. "Nothing you can do or say will make me feel emotions I don't want to feel."

Then before I can reply, he pushes forward, sinking inside me and making me gasp in outrage as I glare at him while my body responds.

"I own you, Jewel," he says, his eyes shining in passion. Who really owns who, I wonder.

"For a short time," I say, unable to hold back the words that fuel his frustration.

He leans forward and shuts my words up the best way he knows how. Although I can't help but kiss him back, I hate him and myself just a little more over the next hour. When we're finished, I'm well aware I've been used, but that's what I offered. He stands up and dresses, making me feel even cheaper.

"By the way, you have a dress fitting in an hour. We'll attend a function on Friday, and you need proper attire."

He doesn't wait for my response, but instead leaves the room. I get up, shower, then make my way down the stairs, surprised to find him still here. I don't say a word. I want to return to my place, but I can't because of the fitting. I move into the kitchen and make coffee and food for myself. I'm *not* serving him.

I'm relieved when the doorbell rings after half an hour of uncomfortable silence. I can get through this, then go home. A petite woman walks in, with an assistant dragging a rack with several dresses on it.

A dress fitting — so not me. This is one more thing in a long line of things I never thought I'd have any part of before meeting Blake. It won't be so bad to go to some stuffy event. It isn't like I'll ever socialize with any of the attendees when my time with Blake is over.

"You must be Jewel," the woman says and proceeds to look me up and down with what seems to be a suppressed sneer as she circles me. When Blake leans back on the couch, I feel like screaming. He's going to sit here the entire time and make me uncomfortable. Why? This can't be his idea of a good time.

"I need you to strip down to your panties," the woman says as she pulls out a tape measure.

"Excuse me?" I look over to the young man who's standing silently by the clothing rack.

"I need you to strip down to your panties," she repeats as if she's dealing with a small, disobedient child. I'm about to throw a fit, so that description might fit.

"Can we go to the bathroom, or something?" I ask as I again look at the young man, and then at Blake, who isn't looking at the tablet anymore, his attention fully focused on me.

"No. I need the light and space in this room. You're wasting my time, Jewel," the woman says and takes a step closer. I have no doubt that if I don't strip, the woman will do it for me. And *that* isn't going to happen.

I begin removing my clothes, trying to remind myself this kid has seen it all before. It doesn't ease my humiliation. When I'm down to my panties, which don't cover much, I close my eyes and stand still while the woman tells me to hold out my arms, and moves this way and that.

By the time the measurements are finished, I've been touched and poked, and the woman has had the gall to comment on some of my trouble areas. I don't know how I manage to hold back the scream lodging in my throat. I refuse to make eye contact with Blake.

Next comes a show of dresses. Of course there isn't time to make one from scratch. I'll have to choose, and the woman will tailor it to my body. Blake rejects dress after dress, and by the eighth one I'm sick of slipping them on and off.

"No. This one isn't right. Didn't I give you specific directions on what I want?" Blake snaps. The woman's nose turns up an inch higher at this comment, and I'm surprised. I didn't think sticking that snoot up any higher was humanly possible.

"I assure you I've never not pleased a client, Mr. Astor," she says, her tone respectful even if her expression isn't. She pulls out another dress, and he leans forward. "This one," he says before I have a chance to try it on.

"Let's see how it looks," the woman says in a warning tone as the young man slides it over my head.

The material is similar to a few I've already tried on, but the fit is better, even without tailoring. It dips low in the front and back and ends high on my thighs, but it almost feels like I'm wearing nothing at all, because it's so light.

"Yes, this is the one."

The boy helps me out of the dress, and I stand with my arms crossed, trying to protect my naked body from their view, even though they've been staring at me shamelessly for the past hour.

"I'll have the dress ready by Friday morning," the woman says before making a quick exit. I move over to my discarded clothes and gather them. I move into the bathroom, not saying a word when I return, then leave his apartment. He doesn't try to stop me.

I don't take a good breath until I close and lock my door, leaning against it. How am I going to make it through this? I remind myself that I'm strong. There's nothing I can't do. I'll make it through this nightmare, and come out on the other side stronger.

I'll make it through this nightmare, and come out on the other side stronger

Chapter Review

Jewel

OOOH, THAT'S GOING to leave a mark!"

I spew out water as I pull myself up on the wakeboard. I send a glare straight to Tyler, who's busy laughing as he looks at me; I hope he chokes on his own tongue.

"Don't worry about me. I'm just fine," I snap, determined to master this ridiculous sport.

"I wasn't worried," Tyler assures me as he waits until I'm holding the rope and my feet are firmly planted on the wakeboard. He then holds up his hand, and Blake puts the boat into full throttle as I struggle to stand on my feet.

We're at the lake, and have been here for the past three hours. I haven't spoken a single word to Blake since we left his apartment, and I'm more than happy to continue not speaking to him for the next few days, not after being an absolute ass to me since our discussion over my brother.

He's the one who asked me why I'm doing this job, and then treated me terribly when I spoke the truth. Let him think I'm a liar. I need him for one thing only. I can't believe I had a weak moment and opened up to him.

What has he done in the past weeks to prove I can trust him? Absolutely nothing. I was a fool to tell him anything, but it won't happen again.

At least I don't have to be alone with him right now — and maybe he planned this outing because he, too, doesn't want to be alone with me.

I enjoy Tyler's company. Granted, I'm not as happy being around Byron. He seems as stern and bitter as Blake, so they aren't the best people to hang out with on a hot, sunny day at the lake.

Before I manage to have another thought, I'm going under again. Water immediately floods my open mouth and I panic for a brief moment.

When I come back up, coughing water and taking in much-needed oxygen, I decide I'm finished with this so-called sport. Aren't sports supposed to be fun? Taking my feet out of the boots on the wakeboard, I wait for the fancy black boat to circle back to me, then swim to it.

"Are you giving up already, gorgeous?" Tyler asks as he holds out a hand to help me inside.

"I don't think I'll be able to walk in the morning. I'm done," I gasp, irritated I'm so out of breath, collapsing on one of the benches in the back of the boat.

"You aren't giving yourself enough credit. You got up and lasted a while," Tyler tells me, beaming a proud smile my way and bringing a glow to my cheeks. "That's great for a newbie."

Blake approaches. "Would you quit flirting with my girl?" he gruffly says.

"Oh, come on, Blake. I like Jewel. She's a beast," Tyler tells him. Winking at his brother, he sits down at my feet, lifting them to his lap, and kneads the tender flesh. I moan appreciatively.

"Get your hands off of her," Blake growls and pushes his brother away.

I want to protest the interruption of my foot rub, but with the thunderclouds in Blake's eyes, I decide I'm better off remaining silent.

"You're such a stick in the mud," Tyler says with a huge grin. "All right, Byron, looks like Blake's out for driving. You're at the helm. Give her hell." He grabs his board and jumps into the water.

Blake still doesn't say anything directly to me as we race around the lake, but he also doesn't move away, making me shift involuntarily while he sits beside me, his hand on my leg, obviously staking his claim in front of his brothers. I don't see why he bothers. He's made it perfectly clear he holds no particular fondness for me, and certainly no respect.

"Are you going to continue giving me the silent treatment for the rest of the day?" he finally asks.

"I'm simply minding my own business, Blake."

"I don't like it, Jewel, so stop."

"Well then, what should we talk about? We're civilized people, after all," I remark with sarcasm dripping from my tongue.

He leans in close, his eyes narrowed into slits. "I won't tolerate you speaking to me this way, especially in front of my brothers."

"I'm surprised you don't tell them I'm your personal prostitute, and our time is almost over, and they can have a turn next if they wait a little longer." Where is this cattiness coming from? I don't have a clue, but I suspect I'll come to regret it. And when he leans toward me, rage burning in his eyes, I'm *sure* I will . . . and soon.

"They already know," he says, making my humiliation complete before he continues speaking. "Is that what you want, Jewel? Do you want to be bedded by all three of us? Right now? Want me to find a nice quiet alcove? No, wait, you like the public stuff, don't you? Why don't I find a place where all of the boats are tied together, and you can make your rounds? Don't worry, doll — I know you expect to be paid extra for taking on multiple partners. Not a problem."

The sneer on his face makes me want to slap him. Oh, how I'd love to wipe away his arrogance, if only for a second.

"I'm not a whore," I say, my throat tight.

"Then quit making comments that make you seem like one," he fires back. "You're your own *sales*woman, you know."

"Why don't we go back to not speaking? You're so much more pleasant that way."

Before I can say something else, he pulls me up and places me on his lap. "Don't think for one minute because I allow you to speak your mind, I give a damn about your opinion." I gasp, but don't have a chance to snap at him before he crushes his mouth punishingly against mine.

Don't think for one minute because I allow you to speak your mind, I give a damn about your opinion

When the boat stops, Tyler climbs back on board and gives a catcall. Blake immediately pulls away, and I can see rage flashing in his silver eyes. I fight the urge to cry; there's no way I'm doing that. I've shed enough tears in the last six months to last a lifetime, and Blake

Astor is certainly not worth wasting any of my emotions on.

He releases me and stands. "I'm done. Let's go in," he says to Byron, who's now the captain of the boat.

Everyone falls silent. The boat turns, and I'm relieved when we approach the dock. The sooner this horrible day ends, the better off I'll be. Tyler gives me a questioning look, but says nothing.

It doesn't take long to tie off the boat, and Blake immediately leads me up the ramp and straight to his car. Our night seems destined to be less than pleasant.

When we arrive at our building, though, he sends me to my apartment without even trying to take me to his bed. I'm relieved . . . or I think I am. I gaze at the clock beside my bed and sleep doesn't easily find me; I feel nothing but despair. I tell myself it's because I'm counting the endless hours until my release from this nightmare, and my freedom from Blake Astor is so far away . . . but I'm lying.

What in the hell is wrong with me . . . and how in the world am I getting attached to this man? I'm a fool and an emotional wreck, that's how. Sleep takes a while, but when it finally comes, I sigh as peace fills me.

Chapter Review

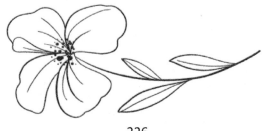

Chapter Twenty Four

Jewel

MY MUSCLES ARE SO sore, I'm barely able to climb out of bed. I somehow manage to stumble into the bathroom. After showering, getting dressed, and putting on makeup, I painfully make my way to the kitchen and head straight to the coffeepot. The apartment is quiet, and I'm relieved to be alone.

I polish off my first cup of coffee and immediately pour another. I have to hurry to get to work on time. I hope Blake is out on a job site today. We've been at each other's throats more than not lately, and I need a break. How much longer will we do this? It's crazy. We only seem to get along when we're in bed together. Do people live years of their lives like this? I couldn't.

I leave the apartment with no time to spare, walking into the large building along with a group of other employees. Everyone's chatting like usual, and I hardly contribute to the conversation as I make my way to my floor and immediately head to my desk.

I'm here for less than a minute when my phone buzzes . . . and I grimace. He must be here and saw me come in. Maybe approaching my boss for a torrid affair hadn't been the wisest decision in my life if I wanted to have some independence.

I need five more minutes, maybe an hour, to fully wake up and get my armor in place before speaking to Blake. Please, I beg, please. But it dings again almost immediately. I can't avoid him forever. I have some defiance, though, so I fire up my computer and pull out a file before I look at my phone after a third message.

Good morning, Jewel, I hope you slept well.

This message confuses me. He's been such a jackass; why is he sending something civilized like this? It makes no sense. Maybe the man's bipolar. Or he suffers from multiple personality disorder. That wouldn't surprise me.

Be ready right after work. You'll be leaving with me.

My stomach tightens. I don't want to spend the evening with him. It's going to be awkward and unpleasant, and I'll end up hating myself . . . again. I sigh. It could be a lot worse. Blake could be into some seriously sick and twisted games. At least I'm not being tied up and flogged, or being forced to have sicko sex in front of an audience.

Get over your tantrum, Jewel, and acknowledge you've seen my messages.

Tantrum? What freaking universe does he inhabit? Or does he own a special cyber helmet that makes every jerky thing he does look and smell like roses?

Fine! I punch in each of these letters in my one-word response with savagery, then drop my phone in a drawer, delighting when it bounces. I look up to one of the cameras facing my desk and give a mocking salute as I firmly close the drawer.

I'm not sure what we're doing tonight, but what I'm wearing will have to do. It's a simple skirt that comes halfway down my thighs, and a decently modest blouse. I get to work. The day passes surprisingly fast as I work diligently, take a lunch break with my co-workers, then continue my work for the rest of the afternoon.

I don't see or hear from Blake again, not that I check my phone often. It's unprofessional, and I want a good reference when I leave. I'm leaning more and more toward Alaska. Sure, it's cold, but it's far away, and no one will know my story. I don't care where I land just as long as Justin is with me. We're all each other has in this world now.

Five o'clock comes before I know it. Everyone leaves their desks. I grab my coat and purse and look at my phone. There are no new messages from Blake. Maybe he's changed his mind. I'm not going to message him to ask. If he's not there, I'll head home, put on my pajamas, and eat ice-cream for dinner. That sounds pretty good.

Blake's waiting outside when I come down. I want to deny the extra thud in my heartbeat, but it's there, and I can't stop it. I'll never be able to stop my reaction to Blake. I can tell myself all day long I hate being with him, but my body calls me a liar.

"Hello, Jewel. You look lovely today."

I stand before him, utterly dumbfounded. He's behaving so differently than he normally does around me. Is this a trick? I have no clue. He smiles as if knowing he's confusing me. He approaches with the confidence I've come to expect from him.

"When a person says hello and offers a compliment, the correct response is usually to offer a greeting in return."

He pulls me against him, and before I'm able to say a word, he kisses me. It isn't a greedy assault on my lips, but a soft, drugging kiss that makes my legs tremble in weakness. When he pulls back and looks in my eyes, I'm too stunned to speak.

"Let's get going," he says with a smile.

I'm surprised with the attitude change. He's treating me like a human being instead of his plaything. I'd do best to remember that this isn't typical, and things can change on a dime.

We go to where his driver, Max, is waiting. I say nothing as he helps me into the backseat, then joins me. We drive for over an hour, chatting about nothing of importance, and I finally start relaxing. I don't care where we're going. When the driver stops and quickly comes around and opens my door, I'm surprised to see we're at a vineyard.

"We're going to a fundraiser tomorrow night, so I thought I'd give you a sampling of good wines while we stretch our legs."

Blake obviously thinks I'm a newbie to wine that needs a corkscrew to open, but I'm not going to get huffy about it . . . well . . . because he's pretty much right.

Soon the two of us are moving through the vineyard. We stop at several stations to taste the local wines from each variety of grown grapes; some leave a sour taste, and some I want more of.

After an hour, he leads me to a private balcony off the main lodge restaurant, where a table is set with wine glasses; food soon arrives.

"I've spent some time mulling over what you said the other day, Jewel, and I jumped too quickly to an unfavorable conclusion."

My heart starts thundering. Does he believe me? I'm fearful to voice the question. His next words make me glad I didn't.

"Though I'm not sure what you're hiding, I believe you have a story to tell."

I've had so much wine — I really should've spit them out as the experts do — so now I have to fight past the fog in my brain. Sure, the glasses have been small and far from full, but I probably have had the equivalent of four to six full glasses by now. I need to eat some

231

food before I can come even close to keeping up with this man.

"I thought you told me you don't care about my story, Blake."

"I shouldn't care, Jewel, but oddly enough, I want to know more about you."

"Why? Our time is going to be short-lived — as if I need to remind you of that. There's nothing else you need to know about me." I pick up a piece of bread and begin eating, hoping it will soak up the alcohol I've downed. I don't dare touch the wine glass in front of me.

"Just because our time will end doesn't mean we can't have a civilized conversation for now."

"I only want to get through our time together," I tell him.

His smile evaporates as he looks at me intently. "I'm trying to be pleasant. I don't appreciate that you're not trying to do the same."

"You can't just suddenly flip a switch and expect me to pour out my heart to you. A few days ago you told me to do my job and not to think of feeling anything about you."

"Maybe I've changed my mind about that," he says. I look at him with confusion. This has to be sarcasm; it *can't* be anything else.

His eyes turn a bit colder after seeing my response, but otherwise he shows no emotion. "So you'd rather I treat you as nothing but an object, something I've bought — no . . . rented?"

"Yes, I do. That will be best for both of us." He's silent for a long time, and then his eyes narrow.

"Fine, Jewel. You want that. You have it," he finally says, and a dangerous gleam appears in his menacing silver gaze.

Our dinner's forgotten. Blake stands and holds out a hand, not as a courtesy but as a command. My stomach dips. But I take his hand, and when I stand, I sway on my feet. Where is he leading me? We end up in a small basement in the large house overlooking the winery, and I panic.

He circles me for a long moment, a predator assessing his prey. I've screwed up, but even knowing this, I can't seem to tuck my pride away, and stop this.

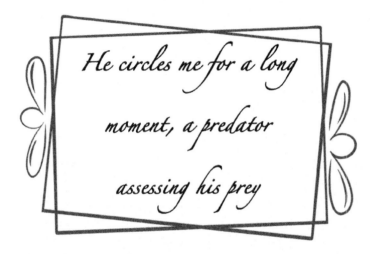

He circles me for a long
moment, a predator
assessing his prey

"Strip for me, Jewel. If you want to be nothing more than an object, do a dance. If you want to try something different, tell me now, and we can go back to dinner and pretend this didn't happen."

The color drains from my face. I approached him the first time by stripping, by offering myself to him so he could help me. He's putting me back in my place, back to the beginning, reminding me of who I am, and what I've done. It's probably for the best. I can't start caring for him. It's best he reminds me of that.

I force myself to erase all thoughts, all emotions, to become nothing but a robot, a sex toy . . . and with defiance, I look him in the eyes and begin taking off my clothes. That dim lantern lighting the room is of small consolation. He sees everything. I can't keep looking him in the eyes, so I sway my hips, and turn as my clothes fall away.

It doesn't take him long to reach for me. We move backward until my back hits the wall. Then he lifts me and I damn us both as he quickly fills me with pleasure, our panting echoing in the small room.

By the time we leave, I've not only stripped and allowed myself to become nothing but a sex worker, but Blake has also stripped another piece of my soul away . . . and this time, it was my choice.

Chapter Review

Jewel

THERE'S NO REASON for me to be standing in the shower with doom hanging over my head. Something more has to be going on. I'm certainly not falling in love with Blake. That's impossible. He's *barely* shown me kindness. Yes, he held me close after the plane nearly crashed — though he insisted he'd been in control the whole time — and in other moments, I've seen small instances of kindness, but not nearly enough.

If anything, anytime he shows the barest amount of humanity, he quickly masks it by letting the dominant, controlling part of his personality take over. I still feel dirty after our *tryst* at the winery. He took his pleasure with me against the wall in silence . . . other than our panting.

I'm relieved our time will soon end. I don't know what will come next. That has to be the source of my doom. After finishing my shower, I slowly get ready for our evening. Tonight is the fundraising dinner with Blake, and the whole idea has my stomach in a constant state of upheaval.

I'm about to enter a world I've only read about. My mother provided a safe and stable home, but we lived on the lower end of the middle-class spectrum. The only fundraisers we attended were small-potato affairs at our public school. This fundraiser will pull in millions of dollars.

Will I pass inspection when Blake picks me up? The mirror gives me no answers. The dress that was tailored specifically for me is exquisite, fitting me like a glove, and in every respect, far more beautiful than anything I've ever worn before. I like it, and I need to thank him. I hope no one will look at me and know exactly what I am, and how much I don't belong rubbing elbows with the rich and famous. The waiting makes things worse.

I spend a lot of time without Blake. He has an incredible work ethic. The man is constantly answering phones, or staying at the office late. I have to admire what he and his brothers have built. It's not only about making money either. He cares about his clients. I've watched him sweating on top of a friend's roof, his button-down shirt thrown off, his expensive slacks ruined. The man looks like he was born to wield a hammer.

I'm now aware that all of the Astor brothers started out on job sites before they created their own company, a business so successful that none of them will ever feel the need to do manual labor again. It shows their character that they can roll up their sleeves and help a friend, and I don't want to be impressed, but I am.

How many other billionaires are willing to climb up on a roof for a man they love and respect? I'd say not many. It doesn't make Blake a good guy, it just makes him less of an . . . ass.

It's best that my time with Blake is temporary. If I stay with Blake too long, I'll be helpless to resist his attention. These glimpses of vulnerability in him try to break through to my heart, and the sex — oh my, the sex . . . it's incredible.

It's funny how things turn out. Well . . . maybe not exactly *funny*. Blake isn't a man a woman stays with. I could have a touch of Stockholm syndrome. Since I'm currently tied to Blake, I need to be with him. Yet how can I feel this way when he can be so awful? My mother didn't raise a masochist.

I remember falling in love for the first time when I was fifteen. What a disaster — I saw the boy kissing my mortal enemy behind the bleachers, and came home in tears. My mother consoled me, told me that it sometimes takes a while to find *the one*, but that someday I'd find him. The man I marry has to be my best friend, my lover, and the person I trust above all others. *Never settle*, my mom said. *Ask for the moon and don't take less than the stars.*

I've never found a man who fits that description.

Instead, I found Blake Astor, who most certainly has none of these traits. And especially not the man I'll marry — if I ever marry at all. Yes, he's a virtuoso lover — perhaps I should use the adjective *masterful* — but he'll never offer me the moon or stars. That isn't who he is. Besides, I have my brother to think about, and it's okay to consider my needs.

The man I marry has to be my best friend, my lover, and the person I trust above all others.

I sit in my sparsely furnished living room. Am I supposed to wait for him or meet in the lobby? Grabbing my phone, I see several messages and grimace.

My driver will pick you up.

Where are you?

Max is waiting in the lobby.

Jewel!

I smile at this last message, practically hearing the growl in his voice. The last message came in ten minutes ago. I'm surprised he didn't add a dozen more exclamation marks to it. His driver is early, so it isn't my fault if he's been kept waiting.

On my way down now. Was getting ready.

After hitting send, I tuck the phone into my purse and do a final check in the entryway mirror before I walk out the door.

"Good evening, Ms. Weston," Max says.

"Good evening, Max. I'm sorry to have kept you waiting."

"It's no problem waiting for a woman," he says. He opens the car door for me and I climb in and get comfortable.

When Max pulls into traffic, I force myself to clear my mind of all doubt. Yes, I'm rubbing my skin raw as I twist my fingers together but realize I'm being stupid. I have to go to this fundraiser, so what good is worrying? None. In fact, it's a *party*, and I might as well try to enjoy it.

We arrive sooner than expected, and I shudder as Max helps me out of the car. And then it worsens when I step up to the door. I look around, but there's no sign of Blake, which means I'm faced with walking in alone. Will they let me enter? I have nothing to prove I'm supposed to be here. What will I do if they send me away? Sighing, I force myself forward. I approach two men in tuxes guarding the entrance of this fancy hotel.

"Invitation?" one asks.

"I . . . uh . . . I don't have one. I'm here with someone," I say, and the answering look in his eyes clearly says he doesn't believe me.

Before I can speak again, Max steps up next to me. "She's with Blake Astor."

The man's attitude instantly changes, and he holds the door open. "I apologize, Ms. Weston. He's waiting for you inside." Wow! I can't imagine what it would be like to possess that much power with nothing but a name.

After stepping through the front doors and being escorted to the fundraiser room, I'm taken aback by the luxury. Sparkling light fixtures hang throughout the room, and the round tables are perfectly set with the finest china, crystal, and what I'm sure is sterling silver.

Waiters silently move through the room, making sure everyone has a fresh drink, not an easy task — the crowd is much larger than I expected. How am I ever going to find Blake in this throng of people?

When a woman's tinkling laughter drifts toward me, I turn to the sound, and my stomach takes a dip. Finding Blake isn't so difficult after all. I just wasn't expecting to find him with a woman clinging to his side. It doesn't matter, of course. But why in the world did he ask me to get dressed up for this glittering event just to leave me standing alone, looking like a fool?

As if he senses my presence, he turns in my direction, and our eyes collide from across the room. I must be frowning, because the smile on his lips vanishes and his eyebrows quizzically rise, then he holds out his hand and gestures for me to join him . . . and the beautiful woman.

It's awkward enough for me being here, without him throwing another woman down my throat. But who cares, right? I'm just a fling. Why in the heck am I such a mess right now?

A man bumps into me, breaking my eye contact with Blake, and when he turns to apologize, he stops and stares, his words trapped in his throat.

"Um . . . excuse me," I say, and try to brush past him.

He subtly blocks me. "What's your name?" His tone is polite. I shouldn't talk to him, but I have nowhere else to go.

"Jewel," I tell him.

"That's a beautiful name." Okay, maybe flirting with this man isn't the best idea I've ever had. Blake will be furious if he sees. He looks at me as *his* possession until our time ends.

"Thank you. I really should be going," I say.

"What's the rush? Why don't you have a drink with me?"

"I'm here with someone," I say as I try to move again.

"I'm better than whomever you're with," he tells me with a cocky gaze.

"The lady's with me."

I'm relieved when Blake breaks in and puts his arm around me, easily taking me from the other man's grasp. The rage shimmering off of him doesn't seem to be directed at me . . . for once.

"I'm sorry, Blake; I didn't realize she was with you," the man says, looking properly chastised.

"Now you know," Blake says. With that, Blake pulls me away, and my heart starts slowing only when we're halfway across the room. Then it picks right back up when the woman I saw him with a few minutes earlier interrupts our escape.

"Blake, aren't you going to introduce us?"

Blake stops, and to my utter amazement, his expression softens, causing instant jealousy to rush through my veins. Who is this snake-charming woman, a woman who can enchant Blake Astor with nothing but a few words? Not that it matters . . . because he isn't mine . . . and I don't want him to be.

"Jewel, this is Monica," Blake says. "Monica, Jewel, my date."

Monica sticks out her hand. "It's a pleasure to meet you, Jewel."

I have no choice but to shake the woman's hand — if I don't, I'll look rude. So I give the obligatory handshake, then move back as quickly as possible. "Nice to meet you as well." This is the biggest lie I've spoken in a long time.

Blake leads us to a corner table and holds out both of our chairs before seating himself between us. Though

I make my face a mask of unconcern, the longer I sit with Blake and Monica, the more irate I become.

How dare he drag me to this worthless event only to ignore me? How dare he flaunt another woman in my face? Okay, it isn't as if I own him. Heck, we aren't even in a real relationship. But still, it's rude.

After we finish dinner, Blake asks me for a dance. I'm less than enthusiastic, but I have to admit feeling the slightest bit of satisfaction that he's asking me and *not* Monica. Though I'm sure he'll trade us off quickly enough.

I'm stiff in his arms when he tries to pull me close, and he looks down with puzzlement. "Aren't you having a nice night? These events can be slightly dry, but the music is good, and the food is better than most."

"I'm fine," I say, my words clipped.

He stops in the middle of the dance floor, not caring if anyone notices us. "Jewel, obviously something is wrong. Is it that man?" he asks as his eyes scan the room.

"No. He's nobody," I say, surprised I've forgotten about him during my uncomfortable time at the table with Blake and Monica.

"Tell me *now*, Jewel!" He isn't as kind now; the domineering Blake has taken over.

"Fine! I think it's rude for you to bring me here when you already had a date. How many does one guy need? Especially since you and *Monica* seem to get along so well," I snap. I instantly regret my words.

His expression goes from shock to confusion and then, to my utter outrage, to amusement. His lips turn up, and before I can say another word, he lets out a chuckle, and then full-blown laughter.

"I'm not going to stand here and take this." To hell with this. I'm out of here.

I whirl around, ready to storm off, but am stopped in my tracks when Blake grabs my arm and begins walking me toward one of the terrace doors. I want to dig in my heels and refuse to accompany him, but I also want to avoid a scene. This entire evening has been a nightmare, and my deepest wish right now is to scurry into some dark corner and hide for a long, *long* time while I lick my wounds.

When Blake and I are alone, he pushes me against the balcony railing, his laughter dying as he looks in my eyes. My breath hitches.

"I shouldn't have laughed, Jewel. I'm actually surprised by it. But I didn't think twice about Monica being here. I've known her since I was ten years old, and she's my best friend, as well as a trusted colleague. She's the only woman I trust."

"That doesn't mean she's not also your lover." I fight the need to squirm.

"Well, considering she's married to one of the starting linebackers for the Seahawks, it pretty much does mean she's *not* my lover," Blake says.

It takes a few moments for his words to sink in, and then I feel like an utter fool. But how was I to know they aren't intimate? I watched them all through dinner, and the two of them shared jokes, laughter, easy touches . . . just like best friends. And now I've shown him I care. Dammit!

He moves closer to me. "I have to admit I like this jealous side of you, even if it's completely unfounded."

"I'm not jealous. I simply don't like feeling like a third wheel." Why don't I sound convincing even to myself?

"I think you're lying. I should punish you for that," he tells me before leaning down and capturing my lips. It doesn't take long to forget about my jealousy and to focus solely on the inexplicable effect Blake has on my body.

When he allows me to come up for air, he speaks seriously. "Jewel, you should be careful what you show the world. There are people who can use your emotions against you."

You should be careful what you show the world. There are people who can use your emotions against you.

I go still as I look at him. Who's he warning me against? Himself? Others? I have no idea.

"I can take care of myself," I say, though a shiver runs through me.

"I don't think you can, Jewel. I think you need someone to take care of you. Is that the real reason you came to me?"

I pause, trying to choose my words carefully. Maybe if he thinks this, he'll drop the subject. It's odd because he seems to want to climb inside my head more as the sand runs through the hourglass.

"I have my reasons," I say. "I don't honestly believe you care. It's your need to be in control."

"You're right, Jewel. I *do* need to be in control. You should remember that, and know I'll eventually get my way."

"Warning accepted," I say as he pulls me against his hard body.

"I don't think you truly know what that means, Jewel. Right now, I still want you . . . and I own you."

"You never let me forget, Blake."

"I don't understand, then, why I need to keep reminding you."

"Maybe because of your own insecurities," I say bold enough to make him tense in my arms.

"You *will* push me too far one of these times."

I have no doubt this is true. What I don't understand is my sudden desire to go back to his place. There really has to be something wrong with me.

Chapter Review

Jewel

I WALK FROM MY BEDROOM early in the morning and listen for sounds. I fell asleep with Blake at his place the night before, but woke in the middle of the night and left, making my way back to my own apartment. He can get into my apartment, which he's done before, but it helps me emotionally pull away from him.

No matter the day of the week, Blake's up early, and usually gone by the time I rise. It gives me a solid hour of alone time before I head to work. Today's Saturday, though. I have something to do today, and I can't let him stop me.

No matter what it takes, I have to see my brother for our weekly visit, and there's no way anything will stop me. Worry wrinkles my brow when I slip into the kitchen to find a full pot of coffee and a note from Blake. A shiver rushes through me. I pick it up, then let out a sigh of relief as I smile.

Be ready by five. I had an emergency, but when I get back, we're going out.

What a relief! I can easily steal away, visit my brother, and be back home in plenty of time without him ever knowing I went anywhere. I can visit Saturday or Sunday, which has been a blessing during my time with Blake. I haven't made a pattern that's made him suspicious.

He has zero trust in me, and he can break this off at any point if he thinks I'm fooling around on him. He won't know I'm gone today, though. Gathering my purse, and leaving my phone off, I walk from the apartment feeling lighter and happier than I have in weeks.

Justin will never understand if I can't come see him. I impatiently wait at a nearby bus stop and don't take my first full breath until I'm out of sight of the ritzy apartment building. It takes an hour, but I finally reach the home my brother's staying at, and, putting on a big smile, I knock on the door. It seems to take an eternity, but when the door finally opens, I can barely resist pushing past the foster mother to get to my brother.

"Is Justin ready for our visit?"

"He's not feeling well today," the woman says, her eyes cold.

I hate that Justin has to live here, and my determination grows stronger as I stand on the woman's threshold. "Then I'll visit with him here," I say. I'm not leaving.

"I don't know if today works."

"I'm not asking for your opinion," I tell her. "The state's given me visitation on the weekends and I *will* see my brother."

I look her in the eyes, making it clear I won't back down. With a deep scowl, the woman opens the door wider, and I don't hesitate to step inside.

"Justin," I call, and the sound of my brother's feet running down the hallway is the sweetest music I've heard. Bracing myself for impact, I easily pull him into my arms, and he clings to me, holding me as if he'll never let go. Soon, this will happen daily.

"They said you might not come today," Justin says when he finally lets go.

"Nothing on this earth can keep me away from you on our special days," I assure him, too angry to look at the woman scowling at us. He isn't sick — clearly, she was lying. Why? Probably because she's a bitter, sadistic woman who wants to use my brother for the measly paycheck the state gives her. I'm taking him away from this woman soon. He needs to be with his sister who adores him.

"That's great — I missed you. Are we going to the pizza place?"

"You bet we are, Bubby. We have three hours, and we're going to have the best time ever." I move to the coat closet and pull out his ratty jacket. I can't wait until he's living with me, and I have the money to give him the things he needs and wants. I already bought him some clothes, but they came up missing after he got them.

I know there are some great foster homes out there, but many terrible ones as well. I'm saving and saving so the day I get him back we'll shop for new things. He'll never feel alone again, never feel abandoned. I'll save my brother . . . and this will save me as well.

"I'm so glad you're here, Sissy. I've had a bad week," he says, his eyes filling with tears.

"Why has your week been bad?" The two of us head to the door, not even acknowledging Justin's foster mother as we pass her and leave the house. *Foster?* Now that's a sick joke as she doesn't know the first thing about encouraging or developing the kids in her care. It's almost as sick as the *mother* part of her name.

"Ms. Penny says I've been misbehaving too much, so she made me stay in my room for two whole days only coming out to use the bathroom," he says.

"Oh, Justin, that's not okay. I'll talk to your social worker." I struggle to moderate my voice so I won't upset him more than he already is.

"I was crying for you the other night, and she told me to shut up, said I needed to start acting like a man, not a crybaby. I try not to cry, but sometimes I miss you so much." His voice quiets, but his little fingers tremble in mine.

I stop and kneel on the sidewalk to see my brother's face, so he can see mine. "Sometimes emotions are too much for us to bear and we have to release them. Never let anyone tell you what you're feeling isn't real. If you have to cry, you do it, and know in a few more weekends we're going to be together for always and not only for a few hours at a time." I give him another hug.

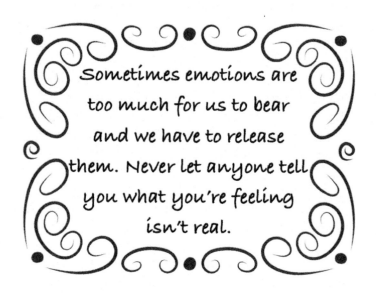

Sometimes emotions are too much for us to bear and we have to release them. Never let anyone tell you what you're feeling isn't real.

"You promise, Sissy. I don't want to be at Ms. Penny's house anymore. She's so mean — nothing like how mama was."

"I promise you no matter what I have to do, I'll get you out of there, and you'll come live with me. You have to give it a little more time and be my brave little man, but not for much longer."

"I know I'm supposed to be brave, but it's so hard . . ." He stops speaking when his voice chokes up.

"You *are* brave, Justin. Keep holding your head high, and know that I'm doing whatever it takes for us to be together. I have a job, a *really* good job, and an apartment, and I'm saving lots of money so we can be together, where we can put up pictures of Mom, and where, if you need to cry, you can without any fear of being made fun of. We're a family, and that means we stick together. No one can keep us apart for long, Bubby."

"I know. I say a prayer every night, asking God to let me come home with you. Why does it take so long for Him to answer my prayer?"

My heart breaks in so many pieces, I don't think it will be healed again. My eyes fill, and a tear falls down my cheek, which I quickly wipe away. "Sometimes it takes a little longer because there are so many people who need so much, but you haven't been forgotten — I promise."

Despite my reassurance, Justin falls silent, perhaps afraid that too much talking will betray his emotion. He holds on tight until we begin walking. I have to keep my promise, no matter what it means for me, and no matter what will come next. I can't let my brother down.

The rest of our visit is wonderful. My little brother comes to life as we have pizza, and he laughs and tells me about school, which is going well. He's always been super smart, and though his grades took a dip after our mother died, I convince him that concentrating on school will help him focus on something happy instead of the overwhelming sadness that's swamped us both since we became orphans.

We eat and play, and even have time to stop at the park where we race down the slide, swing as high as we can, launch ourselves off to land in the soft sand, and get the spinner going so fast we both walk sideways for a while. My heart bleeds when I have to take him back to the terrible foster house. We hug for long minutes before the woman has enough and drags him inside.

After leaving my brother, I rush to the bus stop and shed the tears I refused to shed while we were together.

I pull it together before I get home. As soon as I step off the bus, though, I have a feeling of doom. I move to the apartment complex and come inside two hours before I'm supposed to meet Blake. A shiver rushes through me.

I open my front door . . . then take a step back. Blake's sitting in a chair in my living room and he doesn't appear happy. This isn't going to be pleasant.

He doesn't say a word as I begin moving again. I come inside, reluctantly shutting my door. Nevertheless, I maintain an expression of poise and confidence, though my body shakes with nerves. This is ridiculous. I was out visiting my brother, which is none of his business. What does he care if I'm out? He shouldn't.

It doesn't matter how much of a pep talk I give myself though. As he stands and takes a menacing step toward me, I figure we're heading for a fight in three . . . two . . . one.

Chapter Review

Chapter Twenty Seven

Jewel

GAZING INTO BLAKE'S frigid eyes, I tell myself to be strong, this is only one more bump in the road. He won't physically hurt me — not that anyone will care if he does . . . besides Justin.

Though he might think I'm nothing more than a money-hungry woman wanting whatever I can get from him, *I* know who I am. The mistrust in his expression shakes me up. I've never seen a man so irrationally upset before. His lips remain in a hard line, not a muscle moving on his chiseled face.

"Where were you?"

Ice runs through my veins at his words, spoken deathly quiet. Apparently, *fury* doesn't begin to describe what Blake appears to be feeling.

"I took a walk." Should I simply move past him? Maybe it's wisest to stay right where I am.

"You're lying." I wait for him to say more, but nothing else comes from his tightly pressed lips.

"Do you have any idea of how stir-crazy I get when I'm stuck here all day with very little to do? No, you probably don't, because you leave daily at the crack of dawn. I needed to get out and walk off my cabin fever."

He takes a sinister step forward. "I don't believe you. You snuck off. Why?"

I could tell him what's happening, but at this point I'm pissed off about all of it. I'm ticked at how he's treating me, and ticked at the situation I've been pushed into. How is this happening in the supposedly freest country in the world? It's crap!

His voice rises a little, enough to show me he's truly mad. I don't understand why. We've never agreed I had to tell him my every movement, just as his comings and goings aren't any of my business. Where is his anger coming from? Why is he upset? It makes no sense.

I don't understand why he's acting like an ass, but I'll be damned if I'm going take his verbal beating. If I stand my ground, refuse to back down, refuse to allow him to intimidate me, won't he stop? Isn't that what I was taught years before when I took a self-defense class?

"Look, I wasn't with another man, Blake. I swear to that, and anyway, it makes no sense. I was a virgin before I was with you, so why would I start whoring around now? I needed to be out today, and it's something I don't want to talk about . . . yet." I move forward and edge past him, making sure not to bow my head in submission.

He doesn't grab me, doesn't try to stop me. This is a positive. I move into the room and head straight to the couch, afraid to stand any longer for fear my legs will end up buckling.

"I don't know what your end game is, but if I can't trust you, this isn't going to work between us."

He comes closer but keeps about five feet of distance between us. This is probably a smart move. We're both getting more riled.

"I'm sorry if you don't trust me, but there's no other man. I neither want, nor need, a relationship with anyone, and that includes you. Your suspicions are stupid, and if you were as smart as you think you are, you'd know that. If you want to end this, end it. I can't take it anymore."

Fear flows through me at throwing down this gauntlet. I need him at the courthouse, but I don't deserve to be treated like this. I told Justin I'll do whatever it takes, but maybe I can find some other man on a dating site to help me. It's got to be easier than this.

If the state keeps trying to keep Justin from me, I'll simply kidnap him, and take him away in the middle of the night. The two of us can go somewhere no one will ever find us. Alaska is looking better and better by the second.

It's still in the U.S., and if we're found, Washington state officials might try to take my brother back, but will they search that far? We could live in an Eskimo village. It doesn't matter where we are just as long as we're together.

"Where did you go?" he asks, his voice more controlled as if he's giving up on getting answers from me.

I fold my arms. I need some Advil as my head starts to pound. I glare at him, unwilling to say anything more. Neither one of us seem able to back down.

"Let's go," he says. He turns, confident I'll follow. I don't move.

"Where?" I hate the slight tremble in my voice. Dammit, he's never hurt me, and I don't believe he will now. I hate fighting with anyone. It seems that's all I've been doing since I lost my mom.

He doesn't answer as he continues moving forward. Do I follow or not? Bile rises in my throat. I'm doing all of this for Justin, and because I visited him today, I might've just set myself back several steps.

Tears burn my eyes as I desperately try to find an explanation to calm Blake's temper. But he seems to know when I'm lying. So instead of crying, instead of throwing up, I stand in silence and follow Blake. He presses the button on the elevator, and we ride down and walk into the garage.

When he moves over to a large black pickup truck, I question it. Blake drives expensive sports cars, not trucks that seem more fitting for work. Then I remember he'd been called to work earlier and had most likely been using it on a job.

Still, why is he taking me in it now? Why not just leave the truck here? Maybe because there's a shovel in the back, and he needs to get rid of the evidence . . .

As Blake closes the passenger door and enters the truck on the driver's side, I focus on the windshield and the view straight in front of me, not having a clue where we're going. It doesn't matter. If this allows me to get my brother, I don't care what happens.

A strange sense of peace washes over me, and I turn to look out the side window. This will all be over someday. Soon, no matter what it takes, if I'm alive, I'll be with my brother, and hopefully then, both of our lives can return to somewhat of a normal existence.

This is the only thing I can hope for. Because the alternative will send me into a downward spiral of depression I'll never escape. I won't keep fighting as long as I'm drawing in a breath. To hell with Blake, and to hell with a system that dares to take a child from a loving sister who wants nothing more than to care for him.

I won't keep fighting as long as I'm drawing in a breath.

I clench my fists and try to decide what's coming next. Whatever it is, I won't go down without a fight.

Chapter Review

Blake

FRUSTRATION ROLLS THROUGH me in never-ending waves. The feigned innocence I keep seeing in Jewel's eyes can't conceal the lies she's speaking. I *need* to get the truth, and I want it tonight. If she thinks I easily give up, she has a lot to learn about the real world . . . and about me.

I'm well aware I'm made of ice. How many people have said this? I don't care. Even a man as cold as I am can eventually melt, can feel real emotion. I'm feeling a hell of a lot right now.

Only my brothers have ever been allowed in, and only because of the horror the three of us share. It's us against the world. So why am I letting this woman, this insignificant woman, affect my moods?

Even a man as cold as I am can eventually melt

As I point my truck away from the city, I stealthily watch Jewel. Absurdly enough, I want to reach across the seat and haul her to my side. Her tantalizing scent surrounds me and muddies my thoughts. In a very short time she's changed me in ways I don't understand.

What I should do is take her back to the apartment, drop her off, and never look back. That isn't going to happen . . . not yet. I need to drive, think before I let her go. I need to make her talk.

When I start down a road with no streetlights as the sun sinks, she turns toward me. Her face is barely visible in the insignificant light from the dash, but I have no doubt she's worried. Good. Let her worry. She's caused me an unbearable rush of emotion today. She can deal with some of her own.

About ten miles out in the middle of nowhere, she finally speaks. "Where are we going?"

"I don't know." My tone is curt. I can't seem to stop it.

"Blake—"

She breaks off, leaving me with no idea of what she was going to say, because we suddenly hear a loud thumping noise followed by the sound of my tire shredding.

"Dammit!" I yank my foot off the gas and ease the truck to the side of the road. We're miles from town, in the middle of mint fields without a house in sight. I'm irritated for a few more seconds, then I take a deep breath and realize this isn't so bad. I need to feel something other than anger and irritation, and I know exactly what will ease my frustration.

"Come here, Jewel." The dash lights are the only illumination, but I see a shiver race through her body at my words.

I'm waiting for her to climb over to me, and instead, she throws open the passenger door and bolts from the truck. I sit dumbfounded for a full minute, then finally rush out. Both of the truck doors are left wide open, and the light glowing from the truck offers me some assistance in my chase, and yet her shadow is barely visible as she sprints away.

"What the hell, Jewel?" I thunder, then silently rebuke myself. The tone of my voice isn't going to reassure her, and certainly won't persuade her to stop, and if she doesn't, I'll lose her in the dark.

Throwing off my custom jacket, not caring where it lands, I run after her. She doesn't stand a chance. She doesn't make it far when I catch up to her, and scoop her off her feet. Her scream floats into the night.

"Stop!" I shout as I turn and return to the truck with her struggling in my arms.

"Don't do this, Blake. I'm sorry. I wasn't doing anything that will dishonor you, I swear."

"I don't care anymore," I say in a steady voice as we reach the truck.

"What are you going to do?"

I place her on the bed of my truck, spread her legs, and move close, aligning my face perfectly with hers.

"What we both need." With this, I grasp her neck and pull her against me, sealing our mouths together, and only just beginning to scratch the surface of my hunger where this woman's concerned.

She struggles for a brief moment, until I gentle my hold, my anger gone, passion taking its place. Only then does she melt against me, a whimper escaping her throat as I break through the barrier of her lips and plunder her mouth, making sure she thinks of no other man but me.

Wrapping her in my arms, I dominate this moment in the best way I know how. I push away the thoughts of who's truly in control. I'm transported to a place where my problems evaporate, where the endless void of my life paradoxically disappears. Nothing matters when I'm in her arms, when my lips are on hers, when my body sinks inside her. Nothing matters but her. Only passion, heat, and lust are real right now. Only *Jewel* is real.

Only passion, heat, and lust are real right now.

When I pull back, I can't see her face — the light from the truck behind her. I can only hear her deep, panting breaths as I reach for the hem of her shirt and begin tugging on it. I have to feel her skin, I need to taste every single inch of her body.

I slide my fingers over her taut stomach, and her muscles shake beneath my touch, making me feel stronger, invincible, and molten hot. I gasp in pleasure as my fingers glide over her full breasts and peaked nipples, sending a shock wave through me.

Still, she's wearing too many clothes. I carefully nudge her backward, laying her flat on the bed of my truck. I place my fingers beneath the waistband of her jeans and undo them, then drag them and the thin piece of silk barely covering her off of her trembling legs.

I smooth my hands up her thighs and past her stomach, and cup her sweet breasts, making her groan with need. Her response makes me ache. My arousal pulses, and I'm ready to strip away my clothes and take her right now, to plunge within her heat, to feel the walls of her core pulse around me. But I won't rush. My brow beads with sweat as I draw back long enough to rip my shirt buttons as I fling the offending garment to the floor of the truck.

The cloud cover clears, and the light from the full moon gives me a perfect view of her ivory flesh against my dark truck, and the sight of her nearly makes me fall to my knees in appreciation. When she looks up, takes in my chest, and lets out a gasp, I don't know how I remain on my feet.

"I want you now. I want you always. I can't get enough of you," I say as I undo my pants and push them down, leaving me bare before her.

The frustration in her greedy eyes fuels my desire, and I come to her again and run my hands along the inside of her spread thighs. When goosebumps appear on her flesh, I pause.

"Are you cold?" The air is warm, and I'm burning up, but maybe having sex out in the open isn't the best idea.

"No," she whispers with a shake of her head, her voice barely audible.

"Are you scared?" I hold my breath and wait.

"Not at all," she says. It isn't fear causing her to shake.

Her answer fills me with pride. I was ticked earlier, but I don't want her afraid of me; I want her to desire me, to need me, to not want to let me go . . . even though that's against our rules.

I'm beginning to hate the rules we set, and hate even more how this started. In a short time, she's taken hold of something inside me, though I'm not sure I want to analyze it. Dammit, I'm so confused. I've never felt anything like this with any other woman. I need to think of this as sex . . . and *only* sex.

"I won't hurt you, Jewel. No matter how frustrated I am, I'll never hurt you." I need her to know this and to say she believes me. She's silent, and I wait, my hands resting beneath her heat as I throb.

"Please, Blake," she cries.

"No, Jewel. Tell me you know I won't hurt you," I demand. I slide my hands up her body, stopping them just below the rise and fall of her breasts before moving down to her core, circling her clit, but not quite touching where she needs my touch the most.

"Blake . . ."

I say nothing, but rub my arousal against her slit, letting her know I'm more than ready to plunge inside.

"I know you won't hurt me," she finally gasps in frustration. "Please, please touch me."

I don't need to hear anything more. I move one hand lower, pressing my fingers inside her while the other trails up her body and circles the mound of her breast and over her nipple, making her arch her back and groan into the night.

Lowering my head, I pull her closer, then take her peaked nipple and suck, flicking my tongue over the ridge as she squirms beneath me.

"More, please, more," she begs, reaching out and tugging my hair, holding me tightly against her.

"Here?" I tease as I kiss my way across her perfect mounds, and flick my tongue over her other nipple, wetting it before sucking hard.

"Yes!" she cries, grasping me, clutching me, telling me with her movements that she wants my skin against hers, my body sunk deep inside.

I'm not ready for that yet. I'll go wild and won't be able to give her the pleasure she needs, so I trail my mouth down the tight curve of her stomach. Urged on by her trembling, I skim my mouth across her heat.

At the first swipe of my tongue, her body jumps from the truck bed. Tucking my hands beneath her luscious backside, I hold her in place, spread her core open, and lick along her sweet folds. Pressing my mouth against her pulsing core, I suck the tender flesh of her engorged clit, and glory in her cries of release. I can't get enough of her.

"I need to take you, Jewel — now. I want to make you mine over and over again." I draw her to me, catching her body as I hold her butt and step closer.

Before thrusting inside her, I capture her bottom lip and suck it into my mouth, absorbing the gasp she lets out, all while caressing her. I press closer, and the head of my arousal slips inside her swollen heat.

Her pulse beats hard in the scented skin of her neck, mint drifting all around us from the fields, suddenly becoming my favorite herb, and then I lick her flesh, knowing I'll never get enough of her taste, enough of her body, enough of her.

She moves against me, her body twisting to get closer as the flames of desire quickly build in her. She wants me to fill her, and I won't deny her any longer. My length rests inside her, but I pull back to look in her eyes before I push forward in a slow, sure thrust that has me coming unglued.

When she sinks her teeth into the side of my neck, I nearly spill my seed. "Hold on," I gasp, trying to regain control over my body. This seems to encourage her to push me to my very limits. Bringing her head up, I close my mouth over hers, my kiss hungry, desperate, full of want, need, and emotion I can't identify.

I don't try to hold back any longer, fully plunging in and out of her body, propelling us higher and higher, our groans filling the night sky, our passion seemingly infinite. I fight for self-control, fight to slow this down, but it's no use. Her legs circle my back, and I drive deeper, faster, harder, until she cries out again, her body tensing around me as she comes.

Pleasure rushes through me, and I cry out, my body pulsing within hers, my pleasure complete as I pump deep inside her tight sheath. The shudders of our bodies don't soon die.

When our breathing finally approaches a normal level, she lifts her head, showing me bright eyes and rosy cheeks. "I didn't know I needed that."

She tries to sit up. I help her, feeling somewhat deflated by her words. I'm not sure what I was expecting. I help her get down from the truck, leaving her standing before me naked and trembling.

I don't know what to say or do. I turn and pick up my pants, slipping them on before I move around and grab the spare tire. She dresses in silence and then climbs into the cab. I don't know what I'm feeling as I wrench down the nuts with more force than needed.

I finish and climb into the cab of the truck. We sit for several minutes without either of us saying a word. I'm so damn confused I don't know what to think. I've never felt this before.

"I'd really like for you to talk to me," I say, my voice resigned.

I don't look over at her, hoping that if we aren't making eye contact, maybe, just maybe, she'll open up. I understand I haven't exactly been a safe place for her to do this . . . and even now, I can't seem to offer words that might comfort her enough to open up to me.

"I will . . . eventually," she says with a sad sigh.

I nod as I start the truck. This isn't good enough. "Then we're done," I tell her. I'm not filled with anger. I'm simply resigned. I'm getting too attached, and I don't trust her. This is just how it was with my mother. She started with lies . . . and then she got my father killed along with herself right in front of the three sons she clearly didn't love. I won't trust a woman who's lying to me. I don't think I can ever trust a woman for any reason.

We drive back to the apartment complex without saying a word. There's nothing else to say. I should feel peace. I don't understand the tightening in my chest. The closer we come to the complex, the more my pulse picks up. When we reach home, the ache is worse. I sit in the truck, and she climbs out . . . and I let her walk away.

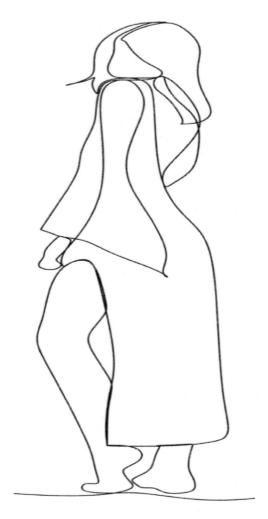

Chapter Review

Max

I'VE WORKED FOR BLAKE for a very long time, long enough to know when I step inside his apartment on Monday morning, that something is seriously wrong with my boss . . . and friend. None of us have heard from him since Saturday, which has never happened before. He's *always* available, even if only by phone. I'm worried about what I'm going to find.

I make my way to the living room, and see Blake sprawled on the couch wearing only a pair of sweats, and with at least two days' growth of a beard. The smell of expensive Scotch hangs heavy in the air.

Slowly approaching, I shake my boss's shoulder and am relieved to hear him emit a groan. I make a fresh pot of coffee, then pour a cup and return to the living room, shaking Blake until he wakes.

"What are you doing?" Blake grumbles as he sits up with some effort and shoots me a vicious glare.

"I think the bigger question is, what are *you* doing?" I counter.

"It's none of your damn business, Max. If I wanted company, I would've called," Blake says. He grabs the cup of coffee and downs half of it before wincing as he feels the hot liquid scorch his throat.

"Is this about Jewel?" I boldly ask, and I'm rewarded with another glare.

"No woman has the power to affect me," Blake snarls. It's always a woman. I barely manage to keep my smile at bay. Even the strongest of men can be taken down by a woman. It fascinates me. Wars are won and lost over women. If only they truly understood the power they wield by the luck of the draw in being born female.

"I followed her on Saturday," I say, knowing this will get his attention. The room goes utterly silent. I can see that Blake's wondering why he hasn't thought to ask me whether I'd done that. It could've saved him a hell of a lot of misery.

"And?" Blake obviously isn't in the mood for suspense.

"She was obviously sneaking off with how often she was looking around her to make sure she wasn't being followed. I knew you'd want to know where she was going. You know, I actually like this girl more and more each day," I say with a chuckle.

"I don't give a damn if you like her," Blake thunders. "Tell me where she went. She refused to tell me." Blake isn't often refused. My like factor goes up another few notches for Jewel.

"She went to a house — by bus, if you're interested — and then emerged with a boy, a young boy. They went to a pizza place and a park, and three hours later, she returned him. There was some clinging and tears. I wanted to step in and help, but didn't know what I should do. Do you want me find out who the boy is?" I wait, surprised when I see the little color in my boss's face drain away. I have no idea what this means, so I wait, knowing Blake's still processing my words.

"She does have a brother . . ."

While I look at him blankly, Blake stares silently at the floor. When my boss stands up and moves to the stairs, I remain where I'm standing, having no idea what's coming next.

One Month Later
Blake

Sitting in my den with the lights turned low, a pleasant crackling sound coming from the fireplace, and a perfect cognac warming my belly, I stare out the window, though I see nothing but black. It's quite fitting — since blackness has been all I've felt for far too long. Seeing the darkness is almost soothing.

But a smile turns up my lips, if only a few millimeters, for tonight some of this blackness will fade. It won't disappear — it never will. But tonight I'll have Jewel back. I could've stepped in sooner, but there were cards I had to put in play before making my next move.

She still works for my company, but I've left her alone. She still lives in my apartment building, but I haven't passed by her. I gave her space, but I followed her movements. She's getting too close to making a mistake I can't allow to happen. She's mine whether I like it or not. I can't purge her from my system, can't go a single hour without thinking about her.

Tonight all of this is going to change.

Max looks at me, his face grim. "Are you sure you want to do this? You've already royally screwed things up."

I send him a glare. "I didn't screw up anything, dammit. How dare you speak to me this way?"

"You can save your bark for someone who might actually be intimidated by it," he easily replies.

You can save your bark for someone who might actually be intimidated by it.

The only reason Max Kane is still standing in my den instead of being thrown out onto the street is because he's worked for me for the past ten years and has always been loyal and discreet. I trust him. And that isn't something that can be said of many people in my life.

"I'll have her back, and it will work. I'll finally know exactly who she is," I say when Max doesn't change his stand.

"Didn't who she is become obvious a month ago?" Max asks.

"Just because she says one truth doesn't mean the rest of what she says is honest." I shake my head. Why am I saying this? It doesn't matter. I know who she is, and I still want her. Is this how my father felt?

"When did she lie to you? She told you the truth about her brother," Max points out. "And then you drank yourself into oblivion for days."

"Do I need to repeat myself, Max? She was out for what she could get. Yes, she gave me a sob story . . ."

"A story that checked out, boss."

"I don't know," I say, frustration rolling through me. I'm so damned confused. "Look," I say. "She lied by omission. She owes me."

Max shakes his head. "Owes you for what?"

"Do you enjoy pissing me off?" I ask. "I'll focus on the services she and I agreed to, but I didn't receive."

"Seriously, Blake? I've known you for a long time, and though the rest of the world thinks you're an asshole, I've been privileged enough to see another side of you. But in what you're saying now, you're proving the world right." Max exhales in an exasperated rush, and begins pacing.

"Good," I say. "This is who I am. If you don't like it, you know where the door is."

"It would do you good if I walked out — you really need a kick in the posterior — but you know I won't," Max says before helping himself to a beer. "It's a wonder I don't drink a lot more, working for you."

"When did it become okay for you to put down your boss?"

"I'm not putting you down, *sir*. I'm simply speaking the truth," Max retorts.

Tension hangs heavy in the room, and my heart's pounding, my every sense on high alert. I got rid of the date she set up with a new man she wants to replace me with. That won't happen. I don't give away what belongs to me.

I don't give away what belongs to me

My new contract will be a surprise. I need to keep her off-kilter. After our last night together, I can still taste the mint in the air, can still hear her gasps of pleasure, can still feel her body tightening around me. I tried to forget her, but wasn't able to keep her from my thoughts. And now I found a reason to be with her again.

Finding out that she wasn't cheating on me, that she really does have a brother, changed things for me in ways that would surprise a lot of people if they knew the whole story.

"Okay, Max, I admit she tried telling me the truth and I shut her down. But still, Jewel and I have unfinished business. When our business is done, we *will* change our relationship — after we both get what we need," I say. "Does that sound more reasonable?"

"I think you're lying to yourself, and you're being more than a little irrational. This woman is more than you're making her out to be. Give her a chance. Don't continue making her into the prostitute you've decided she is."

"I don't need to know her. She's a woman, and you know how I feel about women. I want her lying beneath me — or on top. I'm an equal-opportunity kind of guy," I say with a smirk.

"You can have any woman you want lying in your bed. But it's Jewel you choose — that means something."

I know I'm being unreasonable, but I won't confess this out loud. I want Jewel with a passion I can't explain. It's much easier if I play a bad guy. I can justify being a villain. Actually caring for a woman is something I certainly can't accept. Anyone who does is a complete sap in my opinion.

"I'll repeat myself," Max continues. "I think there's more between you and Jewel than you're ready to admit, and I won't push you, but I'll tell you to be careful. If you're cruel, you won't stand a chance with her, and you won't like the way things end."

"If I want counseling, I'll seek a professional," I reply, and look at my watch for the hundredth time.

"Don't worry; I throw in counseling services free of charge," Max says with a grin.

"How about I pay you extra to keep your mouth shut?"

Max laughs. "You can try."

"It doesn't matter. I'll soon grow weary of her, and then I'll send her on her way — in my own time, and without advice from you or anyone else."

"Who are you trying to convince here, boss? Me . . . or yourself?"

"I don't have to convince anyone," I say, "and I don't have to justify myself."

"If that's true, why are you so upset?"

"I'm not upset, Max," I shout. In any normal building, the walls would be visibly shaking.

"Whatever you say, boss. But if you want some real advice, set her free, and see if she still wants to be with you."

"Set her free? Have you gone bonkers, Max? She's the one who came to me with her idea. She's the one who propositioned *me*. I got ticked, and walked away. With this new contract, she won't be able to turn away. She'll get what she wants . . . and so will I."

"If you want to control her, go ahead and play this out any which way you want, but if you're truly interested in Jewel, you're going to have to change your strategy."

"I'm lost. What are you saying?" I follow Max's lead and begin pacing the room. I shouldn't be listening to this, but I have a lot of respect for my employee.

"Instead of owning her, offer to be a partner," Max says. "Help her do the one thing she's been trying to do for months."

"I am helping her." I'm confused and don't know what to think of my crazy driver.

"She needs more than to be in your bed. Give her whatever it takes to get her brother back. You have power, influence, money. You can get her brother back in a week. Do that, and she'll willingly be yours."

"But she's already mine."

"You have her until she has her brother," Max points out. "Are you so sure you can keep her after that if you've treated her with nothing but disdain?"

"I don't know what you want me to do." My frustration is growing. I'm wavering. What if Max has valid points? No! He doesn't, right?

Max speaks again. "I'm going to get some paperwork done, boss. Let me know when you're ready to leave." He stands and walks from the room.

I sit back down, close my eyes, and run a hand through my hair. Max has always been the voice of reason when nothing else seems to make sense. I don't want to silence him. Well, maybe I want to silence him right now, and anytime the subject is about this particular woman. But overall, I do need one person I can talk to who won't hold anything back. And Max is certainly not a yes-man.

Though I've only physically spent a few weeks with Jewel, it's affected me far more than I care to admit, even to myself. The woman intrigues me, makes me feel things I've never felt. But there's no way these feelings can last. She and I simply need to play our story out . . . then we can both come to a satisfying conclusion.

Once this happens — my hypothetical shrink would probably call it *closure* — I'll be able to let her go and never think of her again. I needed to let her go last month in order to do what needed to be done . . . and in order to clear my conscience of what I already did to her.

I hadn't realized how strong her impact on me was until I'd watched her walk away from me a month ago. The sick feeling in my gut should make me steer clear of ever seeing her again. Obviously, it hasn't. I shouldn't be playing with fire. But I'm a fool, just as so many men are when it comes to women.

I shouldn't be playing with fire. But I'm a fool, just as so many men are when it comes to women.

My father sure as hell had been the biggest fool of them all, and his weakness for a woman had cost him his life . . . and traumatized his children in the process. I'll never be as weak as my father. It's why I'm determined to purge Jewel from my system, and purge her I will . . . *when* I'm ready.

Still, a piece of me knows if I throw her away, it will ruin all of my chances of making any other relationships work. Or maybe both of us are simply fated for damnation. I'll soon find out.

Chapter Review

Jewel

I'M EXHAUSTED WHEN I get home. Work has been offering overtime for the past few weeks, and I need the money and have nothing else to do, so I've taken them up on it. This means all I do is work, eat, and sleep ... and of course, see Justin on the weekends.

It hurts more each time I leave my brother. I can't do it much longer. I'm going to save for another month or so, and if the court won't give him to me, I'm taking him, and we'll run away together. I don't want to always be on the run, but if I have no other choice, that's what I'll do.

I've talked to a man for two weeks, and he seems more than willing to help me. I was sick to my stomach acting like a call girl, offering my body to him to come to court with me, to say we live together, and are in a happy relationship. I promised to do whatever it takes for my brother, and I mean it, I'll do *whatever* it takes.

Entering my apartment, the air shifts. Something's off. I set my coat and bag down and slowly move forward, carefully walking down the hallway. The light is on in the room I've been using as a very sparse office; only a chair and small table are in there. I'm scared as I creep forward, thinking I must've left it on when I went to work this morning.

I'm wrong. I step inside . . . and freeze.

A man looking out the window takes his time turning, and the color drains from my face. I'd almost prefer some sadistic robber to be facing me instead of *him*. His eyes are hard and unreadable, his muscles tight. He looks ready to pounce, and my throat closes with nervous tension.

"Good evening, Jewel."

Shock . . . fear . . . relief . . .

Why do I feel relief? No. I don't want Blake Astor here. Just the sound of his voice slams into my already fractured nerves, leaving me barely able to remain standing. I was with this man for weeks and barely survived the ups and downs. Why is he here now? He's the one who told me to go.

Yet here he is, standing before me in all of his dark glory, his custom suit molded to his shoulders, his gray eyes boring into mine, his very presence overwhelming me, sucking all the air from the room where he seems so out of place. This place is elegant as sin, and the Blake Astors of the world live on a far higher level.

Without moving a muscle or saying a word, he commands this room . . . hell, any room he's in . . . he also commands me — though I hope to the highest reaches of heaven that he isn't aware of this. The man possesses raw power. He doesn't need me to give him more.

When he takes a step toward me, I'm riveted to the floor. Every instinct tells me to run, that retreat is my only option. I thought I'd seen the last of him . . . I was obviously wrong.

As my heart continues to thud violently, I watch his slow and deliberate approach and wonder if I'll pass out.

That wouldn't be surprising since I can't seem to catch my breath.

When his eyes caress my body from the tips of my toes to what seems like every last strand of my hair, a shudder rolls through me. His expression should freeze me, but it does the opposite as I'm heated to my very core.

"Why are you here?"

His lips turn up in the tiniest of smiles as he invades my personal space, seeming to drain my very essence as he lifts a hand and runs a finger along my cheekbone. Looking into Blake's eyes becomes way too much for me, and I briefly close my eyes as I breathe in and try to gain back some semblance of strength.

"May I offer you something to drink?"

It takes a moment for me to realize that someone else has entered the room. Opening my eyes, I turn to find an attractive woman in her early thirties wearing a neutral expression as she gazes between Blake and me.

"I . . . Where did you come from?" I ask.

"I hired her." He turns to the woman. "No," he says. "You're dismissed for the evening, Elsa." The woman turns and immediately disappears.

"Blake, I don't understand," I say, the shock beginning to wear off as agitation takes its place. "I have a strange woman mysteriously popping into my home, and you . . . and . . . I don't understand," I finish as I twist my fingers together.

"Let's go sit down, Jewel."

I wait for him to continue, and when he doesn't, I turn and walk from the small room. I don't want to be in here with him. I rush to the living room, but I don't sit. I won't be his puppet again.

He follows me, wearing a smile. "If you don't want to sit, we could go straight into the bedroom."

I won't be

his puppet

There's no mistaking the desire in his eyes. I'm also well aware of how quickly he can seduce me. I move backward, somehow find a chair, and fall into it.

"I don't know why you're here when you dismissed me. None of this makes sense, Blake. This isn't what you want — not really. This has to be about power . . . or revenge . . . or something I can't fathom." He walks up to me and leans down, caging me against my chair, making my breath rush out.

I can't read the look in his eyes, and I can't figure out what's going on inside his head, but I know, no matter what he's thinking, it can't be good.

"We have things to discuss, Jewel. The two of us began a journey two months ago, a journey we haven't come close to finishing," he says, his tone smooth, his eyes on fire.

I answer in a voice barely above a whisper. "Our journey's over, Blake."

"That's where you're wrong, Jewel. I'm not done with you yet." He leans down closer, and lets his breath wash over my heated skin.

"No . . ." I almost wail, as my body quakes.

"Oh, yes, Jewel. We're only now beginning."

We're only now beginning

Chapter Review

Jewel

I CLOSE MY EYES AND try to think, try to get my head around what's happening. "You don't want me," I tell him, not sure if I'm trying to convince myself or Blake. "You know you don't."

"Yes, I want you, Jewel. Just as much as you want me. I'm always sure, and always to the point. By the way, I became acquainted with some facts after you were gone."

"You mean after you screwed me on your truck and dumped me off like a trashy whore."

He laughs, actually laughs at this. I want to reach out and slap the smug look right off of his face. How dare such a worthless, perverted man laugh at me? He's in serious danger right now, and from the continued mirth I see dancing in his eyes, it's apparent he knows — and isn't in the least worried.

"Calm down, Jewel. We're not getting anywhere with your burst of temper. Though, I must say, it turns me on to see such fire light your eyes," he says with a wink. "You're cute when you're mad. But we can certainly put your heightened emotions to better use than venting."

Oh how I wish I could be as cold and unaffected as this ice sculpture of a man. He wouldn't know true human emotion if it was right in front of him, which it is now as I'm filled with it.

"Why are you the way you are, Blake? How can you be so cavalier and unfeeling? Don't you care at all about anyone other than yourself?" I'm vulnerable, angry, and struggling with other emotions I don't know how to name.

"I see nothing wrong with the way I act," he says, refusing to back away despite my words. As a matter of fact, he draws nearer, and there isn't much nearer to go. "I like who I am, and I know you lose all sense of control when you're anywhere near me. No one can make you *feel* emotion, Jewel. *We* choose how we feel; *we* choose what we think, what *we* want, what we desire. You can *choose* to enjoy this, or you can choose to run from it. But either way, you're mine, and I know you want me. You want *all* of this. To try to escape when we've come this far would be an act of idiocy. And you're not dumb."

The way his breath whispers over my flesh, across my cheek, my lips, and my neck, sends shivers. To deny it would be a wasted effort — we'd both know I'm lying.

Instead I do something I'll later regret because I act with emotion, with rage, and with desire. I clench my fist, and watch, almost as an outsider, as my arm rises and my fist slams into the side of his smug face.

We choose how we feel; we choose what we think, what we want, what we desire

His expression remains neutral, and though he flinches, it's almost imperceptible. He simply stares at me with eyes that are too knowing. I lose it further. I pull back and slam my fist into his jaw.

When I still don't get a reaction, I lose the last vestiges of my sanity, and lift both hands, my claws coming out as I reach for him and tug on his hair. I'm beyond reason and control now, lost in a blaze of fury. The past months have come to a head.

Who in the hell does he think he is? It isn't fair that he can so easily mess with my emotions and choose my destiny. He has no right to make me feel anything. This is a battle I can't win. And what I've just done makes me utterly ashamed. Am I really this woman . . . no better than an animal?

For some reason I can't retreat. "I hate you," I snap. He still shows no reaction. I'm about to fall off the deep end.

Then, so quickly I have zero chance of stopping him, he thrusts out one hand and grabs both of mine, then jerks my arms up while the fingers of his other hand snake behind my head and tangle in my hair.

Before I can think of struggling, I'm being pulled from the chair and shoved backward until I'm flat against the wall, his body a mass of steel, boxing me in. My arms are stretched high above my head, my heart thundering and my breath gone.

Blake displays a hint of emotion as he pushes against me, and I can't mistake how hard our struggle has made him. This somehow turns my rage into a burning passion — a passion I despise myself for feeling.

Before I'm able to recover, to firmly lock away anything other than hatred for the man who's trapped me, his eyes narrow, and he goes on the attack. He bends his head and captures my mouth in a kiss of possession.

The month we've been apart evaporates in an instant and I'm back with him, right where we were on our last night together, where anger and frustration have morphed into heat and ecstasy.

His kiss is masterful, and it doesn't take him long to part my closed lips and access the warm recesses of my needy mouth. There's hunger, danger, and so much more in the way he holds my body, the way he devours me, leaving no room for thoughts of anything or anyone but him.

One feeling merges into the next as he plunders my mouth, intimately reacquainting himself with the touch of me, making my knees grow weak, my heart thump erratically, and my core heat to the point of boiling. This is raw sex at its most basic level.

His fingers tighten in my hair, and he moves his body rhythmically against mine, his arousal pressing as intimately against my womanhood as our clothes allow. I'm ready, so ready, for him to take me.

"I want you, Jewel; I want you more than I ever wanted any other woman. You make me burn," he says when he pulls back for air. He trails his lips down my throat after his words make my insides dissolve.

I try to remember why this is wrong, to regain my equilibrium, but I can't think, can't move, can't breathe, let alone resist this pull he has on me. I know I'll hate him and myself even more, but I can't stop responding. The only way this will end is if *he* puts on the brakes.

But Blake obviously isn't finished. He frees my hands to let his fingers glide down my body, stroking the sensitive flesh of my sides, hips, and ass. My head falls back, and a sigh escapes my lips while he caresses the skin of my neck. And then it stops as quickly as it began.

It takes a long moment for me to realize he's stilled. He rests his hands on my hips, and his mouth is no longer making its seductive way along my skin. I slowly tilt my head forward, and once again, find my eyes captured by his ardent gaze.

We must stand here for an eternity, neither of us saying a word, our breathing returning to something like normal — though my body will never be normal again. I don't know what to say, and I can't think with his hard body pressed against mine.

But the silence gets to me, and just when I can't take it another second, I finally open my lips, run my tongue slowly along their swollen edges, and take a deep breath before I speak.

"That didn't prove anything," is all that comes out, but not nearly as strongly as I'd intended.

Blake throws me a hint of a smile and leans a little closer. When he finally replies, his mouth is within an inch of mine.

"I think it proved exactly what it was supposed to, Jewel."

"And what is that, Blake? That you have power over me? That no matter what I do or say, you'll still get exactly what you want? Well, if that's what you're trying to prove, congratulations, you did it. Yes, you can force me to do what you want. You're bigger, stronger, and far more manipulative than I am." I hope I've infused my voice with utter disdain.

"You've developed some bite in the time we've been apart," he says, his voice smooth and . . . impressed. I'm trying to sound fierce, intimidating, frightening. I'm not supposed to be turning him on more.

"Yes, I have. In the month since you discarded me so carelessly, I developed a spine. You'll find I'm not the same submissive little girl you abused to your heart's desire. Oh, sorry — you never had a heart. But you wasted your time, Blake Astor, because I won't be what you want."

"Oh, Jewel, I know exactly what I want," he says, running his hand through my hair again. "And it's most certainly you. Besides, wasn't the original deal *anything* I want?"

"We broke that deal," I tell him, but I'm losing the fight in me. I promised my brother. And here's Blake, a sure thing where the other guy could flake out.

"We can make a new deal." He seems quite happy to do this. I want to say no, but then I have an idea.

"How bad do you want to make the deal?" I question, my fight returning. "If you want a new deal, I want an official contract, one you sign saying you'll come to court, that you'll say what needs to be said." My spine is straight against the wall I'm still backed into.

He doesn't look fazed. "Deal," he says. "I was going to say a contract is a good idea to protect us both."

He has no advantage with a contract. Technically, he can't take me to court if I decide to not have sex with him. But, then again, could I really take him to court if he doesn't go with me to Justin's hearing? Probably not. What am I going to say? *I had sex with him again and again, and he won't come in here and lie to you.* Yep, that's not going to get me custody of my brother. I'm desperate though, and he knows it.

"Just so you know, I won't enjoy this, nor will I try to make it better for you. Be warned."

He laughs. "That's where we'll agree to disagree," he whispers. "I know for a fact that you'll not only enjoy it, but will beg me for more . . . and more . . . and more."

299

With these last six words, he brushes his lips against mine. "And I'll definitely give it to you."

Liquid heat flows through my veins. Yes, he's given me pleasure, pleasure beyond anything I've felt before. But he's also given me pain. And the pain is what I'm afraid of. I've suffered enough emotional trauma to last a lifetime.

He can so easily destroy me — I have no doubt of this. But I'm once again agreeing to this deal. Why fight it? Because even though he might own my body, he can't own my mind, my heart, or my soul, or at least the pieces of those I still have.

He might own my body, but he can't own my mind, my heart, or my soul

"You know I'll hate you forever, Mr. Astor."

Only a tiny spark igniting in his eyes shows my words have registered. When his lips part, I wait for the backlash. I don't get it.

"I don't require any emotion from you except passion," he says dismissively. "A nice, basic animal response." The words sting more than I'll ever admit.

"Then we're on the same page," I tell him. "Because you won't get anything other than my body." How desperately I wish he'd give me just a bit of breathing room.

"Ah, Jewel, the fire in you is what made me come back, what makes me have to see this through to the end."

"You mean until I get my brother back." He stares at me in silence, showing nothing in his ice-cold eyes. I won't break the silence, though. This is up to him.

"No, Jewel. We won't be done until I'm finished with you."

I have no idea what this can possibly mean . . . but I have no doubt this won't be easy. It never is with this man.

Chapter Review

Jewel

I T'S EXCRUCIATING. MY emotions continue a chaotic dance as Blake leans closer. But then, almost on a dime, he steps back and breaks into something like an actual smile. "Follow me."

Without waiting to see whether I'll obey, he pivots on his heel and walks from the room, leaving me sagging against the wall as I pray my knees won't give out. Less than thirty minutes in Blake's presence and I'm once again a complete mess.

I keep my distance, not because I'm afraid he'll physically hurt me, but because I know what will happen if I end up in his arms again — I won't be able to deny how much I'm attracted to this despicable man. I'm better than this . . . but I'm still here.

Forcing myself to follow, he's in the kitchen making a pot of coffee, even though it's late. I probably need the caffeine. My apartment is light and airy, but having Blake in here makes the place shrink and grow dark. This is his domain, not mine. I'm his paid mistress, and I feel it in every bone — no, in every *cell* — of my body.

When the coffee is ready, Blake pours us each a cup and, without a word, leads me to the sitting room. He makes himself comfortable, and I bet he enjoys watching how *un*comfortable I am.

With my legs trembling, I decide it's best if I sit on the nearest couch and focus on my coffee. No matter how long he drags this out, I'll figure out his next move soon. And why worry about any of it? In this game, he's fated to be the only winner.

"You seem unhappy, Jewel."

"Do you honestly think I'm happy you're buying me?"

"I expected a bit of appreciation."

"You amaze me, Blake . . ."

He quickly interrupts. "Thank you."

"That wasn't meant as a compliment."

"I'll take it as one," he replies. "You may be fighting me, but you aren't disappointed I'm back."

"Can we quit dancing around this, and you tell me what you expect?" He looks at me for several long moments. I bite my tongue to keep from asking him to speed it up.

"What do you think I want, Jewel?"

"To prove your power. You can't control me, so you're back for another chance to put the win in your column."

"If that's all I wanted, I could have it right now. This is just the beginning, but the ending isn't in doubt here, because you want me as much as I want you. If I was in the mood to play power games, I'd do it in the boardroom. The way things play out there is less predictable, though even there, I *always* win."

"Damn, you're arrogant."

"It's not arrogance when it's true."

There's no arguing with him. "Let's get this over with, Blake. I've had a long day — a long year, for that matter — and the sooner this song and dance ends, the sooner I can rest."

Utter exhaustion threatens to pull me under. I've run the gamut of emotions over the last few months, especially today, and I'm now barely able to stay awake, much less agile enough to spar with him. When Blake stands and moves over to sit by me, I don't object.

"It doesn't matter, you know," I say, my defenses down.

"What doesn't matter?" he asks while reaching for my hand, which I allow him to take. When he rests our joined fingers on his leg, I feel a spark, but I repress it.

"Anything," I tell him. "What I feel, what I want. None of it matters."

"I don't agree, Jewel. What you want is very important." This contradicts everything he's been saying to me, everything he's doing. I can't keep up with him.

When he pulls me onto his lap and draws my head against his chest, I know I should resist, but I'm too tired. This man, who causes me so much pain, also seems to be the one shouldering it. It makes no sense, but what in my world makes sense anymore?

This man, who causes me so much pain, also seems to be the one shouldering it.

Since the death of my mother, I've felt like a passenger on a roller coaster without brakes, and all I can do is pray that at some point the ride will stop, and I'll end up safely back on solid ground.

"How long will this go on? Do you want me broken? If that's the case, it's close to happening." Damnation. I'll regret these words later, when I feel stronger. *If* I ever feel stronger.

"I don't want to break you, Jewel," he says, letting his fingers sift through my hair.

"I thought that's what you love to do, Blake — break women."

"I won't deny it's brought me pleasure in the past. But a person can change."

"No. Not that much. I don't think anyone can change entirely from who they are. Especially if they don't want to."

"It's simple, Jewel. I've decided I don't want to let you go," he says.

"And what if I don't go along with your plan?"

"I have something you want, so I think you will." His voice is filled with the utmost confidence.

"There's nothing you have that will make me *want* to stay past the end date," I say, my voice a bit stronger.

"You don't know what I have, Jewel."

I don't want to ask him, don't want to know what he's holding over me, besides, this night won't end until he gets to make his point.

"What is it, Blake? What do you have?" My heart pounds during the long moments of silence. But at last, Blake speaks.

"I have access to your brother."

A few minutes might pass, perhaps even an hour. I have no idea, because after Blake speaks of my brother, my heart stops.

"What's going on?"

307

"Let's just say I've done some research, Jewel. I've found out quite a lot."

"Why are you doing this to me? Is this your idea of a cruel joke? Do you find my pain amusing?" He releases me, and I jump up and begin pacing as I wait for his response.

He slowly stands and approaches me with measured strides, intimidating in his masculinity. I back away, but once again am against the wall, with Blake trapping me.

"I don't joke," he says, his words low and ringing with the sound of truth.

"But . . ."

"I found out everything about your brother. As I told you, I have access."

"I'll ask again, Blake. How? And what's the price you want from me?"

"Does it make a difference?"

His words are a clear challenge, and all of the fight leaves me. "No." I'll do anything to have Justin. Haven't I already proven that when I stripped for this man?

He rests his fingers against my hip. "Are you going to keep defying me?"

"Yes." I'm surprised when the word emerges. How can I be so foolish as to risk this? I won't. But before I can correct myself, he leans against me and brushes my mouth.

"Good. I wouldn't have it any other way," he says, his words vibrating against my lips.

"I didn't mean that. I'll do whatever it takes to get my brother."

"I didn't say I'd give him to you. I said I have access."

"What in the hell does that mean?"

"I need to know more, Jewel."

"And what is that?" I snap. "What more do you need to know?"

There's a long pause before he speaks again.

"That you're not after my money."

"Seriously, Blake? I'm a lot better person than you'll ever be."

"I don't make a habit of it doing what I've been doing with you, Jewel."

"Obviously, I *haven't* either, and you know it. But you win. You can have whatever you want," I say, though everything in me fights against saying these words.

"Don't become boring and predictable, Jewel." He presses his arousal against me. "Don't make it too easy to tame you."

"I don't think that's something you'll have to worry about, Blake, because I can't even figure myself out. None of this is right, and none of it's predictable, but I guarantee, no matter what you do, you'll never own me."

"That's where you're wrong, *very* wrong. I won't settle for less than all of you."

I don't want to desire this man, and even though I'm well aware he's a monster, I also know how good it feels to lie in his arms. I want him, and I hate both of us for it.

"You'll be disappointed then, Blake. But you're a man of your word. You've earned the right to my body. And, because of Justin, you've bought my obedience. But the fact that you have this — and even that I desire you — doesn't mean I've agreed to give you any other piece of me."

"I can have anything I want, Jewel."

"Not quite, Blake. You can have anything that money and power can buy you."

"I own you," he points out.

"Actually, you've simply *rented* me, and not all of me at that. If it wasn't clear before, I hate you, and always will."

His eyes flash at these words and the tone I'm using, and I wait for punishment. I have to learn not to respond when he goads me, or my time with him will be unbearable. No matter what I can possibly do to him, he can do it to me ten times as painfully without breaking a sweat.

"If I believed that, we'd be done." He tugs my hair with a firm hand. Before I can respond, he crushes his lips against mine. I fight for a brief moment before all thoughts evaporate. This is the power he wields. No matter how angry he makes me, a few seconds in his arms and I'm completely under his spell.

When I fully submit to him, he releases me. I open my eyes and see unmitigated triumph in his expression, and once the fog clears, I stiffen.

"I hope you don't take any of this as something more than an instinctive reaction, Blake. I can despise you and still be turned on. After all, you're a pretty good lay."

He lets go of me and turns his back, leaving me against the wall. After a few heartbeats, he swings back around and gives me an unreadable smile.

"You'll eventually learn more about me, Jewel, about what makes me tick. We obviously haven't spent enough time together if you think I'm so easily discouraged. But that's okay — we have all of the time in the world to get to know each other."

I ignore this. "When will I get my brother? Do I have to please you before I can bring him home?" Blake moves back to the couch and sits as if he has no other place to be.

"Don't worry. You'll see your brother."

"When?" I ask through gritted teeth.

"Depends on you," he says nonchalantly.

"What do you get out of this, Blake?"

The smile forming on his lips is my first sign I'm not going to like his next words any more than I've liked anything he's had to say so far. I'll probably like them less. The confidence emanating from him intensifies the sick feeling in my stomach.

"We've gone over this ground before. I get everything I want, don't I, Jewel?"

"No, Blake. No one gets *everything* they want," I tell him. "I'm not arguing with you. I'm simply speaking the truth."

He throws me another smile, one making it clear that my words haven't put him out one little bit. It seems nothing I do or say will throw him off his high horse.

When he stands, I wait for his next assault, but instead of coming toward me, he's heading away.

"What are you doing now?" I ask.

"I'm done for the night. We'll discuss this more tomorrow," he says and keeps walking away. Before I'm able to say another word, the front door opens and closes. He's gone just like that.

I slowly walk to my bedroom. I sag into bed, not bothering to change clothes, and not bothering to open my eyes once they drift shut.

Blake Astor has reappeared in my life with a hurricane-like force, disrupting everything in his path. But unlike a hurricane, he isn't going to grow weaker as he continues on his journey, much less drift out to wherever he came from. No. There will be no calm after the storm. That isn't his style. He'll return again and again until he gets what he wants. And there's nothing I can do to stop him.

There will be no calm after the storm

Chapter Review

Jewel

I HANG UP MY PHONE and have to fight tears while I wait outside the office. I can't walk into this building with tears streaming down my cheeks . . . not with the number of cameras everywhere. I don't want Blake to see how upset I am.

My call with Justin's caseworker didn't go well. What in the hell do these people want? Do I need to join the circus and walk the high wire to prove myself? Should I rush into a burning building and rescue kittens? I've done everything they've asked: gotten a job, an apartment, and even said I'm dating a reliable, successful businessman. Still, they're telling me this process can take months. I hate the system, and despise that they're keeping me apart from my brother who desperately needs his sister.

I take in some deep breaths, then finally walk back inside the building. I paste a fake smile on as I pass the guards, then move to the elevators. I'm about ten minutes early. I was going to grab a sandwich, but the phone call ruined my appetite. My stomach's churning too much for me to eat. I'm not at my desk long when McKenzie comes by.

"Hello, Jewel, how are you?"

I give her a fake smile. "Great. Love working here."

She chuckles. "This is a wonderful place to work, but that smile looks about as fake as it gets."

"Nope, I'm good," I say. We both know I'm lying.

"Well, things might go better or worse in a second," she says, taking a notch away from my smile. "Mr. Astor would like you to report to his office."

"Which Mr. Astor?" I question, though I'm well aware of which one.

"Blake. He said to come up right away." She doesn't look like she sees anything wrong with the request. I can refuse, but I can't afford to lose my job. However my irritation level grows a few notches. McKenzie walks away, and I figure I'd better get this over with.

What in the heck will I do about my brother? I make my way to the top floor. Blake's secretary isn't at her desk, so I move around it and go to his closed door. Should I knock? I stand for a minute, staring at his door. The longer I remain, the more my fury brews. I'm so mad right now, mad at the world, mad at how horrific the justice system is, and mad at life itself.

Will I come across as stark raving mad? Probably. Maybe he'll call the authorities and have me hauled off to a mental hospital . . . which I might need. At least then I can say I've done all I could for my brother, and it's out of my hands.

I shake my head as I have this thought. No. I won't do anything that will cause that to happen. I'm not one to give up, not without one hell of a fight. All I know right now is that I'm ticked with the world, and the person I currently want to take out my anger on is Blake Astor.

When I hear my own knock on his door, I jump. What is wrong with me? Maybe a person really can snap. One too many kicks backward on the path of life and you simply can't take it anymore.

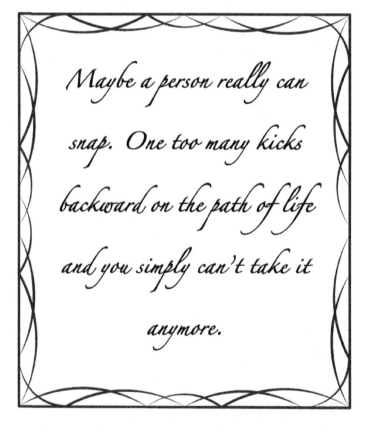

Maybe a person really can snap. One too many kicks backward on the path of life and you simply can't take it anymore.

When I see Blake in front of me, I freeze. He stands before me in all his beautiful glory, wearing custom-made pants, a button-up shirt with the top buttons undone, and a confident smirk that intensifies my rage. I hate how breathtaking he is, hate how he makes my heart skip a beat even though I consider him the enemy.

Without saying a word, he beckons me into his office with the crook of his finger. All I can think of is the line, *Will you walk into my parlor, said the spider to the fly.* Not good. Still, amid the oppressive silence, my feet move, being drawn into his web.

"Have you adjusted yet?"

All of the agony of the past six months of losing my mother, losing Justin, and becoming Blake's slave comes to a head, and because he's the person standing before me, he's about to be the one to feel my wrath. A sound unlike anything I've ever heard escape my mouth, and I rush toward him with a yell, not knowing what I'm going to do. But I never get the chance to unload on him.

With a growl of satisfaction, he grabs my hair and pulls me forward, no gentleness in his touch as he shows me exactly who's in control. I should stop this, but I can't pull away from him mentally any more than I can physically.

His lips take mine as he grinds his hips against me, and I feel how hard he is. Oh yes, Blake likes it rough, and he likes it kinky. *Plain vanilla* isn't in his sexual vocabulary. And though I hate myself for it, I love the way he consumes me.

I knew this was exactly where the two of us were heading from the second I was summoned to his office. From the moment he made his magical reappearance in my world, the two of us have had no other option but to end up right here.

He releases my lips, and I gasp for air, but nothing seems to be tamping down this hunger, this passion, this raw craving rushing through my blood. This isn't about sex, it's about need, the need to feel anything other than hopelessness.

Blake runs his hand down my back and presses me against his bare chest, making me cry out as the thin material of my bra scratches my hardened nipples. I can't breathe, can't focus, can't figure out what I need most.

"Quit thinking, Jewel. Do nothing but feel," he orders before tugging on my hair and fusing our lips together again.

I do exactly as he commands, letting my mind go blank as my body homes in on the flood of sensation flowing through it. This man, *only* this man, knows how to make me forget the world, how to propel me to the highest reaches of ecstasy. It doesn't matter if I hate myself for it. Whatever I do now, I'll despise myself afterward. So why not take what pleasure I can in his arms? Why not push the pain away for at least a moment?

I whimper in submission as he smooths his hands down my back and cups the curve of my rear so he can pull me into his hardness. He grasps my bottom lip with his teeth and bites down enough to send a flash of pain through me before his tongue soothes the spot and rocks me with currents of desire.

Time has no meaning as his hands and lips send a tsunami of desire through my body, leaving me wet, needy, and hungry for more. When he ends the kiss and steps back, I moan despairingly, but he doesn't leave me for long. He tears his shirt off, then pushes me against the wall, strips my shirt and bra from my body, and pins my hands above my head.

I hardly notice when Blake takes off my pants and panties in a sudden rush. I'm standing with him, his naked chest pressed against mine, my nipples rubbing against his smooth, solid skin, his hands squeezing the flesh of my behind, his mouth owning me.

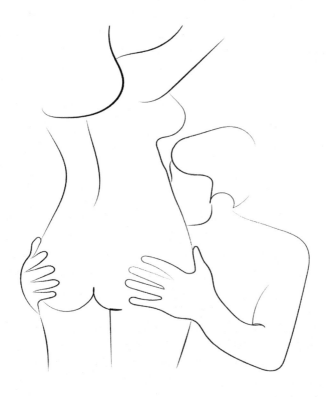

When I can't possibly take any more without crumpling at his feet, his lips skim my neck and move over my breasts before he takes each nipple into his mouth long enough to make them bead in pleasure. Then he drops to his knees and nuzzles my stomach.

"Blake . . ." I cry, digging my fingers into his hair. I don't know what I'm asking of him, but he certainly docs. Moving lower, he worships the sensitive skin right above my heated core, caressing me with his tongue, and his fingers open me up to his demanding mouth.

My internal temperature soars as he sucks my swollen bud, and his tongue swipes against it, once . . . twice . . . a third time, and more, until I lose count. I suddenly feel an explosion rip through me, my core tightening around the fingers he's using to stroke my G-spot, and my legs threatening to buckle as wave after wave of release overtakes me.

Before the last of my tremors die, he surges to his feet and catches my hips in his strong hands, lifting me against the wall and swinging my legs around him. His hardness is ready, and he pulls me down his length, coating himself with my pleasure, before lifting me back up and pushing me down hard around him. I gasp in pleasure and meet his desire-filled gaze.

"You're so tight, so perfect, my Jewel," he groans as he keeps withdrawing almost completely before plunging back inside. He loses every shred of control as he grips my hips tightly and thrusts in and out of me, the friction of our lovemaking sending me rapidly toward a more explosive finish than the last.

I grab his shoulders, lean my head against his neck, and bite the salty skin while he continues pumping with such force, I'm not sure how the wall behind me remains intact.

"Oh, please, Blake, please . . ." I beg for release — the intensity of our union too much to bear for a single minute longer.

With a few more hard thrusts, he gives me exactly what I need, and this time fireworks explode behind my tightly closed eyes as my body contracts and pulses around him, screaming my ecstasy against the flesh of his bruised shoulder. It takes a moment before I realize he's shaking as he cries out with his own release and sends his seed through me.

When it's over, I slump against him, my legs clamped tight against his back — the only thing keeping me from falling. The rest of my body feels like a mass of jelly, and I'm afraid if he lets me go, I'll slide down the wall into a boneless heap, never able to stand again.

"I need more," he groans against the top of my head.

How? There's nothing else I can possibly give, nothing else he can either. Our joining has been soul and body shattering, and if we attempt to continue, neither of us will make it out in one piece.

I'm beginning to drift out of consciousness when movement jars me awake. Is it us, or has an earthquake hit Seattle? I lack the strength to open my eyes. But his arms loosen around me, and I fall backward. My eyes open with a start when I land against the coolness of his couch, his scent surrounding me setting off another rumble of need low in my belly.

He'd only pushed his pants out of the way when he took me against the wall. I watch now as he sheds them and climbs over me, his eyes staring intently into mine as he spreads my legs with his knees, and poises his arousal — still hard — above my core.

"What? We can't . . ." I cry as he slips the tip inside.

"Yes, we can." He thrusts inside and wrenches a moan of pleasure from deep within me. He lies fully against me, gripping the back of my thigh with one hand and pulling my leg up, opening me farther so he can slide all of the way in.

Soon he's thrusting his tongue in my mouth in a perfect rhythm with his body; my stomach quivers as the pleasure rises unbearably higher. As he skillfully moves his hips, his hardness fills me in ways only he can — and only he has — while I convulse around him again and again, shattering in immeasurable wonder.

Blake makes love to me in a way he never has before. There's desperation and urgency, but also moments of tenderness and passion beyond anything we've done. His tongue traces my tender lips, his words washing over my skin, his body fit perfectly against mine, and I beg him to never stop.

When he does pull from me, he trails his lips down my neck, takes my peaked nipple into his mouth and, instead of soothing it, makes it ache even more. Then he moves down and tastes the passion he and I have already shared, before he climbs back up, and allows me to taste us in his drugging kiss.

He slips back inside my molten core and commands me to look at him. "Open your eyes, Jewel. I want to see the explosion this time. Do not close them under any circumstance!"

I try to disobey, but he bites my lip, causing me to gasp, and I'm too weak to fight him. I can barely keep my eyes open, but I manage as he moves faster. I come apart, the climax savagely tearing through me, taking every bit of energy I have left. I gaze into his nearly black eyes and watch their depths sparkle with satisfaction. That's it, I'm done. I close my eyes and gladly give into the darkness.

i love you

Chapter Review

Blake

I M LYING ON TOP OF Jewel and very aware the
second she loses consciousness. She obviously
needs the rest, but the thought of leaving her
causes me physical pain. The need for her is churning
my insides. I've spent a month thinking of no other
woman but her, and during that time I've felt . . .
bereft . . . which infuriates me.

No woman has ever lodged herself so deeply inside
me . . . not even come close. What makes Jewel
different? Why does it seem I'll never get enough of
her? I've tried to reason it away, tried to tell myself it's
nothing but raw hunger, but doesn't hunger eventually
fade with repeated satiation?

This woman has barreled into my life, and in a minuscule amount of time has shaken up my world. It should be impossible.

Rolling carefully off of Jewel, I lie tightly at her side and trail my hand down her body. I've taken her for what seem like hours, have come twice inside her, but am only feeling a modicum of relief from the damn sexual tension that's been with me ever since I met her. As I continue touching her soft skin, I begin stirring once more.

Jewel's eyelashes flutter, and I can't let her go, not at any time in the near future, at least. I justify my control because I need her. Damn the consequences, and damn the cost to myself or anyone else.

My heart stopped its frantic thudding, and my breathing slowed, but I'm well aware we will both go into overdrive the moment I sink back inside her glorious heat. Her eyes float open, and she looks dazed and sated. For one brief second her guard is down. Maybe this is the key. I'll simply keep her in bed, where I can look into her depths when she's too defenseless to hold me at bay. But the problem is that when she's like this, *I'm* also vulnerable. I can't afford to be weak.

"I've missed you. My body missed you, and I feel as if I can't get enough." I caress her nipples, and feel them harden. "You're mine." I lower my head, and when my mouth takes the place of my hand, her exquisite flavor makes my taste buds explode. She gasps as I move my hand down her stomach and run my fingers along the outside of her core.

"No. I . . . uh . . . I have to get back to work . . ." she says, weakly shutting her legs and trapping my hand. I can easily pry her legs back open, and quickly have her begging me to take her, but that's not what I want. I want her to own this, want her to need me as much as I need her. I want her to give herself freely, without coercion.

"I don't want you to leave; I'll tell them you're busy for the rest of the day," I say, removing my hand and resting it on her shaking stomach.

"I . . . I can't think, Blake. Please stop touching me." The hint of desperation in her voice makes me pause. Though it pains me to pull back, I do.

"You don't need to think, Jewel. When you're in my arms, all you need to do is feel." Okay, that's a bit sappy. To save face, I accompany my words with a cocky smile, one that instantly irritates her.

Why can't I seem to stop pushing her buttons, even when I want to? Maybe it's because the fire in her eyes turns me on, or maybe it's my armor locking into place. Whatever the reason, I can see her pulling back from me.

I stand, and feel satisfaction as her eyes move to my arousal. I go to the phone and tell her team lead she'll be busy for the rest of the day. I then turn back to her. She doesn't look pleased with me, but her eyes keep straying to my lower half which is growing harder by the second.

"You can climb on, and I'll take you for a ride." These words earn me a glare.

"How can a person think about nothing but sex?" she asks.

"I find it very easy when I have such a captivating partner, Jewel."

"If you're kidnapping me, we need to talk."

"Talking's the last thing I'm in the mood for right now."

"You can keep me in a sex coma for only so long, Blake." With an exaggerated show of throwing up my hands in defeat, I back off, surprising myself.

"So, what do we need to discuss?" I ask.

"My brother. What else?" she says as she sits up and grabs her clothes, holding them over her naked body and taking away my view.

"I told you I'll help you get him."

"But how? I want to know *how*."

"I know people," I say. My arousal dies at the depressing topic. I grab my pants and yank them on, frustrated this isn't playing out the way I'd hoped.

"You got your sex," Jewel firmly says. "Now give me my brother."

"Do you think I'm *that* easy, Jewel?" I ask in a suddenly cold voice.

"Yes. I think you're an emotionless drone and you'll do anything it takes to get what you want. You wanted sex. You got it. I *want* my brother. I've earned the right to get what you offered." Her chin tilts up in the stubborn way I love.

"Do you think you've done enough for us to be over?"

"I do," she says.

"You aren't stupid, Jewel. So why do you insist on acting like you are?"

"I'm not acting stupid, Blake. I'm trying to get you to honor your word."

"I'm not letting you go this soon."

"So you won't hold up to your word? Obviously not your word of *honor*. You wouldn't know *that* word." Her expression hardens. "How long do you need me in your bed, Blake?"

The question makes me smile. It's the smile of a shark about to fasten its teeth upon its prey. "Do you truly want to hear my answer, Jewel?"

"What? A month? A year?"

"Ah, Jewel, you underestimate yourself. I'm not letting you go, Jewel — maybe not ever. Quit planning your escape, quit trying to leave, and agree to belong to me for as long as I want."

"I don't *belong* to anyone, Blake. And what makes you think I'll keep my word? I can tell you anything you want to hear, and then walk out anyway when I have what I came here for."

This stops me in my tracks. She's correct. I think back to my conversation with my brothers, then my smile grows. She leans away from me, instinctively knowing she's not going to like what I have to say next.

"We're at a crossroads, aren't we?"

She nods. "I guess so."

My smile grows. This hadn't been what I was expecting to say but it makes sense in my frazzled brain. I'm not doing this because I'm obsessed with this woman, I'm doing it because it will help the company.

"My brothers and I have spoken with Stanley. He doesn't believe we're becoming more settled, which means the deal between you and me isn't helping. There's one solution that will benefit both of us."

She warily gazes at me. "I'm not going to like this, am I?"

I laugh, actually feeling much better. I don't even care if I've officially lost my mind. It was bound to happen one of these days. It's shocking I haven't broken yet.

"We'll get married. We'll have an airtight prenup. You'll have your brother within days of the marriage where we'll share custody. No court will say no. Then, Astor Corp will have the deal with Stanley. It's an all-around win-win."

Her mouth drops, and I kiss her and seal the deal. In my eyes this is done. I'll call the attorneys today and set it in motion . . .

Chapter Review

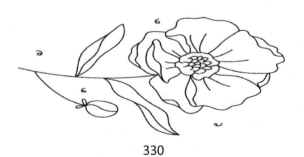

Jewel

WHOOSH! MY LUNGS are robbed of oxygen. I must have heard Blake wrong — he can't have said the price I have to pay to get my brother back is marriage. Why in the world would a billionaire like him want to marry me? Sure, he's saying it's for a business deal, but it doesn't make sense . . . none at all.

When he finally releases me from his grasp, I stumble backward, still clutching my clothes to me as if my life depends on it. Maybe it does. Everyone talks about security blankets . . . well, security clothes are my new thing. These clothes represent my sanity, and if I lose my hold on the thin pieces of fabric, I might also lose my hold on my sanity. Heck, this makes as much sense as Blake's demand that I marry him.

And yet these strange thoughts give me new determination, and I change my focus. I won't reply to his off-the-wall proposal. If I don't reply, then it's all a nonissue, right? Of course it is. So instead of looking at the man, I move away from him, and start gathering the rest of my clothes. Those I'm not clutching are strewn about, and some are rather worse for the wear — and tear.

Maintaining a resolute silence, I walk into his private bathroom and firmly shut the door. The next thing I know, I'm in the large shower. I'm on autopilot. What am I going to do? It should be an easy decision. So what if I marry this man? It doesn't matter. Something inside of me realizes how wrong this is. With these happy reflections, I wash my hair and keep scrubbing my body. When the bathroom is thick with steam, I shut off the water, climb from the massive shower, and take my sweet time toweling off.

When my clothes are firmly back in place, offering me a measure of protection from Blake — yeah, right, just as they had earlier — I decide I can't hide out in his bathroom any longer. I need to get out of his office so I can *try* to figure out what I'm going to do next.

Why have his words shocked me so much? I planned on marrying someday so why should a piece of paper upset me? Maybe because, at one time in my life, marriage actually meant something special. It had been a cherished dream of mine to fall in love, to have a storybook wedding with a meaningful church ceremony, and then add a few children and two cats in the backyard. But that dream seemed to die around the time I buried my mother.

Maybe, in spite of it all, a small piece of me still holds hope of a brighter tomorrow. But with the way Blake is eclipsing the sun from my life, it's unlikely. Maybe I simply need to accept that some people don't get the fairy tale they believe they deserve.

Deep down inside, even in my darkest moments of despair, I know life will change, that things will eventually even out and I'll have days of true happiness. How can I not? Life can't be completely unfair, can it?

But I don't understand why Blake is choosing me to marry. He can have anyone; he can be with the wealthiest of the wealthy, with aristocrats, even with royalty. Why in the world would he choose me? I'm a nobody, someone who can't do anything for him . . . other than pretend we're a happy couple.

I finally slip on my shoes and am ready to flee, but when I step from the bathroom, he's standing near the door, his face a mask. There's no way of escaping unless I suddenly develop some prize football prowess and can knock him on his ass and vault right over him. This nearly makes me smile — almost, but not quite.

"I need to go," I tell him, standing far enough away that he can't snake out his arms and grab me.

"You haven't responded to my request yet, Jewel. You're the one who wanted to talk, and when I did, you rushed off into another room for an hour and now you're heading straight for the door. To me, that's not talking."

Taking a calming breath, I look at his nose, knowing better than to meet his eyes. "Yes, I wanted to talk. I was wrong. I . . . this . . . I can't think," I stammer, frustrated I can't find the words I'm searching for. "You already have me in your bed. I don't understand why you want more than that. It doesn't make sense, and my head's too muddled to try to make it sound better, so I need to be alone. *Please*." He doesn't move.

So much for attempting to reason with him. "Look, Blake, I'll do anything to get my brother back, but this is extreme." He still doesn't move, which makes me even more nervous.

"Why don't you want to marry me?" I stop squirming and finally look in his eyes, but as usual, I read nothing.

"Because even though I'll probably never get married, the act of marriage still means something to me. The institution isn't a mere charade in my way of thinking. Yes, a lot of people seem to see it as a meaningless piece of paper, legally binding two people until they tire of each other. I, however, was taught that it means more than that . . ."

"Our marriage will be real," he calmly tells me.

"There can't be a marriage, Blake. I don't know when or how you came up with this idea, but it's not going to happen," I say, my voice rising with each word.

"I met with the judge, Jewel, and he told me that because you don't meet the conditions the court has set, you'll have a very slim chance of getting your brother back. If you do get him, it will take months. Our marriage will speed this up . . . significantly." This is too close to what the attorney said to me.

"I . . . I . . . How can they put this sort of condition on getting custody? It's wrong," I say, my head spinning.

"It is what it is, Jewel." He's speaking so casually — as if he has conversations like this every day. He looks at me intently for several moments.

"Why me, though? Why on earth do you want to marry someone like *me*? I'm sure you can find a hundred other women — socially acceptable women — who won't hesitate to take your name, and who'll help you lock in your business deal with no problem."

"I want *you*. And you need me. It's that simple," he says. "This way we both get something important to us, and you won't have the constant urge to run and hide."

"I can still run, even if we're married."

"Not if we both have custody of Justin."

"You think I'll give up my rights to him as soon as I get him back?"

"You won't get him back without me, Jewel."

"What sort of man are you?"

"I'm the sort of man who knows what he wants and goes after it."

I'm the sort of man who knows what he wants and goes after it

"I hate to tell you this, Blake, but you can't own another person."

"You're very wrong, Jewel. I can own you," he says, and the shiver that runs through my veins has nothing to do with the temperature of the room.

My eyes flash dangerously. "Do you know what you're getting yourself into? Do you know how much work caring for a child is, especially one who's been through the trauma Justin's been through? You can't do whatever you want whenever you want if you have a boy of his age and circumstances living in your home. Children are messy, they're demanding, and they're exhausting. Why don't you give me back my brother, if you can, and go and find some easy woman, one who's willing to bend all the rules for you? Why are you hell-bent on making a bad situation worse?"

"I've already told you this, numerous times. I want you, and I won't change my mind." The steel in his voice tells me he's speaking the truth, and the anxiety in my stomach tells me the same. He isn't going to back down.

"You aren't giving me a choice, and you know it."

"I've told you what I want and expect, Jewel." He then moves from the door and goes to his desk where he leans on it. Is this a test? Is he going to let me go now? I pull open the door and take a step toward freedom when I feel his fingers grip my arm. Yep. I knew he wouldn't make it easy.

"Something to remind you of what we have together," he says before his lips descend and he's kissing my breath away . . . again. When I sway toward him, he releases me. "We're good together, Jewel. We both know in the end you'll agree, but if you need to fight this so you feel better about yourself, take your time to do it."

With that, he steps back once again, indicating with a gesture that I can go or I can stay. I flee. I don't know if I'll ever stop running, and I don't even know who I'm running from — Blake or myself. Most likely both. I will bend . . . it's just a matter of time.

Chapter Review

Chapter Thirty Six

Jewel

I SOMEHOW MAKE IT BACK to my apartment building. After stumbling into my front hall, I take extra time to fasten all of the locks on my door. Not that the strongest lock will keep Blake out, especially since the man has the keys to the apartment, but the symbolism of doing it makes me feel immeasurably better. I head to my room and fall onto the bed, where I know I'll lie awake for hours without the possibility of sleep.

Haven't I promised Justin I'll get him back any way I can? Yes. So why in the world am I balking at the idea of marriage? It's selfish of me, and I know it. My brother is the only one who matters. He's the reason I've

339

done all of this, the reason I propositioned Blake in the first place. I'm not blaming my brother . . . not at all. I'm an adult, and I've made my choices. I had a wonderful life while growing up. It's time for my brother to have the same privilege.

I toss and turn the entire day and night, and when I finally find a few minutes of peaceful slumber, nightmares of my brother being dragged away wake me. At the crack of dawn, when my chances of more sleep have hit nil, I give up.

I can continue to fight Blake, but he'll win. He has power, and I have none. This seems to be the way of the world for the haves and the have-nots. It's why he isn't worried about my answer. That he told me he'll give me time to think is almost amusing. It's like giving a starving animal a choice on whether to eat or not. No matter how distrustful they might be, they'll eventually take the food that's being handed to them . . . even if it's filled with poison.

I should call Blake now and tell him he's won. But the defiant part of me decides to put it off for a little while. Maybe I'm holding out hope he'll change his mind, that he'll help without us having to marry. But, I know it's not going to happen. In the short amount of time I've known Blake, I've come to realize that once he decides on something, he considers it done.

I don't want to end this with him anyway. I might hate relying on him, but as much as I want to despise the man, I don't. This is more about me wanting to be independent, more about getting choices in my unstable life.

The last time Blake ended things, it didn't work out too well for me. It's only made me take longer to get my brother back. I climb from bed, wander into my kitchen, and impatiently watch coffee drip into the pot. This morning ritual gives me a measure of comfort, which might be slightly pathetic.

When the coffee's ready, I add a nice splash of flavored cream, and sit in the living room gazing at one of the soulless, impersonal art pieces hanging on the stark white walls. How have I fallen so far? I went from a college graduate with a great job, to a pathetic creature who has a difficult time looking at myself in the mirror.

My doorbell rings and I sigh. I thought I'd have longer to make this choice. I set my coffee cup down and move to the door. When I open it, I'm shocked to see Tyler, Blake's youngest brother, standing before me. Before I'm able to say a word, he flashes a big smile and pulls me in for a hug.

"Hi. I've missed ya, Jewel." His affection fills me with warmth. I need friends.

Tyler's certainly as good-looking as his brother, with wide shoulders, dark, slightly messy hair, and a dimple in his cheek that gives him a boyish charm that neither of his brothers come close to possessing. He's also the first to smile and show his emotions, whereas Blake and the other Astor brother, Byron, make a point of playing everything close to the vest.

All three brothers are far more handsome than is good for them, or the poor females who happen to stumble into their paths. And what makes it harder to resist is the command, the raw strength that radiates from them in waves. There's something about a man who knows exactly who he is that makes a woman want to give him anything and everything he could ever possibly desire.

"What are you doing here?" I ask.

"I took a chance you'd be home," he says. "My brother likes to keep you all to himself, but I decided to pop in for a little unannounced visit. That way you can't turn me away." He pauses as he sniffs the air. "Is that fresh coffee I smell?" Without waiting for an invitation, he walks inside and makes his way to my kitchen.

I follow and find him rummaging through my cupboards for a mug. He grabs my empty cup and pours fresh coffee for both of us. Smiling, I add cream to mine and lead Tyler to the kitchen table.

"Don't you have work or something more important to do than sit around and chat with me, Tyler?"

"I like visiting with you, but even more importantly I need information," he says.

"What information?" I question, though I'm sure I know his answer.

"We can trade small talk all day, Jewel, but why don't we cut to the chase and you can tell me why you were gone for a month, why my brother was a bear during that month, and why you now have crater-sized dark circles beneath your eyes?" He softens the interrogation with a wink and a grin. My smile vanishes while he speaks.

"Your brother can answer all of these questions," I tell him with a brittle laugh.

Tyler reaches across the table and takes my hand. "I'm not asking Blake. I'm asking you."

I'm so close to tears that I have to turn my head away. If only I had a single friend I could talk to. If I did, maybe I wouldn't be feeling this insane urge to spill my guts to Blake's brother. But it's so difficult to hold everything in when he's looking at me with these openly friendly eyes of his.

"It's complicated," I finally say.

"I'm not going to pretend that I understand everything, Jewel, but I've been able to tell from the first moment I met you that you're a truly good person. And though I love my brother very much, I know he can sometimes give people the wrong impression of who he is. There's a long story there, but it isn't my place to tell it."

"You two are so different from each other," I say. I'm avoiding his questions, but I'm also curious how Tyler is so full of joy while Blake seems like the weight of the world rests on his shoulders.

"Some people — maybe most of us — have lousy childhoods, but let me tell you that ours was a doozy. I was too young to be affected as badly as Blake and Byron were by the disasters of our past. As I got older and saw the hell they were going through, I decided I had a choice of being happy or being angry like they were. I much prefer happiness."

"I had an incredible childhood. My mother was amazing."

343

"You're very lucky. I consider myself lucky too. I have two brothers who'd do anything for me. I have friends as well." He pauses another long moment. "Sometimes it really does help to get things off your chest, and to talk to someone. I want to be your friend."

The man is practically begging me to open up to him, and I'm oh so tempted to. But what if it backfires, and makes my situation worse? Then again, it can't seem to get much worse than it is now.

Before I'm able to stop myself, I'm letting out the entire story. To his credit, Tyler doesn't interrupt, not even once. His eyes grow wider and he grips his coffee cup tightly a few times, but he doesn't release my hand, and he doesn't ask questions.

"So yesterday, he strongly pushed for marriage, and I don't have any prospects of ever getting married to anyone else, so what difference should it make? But at the same time, I believe in the institution, of two becoming one in the eyes of God and all of that, and . . . I don't know. I'm so confused right now." Having finished my long, sad story, I'm now trying desperately not to give in to tears. How I hate the dang tears.

I've only been around Tyler a couple of times, but I feel better telling my story to another person, a guy who seems to want nothing from me. He's quiet for long enough, though, that I grow uncomfortable.

"I'm sorry," I say, my voice barely above a whisper.

"Oh, Jewel, I'm the one who's sorry. You've been shouldering far too much for too long. I believe my brother has honorable intentions toward you, but he's clearly not going about it in the right way. I'm glad you've talked to me. My brothers and I may not always see eye to eye on things, but nothing will ever rip us apart. We do need each other to step in once in a while and help the other out. This might be one of those times." His lips finally show a hint of a smile.

344

"Tyler, I don't want you going to battle for me," I say, now wondering if I should've spilled my story. "Maybe you should simply forget I told you all of this?"

"It can't be undone, Jewel, and it shouldn't be. You need someone in your corner. I'll speak with my brother." He stands up.

"Right now?" I squeal.

"The sooner, the better," he tells me, and he starts off toward the door.

"Tyler, I don't think this is a good idea."

"I guarantee there won't be any backlash, Jewel," Tyler says, and then he's gone, my front door closing behind him.

I walk into my sitting room and slump down on the sofa, praying I haven't screwed up my only way to get Justin back. What if Blake gives up on me and I lose Justin forever? I'll have only myself to blame.

All I can do is wait and see what Blake's next move will be . . . but the waiting might very well kill me. Once again though, I have no choice but to sit and wait . . . and wait . . . and wait.

Chapter Review

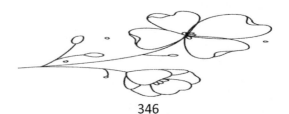

Blake

AS OFTEN HAPPENS, I head to my office building on a Saturday. My brother called earlier, snapping at me, which isn't like Tyler, and demanded a meeting. I'm confused. Tyler's the peacemaker of our family, the one who never loses his cool. From a few of the things he growled at me, I have no doubt he's been by to see Jewel. It seems she might have told him everything. Instead of being upset about this, I'm happy to see, or at least suspect, that she's still fighting.

I'm not as happy about Tyler being so protective of Jewel, but I also know he won't overstep his bounds when it comes to her. We never poach on each other's territory . . . though we aren't beyond pretending to do so.

As I near the office, I wonder what Tyler will say. The funny thing is, if I listen to anyone other than Max, it will be to one of my brothers, and *especially* to Tyler, since Tyler's always the voice of reason when anger seems to consume me to the depths of my soul — if I even have a soul. But Tyler sure as hell wasn't the voice of reason an hour ago. He'd been too busy snapping at me.

I park and walk to my office, then decide to wait for a while before buzzing my brother. It's such a rarity to find Tyler in a bad mood that I can't help but add fuel to the fire. Granted, this move might come back to bite me in the ass, but I can't help myself. A man has to do what a man has to do.

After about ten minutes, my intercom sounds, and I know it's Tyler. He most likely told security to notify him the minute I entered the building.

"Yes, Tyler?" I say in a chipper tone.

"We're supposed to be meeting, Blake."

I lean back. "I'm sitting here waiting for you, bro." The line disconnects. I school my expression and watch as a moment later my door's thrust open, and Tyler enters the room.

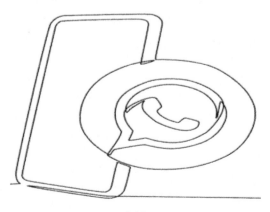

"I've known you to do some pretty dumb things, Blake, but this has to be a new low for you." Well, this is a civil greeting . . . not.

"It's been a few days, brother," I tell him with a smile. "It's good to see you too."

"Don't play games, Blake. I'm not one of the boneheads you employ, one of the yes-men who bow and scrape to you to keep from pissing you off," Tyler says. I laugh.

"Do you like being feared?" Tyler asks.

The question takes me by surprise, and I lose a trace of my grin. "Yes," I say, but is this as true today as it was a year ago — heck, even a few months ago? I honestly don't know.

"And do you like scaring women and children?"

"I'm not trying to scare Jewel." I don't like how this conversation is going. It's not at all what I was expecting.

"Whether you're trying to or not, you scared her. She's already alone and desperate, so she certainly doesn't need to be afraid too," Tyler says. Some of his irritation seems to evaporate as he moves to the couch and sits.

This shames me more than I'll ever admit. "I'm good to Jewel," I say in my own defense.

"If she's only with you out of desperation, that's not being good to her, Blake. You have to earn someone's love and trust, not demand it."

"I don't need her love or trust. I just need her." I'm not willing to delve into my emotions . . . not even with myself, let alone with my brother. This isn't going to turn into a bonding moment for the two of us where we can hug, say *I love you, man*, and sing campfire songs.

"Don't trap her if you don't care. Help her, then let her go," Tyler tells me. "Give her back her brother — you have the power to do it — and let them be free."

If she's only with you out of desperation, that's not being good to her. You have to earn someone's love and trust, not demand it.

"Things are complicated. I can't let her go."

"Then I'll step in and help her," Tyler says. "Nothing complicated about it."

The threat comes as a total shock. I stare at my brother, wondering whether I've been wrong to think Tyler won't mess with my woman. The look on his face isn't love, though . . . it's compassion and generosity. He came across a woman who needs protection, and he feels compelled to give it to her. It's simply who Tyler is.

"This really isn't your business, Tyler."

Tyler's about to say something, but his mouth closes, and he leans back, his brows wrinkled. He stares at me for so long it makes me shift in my seat, something that never happens. *I'm* the one who makes *other*s blink, not the other way around.

"Do you love her, Blake?"

"No!" I practically shout this monosyllable before I calm myself. "No, I don't love her. I just don't want to let her go. I have my reasons."

"And you'll use a child to bribe her into staying with you, even when she can't stand the sight of you?" Tyler asks. This hits below the belt.

"I promise you she wants me just as much as I want her."

"That isn't the impression I got from her today. She seems depressed, defeated, and out of options. Do you really want her to be with you because you're her last resort?"

I sit back and think about my time with Jewel, and the month of agony without her. Yes, our time together has been relatively short, but during our time apart I thought of no other woman but her . . . something that's never happened before.

"She and I *will* marry, Tyler. It's not as if that has to lock us together for life. But if I marry her, she'll easily get custody of her brother . . . and I get her." I try to infuse arrogance into my voice, but I've failed.

"You're nothing but show right now — do you know that?" Tyler says, and then he laughs. His laugh gets beneath my skin far more than the lecture he's giving me.

"What in the hell are you talking about, Tyler?"

"You won't admit it — hard to believe — but it's clear you care about her. Are you afraid of telling *me* how you feel, or are you afraid of telling *yourself*?"

"I'm afraid of no one," I snap.

"Why not date the woman properly instead of making her feel cheap?"

"Jewel's the one who put herself in this situation," I remind my brother. "*She* came to *me*."

"You know perfectly well she had no choice. She'll do anything for her brother, just as I'd do anything for you and Byron."

"And I'll do *anything* to be with her."

"What does that mean?" Tyler asks "You'll do anything to have sex with her?"

"It's more than sex. It's something so powerful you can't possibly comprehend it, little brother."

"Just because it's great sex doesn't mean you have the right to take it when it's not offered freely."

Just because it's great sex doesn't mean you have the right to take it when it's not offered freely

"Believe me when I say that our sex life is no hardship on her," I smugly tell him.

"You're demanding marriage, Blake. Great sex will fade, then you'll find yourself living with a woman who resents you."

"I don't think so. I've been with a lot of women, and I've never had a connection like the one I share with Jewel. She knows this too — she's just fighting her feelings."

"Do you honestly believe the shit you're spouting?" Tyler asks.

"I believe we're meant to be together." I might not want to open up my chest and wear my confounded emotions on my sleeves, but I do want to show Tyler I'm not trying to hurt Jewel, and I do feel something, even if I'm unsure of exactly what that is. In fact, I'm trying to help her.

Tyler rolls his eyes. "I'll be watching you, Blake."

"I wouldn't have it any other way," I say. I stand and Tyler rises as well.

"Don't screw this up," Tyler says.

"We've always trusted each other, Tyler. Don't lose faith in me." I lean in and give my brother a hug. I don't often show vulnerability, but I let my guard down just a tad.

Tyler nods, then steps back and looks at me again, making me feel as if I'm beneath a microscope, and then, without another word, he leaves. I sit back down and turn my chair away from my open door.

Closing my eyes, I think about the previous day with Jewel. It was perfect, as usual, but it wasn't enough, even if we were finally together again, it's never enough. I constantly want more. With her it will *never* be enough.

I shift in my seat and groan as my body hardens. I can practically smell and taste her on my tongue. Only Jewel has been able to make me hard with only a single thought of her. She isn't something to let go of.

But what if Jewel really is afraid of me? No, that's not possible. I'm demanding, sure, and I expect a certain amount of respect from her, but I'm also willing to offer her everything she could ever desire. We have something, and she knows it. She doesn't fear me — that's impossible. She simply wants to establish her independence. This will all be fine . . . won't it?

Scorpio

Chapter Review

Chapter Thirty Eight

Jewel

"D AMMIT!"

I look at the blood on my finger, scurry to the kitchen sink, and wash the shallow wound before grabbing a paper towel and wrapping it so I can get to my bathroom without making my apartment look like a crime scene.

My mood's less than stellar. It's been three days since Tyler was at my place, three long days and three even longer nights without a single word from him . . . or Blake. I went to work and haven't seen any of the Astor men.

Blake said he'd give me a couple of days to think, and those days have come and gone. What in the heck is going on? Did Tyler speak to him? Is he going to back off? Is he giving up?

All it will take to find out is a simple phone call, but as many times as I've picked up my phone, I haven't managed to dial his number. What if the pot's on a low simmer, and I accidentally set it to boiling?

I made phone calls Monday and Tuesday, but they weren't to Blake, and they got me nowhere. I feel like I'm on a first-name basis with the court clerks now. The children's services division hasn't been any help, and I'm growing more and more desperate.

Maybe Blake's waiting me out. Tyler must not have been able to help me. The stupidest part about all of this, what I'm most terrified of, besides losing my brother, is falling in love with a man who can never love me back.

When I can't stand being alone with my own thoughts a single minute longer without flipping out, I grab my coat and head to the elevator. Getting away from phones will keep me from making a call I'm sure to regret. I go to a corner pub not far from my place and don't hesitate to take up residence on one of the barstools.

"What can I get for you?"

"Something sweet and strong," I answer.

"Ah, having one of *those* days, huh?" says the woman behind the bar.

"I'm having one of those weeks . . . or months . . . or maybe even years," I reply as the bartender mixes a drink.

"You know it's a bad day when drinking starts at two in the afternoon," the woman replies, not unkindly. "Here ya go, sweetie. The first one's on the house."

Strangely, the bartender's kindness nearly does me in. "Thank you," I say as I accept the tall, fruity drink and take a long swallow. "Oh, this is exactly what I needed. What's it called?"

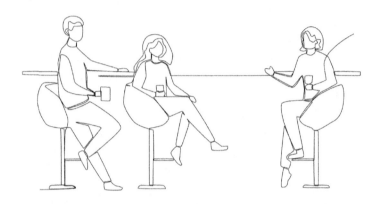

"You probably don't want to know. But yes, it has magical powers. Or maybe if you drink enough of them, your head gets so fuzzy, it simply *feels* like they have magical powers. I'm Tina."

"I'm Jewel." A group of young men come in, and the bartender's busy for the next several minutes as she checks their IDs and makes drinks. One of the kids, who can't be more than a few months over twenty-one, comes and sits by me.

"Can I buy your next drink?" he asks.

I give him a smile. "Trust me, you're going to be much better off buying it for one of the young ladies over there," I say, and point to a group of college-age girls sitting at a table in the corner.

"Nah, the girls my age are too shallow. I'm Dale," he says with a wink as he motions for Tina to come over. "Can I get another drink for the lady?"

Tina looks at me, and I shrug, shocked to see my first drink is already finished. Obviously I needed it more than I realized. Tina makes another one, and I smile as I sip on it and start an interesting conversation with Dale, who invites his friends over as we share a third drink together. I'm laughing with the entire group of boys, who I learn are attending the University of Washington.

I decide no more drinking after the fourth one arrives; I don't want to end up doing something foolish, and if I keep going, I'm cruising in that direction. I excuse myself and move to the waiting line for the bathroom.

"Are you giving up on men and going for boys now?" I turn to see McKenzie standing near me. The smile in her voice takes away the sting of her words.

"Maybe. Men are too complicated," I reply, happy to see her. "Are you following me?"

"I might be," McKenzie says with a brittle laugh. "Or I might be having just as bad a day as you, and I needed to escape my troubles with a few drinks of my own."

"It's so easy to look at others and think they have picturesque lives. I'm not saying this to be mean, but it makes me feel a little better to see someone as beautiful and successful as you having a bad day." I probably would never say something like this if not for the four drinks I've consumed.

McKenzie laughs. "Well, you made me feel better. I'm glad my pain helps," she says. "Good luck with the boys." She walks away smiling as I slip into the bathroom. When I come out, she's gone.

I walk back to the college kids, and although I'm immeasurably better than I was when I walked into the bar, it's time to go. I thank the boys and Tina, and announce I'm heading home. I'd much rather eat at my own place than consume a bunch of deep-fried bar food.

My companions lodge protests, but they don't hassle me too much. I make my way back down the street in a decent mood because of my adventure. But my good mood immediately disappears when I walk through my door and hear laughter coming from the living room.

My stomach clenches when a male voice pipes in. The part-time housekeeper Blake sends to my home twice a week, even though I've told him it isn't necessary, isn't alone, and I know who's with Elsa. *He* gets to disappear for days and then show up whenever he feels like it. It instantly ticks me off.

When I stop in the doorway and see Blake with a smile on his normally stern face, I have an odd surge of jealousy. This is ridiculous. If he wants to run off with the housekeeper, a woman he's hired, that will save me a lot of hassle. I should leave them to their fun . . . and walk away in relief. That isn't what I do. Instead, I take another step forward.

My eyes are drawn to the laugh lines by his eyes; they make his face seem more open, more human. He's wearing a pair of jeans that hug his thighs to perfection, and a shirt that's molded to his sculpted chest.

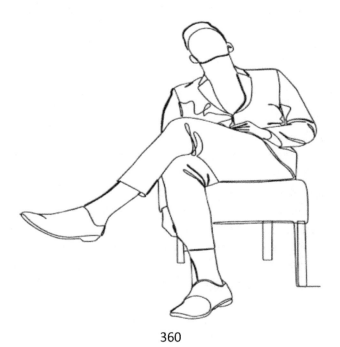

My stomach tightens with raw need, and my head starts to spin. When I try to take another step, I grip the doorjamb and holding on for dear life. I'm glad that neither Blake nor Elsa have noticed me, because it gives me a moment to compose my features, to pull myself together. I'm starting to regret the drinks I downed.

Blake's shoulders tense, and he turns his head an inch in my direction. He's now aware of my presence. There's no use in hiding, so I let go of the doorjamb and move into the room, hoping my voice will sound normal if I'm expected to speak.

"Hello, Ms. Weston, let me get dinner started for you," Elsa says as she immediately stands.

"It's fine, Elsa. I'm not hungry," I reply.

"Oh, it's not a problem," Elsa says. I notice how she practically bats her eyes at Blake, and I fight not to grit my teeth together. It looks like Elsa and Blake have enjoyed each other's company quite a bit. I'm not proud of myself for being jealous. What in the heck is wrong with me?

"Don't let me interrupt you guys," I say. "I need to take a shower."

"I'll have dinner ready in half an hour," Elsa says.

Elsa goes to the kitchen, and I hightail it out of the room, shut and lock my door, then lean against it. After catching my breath, I go into the bathroom and take an extra-long shower. When I come out the apartment smells delicious . . . but I have no appetite. I move to the table that's already set. I want to be petty, but realize I'm acting ridiculous. I take a seat and Blake comes over and chooses a seat too close for my frayed nerves.

I focus on the food in front of me because I'm not sure what in the hell I'm feeling right now. I take bites without looking up as the silence begins growing to oppressive levels. I can't help but think of all of the meals I've shared with Blake where most ended with me as Blake's final course. The confusing part of all of this is that I wouldn't mind reenacting a few of those moments right here and now. I'm too rattled to eat anything more so I push my food around my plate hoping Blake won't notice.

"You've lost weight, Jewel. Please don't let my presence stop you from eating. You obviously need the calories." When I don't look up, I hear movement, and then his fingers are beneath my chin, tilting it up, and forcing our eyes to meet.

"I might have a bug or something," I say. It's the only excuse I can think of on the spur of the moment. He gives me a long look that makes me feel guilty about the lie.

He takes my hand. "It's been pointed out that I'm not good at communication. I'm also not good with sharing . . . feelings." He pauses for so long I think he's finished. But then he looks up, and brings my hand to his lips, gently kissing my palm, sending tingles through my entire body.

"I've backed you into a corner one too many times. I don't know if I can change, but I'm willing to give it a try."

He shocks me further when he stands. He grabs both of our plates, takes them into the kitchen, rinses them, and loads them into the dishwasher all while I stare at him, unsure of what's going on.

"Thank you for sharing dinner with me." He then turns and walks toward my door.

"You're leaving?" I ask, so confused I don't move. I'm not drunk anymore . . . or at least I don't think I am.

"For tonight. Goodnight and sweet dreams." He then walks out the door, leaving me staring at the space, not understanding what just happened. He hadn't tried to kiss me, had barely touched me. He'd treated this like a first date. I have absolutely zero idea what this means . . . but I wish he hadn't left . . .

Chapter Review

Jewel

S ILENCE IS WHAT I experience for two days after Blake's dinner visit . . . and his unusual exit. I don't like not talking to him. How have I gone from wanting to avoid him to desperately wishing he was here? This morning I wake up and something feels different. I can't figure out what it is . . . until I hear his words whisper in my ear.

"Open your eyes, Jewel." My body instantly heats. His voice has been in my dreams, in my thoughts, and in my soul for every minute of every day ever since I first met him. I try keeping my eyes closed, but curiosity is too much, and I slowly slide them open and gaze at this man who looks far too good to not be considered a hazard to every woman's health.

His voice has been in my dreams, in my thoughts, and in my soul for every minute of every day ever since I first met him.

"What are you doing, Blake?"

"I gave you enough time to think about all of this. Giving you space doesn't seem to be helping." He's leaning over me, making it hard to breathe. He slips his hand beneath the covers and cups my breast, only a thin piece of cotton separating his hot touch from my skin.

My traitorous body instantly responds, my nipples hardening, my stomach quivering, and my breath hitching, unable to hide this from him. He leans over and kisses me, and I'm quickly falling. He kisses his way down my neck, and my body arches.

I've fought this man for so long, but it's impossible when I want him this dang much. If only my guilt over my desire wasn't constantly nagging me, I could let go . . . and simply enjoy every second of this.

Blake looks into my eyes again, a sexy smile resting on his lips. "You can either stay right here where I'll strip away your jammies and make you scream my name over and over again . . ." he says, the low timbre of his voice sending heat straight to my core, and befuddling my brain. He kisses me again as his skillful fingers squeeze my nipple.

"Or you can get up and come out for an adventure." He continues touching me, and it takes several heartbeats for me to process his last sentence.

"Adventure?" I huskily ask.

My shirt inches up as his magical fingers trail across my skin. His breath on my nipple as he leans down and slowly runs his tongue across it, makes me moan. He takes his time licking and sucking before he leans back. I protest before I realize I'm doing it.

"Choice A or B?"

I look at him in confusion. "What?"

He chuckles. "Is it bed or adventure?"

Isn't being in bed with him an adventure? I barely keep from saying that. I want to stay right here and finish what he started. But he seems so relaxed, so excited . . . and not just about sex . . . that I want to know what this adventure is. He's hard to resist when he's cold and demanding. This more playful side of him is impossible to pull away from.

"I guess adventure." I instantly want to kick myself. I know I'll enjoy spending a day in bed with him. I'm not so sure the adventure will be good.

"Better shower then," he says before he rolls off the bed, only seeming a little disappointed. When he stands, I see he's only wearing a pair of silk briefs . . . that hide absolutely *nothing* from my view. It makes me want to change my mind.

He laughs. "Nope, you made your choice," he tells me as he walks from my room. I let out a groan, flop back on the bed, then five minutes later, climb out and slowly walk into my bathroom. It takes fifteen minutes to get out of the hot shower. I dress in jeans and a sweater, unsure what we're going to do next. Blake's sitting at the bar, drinking coffee, and reading a newspaper on his iPad.

"Where are we going?" I ask, pouring myself a cup.

"To the marina."

"What are we doing?"

"You'll see. I have plans," Blake says. This is a playful side of him I've never seen before. It's really throwing me off.

We finish our coffee, then he grabs my jacket from the coat closet, and helps me into it, letting his hands linger on my shoulders before he smooths them down my sides. Another shudder passes through my body, but before this leads us back into the bedroom, he takes my hand, and we walk out the door.

He says nothing as we step into the elevator, and then suddenly, it's as if a dam breaks, because I'm pressed against the elevator wall, with Blake's body covering mine, and his head descending. The kiss he gives me leaves my knees weak. His hands travel up and down my back, and my body melts underneath his possession. What was I thinking to turn down lovemaking in favor of going out?

Just as his fingers are slipping beneath my shirt, the bell on the elevator chimes, and he steps back and helps me tug my clothes back into place. We exit the elevator as if that didn't just happen. We go outside and find a waiting car.

"To the marina, sir?" Max asks. Blake nods. After we climb into the backseat, he lifts my hand to his mouth and feathers kisses across my knuckles, making my stomach twist.

Max says nothing; he doesn't so much as look in the rearview mirror as Blake once again seduces me right here in the car. His hand trails down my thigh, slowly . . . deliberately . . . unbearably.

When we arrive at the docks, I'm breathing hard, and it takes several moments to realize the vehicle's come to a stop . . . and Blake's no longer touching me.

"We should've stayed home," he says with a laugh.

"I agree," I say before I can take the words back. The grin he gives me makes me glad I can't.

"Let's go."

I'm wobbly as we exit the vehicle. I lean on him as we walk down the dock where huge boats bob along the pier. I stop to look at the biggest boat I've ever seen in person.

"Wow!"

"What?" he asks. I turn to him in shock.

"Are you so used to this much wealth that you don't see what's right in front of you?"

I gaze at the yacht gently bobbing beside the dock in front of us. He's gazing at it too as if seeing it through new eyes. He then looks at me with a bit of a smile.

"You might be right. I see this so much I hardly notice it anymore. You might be opening my eyes. There never was a time I was exactly poor, but my brothers and I have built our company from the ground up, and I do appreciate what I have, just not as much as I should. Want to step on board?"

"I'm not sure. Honestly, it scares me a little," I admit, which makes him laugh.

"Come on, let's look it over." He grabs my hand and helps me board the nearly two-hundred-foot vessel.

"I honestly had no idea boats could get this big. Is this yours, Blake?"

I don't notice when he doesn't exactly answer. "Many people in the world own boats this large . . . and even bigger ones. Many live on them."

"Sort of like Tom Hanks in *Sleepless in Seattle*," I say with a nervous giggle.

"Well, his wasn't *quite* this big."

"Very true." My voice is hushed.

We're silent as we pass top-of-the-line furniture and exquisite tables. I look everywhere as I try to take it all in. We step through a door, and we're inside a gigantic . . . bedroom. I gasp in delight.

The walls are mahogany with wide open windows and gleaming glass doors leading to a private balcony. The gilded ceiling looks like the boat was taken straight from a classic English country house. In the middle of it all sits a huge four-poster bed that's far too inviting.

"Jewel," he whispers, and a shiver rushes through me at the need in his voice. I turn and look at him. He smiles as he walks up to me and places his fingers beneath my chin, then backs me up against a built-in bookcase filled with rare books, books I'd love to explore at another time.

"I'm going to peel your clothes away, piece by piece, slowly and completely, and then take you long and slow, and then hard and fast. And then we'll start all over again, and do it for days on end. I'm going to please you so much you'll never be able to tell me no again."

"But . . . this . . . here . . . now?"

"Right here. Right now." Blake presses his body up against mine, letting me feel how ready he is to take me.

"This is your boat, isn't it?" I look around nervously, finally realizing the décor isn't exactly his style.

"Why do you ask? Are you afraid of being caught?"

"Yes," I say nervously, looking away from him to the door he firmly shut behind us.

"That's all a part of the appeal." I feel his excitement building.

"I don't know if this is a good idea," I tell him, but there's no stopping us.

He leans forward and kisses me, and all other protests evaporate as I fall into his arms, not caring if the rest of the world tries to stop us . . . because I don't think anyone can anymore.

Chapter Review

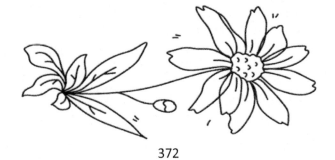

Chapter Forty

Jewel

F IRE AND ICE. I'M molten as Blake pulls me into his arms. The air weighs down on my lungs, and my entire body undulates with desire. His power, my loss of control, the pure lust shining from his eyes fills me with so much heat I'm going to burn alive. I'm his, no reservation left.

"This is why we can't part, Jewel. You're as powerless as I am to resist what's happening between us," he says before sinking his teeth into my shoulder, making me cry out in painful pleasure. I need more. I slide my hand down and cup him, desperate to feel the raw power residing between his legs.

My clothes fall away, scattering in all directions, and before I can blink, I'm standing before him in only the thin lace of my panties. He draws back and gazes at me in reverence, making me glow hotter.

"You're so unbelievably gorgeous," he whispers.

I want to repeat these words to him as he unbuttons his shirt and lets it slide down, revealing his sculpted chest. Then he undoes his belt and the top button on his pants, and my mouth waters in anticipation of seeing him in all of his naked magnificence. But he stops, and I'm sorely tempted to scream.

"Lie on the bed," he huskily whispers. "Leave your panties on, but spread your legs for me."

"No." His eyebrows raise at my refusal.

"You finish undressing first, Blake." He smiles at me, a predator's gleam in his eyes. He loves our battle of wills. The shocking thing is, I'm loving it too, even in the heat of the moment. He's always the one in charge, and I think the tables should turn.

"Maybe I want *you* to do what *I* say," I tell him. My sudden boldness stuns me. I've always been a good girl — okay, until I went to this man's office, stripped, and offered myself to him on a silver platter. I'm changing the longer I battle with Blake.

His eyes twinkle. "I love it when you fight me, Jewel," he says. He moves toward me with lightning speed, spins me around, and traps my hands behind my back. Pulses of heat shoot through my core as pure, unadulterated lust consumes me. He holds me with one hand as I hear the whoosh of his belt slipping through the loops of his slacks . . . and then the leather wraps around my wrists.

"What are you doing, Blake?"

"Whatever I want," he whispers against my ear. He pushes me forward, making my knees hit the bed. Within seconds he lifts me, leaving my derrière high in the air, my face on the bed, my hands secured tightly behind my back.

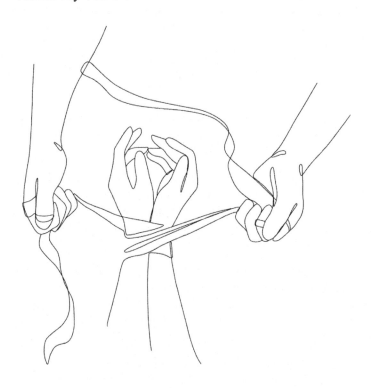

He caresses my backside, then slips a finger inside the edge of my panties and feels my undeniable wetness. No question that I'm turned on.

"You can try to run, Jewel, but we're meant to be together. Your body tells me how much you enjoy this, exactly how much you want me . . . just as much as I want you."

His fingers slide across my curves before he lifts his palm and then comes down. I let out a shocked cry when he makes contact with the tender flesh of my backside. The blow isn't hard enough to hurt me; it's just enough to warm my skin, and send a ripple of pleasure through my core.

"I don't think I'm going to give you your next orgasm until you beg," Blake says with hunger in his voice. He leans over and his teeth and tongue run along my buttock.

I'm melting, but I don't easily give him victories. "I don't beg," I say, my words bellied by the panting in my voice.

"Oh, you *will* beg, Jewel. I guarantee it."

Before he says anything more, a pounding fist slams on the door, instantly sending a cold chill through my body.

"Who's in there?" someone yells. "Why is this door locked?" The knocking grows in volume.

"Go away," Blake shouts, his powerful voice enough to scare most people into doing exactly what he wants.

I gulp. "I watched you use a card to get on this dock, Blake. Isn't this your boat?"

The man on the other side of the door calls out again. "I most certainly will not go away. This is private property — *my* boss's property — and you're trespassing. I'm calling the cops."

"You don't have permission to be here?" I ask. I'm squirming to get away, but Blake has his hand tightly on my hip.

"It belongs to a business associate of mine who's in the process of selling it. It will be mine in one minute," Blake says, and he releases me, though all I can do is roll onto my side. The belt around my hands doesn't allow me to cover myself.

"Let me out of this," I beg, but Blake doesn't seem to hear.

He moves over to his jacket and pulls out what appears to be a checkbook. He scribbles something furiously and goes over to the door without bothering to put on a shirt . . . or to button his pants.

When he opens the door, he obscures any view inside the room. Blake must be a fearsome sight, because the man on the other side of the door takes a quick step back. All I can see are his feet through Blake's firmly planted legs.

"What in the hell do you think you're doing?" the man asks in protest, but he isn't speaking quite as loudly as he had been just a moment before. "This is private property."

"This is *my* boat now. Get the hell off my property," Blake growls as he lifts the check he's just written and slams it against the stunned man's chest.

"I . . . what?" the man gasps.

"Call your boss." Without another word, Blake shuts the door with a final click, and bolts the lock, then turns and shoots me a look filled with so much heat it's a wonder I don't melt against the still-made bed.

"We won't be interrupted again," he says as he stalks toward me.

"What if he doesn't want to sell his boat?" I ask.

"I told you I know the seller. I gave him more than he was asking. The boat is now mine."

"You can't just buy a boat without the proper paperwork, Blake."

"*I* can." This mind-set and this kind of wealth don't compute for me.

"So where were we?" Blake asks, hunger burning in his gaze.

"I'm not in the mood anymore," I say, still in shock over the events of the past few minutes.

"Don't worry. I'll get you there."

With these words he unbuttons the rest of his pants, and lets them fall to the floor. Apparently, the interruption has done nothing to put a damper on his excitement — he springs free, thick, long, and hard, and another rush of liquid heat coats my core.

I can't tear my gaze away from Blake as he walks to the bed and stares down at me. Then, when he sits, his erection is close to my face. I try not to be affected, but it's impossible.

"Taste me, Jewel," he offers, and my throat tightens. I need to put my lips around him, and I want to feel his pleasure on my tongue.

I want to feel his pleasure on my tongue.

He shifts his body and pulls me back up so I'm on my knees, my mouth only inches from his gleaming shaft. When he brings me to his arousal, I don't hesitate; I simply open my lips to take him inside the recesses of my mouth.

"Yes, Jewel, just like that." He guides my head slowly up and down. I suck his velvet skin and smile around his manhood when I taste his salty flavor.

He supports my head with one hand so I won't fall against him, and he reaches around my throat with the other and glides down until he's holding my breast. He rubs his palm against my aching nipple, then pinches, making me cry out as I suck on him, and I take him deeper into my throat.

"Enough," he groans, lifting my head from him. The sight of him wet with my saliva makes my core throb.

"Please," I groan.

"I thought you wouldn't beg." I don't respond. I should've known better. I always beg while in his arms. He undoes me; that will never stop. But I bite my tongue. I can't give him more of an ego than he already has. I hear a low chuckle.

The bed shifts as I'm left on my knees with my ass arched in the air, and my hands still trapped behind my back . . . the lights shut off, leaving us in darkness. I wait for his touch . . . and nothing happens.

My body's aching, and I twist where I am, my breasts tight, my core on fire. He's going to make me beg. I refuse . . . for a little longer. I'm well aware of what he's doing, but I need him. A frustrated sigh escapes me.

"Fine! Touch me," I say in a whimper filled with frustration. Here goes my pride.

"My pleasure," he purrs before pulling me backward to the edge of the bed. Before a heartbeat passes, I feel his hot breath on the sensitive flesh of my backside. His tongue flicks out, and runs down one butt cheek and up the other before he spreads my legs wide open and licks along the lips of my core.

"More," I practically sob. The sensation of his rough tongue and hot breath are almost more than I can bear.

"Arch your back," he commands before licking my most sensitive areas, then he sucks my swollen bud into his mouth, making me cry out over and over again. Just as I begin to reach my peak . . . he stops.

"Please, Blake, don't stop now," I beg, but to no avail. A sob rips through me when I feel the bed shift, feel him draw his mouth away from where I need it most.

"It's not time yet," he tells me as he spreads my thighs wider and fits himself between them. The tip of his thickness is pressed to the outside of my core, and I wiggle in his grasp, trying to force him to enter me. With a groan, Blake finally pushes forward and does as I bid, sinking deep inside of me with one powerful thrust, taking my breath away.

He slowly pulls back, then thrusts forward over and over again, not fast enough to allow me to come, but at a pace designed to keep me on the edge of the cliff. I plead with him to free me from the mass of tension that builds higher and higher within me, but he keeps me hanging for what seems like hours.

When I can't stand it for another second, I feel him untie the knot on the belt that binds my hands, and he's laying me on my stomach. Still buried deep inside of me, he lifts my hands and begins massaging my numb arms. I hadn't realized they'd gone numb — I was so focused on the pleasure there was no room for pain.

When he's finished massaging me, he withdraws from my body, making me cry out in protest, but I'm flipped over and he's poised above me. He moves us both to the top of the bed, and my head hits the pillows.

He reaches over, switches on the bedside lamp, and looks down at me, his eyes wild with passion. "I need to see your face when I make you come," he says, and he plunges back inside me.

Blake holds nothing back, no longer interested in games. He continues rapidly thrusting in and out, his face a picture of ecstasy, and I lose focus as my body releases all of the pressure that's built over the last couple of hours. I don't try to hold back my scream.

I barely maintain consciousness when I hear his thundering groan, and feel the pulsing of his manhood as he empties himself into me, coating my slick walls. Silence engulfs us as he pulls me against his chest and holds me tight. When my heart's erratic beat settles down, I nearly don't hear his whispered words.

"It will only get better, Jewel. We're meant to be together."

Chapter Review

Chapter Forty-One

Jewel

WHEN I BREAK AWAY from the bonds of sleep, I'm disoriented. Where in heaven's name am I? The sheets don't feel like mine. My adrenaline spikes, but Blake's body is next to me, his arm draped around my back, and his heartbeat beneath my hand.

My eyes are still closed, and I savor the moment, letting my guard down as I enjoy being held with tenderness. If only I allowed myself to admit to Blake how much I need this.

The sex was wonderful — unbelievable, in fact — but right here, right now is what I need more than anything else. I *need* to be comforted by another person . . . by Blake. I shouldn't be feeling this strongly toward him, but my heart seems to have made its choice.

True, he's demanding, and he made no real promises to me, but how can I not feel emotion toward a man who's changed my world so dramatically? Would it really be so bad to take his name, if that's what he still wants?

It's bad because I'm going to fall in love with him, and that's something my fragile heart can't afford to do. I'm already too dependent on him. When he disappears for days — as he has often, in fact, since he's reappeared in my life — I've felt unmotivated, almost listless. What will it be like if I'm with him for months, or years, and then he decides to toss me aside?

Can I be tied to him without giving him my heart? Not likely. But what other choice do I have at this point? This is the fundamental question I need to answer.

"Are you hungry?"

The sound of Blake's voice jolts me out of my reverie, but unsure what to say, I say nothing. Damn. Holding my tongue is becoming such a habit around him.

"Are you in a sex coma, Jewel?" he asks with a laugh as he turns me to face him.

I'm afraid to open my eyes. Maybe if I stay as I am for a while longer, there will be no stress, no worries, nothing to upset this beautiful moment. I need a few more minutes to savor the contentment I feel at being in his arms.

"Ve haf vays of makink you talk," he says in an accent I've never heard him use before. Is he joking with me?

"I . . . uh . . . I'm awake," I finally say, letting my eyes slowly drift open.

"I think I'll enjoy this boat," he tells me as he rubs his hands up and down my back.

"I can't believe anyone would pay so much to have sex," I blurt, and then feel my cheeks turning crimson. He just shelled out millions for this boat so we could get to the end of our horizontal tango.

"I was already thinking about buying it. I came down here to take it for a spin, but got a message right when we arrived that the captain had an emergency. You in here . . . naked, sealed the decision."

"I should complain, but I feel too good," I admit, which makes him laugh. "How are you always so calm and determined?"

"I know what I want in life, and I go after it. I wanted this boat . . . and I want you. Life's one big business deal, so whether you're buying a house, a boat, a business, or planning a marriage, it can all be wrapped up in business," he says, his voice calm and practical even though none of this is *practical* to me . . . it's dang emotional.

I know what I want in life, and I go after it . . . and I want you

I pause, looking into this handsome man's eyes, then take a deep breath. It's so hard to think with a clear head when my body's so completely satisfied.

"Don't forget that my little brother comes with me, and this impacts any deals we make, Blake."

He doesn't even hesitate. "I like kids."

"Have you ever even been around them for any length of time?"

"I was a child once."

I have a hard time believing this. It more likely he sprang from the womb full-grown. I can't imagine Blake smiling with dirt smeared on his cheeks, or running around playing cops and robbers. Yes, he works on construction sites even now, but that's different from making mud pies and building forts.

"I don't think you know how to be carefree and go with the flow," I tell him. "Did you even know how to play games as a child? You're too set in your ways. I'm scared it won't be a fun and carefree experience for Justin in your home. You'll realize we're both a burden, then he's the one who will pay the price." I don't care what happens to me, but I don't want Justin to pay for my mistakes.

He's quiet for so long that I figure my words have finally gotten through to him and he's deciding to break things off. I hate the pang inside of my chest. I don't want our relationship to end. But I know it will hurt more if it ends later when I'm more attached.

"Once I decide on a course of action, I don't change my mind, Jewel. I'm not letting you go, so it's a waste your time worrying about it."

"I don't want to keep arguing. I don't know why I started it," I admit.

He rubs my shoulders for a moment. "Because you're strong and stubborn. These two things I thought would drive me crazy, actually turn me on. We do have to get dressed though." He doesn't appear pleased with this. I don't reply, and he lets me go, instantly chilling me.

He stands, and as unsure as I am about the future, I can't help but look at the beauty of his naked behind. I frown when he takes away my view by pulling up his slacks, covering up the prime view.

He turns and smiles at me as if he can read my thoughts. I blush, and hate myself for it. He comes back to the bed, leans down, and kisses me for a heart stopping moment. I sigh as he pulls back.

"I'm going to leave so you can get up and dress. Our day isn't over yet."

He turns and leaves the room. There's no fight left in me. This man desires me, and I desire him . . . and much more. I'm going to say yes. I'm going to become his wife. What this means for the two of us doesn't matter anymore, because there are no more options left. I'm in too deep, and I have to finish this ride.

My stubbornness keeps me from telling him, or maybe I'm waiting for something more. I'm a fool if that's what it is. I'll be as surprised as he is when the answer comes to me . . . and then share it with him.

Chapter Review

Blake

I WEAR OUT THE DEN'S carpet at my brother Byron's house as I pace his floor while he, Tyler, and our family friend Bill, gaze at me as if I've lost my mind. It's quite possible I have.

"I don't understand what I'm doing wrong. I've put a lot of effort into changing my ways, and to romance Jewel, and it doesn't seem to change anything," I say, my voice tight, my muscles clenched. "She's still not agreeing to marry me."

"I don't understand this at all," Byron says. He's nearly as irritated as I am. "Why don't you let this go?"

Bill chuckles. "I disagree with your brother. You have a solid plan. I also believe this has become more than a simple business deal."

"This isn't love," Byron says with a roll of his eyes. "It's lust. Don't try to mess with his head, Bill."

I look at both of them. "This isn't about the two of you, it's about me," I remind them.

Tyler sits with a lazy smile resting on his lips. "It's entertaining to see you such a mess. Does that count as it being about us?"

"Shut it," both Byron and I say as we glare at our youngest brother.

"I'm telling you, Blake, this woman means more to you than you're willing to admit," Bill says. "I'll give you a piece of unsolicited advice, though. If you treat her like shit, she'll walk away and never look back no matter how badly she wants to do the right thing by her brother. A woman can only take so much before you break her spirit."

A woman can only take so much before you break her spirit

"Give me a break," Byron says. "I can't listen to this nonsense." He rises and walks from the room. Yep, something's definitely going on with him. I'm not sure what, but we've always respected each other's choices. If he needs space, I'll give it to him. He'll come to me when he's ready.

"Byron's dealing with something," Tyler says as if reading my mind.

"The problem with all three of you is, you focus so much on other people that you don't take the time to look within yourselves," Bill says. "If you took a few moments to find out what you truly want, maybe you wouldn't be so miserable."

"Are you a counselor now?" I ask.

"I've done some counseling through the years," Bill says, not at all offended at my tone.

"I'm not sure how much advice a craggy old man can give," Tyler says with a laugh. Bill shoots him a glare.

"Don't knock my age, boy. It won't take too long before you're knocking on the same door."

Tyler looks horrified at the idea of getting old. I'm not exactly thrilled about it, but it doesn't scare me. It's simply a part of the circle of life.

"This marriage will help both of us. I don't know why she has to be a pain about it," I say, bringing the conversation back to my problem.

Bill meets my eyes. "This is about being in control. Maybe if you told her your true feelings she'd accept the proposal."

"I've spoken about feelings. Yes, I like control . . . and you know why. That doesn't mean I haven't been good to her," I remind him.

"You've never hurt her?" Bill pushes.

This makes me pause. "Not physically," I say with confidence.

"I don't know, Blake. She's pretty broken. She needs a friend, and she needs someone who will give her what she needs most without taking too much more from her. She doesn't have enough left to give and still survive."

"I agree," Tyler says. "You have the power to either break her or save her. The choice is in your hands."

You have the power

to either break her

or save her

"I don't want to break her," I say, moving over to the liquor cabinet and pouring myself a stiff drink. I don't down it in one shot. Instead, I move to the window and stare out while I sip the fine bourbon. How has my life become this complicated? It makes no sense. We've all had a plan for a long time, and it's never come even close to breaking. Now, it seems nothing can go right.

"Then do what's right and help her without her agreeing to a marriage of convenience," Bill suggests.

"If I do that she might walk away," I say. This makes my throat tighten.

"Yes, she might, but she could also choose to stay, then you'd have no doubt that it's her choice, not because you paid for obedience," Bill says.

"I don't know . . ." My voice trails off. I can't look at Bill or my brother. I'm afraid I'll do exactly what they want if I do . . . and I don't want to take a chance that she'll leave me.

"I loved you from the moment you were born. I'll love you to the day I die. I have faith this will all work out," Bill says.

"I wish I had as much faith as you do," I murmur, the words almost too quiet for him to hear.

Bill stands. He moves over and pats my shoulder. "You'll do the right thing." With this he turns and exits the room.

Tyler chuckles. "You really know how to clear out a space," he says.

"You're a pain in the ass," I tell him.

"I know. It's only one of a million reasons why you love me," Tyler says. Then he exits the room, leaving me as the last man standing. I stay for a long time.

When I finally do leave, I'm no closer to figuring out what I'm going to do . . . or how I'm going to get what I want.

Chapter Review

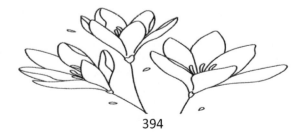

Jewel

I WALK INTO TYLER'S home in shock as I hear the chatter of voices. Why did I accept his invitation to come over? He said it's a company party, and it's good for me to rub elbows with people. I'm still not in the mood . . . and it feels wrong to be going to Tyler's without Blake.

"Jewel, you're here." I turn and McKenzie's walking up to me, looking poised and effortless as usual.

"I honestly don't know why," I tell her nervously.

"You came because it's good to get out into the real world."

I'm feeling off because I visited with my brother today. It was another heartbreaking experience. He clung on tight to me and begged me to take him away from the foster home. I told him I was doing everything in my power to make it happen. Am I really, though?

The answer is no. I need to suck it up and agree to marry Blake. I'm going to get the courage tonight and say yes. Whatever happens down the road after, I'll figure it out. I can't leave Justin in a place he isn't loved for weeks, or possibly months.

I'm pulled out of my thoughts as Tyler moves toward us, his trademark smile resting on his lips. "Hello, Beautiful, I've missed you," he says before wrapping me in his arms and lifting me into a bone-crunching hug.

"Do you have these parties often?" I ask when he finally lets me go.

"I like to have people over. It's no big deal," he says. He puts my arm through his and leads us out where too many people are milling about. "Besides, Jewel, you need people in your corner." He points out a man engaged in conversation. "That man over there is a DA. The guy he's speaking to is a judge. It will benefit you to mingle, and to show all of these people what a great guardian you'll be for Justin."

"I'm not good at mingling," I say. I have to stave off panic.

"It's a piece of cake," he tells me. "Simply walk up to someone and ask a question. Everyone loves to talk about themselves. Ask about their families, work, hobbies, and interests. You can have an entire conversation by only saying a dozen words. The beauty of this is you'll get to know them, and they'll walk away feeling like they've had a great conversation."

"I'll give it a go," I say.

McKenzie walks away with me and starts introducing me to people. I'm soon lost as I move around the large property, with no chance of keeping all of the people's stories straight. If I can meet someone who can help me win Justin back sooner, it's all worth the stress and chaos.

After a couple of hours, I hide in a dark corner to give myself a moment to breathe . . . and instead find Blake leaning against a wall looking devastatingly handsome . . . as usual.

"Having a good time, Jewel?" he casually asks.

"Not the best time of my life," I honestly tell him.

"Can I help?" he asks. He takes my hands and leads me away from the partygoers to a dark gazebo with benches. The two of us sit, relieving my aching feet.

"No, I'm not in the best of moods tonight, and it's difficult to speak to strangers. I recognize some people from the office, but there are far more people who I don't know," I tell him.

"I should take you out more," he says.

"This one's on me, not you," I tell him. I realize Blake puts a lot on his shoulders. He might initially come across as arrogant and controlling, but it's because he's harder on himself than he is on everyone else.

His hand's in mine as he strokes my palm, lowering my stress the longer I'm with him. I can't look him in the eyes though. We're surrounded by people, even if they aren't directly in front of us at this very moment. When I look into his eyes, I'm well aware of what happens next.

"I'm trying to give you more respect, Jewel, trying to be a better person," he says, leaving me absolutely shocked. "My brothers seem to think I act too much like an ass."

I chuckle. "You said it, not me."

"A person can change," he says.

I think on this for a moment. "Not too many do," I slowly tell him. I don't want to fight with him though, not when he's being open.

"I'm trying, Jewel. I've decided it's better to listen to others when more than one person says old Blake isn't providing *customer satisfaction*," he replies as he continues stroking my hand. I don't know what this means.

My head's spinning as he moves to caress my knuckles. "I . . . uh . . . I don't know what to think."

"You don't have to think, Jewel. Very few things in life are black and white, and sometimes it's better to trust our gut. We can't predict what will happen every minute of every day, but we can learn to roll with the changes. Or the punches. Or whatever cliché you want to use."

"It's easy to think like that when a person doesn't have a lot to lose," I tell him.

"That makes sense," he says. Then he grips my chin and forces me to look in his eyes. It's dark out, but there's enough light for me to see his smile.

"I bought a house," he spits out, leaving me stunned.

"A house?" I ask, confused.

"We're going to have a child living with us, so I figure we need a yard." In his world it's easy to want something and immediately get it. How nice would that be?

"You bought a house because of Justin and me?" My head's spinning all over again.

"Yes, for the three of us," he says. He sighs as he allows me to look away again. "I've never wanted to be in a relationship before . . . at least not a real one. We're in one, though, whether we care to admit it or not. It's not perfect, but what relationship in life is? We'll have problems, and we'll work through them. At least we'll have a house to do it in."

I cling to the one thing that I can focus on and manage to give him the barest of smiles.

"Are you admitting that you aren't perfect, Blake?"

He looks horrified at this statement. "I'd never say such a thing." The laughter in his voice makes me realize the man truly does have a good sense of humor. Maybe it's hard for him to let this side of him show . . . like it's hard for me to allow myself to be vulnerable.

"I don't know, it sounds to me like you're admitting you aren't perfect," I push.

"Well, to be honest, anyone who knows me realizes that I'm about as close to perfection as it gets," he says with a cocky grin.

"I wish I had half of your self-confidence."

"Why shouldn't I? I know who I am, and I know what I want. To top it off, I also *always* get what I go after."

"Yeah. Yeah. I get it. You're the cat's meow," I say, trying to keep a straight face, but not succeeding. I smile, as if we're in this intimate bubble I don't care to pop.

"Things are rarely black and white," he says after a heartbeat. This is his vulnerable side he rarely shows. I'm well aware there's more to his story than he's shared.

I know who I am, and

I know what I want

"I know, Blake, probably more than anyone else," I say. He turns so we can see each other again, and I watch as he fights whatever demons reside inside him.

"I'm about to do something I've never done before," he says.

I feel like this is a make-or-break moment for us. "What are you going to do?"

He pauses for so long I wonder if he's already changing his mind. But then he sighs, not turning away from me this time, raw determination in his tone.

"I'm going to tell you the truth. If you can give me a chance when I'm finished, it's worth it. Whatever you choose, though, you're getting your brother back . . . and very soon. The wheels are already spinning."

He stops for a moment as my heart thunders in my ears. What's coming next? I'm here . . . and there's nothing in me that's telling me to run.

Chapter Review

Chapter Forty Four

Blake

I T'S TIME TO TELL Jewel about my family. I'm aware if I don't do something drastic, I'll lose her. This means I need to give a piece of myself up, or else I'll be without her . . . and that's unacceptable.

I'm thankful to my brother and Bill for talking to me, grateful I listened. I'm so used to getting what I want, no matter what I have to do to get it, that somewhere along the way I've forgotten the basic rule that a person gets more with honey than vinegar. I've never tried to sugarcoat anything, but maybe it's time to take some valuable lessons from my youngest brother. I look Jewel in the eyes, then speak, trying to show honesty in my expression.

"You already know that my family's incredibly messed up, right?"

She warily looks at me. "I know there's a story to be told."

"I grew up wealthy. My father was a *very* rich man, and my mother . . . well, my mother was a gold-digging bitch."

Jewel's eyes pop wide open. "Surely, she couldn't have been that bad."

"What do you think of, Jewel, when you hear the word *mother*? Whatever adjectives come to mind *can't* be used to describe the woman who birthed me. She was vain, egotistical, and out to get whatever she could. I don't feel even a glimmer of emotion — unless contempt counts — when describing my mother."

"Is that why you hold everything so close to the vest, Blake? Is that why you push people away from you?"

"That's certainly a part of it."

"But a person can only use past experience for so long to justify being a jerk. At some point you have to take responsibility for your actions." I can't help but agree. But instead of addressing her remark, I continue with my story.

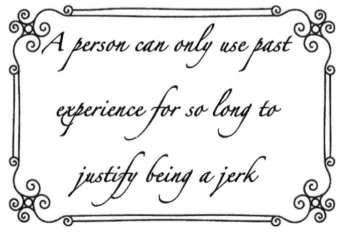

A person can only use past experience for so long to justify being a jerk

"Byron and I remember everything that happened . . . *vividly* — all of the fights, all of the underhanded things our mother did, and the whipped man our father became. She couldn't leave him and walk away with the money because she'd signed an unbreakable prenup. Sure, she could've gotten a lot of money for child support, but it wouldn't have been enough to cover the lifestyle she'd grown accustomed to, *and* she didn't want us. She liked that we had a nanny and she didn't have to deal with us. We barely saw her, and we certainly didn't talk to her. Tyler was too young to be affected by her attitude and actions, but Byron and I remember her very well."

"Lots of children have parents who don't live up to the dream," Jewel points out. "But they don't take that as an excuse to treat everyone around them badly without the least bit of guilt."

"I can't deny that. But how many children watch their parents get killed right before their eyes?"

"Wait! What do you mean?"

When Jewel takes my hand. I'm aware she's trying to comfort me, even if she doesn't realize she's doing it. It's a start, a start I'll take.

"My mother decided she didn't want to be with my father any longer. And she didn't want anything to do with my brothers and me. So she hatched a plan to have my father killed. Because her sons were nothing to her, she wasn't worried about the fallout. If we got hurt or killed in the shuffle, so be it. She could garner more attention at the loss of children than simply the loss of a husband. That's how that evil hag thought."

"That's insane. There's no possible way anything like that can happen," Jewel exclaims, her fingers tightening on my hand.

"It did happen, Jewel. I've told you more than once that the world isn't black and white. People aren't always who they're supposed to be."

"I'm sorry, Blake. I really am. Please tell me what happened."

"My mother was seeing a man, and she told him that if he killed her husband, she'd marry him and share the vast fortune her husband would leave behind. Apparently, the man she was seeing knew she was as big a liar with him as she was with my father. He somehow found out her ultimate plan was to play the victim, throw him to the cops, and run off into the sunset with all of her hundreds of millions of dollars, the money she'd get in my father's will. Her lover told her he was going along with her plan, but the entire time, he had his own agenda. He might not have been smart, but he was angry as hell."

"What were his plans?" Jewel asks.

"I was ten when it happened. My brothers and I were watching a movie in the family room when we heard shouting in the hallway. We ignored the noise — it wasn't abnormal to hear raised voices in our house. We turned up the volume and continued watching our cartoon."

"But this shouting was different," Jewel says when I pause for too long.

"Yes, this shouting was different. Suddenly, these two guys came into the room, and they were pushing my parents ahead of them. Before we knew what was going on, they had each of my parents tied to a chair, and then they bound us, and set us on the couch. I'll never forget the look in my mother's eyes. They were practically glowing with excitement. I thought it had to be some sort of game because she looked anything but worried."

"How could she not be worried?" she asks. "These men bound her."

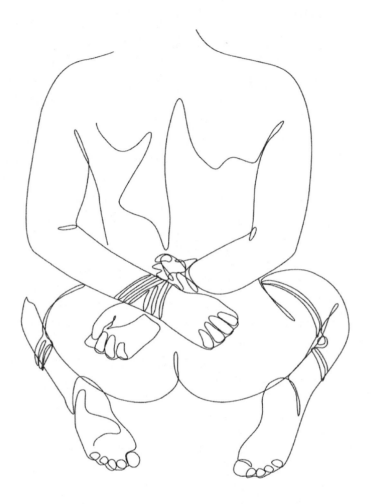

"Yes, but you see, that was all a part of the plan. She couldn't get away unscathed, or the cops would never buy her story. My mother's sick and twisted setup was to have her boyfriend *rape* her and then kill her husband. And this plan included us," I say with a disgusted snort, "because we had to be witnesses to what happened, so when the cops asked, we could say the men hurt her too."

I can see the horror in Jewel's eyes, and she holds on to me so hard, her fingernails dig into my hand. Strangely enough, the pain stabilizes me enough to continue.

"Things obviously didn't go the way my mother intended them to. She figured that out pretty fast, and that's when I saw panic enter her eyes. Her boyfriend told her he knew she was a sadistic bitch, someone out to get anything she could. He told my father and us her entire plot. My dad was weak. He started sobbing, and begged the men to spare his life. They were amused. They began beating him, and his blood splashed across the room. Some of it landed on my mom, some even hit us." I stop to catch my breath.

"Finally," I continue, "our father passed out from the pain, and the men got tired of wasting their energy on him. One of the guys looked right into my eyes and smiled while saying, *"Take this as a life lesson kid. If you let a woman screw you, this is how you'll end up."* Then he put his gun against my father's temple and pulled the trigger. My mother screamed as my dad's brains splattered over the side of her face."

"Oh my gosh, Blake," Jewel whispers, and she's now sobbing.

I have to look away from her. I'll never finish my story if I focus on the sympathy in her eyes. And I *need* to finish.

"My mother thanked the man, then she begged for her life, just like my father had. He laughed at her while he ran the gun up and down her face. He told her if she pleased him really well, he might let her live. The next hour was almost worse than any other part of the evening, because that's exactly what she did, even as the sickening smell our father's blood was filling the room. We closed our eyes, but we heard everything. The two men beat the hell out of my mother while doing unimaginable things to her at the same time. At one point I opened my eyes because she told them to go ahead and kill us too, that we would tell on them if they didn't. She looked at me as she said it. Blood was dripping from her mouth, and all I saw was hatred in her eyes." A strange tightness in my throat shocks me. Why should this upset me? I hate my mother and even hate my father. This story shouldn't affect me anymore . . . but obviously it still does.

"Blake, oh, Blake, I'm so sorry," Jewel says as she rises. Before I can stop her, she sits in my lap and wraps her arms around me.

The tightness in my throat grows harder to fight, but fight it I do. I need to keep talking, to get this over with. It's several moments before I continue, and when I do, my voice is flat. I refuse to keep letting emotion overwhelm me.

"When the men grew bored, they shot my mother in the head and left her lying on the floor, then threw my father over her. I'll never forget the sight of my parents' blood seeping from their bodies. To this day I won't own red carpet." Jewel isn't impressed by my attempt at a joke.

"Don't do that, Blake. Don't try to make light of this to show how strong you are. I know you're strong, I get it, but there are some things no one's strong enough to deal with . . . and this qualifies."

I nod. "They didn't even look at us again before they turned and walked away. My mother had given the staff the day off, because she didn't want adult witnesses, so my brothers and I spent the whole night tied to the couch in a room with our dead parents. When the maid came in the next day, she found us and called the police."

"But every time you close your eyes, it's like being right back there, isn't it?" Jewel asks.

"Not every time, Jewel . . . not since meeting you," I tell her.

"Blake . . ." she begins but I can tell she doesn't know what to say.

"I'm not trying to put this on your shoulders, however, since you've come into my life, it's been different. I don't know what it is, but I'm sleeping better. I want . . . more for my life. I don't want you to go."

She's silent for a while as she snuggles against me. I can practically feel the fight within her as she tries to figure out what to say. I don't love her next words, but she's not pulling away, and for now, it's enough.

"That's a lot of responsibility to put on my shoulders, Blake."

"I'm simply speaking the truth."

"You aren't what you portray to the world, are you?" she asks. I might have shared my story with her, but I also don't want to give her false illusions of who I am. I carefully draw her head back so I can look into her eyes.

"I'm still cold, Jewel. Around you, I *want* to be different, but I'll never fully change," I warn before leaning down and gently taking her lips. I don't want to hurt her. I *need* this woman with me, but I need her to know this is who I am, and this isn't something I can change about myself. Yes, I've been through a traumatic experience, and I still make bad choices in life . . . but I always own my choices.

"I don't think you're as cold as you want the world to think you are," she says. When I'm clearly about to reply, she holds up her hand to stop me. "We're both screwed up, Blake, probably too screwed up to discover real happiness. So, you know what?" She pauses long enough for me to be concerned.

"What?" I ask, the pain of my horrible memory slowly fading while she rests within my arms.

She gives a half-hearted smile. "I'll marry you. I'll do what we both need."

It takes a few moments for her words to sink in. I don't express the triumph I expected at her finally saying she'll be mine. This isn't how I want her to be mine — not at all. I want more, but I don't know what *more* is.

"I don't want a pity acceptance, Jewel."

"Whether you want it or not, you have it. Have you changed your mind about getting married, Blake?"

This stops me. "No, Jewel, I still want to marry you. It won't be a typical marriage filled with a bended knee and roses every night. I don't want to mislead you." I want to buy her flowers, though . . . and shock of all shocks, it's difficult for me *not* to drop to my knees for her.

"I'd never think such a thing," she says, and her sad sigh makes the tightness reappear in my throat.

I have to push these odd emotions aside, though, because I finally have what I wanted for a long time. I won't allow the guilt consuming me to change the course our lives are about to take. Jewel *will* be my wife. We'll have to wait to see what comes next . . . because I can handle just about anything as long as she stays right where I want her most.

Chapter Review

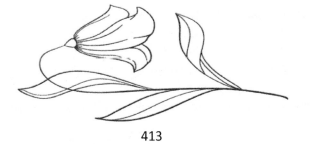

Chapter
Forty
Five

Jewel

S AVE YOURSELF!"
Startled, I lose my hold on my cup of coffee, but am thankful when it bounces into the sink. Timing is everything. I can't help but smile when I turn to see Justin running into the room with Blake hot on his tail.

"Help, Sissy," Justin hollers, the words scrambled because he's laughing so hard.

"There's no help for the two of you," I say with mock weariness, and begin laughing when Justin's socks make him skid across the well-polished tile floors. He lands in a heap near my feet. Thanks to the counter, Blake manages to come to a stop, though just barely.

I've been in fog for the last three weeks. When Blake said he could get things done, he hadn't been fooling around. We had a court date within one week — for mere mortals, that would be miraculous — and we were granted temporary custody of Justin. The three of us have been living in Blake's new house since Justin was removed from foster care.

So quickly it still makes my head spin, we've developed a weekday routine. We get up together and have breakfast, and then Justin goes to school with either Blake or me, and we both head to work. I love my job more and more each day. It gives me purpose now that I'm not worried about Justin, and for the first time in a long while, I'm in control.

Maybe it's not *complete* control, because I'm still unsure of where Blake and I stand, but at least there's stability in my life, and most importantly, Justin's with me. I won't do anything to screw this up.

One thing truly baffles me. Blake hasn't touched me since we've moved in together. I don't share a room with him. Since the time I agreed to our marriage of convenience, I haven't heard him utter another word about it. I fear this is all nothing but a dream, preventing me from bringing it up to him, though it's constantly on my mind.

Blake's standing before me in a low-slung pair of sweats and a tight T-shirt, his normal morning attire. When he reaches for a mug and pours himself some coffee, I can't help but appreciate his incredible physique.

I also wonder whether he thinks this togetherness isn't such a great idea after all. He's amazing with Justin. Maybe he just needs someone to make his business deal go through, but in the meantime, he's getting attached to my little brother.

Elsa works for us, cleaning and cooking on occasion, but other than that, Blake splits the household responsibilities with me. The two of us seem to be nothing more than housemates . . . and I don't like it.

"What are your plans tonight?" he asks as he gets out cereal for Justin while my brother reaches into the cupboard for a bowl.

"The ladies at work asked if I wanted to go out for a drink," I tell him. "I'm pretty excited about it. It's been a long time since I was asked to go anywhere with co-workers — not since before my mother died."

"Oh, that's good," he replies, but the expression on his face doesn't match his words.

"Is something wrong?" I ask as I wrack my brain for something I might've missed. "Is something going on later today that I forgot about?"

"Not at all," he replies, but all of the joy I saw when he and Justin first hurtled into the kitchen is gone. "Go get ready for work."

I nod, but a sense of guilt follows me while I get ready for work. Blake doesn't say anything when I leave to take Justin to school, then head to the office. What am I feeling guilty about? It makes zero sense. Have I done something wrong? Should I not go out? He's encouraged me to have some girl time before. I haven't left Justin's side since he came. I'm confused now.

I push away these feelings as I walk through the doors of the beautiful building. My job might not always be thrilling, but I had enough excitement in the last year to last me a lifetime. What I crave now is peace, normalcy, and the absence of any further disasters in my life.

Do I miss the passion I used to share with Blake? Sure I do, but I've lived most of my life without having it, so I can certainly get used to living without it again. I might have a chance to find true love one day — both romance *and* passion. It isn't like I'm an old maid and past my prime. Heck, it's never too late to find love. Justin will be home with me for the next eight years, but a lot of people have patchwork families. If only the thought of being with another man was in the least bit appealing. When five o'clock finally arrives, I'm more than ready for some girl time.

What I crave now is peace, normalcy, and the absence of any further disasters in my life

"Jewel, let's get the heck out of here. It's Friday and I want to find some cold drinks and some seriously hot men." I look up at my co-worker, Stacy, a single mom in her late twenties who possibly parties a bit too much, but seems like a fun person to hit the town with.

"Who's coming?" I ask after I shut down my computer.

"A couple of women from accounting, and a new receptionist. I hope you plan on staying out late," Stacy says as we make our way to the elevator.

"Not too late. I have my brother to get home to."

"He's fine with Blake. Let's have some fun." I ignore this. I'm already feeling guilty and thinking this wasn't the best idea. I go from excited to guilt-ridden in seconds.

"Are we meeting them?" I ask.

"We're carpooling. Jenna's agreed to be the designated driver tonight," Stacy says, and she grabs my hand and leads me to a minivan in the corner of the garage. Four other women are standing by, waiting.

"I had a crap week," Jenna says. "Let's get to the bar before all of the tables are gone." We pile in. It doesn't take long to get to the bar, and within an hour I'm ready to go home. This isn't my scene, and I'd much rather be spending time with Justin — okay, and possibly with Blake too — than with a bunch of women intent on getting plastered.

"May I have this dance?"

I look up at a nicely dressed man gazing down at me as if I'm his next meal. The refusal is on the tip of my tongue when Stacy leans over and whispers. "Yum . . . he's beyond hot. Go for it."

I'm pushed from my chair and led to the dance floor. Maybe it's the two drinks I had, and maybe it's depression from feeling unwanted by the man I desperately want to need me, but one dance turns into two . . . and then three, and soon I'm sitting at a corner table with Frank. The guy's telling me the story of his entire life! And I couldn't care less, but somehow, I'm still sitting with him.

The only thing keeping me here is the hope that maybe by receiving a little bit of male attention I can somehow push away my all-consuming feelings for Blake . . . so far, it isn't happening.

A long and painful hour later, I'm waiting for a break in the conversation, an acceptable opportunity for me to excuse myself. I'm not attracted to Frank and hope to make it home in time to watch a movie with Justin and Blake. My plan to not think about Blake is failing miserably.

A night on the couch with a huge bowl of popcorn is more my idea of a perfect Friday night than sitting in a bar with a man who's starting to drop heavy hints about the way he wants the evening to progress.

"I've enjoyed spending time with you tonight," Frank says as he reaches across the table and takes my hand before I can pull it away. "I'd like to continue this somewhere . . . quieter." He runs his fingers across my knuckles, and I shudder, *not* a good shudder.

The guy isn't getting the normal social cues I'm giving him, cues that should tell him I'm not interested in what he has to offer. But before I'm able to respond to his suggestion, he continues.

"We're both attractive people with needs, and the two of us have a connection," he says with what he probably thinks is a seductive grin. This needs to stop.

"Frank, I appreciate the dancing tonight, and the drink you bought me, and the company, but I'm not interested in more. I wanted to come out with my girlfriends for a few hours. I'm sure there are plenty of women here looking for something that might last until morning," I tell him with a gentle smile.

"Oh, I wasn't expecting that. It seemed like we had something going on tonight, something more than just . . . well, *that*," he says, still holding my fingers. "Is there any possibility you might change your mind?"

"No. I've had a rough year, and I'm not on the market. Sorry, Frank."

He looks disappointed, but certainly not devastated, which makes me feel better. And why would he be upset? It isn't like we know each other, not after an hour in a loud club.

I look away from him to all the people, men leaning against the bar and flirting with women they've never met before, groups sitting around tables and engaging in serious people-watching, and I can almost guess who's hoping to hook up with someone, and who just wants a little down time after a long workweek. I'm in neither category. I simply wanted some female bonding, but it seems that isn't going to happen.

"I'm out celebrating tonight anyway, Jewel. I wasn't really looking to hook up with someone, but I saw you and couldn't turn away, so I thought *what the heck*. But I get it. I was in a relationship last year that threw me for a loop when it ended. I haven't been serious with anyone since."

"I'm sorry about that. Maybe a bar isn't the best place to go hunting for a nice girl."

"Yeah, you're probably right about that," he says with a chuckle. "But, on the other hand, I found you, and you're certainly nice." This makes me laugh.

"I'm ready to go home," I tell him.

Frank stands and holds out a hand. "Let me walk you out."

I give him my hand and stand, allowing him to escort me back to the table where my co-workers — other than poor Jenna — are feeling a buzz from all of the alcohol they've been consuming. It barely registers when I tell them I'm calling a cab and heading home.

"Good friends?" Frank asks.

I laugh. "Co-workers."

The valet calls a cab and Frank waits with me in the chilly evening air. When the cab arrives, I turn to thank him, and he pulls me in for a hug. "Thank you for a wonderful evening. I hope to run into you again," he says, and I can see he's hoping to get my number.

"I don't think that will happen, but it was nice talking with you tonight."

"I can always hope," he says as he holds open the cab door. I don't bother replying this time. This is my last ladies' night out. I tried and it failed.

The cab ride doesn't take long. When I pull up to the house, the lights are off in the living room, and my hopes of a movie and popcorn are dashed. It isn't all that late in the evening, but a lot has happened these past two weeks for Justin: a new school, a new home, and moving in with a man he doesn't know, although he's quickly come to like and respect Blake.

My brother's a real trouper to have such a positive attitude after so many changes were thrown at him. I pay the cab driver, make my way up the path to the front door, and fumble in my purse for what has to be a full minute before I find my keys and let myself inside.

All of a sudden, loneliness like I haven't experienced recently weighs me down, and I fight the urge to run to Blake's room and demand he give me some TLC. But this will only ease the loneliness for a short time. I need a long-term solution.

If I wasn't so afraid of rocking the boat, I might open up and tell him how I feel. But what if he's somehow disgusted and gets rid of me? Justin's life will once again be thrown into upheaval. No. It's better to go with the flow, even if I'm constantly fighting the current.

I set down my purse, and smile when I hear a squeak. The kitten we got the day after Justin came home is winding its tiny orange body around my feet.

"At least someone missed me," I whisper. I lift up the little girl and nuzzle her soft fur, delighting in the purrs she releases amid her high-pitched mews of satisfaction at being held. When I step into the living room and find Blake sitting back with only a dim lamp lit and an unreadable expression on his face, I stop.

It's better to go with the flow, even if I'm constantly fighting the current

"Why are you sitting in the dark?" I ask.

When Blake's home, he's almost always working, either in his office or in his favorite chair in the living room, and one thing I know about him is that he likes a lot of lights on. I'm always turning them off in the rooms he exits. I move closer and see a bottle of bourbon on the table beside him, and an empty crystal glass next to it. This doesn't look good.

As I draw nearer, I notice his muscles are tense, and the look in his eyes isn't as casual as I first thought. No, his eyes seem cold . . . or hot . . . or something in between. I've seen this look before, and I don't like it.

"Is everything okay, Blake? Is Justin okay?" I ask, getting ready to bolt up the stairs to assure myself that Justin's still here, and he's fine.

"Justin went to sleep an hour ago. It's been a busy week for him," Blake says, and my heartbeat slows the tiniest bit until he stands and moves toward me.

I don't know why, but I take a step backward. There's something dangerous in his eyes, and every muscle in my body is screaming at me to run. This is foolish, but at the same time, my instincts are often right. Is he going to box me in? Up against the wall? Damn! This excites me.

"Put down the kitten, Jewel," he tells me as he draws closer.

I've almost forgotten about the kitten. "Oh," I say as I free the little fur ball and watch as she runs off, probably to destroy something.

"You're worrying me, Blake. What's the matter?" I take another involuntary step backward.

"I gave you time to adjust, waited for you to tell me you're ready, moved us in together, reunited you and your brother, and *still* I've waited, but I haven't gotten the green light from you," he says. "Not once."

I step back again. "What in the world are you talking about, Blake?"

"It's been over a month since the last time we were together — *over a month*, Jewel. And then tonight you go out with another man," he says, his muscles flexing, his eyes sparking.

"What? I didn't go out with a man," I heatedly tell him.

"Max was at the bar," he tells me.

"I didn't see him," I begin before stopping to think. "Max . . . then why in the world didn't he give me a ride home?"

"I wanted him there to make sure you were safe. Apparently, you were more than safe," Blake says, his voice menacingly low.

"I don't need someone spying on me, Blake." I don't say anything more, though.

Blake decides our conversation is over, because one second we're facing off against each other, and the next second I'm completely out of breath. He reaches out and grabs me, hauling my body against his before lifting me in the air . . . then we're moving — right toward his bedroom . . . finally.

Chapter Review

Chapter Forty Six

Jewel

BLAKE PUSHES HIS bedroom door open with his foot, and shuts it the same way. I'm so shocked by his behavior that I've failed to utter a single protest. And then I'm airborne for a brief moment before the bed catches me. I'm trying to clear my head, but his scent envelopes me, and all I can do is inhale the musk of the only man I've ever desired.

Still, he's behaving like a brute, and I briefly think about stopping him — for about one second — then he's on the bed with me, his legs pinning mine down as he pulls off my coat, shirt, and bra in a quick sweep, leaving my upper half bare for his viewing. He moves to the side, but only to yank off my slacks and minuscule panties, then he rips his own clothes away.

It's so fast — all of it's happening too fast. Blake stretches his naked body on top of mine, and the feel of his solid chest pressing against my tender breasts makes me cry out his name in pleasure.

"Yes, Jewel," he tells me, "I *only* want my name on your lips." He kisses me hard, and I groan against his lips. I can't breathe because I'm so turned on. He leaves my mouth and I whimper as his lips trail down the side of my throat, where he can feel the pounding of my pulse.

"I can't believe I refrained from touching you for so long," he says, and he circles my nipples with his lips and nips the tender peaks before soothing them with his tongue.

He slowly moves his mouth between my breasts and he's kissing me again, invading my mouth with his tongue while his solid erection presses against my core. I spread my legs wider as my body begs his to complete me.

"Please, Blake, please fill me," I groan. I plant my feet on the bed and lift my hips, urging him to join us.

It's been too long since we last made love, and I want fulfillment; I want the two of us to be one, and I want it right now. My passion is overwhelming in its intensity.

Blake doesn't answer my plea; instead he grips my hair and angles my head the way he wants it, the better to devour my mouth, while he rubs his hardness on the outside of my wet heat, letting it lubricate him, to prepare him for entry.

"Now, Blake, please," I say again as I push against him. I rake my fingernails down his back and grip his muscular behind in my desperation to have him inside me. If he wants me to beg, I'll beg.

"How much do you want me, Jewel?" he asks as he reaches for my hands, takes them both, and, holding my wrists with one hand, pushes my arms above my head.

"I want you, Blake. I need you. I need you now," I practically sob. To hell with power games. I'm not in the mood for anything but completion.

He rewards me for these words by reaching between us and slipping two fingers inside my hot core while stroking my aching bundle of nerves with his thumb. I cry out when only a few flicks of his masterful fingers bring me release, my body tightening, my heart thundering.

"Yes," he sighs. "You're so responsive, my Jewel." And before I think about catching my breath, he pulls his fingers from me and moves them up to cup my breast and squeeze my nipple as he thrusts inside of me with so much force it knocks out my breath.

Time loses meaning, and something seems to come over Blake. I feel his thrusts, each and every one of them. Moans tumble from my throat while he growls words of praise and pleasure almost in time to our frantic lovemaking.

Sweat slicks our bodies as the inferno builds higher and higher, and each time Blake ravages my mouth along with my body, it's almost as if I'm floating above myself, watching this exquisite moment from afar. I'm forever lost to this man, because no matter how long we're apart, the instant I'm in his arms again, I belong to him, *only* him, and it's right where I need and want to be.

"Come for me, Jewel. Squeeze me tight," he commands.

I give him exactly what he wants. My body lets go and I cry out his name over and over again as my body convulses around him, feeling the release in every cell, every atom in my body. He continues pumping, drawing the orgasm out, making me shatter over and over again until I can't bear it any longer.

I'm floating above, and when my pleasure begins to ebb, he cries out as he tenses, buried deep inside me, shaking as his own climax washes through him, his seed buried deep within my womb.

Blake collapses against me, our bodies burning up. I tightly cling to him, not willing to let the moment go, not willing to free him from my hold. Fear, fear that this moment will end the second we speak, keeps me cleaving desperately to his embrace.

But the moment fades all too soon, and I'm bereft when Blake rolls off me. My limbs grow cold, and an ache and emptiness unlike anything I've known fills me.

"You belong to me, Jewel. I *won't* share you with others," Blake warns. "Do you hear that?" He reaches for me again, pulling me close to his side.

"What are you talking about, Blake?"

"The man at the bar. You shouldn't have done that."

"The man at the bar?" I'm lost for a few moments in my sex-induced coma. Then my eyes snap open, and I draw back so I can look at him. "Wait! Is that what this was about? Another man spoke to me, so you had to screw me into submission to show me you're better?" I ask with horror.

"No," he says, his voice almost deadly. "I was holding back because I thought that was what you wanted — needed. When you allowed yourself to be vulnerable with another man, I decided it was time for me to remind you I'm here," he tells me, not releasing his hold on me. "Ready, and *definitely* waiting."

"But . . . this makes no sense, Blake. We've seen each other almost daily for weeks and you haven't touched me. Why would speaking to another man upset you?"

"I told you, I was trying to give you space. But I'm done with that. I'm so hungry for you, I can't think straight. And you're just as hungry for me. We belong together." He rolls back on top of me and presses his manhood against my core. I'm not surprised when my body instantly responds to his.

I'm so hungry for you, I can't think straight

"I assumed you didn't want me anymore," I tell him. While lying in his arms fully naked, I can't hide any of my body's secrets from him. I might as well open my heart too. If he's going to crush me, I'd rather he do it in one fell swoop than keep dragging the suffering out.

"You assumed wrong, Jewel. What we have is a failure to communicate, and that's going to end right now. I *will* marry you soon."

He doesn't proclaim love, and this hurts. But at least I have him. It doesn't seem our passion is ending soon, so I should have him for a very long time. Will it be enough? I hope so, because he's an obsession . . . and I can't walk away.

I cover my sadness by reaching for his head and pulling him down to me, being the one to initiate the kiss this time. When he groans into my mouth, the sense of emptiness begins to ease. Yes, our relationship is nowhere near perfect or conventional, but it's working.

"I want you, Blake," I say, instead of saying what I so desperately want to say. Blake doesn't reply. His body joins with mine, and he loves me again and again until the early hours of the morning. This is enough. I'm convinced I'll believe this if I say it enough times.

Chapter Review

Chapter Forty Seven

Jewel

THE SUN IS SETTING as I walk by Blake's side, my hand in his, sounds from his old neighborhood our background music. I'm taking it all in, and grateful that we're here. This is progress . . . This is about so much more than just a walk. This is us in an almost normal relationship . . . and I love it.

Justin's hanging with his new favorite uncle Tyler and assured us to take as long as we want. I think we're both smothering him a little too much and he wants some fun uncle bonding time where he isn't asked every two minutes if he's okay.

"I have a lot of fond memories from living in this neighborhood," he tells me, seeming far mellower than I've seen him before.

"Yes, growing up with good people can do that. Before my mother died, she was my best friend. I don't understand how people can so easily dismiss their parents these days. Kids think they're smarter than their parents, and they simply don't value them. I'd give anything for one more day with my mom to tell her thank you for all she did for me." As soon as the words come out, I want to take them back. His fingers tense while holding my hand. Before I can apologize, he speaks.

"Not all parents deserve honor or respect," he says. "And not all parents are those who gave you their DNA." I fully agree with this. Family can be so much more than blood.

"Do you consider Bill and Vivian Berkshire as replacement parents?" I ask as we stop in front of the home Bill still occupies, though it doesn't appear as if Blake and I are going inside.

"No. Bill was best friends with my grandpa, so they were far more like grandparents, but they've always had all of our respect. It hurt when Vivian died. And there's nothing we won't do for Bill today . . . if the stubborn old man will simply let us," Blake says with a rare laugh.

"That's a bit like the pot calling the kettle black, don't you think?"

"Yes, I know. But there's stubborn and then there's *stubborn*," he says with a roll of the eyes.

"If it makes you feel better, I'll let you think Bill's more stubborn than you," I tell him.

We're moving forward. I'm a little disappointed not to stop in and see Bill, but I'm not sure what Blake has planned tonight. He parked at the coffee shop around the corner, and we've been walking through his old stomping grounds since. It's actually pretty dang close to perfect.

"What made growing up here special?" I ask as the two of us approach an empty playground.

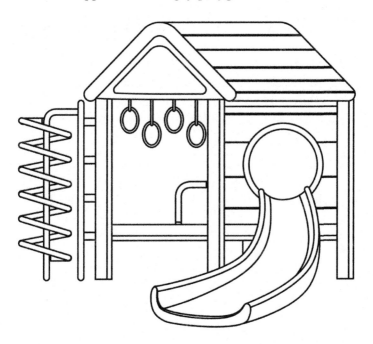

"I don't know. Maybe it was the normality of living here. Tyler broke his arm over there on the baseball field when he was five, and Byron and I got into a fight with a couple of older kids over a girl Byron had kissed behind those bleachers," he says, pointing to a set of bleachers that appear to be in pretty good shape. I bet he gave the money to keep this neighborhood looking so beautiful and quaint. He won't admit it if I ask.

For a man who has so much pride and likes to act like he rules the world, I'm discovering he's not who he portrays. He gives a lot, and he does it with zero fanfare.

With every bit of information I learn about him, it makes me love him more.

"Who won?" I ask as we approach a swing set.

"I'd love to say us, but we got our asses kicked," he tells me as he gets behind a swing and motions for me to sit.

"What are we doing?" I ask, looking pointedly at the swing.

"I'm giving you a date," he says.

My eyebrows raise. "This is a date?"

"Yep." He pats the seat of the swing.

"Whose idea was this?" I move forward and sit.

He grips the sides of the swing, and I'm being pulled backward before he releases me. My legs automatically go out and then tuck in as I return back to him. The feel of his hands against my lower back as he pushes me to fly forward again, sends a surge of awareness through me.

"I'm not divulging my secrets," he says.

And then, miracle of all miracles, I relax as I go higher and higher with each push Blake gives. Soon, I'm giggling like a young girl on a playground — exactly how I feel . . . and, well, exactly where I am.

After several minutes, he stops pushing, and I come to a stop in front of him. Turning, I barely see him under the dim lights, but I can't miss the smile on his face. My how it changes him to see him looking this carefree. He's always gorgeous, but in the moonlight with no stress marring his features, he's spectacular.

"I can't remember the last time I've had so much fun," I admit.

"Then the date's a success so far," he tells me before he comes around the front of me and pulls me from the swing and straight into his arms.

"The date's most certainly a success," I breathlessly reply. Bending down, he runs his lips across mine before drawing back.

"I want you right now," he says in a growl that sits low in my stomach.

"I *always* want you, Blake."

I wish I could see his eyes better, but rays of light from the moon have begun, and the lighting around the playground is inefficient at best.

"Come on," he tells me.

But he doesn't drag me to the nearest cave to have his wicked way with me. We fill the next half hour with our laughter as we move through the growing shadows of the park, swinging across the monkey bars, trying out the teeter-totter, and taking a turn on the merry-go-round. Blake nearly flies off it when he puts out his leg to spin us faster.

"I might need to have one of these installed in the backyard. I see definite possibilities," Blake tells me when the spinning stops, and I lie back on it. He leans over me, and my laughter dies as passion quickly takes its place.

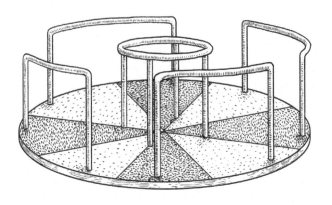

"Hmm, we might be a little too old for playground equipment," I tell him, but a few ideas of my own pop up in my mind.

"We're only as old as we allow ourselves to be, Jewel."

I don't get a chance to reply, because he's covering my mouth, and this time the kiss isn't nearly as gentle, and with the hardness of his desire pressed against my core, I begin to seriously think about adult playtime.

Minutes pass and I'm ready for Blake to take me right here on the playground when we hear voices closing in on us. Blake lifts his head and groans in frustration. Then he sits up and helps me to my feet.

"Let's go home." I smile in anticipation as the two of us run from the park. Even in our haste, we still don't make it home for quite some time as we get lost in each other's arms on an old road in the front seat of his car. I'll never get enough of his touch, and I'm truly accepting this now, and even more scary, I'm getting used to it.

Chapter Review

Jewel

TYLER AND BYRON LOOK at Blake and me with differing expressions. I shift nervously on my feet, glance up at Byron's black eyes, then down at the floor. I always thought Blake was intimidating. Well, Blake seems to have nothing on his little brother. Byron's downright terrifying.

When I manage to lift my gaze, Tyler beams at me, and before I can think of stopping him, he rushes over, takes me from Blake's arms, and wraps me in his. "Congratulations, Jewel. I'm delighted to welcome you to our family," he says. He bends down and gives me a loud, smacking kiss . . . right on the lips.

"Okay, that's enough," Blake grumbles as he pulls me away from his overly enthusiastic brother.

"Aw, come on, Blake. She isn't married yet," Tyler says with a laugh, and I have to cover my smile when I see Blake's eyelid twitch. This is the first warning he might blow.

I gently rub his arm, and Blake turns his look from his brother to me, and I watch a miracle happen — his shoulders relax and the sparkle returns to his eyes.

"Sorry, Jewel. I know Tyler's doing this to get a reaction from me, but when I think of another man touching you . . ." With a rueful smile, he brushes his lips lightly against mine.

"I'm going to tell you one of *my* secrets," I quietly say, and he leans closer. "I love that you're possessive. Just don't be ridiculously so," I add, and give him a kiss. There's protective, and then there's psycho. I don't want Blake to cross over the line into boiling bunnies on my kitchen stove.

There's protective, and then there's psycho.

"I knew this was going to happen pretty much from the beginning. Blake's been a mess ever since meeting you," Tyler says.

Blake stiffens. "I'm not a mess, Tyler, and never have been," he indignantly says.

"Sure, brother," Tyler tells him. "It's okay; really it is. Even the biggest asses hit the ground eventually. The harder they come . . ."

"I don't see that it's funny to mock a man who's under the thumb of a woman," Byron says. Then he turns his eyes on me, and I certainly feel singed.

"Back off, Byron," Blake warns his brother. "This isn't about you."

"It sure as hell is about me. Anything to do with our family is about *all* of us," Byron says. I watch as both brothers' shoulders stiffen, knowing this could turn ugly fast.

"Oh, come on, guys. This is a special occasion," Tyler says, and I notice how he moves just the slightest bit, to put himself between his two brothers.

Is fighting such a normal thing in this family? Does Tyler often break it up? I'm too horrified to say a word as the tension continues to mount despite the youngest brother's attempt at intervention.

"And when is the happy day?" Byron's practically sneering when he throws out this question.

I really wish I wasn't standing here right now — it seems the fireworks are about to explode. But Blake's arm is wrapped around me, and I have no choice but to witness the explosion when Blake answers Byron's question.

"Tomorrow," Blake says.

"Tomorrow?" Byron practically thunders.

"Do you have a problem with my wedding date?" Blake curtly asks.

442

"Why in the hell are you rushing this?"

"I don't see why that's any of your business."

"It's my business," Byron tells him, "because I don't understand why you're allowing yourself to be snatched up by some woman who's obviously out to get whatever she can from you."

My mouth drops when Blake releases me so fast I nearly trip, then I'm watching his fist come up and knock Byron in the side of his jaw. I have no idea what to do. I'm sure Byron will retaliate.

Instead, after turning his head and spitting out a bit of blood, Byron looks straight at his brother, who's staring daggers at him. "I'll let that one pass, Blake, since you're obviously screwed in the head right now."

"Who in the hell do you think you are?" Blake shouts.

"I'm your freaking brother, and I've been with you through thick and thin. I'm also the one you'd normally listen to. Don't you realize that this woman has you so messed up that you're choosing to please her even if it upsets the balance of our family?"

"Look, guys, emotions are running high right now," Tyler interjects, "but we really don't want to say something that can't be taken back."

"I don't regret anything I'm saying," Byron shouts.

"No, because you're a complete asshole, Byron," Blake tells him. "Jewel *will* become my wife tomorrow, and I'd like to have you there, but if you can't come, I understand." And he finally takes a step back. This allows me to gulp in a breath of air. It looks like the fight might be over.

"I'll be there, Blake, not because I support this marriage, but because you're going to need me when you realize what a monumental mistake you've made," Byron says as he looks at me and pierces me with his brutal gaze.

"I'm sorry you're so bitter," I tell him before he can speak. "But you're wrong, Byron. I don't want to take anything from your brother."

"Ha. A woman always has a plan," Byron replies, dismissing my words as easily as he's dismissing me.

"I won't have you here if you can't treat Jewel with respect," Blake warns.

"I won't say another word to her," Byron says. "No problem."

He might not be saying another word to me, but I can feel his animosity; the very air around us is thick with it. I suspect Byron and I will never be friends, not because I believe he's evil — though he shows signs of being pretty dang close — but because Byron doesn't seem to allow anyone to get close to him. I feel sad for him. What a lonely, thankless life he must lead.

"Well, we got that out of the way, so why don't we celebrate with a nice dinner?" Tyler says a little too eagerly.

"That sounds good, Tyler," Blake tells him.

I'm more than happy when we leave the park in front of the office building, where Blake decided to inform his brothers about tomorrow's wedding. It isn't going to be a fancy wedding. It isn't about love, after all. But still, he managed to arrange a simple ceremony at our house. Well, at *his* house. I don't know whether I'll ever consider it mine.

For the past couple of weeks, the two of us have gotten along. Blake went from demanding and arrogant to more considerate and asking my opinion. Well, everywhere except for the bedroom. There, he's insatiable and very, *very* demanding. And I love it.

His business deal has to be going well, because he's happier than I've ever seen him. I just wish he was happy for a different reason. We don't speak of love, and I'm not under the illusion that we're marrying because of the sloppy emotion. That kind of sucks, because somehow in the midst of all of this, I've fallen in love with him.

I can't pinpoint the moment it began. Maybe it's like those survivor stories where two people under extreme circumstances fall in love with each other. *The Stockholm syndrome, perhaps?* I think with a grim chuckle. Maybe it's because I'm dependent on him. Whatever the reason, I'm simultaneously excited about my marriage to him . . . *and* dreading it.

This is a fairy tale, but a fractured one. I'm not a princess, and Blake most certainly is *not* Prince Charming. This long, strange dream seems almost certain to end in a rude awakening. But we're here for now, and I don't want to run away.

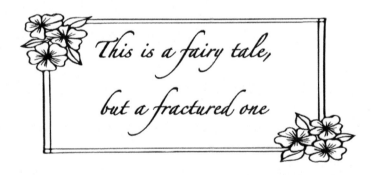

This is a fairy tale, but a fractured one

Byron backs down a little during the dinner, and later in the night the brothers take Blake with them for an impromptu bachelor party. I'm restless, tossing and turning for hours in my lonely bed with him gone.

Isn't the night before a woman's wedding day supposed to be filled with dreams of happily-ever-afters? Not for me. Haven't I decided long ago that I'm not one of those people who are destined to win a perfect life? Still, I'm luckier than most, I remind myself.

I have my brother, and I have Blake — and that's all I need.

Chapter Review

Jewel

YOU DO REALIZE IF you don't breathe, you're going to pass out, don't you?"

I meet McKenzie's gaze in the mirror and attempt a smile, but no power is strong enough to accomplish that. My stomach's nervous, my eyes almost wild. My body feels like it doesn't belong to me.

"What if I'm making the biggest mistake of my life?" I ask.

McKenzie kneels down by me and grabs my chair. "Jewel, I've made many mistakes in my lifetime, so trust me when I tell you this isn't a mistake." She surprises me by leaning in and giving me a hug.

McKenzie looks so much softer in her light blue chiffon dress that brushes the top of her knees in the front and flows down in the back. Her makeup is minimal — she possesses an amazing natural beauty — and her hair's up in a stylish bun with a few strands falling around her face in a lovely frame.

"You've been good to me these last few months, McKenzie. I don't know how I can ever repay you," I say, feeling tears trying to break through.

"I like you, Jewel. I didn't expect to find friendship with you, but I *genuinely* like you," McKenzie tells me.

"I like you too, McKenzie. And maybe someday you'll tell me your story. You know mine, after all."

McKenzie doesn't retreat into silence the way I expect her to. "I might just do that, Jewel," she says. "But right now it's *your* wedding day, and you have an anxious groom waiting out there."

"I don't think he's anxious, McKenzie. Remember, this is a business deal," I say with more sadness than I care to admit. "So I can have Justin."

"You can say anything you want to make yourself feel better, but I know that look in a woman's eyes. You love him, Jewel."

"I . . . I'm doing this for Justin," I insist, though the words nearly get trapped in my throat.

"You've done a lot for your brother," McKenzie says, and then something in her eyes alerts me to the depths of pain this woman has borne for some unknown reason. "Just remember not to lose yourself," she adds. "Enough of this, though. Let's focus on what matters today — your wedding."

"If you need to talk, I'm always here."

"I realize that," McKenzie tells me with a shaky smile. "Now keep still. We need to get this veil on you and march you down the aisle. The groom will start manhandling people if you don't get out there on time."

If only that were true. But this is a business deal no matter what McKenzie says. My feelings for Blake don't matter. This isn't about me, or about Blake for that matter. It's about my little brother, and doing everything I can for him.

It's absurd to want more. I'm getting a second chance at life, and if I ask for too much, I'm setting myself up for heartbreak. I have Justin, an incredible sex life with Blake, and security. That's more than most people have, so I'm damn well going to smile and appreciate my blessings instead of focusing on what I lack.

My veil in place, I look at my image in the mirror. My gown is simple, made of white chiffon that flows to the ground, with delicate beadwork on the bodice and sleeves that billow until they reach my wrists. The dress is molded to my torso and floats around my legs, making me feel like I'm walking through a breeze.

Even my jewel-encrusted shoes sparkle as my toes peek out with each step I take. I look like a happy bride. I'm surprised by how quickly the wedding came together. I expected nothing more than a quick exchange of vows in front of the justice of the peace at the county courthouse. This is better.

We're about to wed in the backyard of our home, and every time I sit out on the deck, I'll be able to remember this day. And when the marriage ends, as it inevitably will, I'll leave this home behind and, if I'm lucky, leave the memories behind too.

"You look stunning," McKenzie says as she stands beside me. "Blake's a very lucky man."

"Sissy, are you ready?"

Justin is standing in the doorway. He's so grown up at only ten, looking more handsome than ever in his little black tux, his hair combed into place, and no dirt smudges on his cheeks.

"Oh, Justin, you look so handsome," I say as I bend down and hold out my arms.

He doesn't hesitate to run over and hug me as hard as I hug him. "I love you so much," I tell him, squeezing a little too tight, not caring if it musses my dress.

"I love you too, Sissy," he responds before he backs away as he pulls himself together. I take my brother's hand, and we follow McKenzie to the back doors of the house, where I hear music begin.

"I'm so glad you're walking with me," I tell Justin, "because from here on out everything we do will be together."

"I love Blake, Sissy," he says, his eyes shining up at me.

"I know you do, Bubby. He loves you too."

We stop talking as the two of us proceed through the doors and begin the short walk down the red-carpeted path to the stage. When I look up, my gaze meets Blake's and I stop for a moment, my heart racing at the expression in his eyes.

For one moment, I let go of all of my worries, of all of the pain I've been through, and I let go of my doubts.

I imagine this is all real, and I'm walking down the aisle toward a man I can't live without, and who can't live without me. My lips lift, and my smile grows when I see the possessiveness in his eyes. His look is all for me. It's just the two of us, and everyone else fades away.

His look is all for me

Bright red and orange splashes across the sky as the sun slowly sinks over the horizon, and with the music playing, no scene could be more perfect. Only a few people are here to witness our marriage, just the way I want it.

Standing next to Blake is Tyler, and, surprisingly, Byron. Though Byron doesn't support our marriage, he does support his brother; the man isn't as hard as he wants everyone to think he is. There's hope for him yet.

I arrive at the altar, and Justin takes his role very seriously as he hands me over to Blake then moves to stand beside him, beside the man who will raise him — at least for as long as Blake wants to remain a part of our lives. I only have McKenzie next to me, and that's fine. She's become a true friend.

The ceremony starts without fuss, and Blake and I repeat the pastor's words, but if someone quizzes me later on what was said, I'll fail miserably. All I can do is repeat what I'm supposed to as I gaze into Blake's eyes. He looks back at me with an intensity that puzzles me.

Yes, McKenzie's right. I'm completely in love with Blake — a man I never should've fallen in love with. And I no longer care about my weakness. A person can choose the people to be friends with, but can't choose the one their heart decides to let in.

> A person can choose the people to be friends with, but can't choose the one their heart decides to let in

"I now pronounce you husband and wife. You may kiss the bride."

Air sweeps from my lungs as Blake pulls me into his arms and takes my mouth in a kiss that seals us as one. I melt against him, in a daze when he pulls back, and look at the sparkle in his eyes.

"Now you're forever mine, Jewel," he whispers for only me to hear.

"I've been yours from the day we met," I reply, making his lips turn up.

"We're a family now," Blake tells me, and he holds out his free arm to Justin, who steps up and throws his arms around his new uncle ... or brother ... or whatever we all are now.

"Yes, we are," I say as tears flow down my cheeks. As the three of us walk down the aisle, my heart's overflowing with joy. My only hope is that this joy will pass the test of time. It started so rocky. Can we have a happily ever after? A glimmer of hope tells me we might possibly be able to have just that.

Chapter Review

Blake

HOW LONG CAN IT possibly take someone to change clothes?" I slam down a shot of bourbon and glare at my brothers. I want to be alone with my new bride. Patience is certainly not one of my virtues. Tyler laughs and Byron scoffs as we stand at the bar and gaze at the lights hanging from the trees.

"You know women, Blake. They have to be perfect before we're allowed to see them," Tyler says.

Byron downs his shot. "Or they like to play games and see how antsy they can make us," Byron adds as he sends a glare toward McKenzie, who's dancing with Justin. What in the hell is going on with this? For a man who hates women as much as he does, he sure seems interested in McKenzie all of a sudden. I wouldn't bet on my brother when it comes to this intelligent woman I've worked with for a long time. She has more bite than he can handle. It will be amusing if he pursues her, though.

She has
more bite than
he can handle

"You seem to be staring at Ms. Beaumont quite a bit," Tyler says, and he punches Byron in the arm.

"What in the hell are you talking about?" Byron snaps.

"I just call it as I see it," Tyler says with a wink and a shrug.

"I was preoccupied today, to say the least, and even *I* noticed your obsession with the woman," I say with the first smile I've displayed since Jewel left the room.

"You can both go to hell. I think I'm going to have a talk with Ms. Beaumont," Byron says, and he storms off.

Tyler watches McKenzie tense when Byron walks up to her. "Should we protect her?"

"Hell, I think we should protect Byron," I reply. "McKenzie's one tough woman."

"You may be right," Tyler says with a chuckle as we watch McKenzie shove Byron away and storm off. "Quite impressive she can stomp off with such elegance, *and* while wearing those stilt-like heels."

The temporary distraction helps, but as soon as the conversation dies down, I'm once again eager and anxious to see my new bride. She looked beyond beautiful in her wedding gown, and as she'd glided toward me earlier, it had taken all of my finely-honed willpower to remain standing. I was sorely tempted to rush to her side and sweep her into my arms, and my heart hasn't slowed its beat since.

She's mine, more than I'm admitting. She means more to me than I'll tell anyone. I vowed for so long to not fall for a woman that I'm not dealing with this well . . . not at all. I'm starting to accept my feelings though, accepting this isn't temporary. She's not like my mother. The sooner I come to terms with that, the better off we'll be.

"I'm done here," I say.

Tyler blinks in confusion. "Huh, what?"

"I want to be with my bride."

And that's the end of our conversation. I walk away from Tyler, knowing my brother. Justin's going to stay at McKenzie's house for the night, and everything else is taken care of. Jewel and I will have the entire night to ourselves without the world interrupting. We need this . . . I *need* this.

Something about this woman makes me feel like a caged animal who's finally set free. I spent the better part of my life as a shell of a man, not feeling the colors of life, instead living in black and white. Jewel makes me feel and do things I've never wanted to feel or do before. She makes me see all of the colors. And I sort of like being out of control, sometimes powerless because of her.

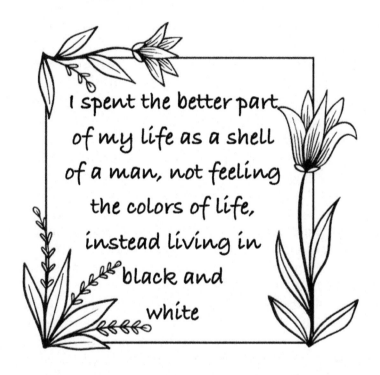

I spent the better part of my life as a shell of a man, not feeling the colors of life, instead living in black and white

I bound up the stairs three at a time, but pause at our bedroom door and take a deep breath. I don't want to frighten her with my impatience. This night is ours together — for once it isn't all about me.

When I push the door open, my heart nearly stops when I see Jewel lying on our bed in a silk nightgown. The sound of the door makes her jump, then our eyes meet, and my heart hammers out of control again.

"I was wondering when you'd get here," she says, looking . . . hell, looking almost shy.

"You take my breath away, Jewel." I stride to the bed and drop to my knees, my desire to worship her overpowering.

She sits up with her legs dangling off the bed, reaches for me, and her fingers sift through my hair. "I was going to say the same about you," she softly replies. Something's different in her eyes as if maybe, just maybe, this marriage means something more to her as well.

I can't move for a few seconds. The urge to rip her nightie from her body and plunge inside her is so potent I'm afraid I might turn into a complete animal if I don't get myself under control.

We've made love frantically many times over. Tonight's about a perfect union, binding us together, joining us in a way that will ensure we never part again. I don't want to ruin this moment for either of us.

Instead of shedding our clothes, I tug on her legs to bring her to the edge of the bed and rest my head on her bare thigh, inhaling her perfume as I gently caress her. I savor this moment, and then turn my head and swirl my tongue across her smooth, sweet skin.

A shudder passes through her, and I continue chanting to myself: *go slow; remain calm.* It isn't an easy task when such a delectable treat is right in front of me. "Jewel, you make me come unglued," I whisper before standing up and backing away.

Jewel whimpers when I break contact, and the sound goes straight to my gut. I gently push her up the bed and crawl over her, poised above as she lies beneath me, her chest heaving, her eyes burning.

I tenderly take her lips, caressing them, tasting them, glorying in their softness. "So beautiful," I murmur as I

460

trail my lips down her throat, grasp the strap on her nightgown with my teeth, and pull it down her arm.

Once the gown is removed, leaving her bare before me, I behold her body. "No matter how many times I see you like this, I'm still awed."

She reaches for me, a moan escaping her beautiful lips as she pulls me back, cradling my clothed body with her naked one. Time disappears as I roll with her on the bed, kissing her, touching her, worshipping her.

When I finally stand to remove my clothes, my fingers are shaking. I tell myself it's because I'm so incredibly turned on, but this takes me to a whole new place — a place I never want to leave.

Shedding my clothes in record time, I rejoin her on the bed and sigh at the perfection of our bodies pressing together with no barriers. I kiss every inch of her beautiful skin, then I'm poised above her, but I stop before I enter her.

"Every time I look at you like this, my beautiful Jewel, I can't believe I'm the one who gets to be with you."

Her eyes widen and glisten with tears. "Make love to me, Blake," she demands, bringing her hands up around me and pulling me closer. I surrender to her and sink between her trembling thighs, submerging myself deep within.

She clings to me as I thrust in and out, her hands guiding me, my name a continual cry from her well-kissed lips. And I become lost in her arms, hoping never to be found again as I make love to her — and it *is* love — slowly, tenderly, and with a passion I could never come close to feeling with any other woman.

I become lost in her arms, hoping never to be found again

Looking into her eyes, I move in perfect sync with her, and when her thighs tighten around my waist, her pleasure explodes around me while I follow into the sweet abyss.

"Mine, Jewel — you're mine forever," I tell her as my body rests against hers, and she caresses the heated skin of my back.

"I'm yours right now, Blake."

That isn't good enough. No words can possibly convey what I'm feeling in this moment. It's possession, it's passion, but it's so much more than that. I never was good at expressing the way I feel in words, so I decide to show her in all possible ways that she belongs to me . . . and I belong to her.

When I know my weight is too much for her to bear any longer, I shift our position so she's lying on top of me, still connected, our heartbeats syncing in rhythm with each other. As I cradle her head against my chest, I can't imagine a more perfect wedding night with the wife I chose.

We don't sleep at all. We make love and speak of the future. I give her my heart, something I've never given to anyone else. I might not be able to say the words, but I show her in the only way I know how, with every caress, every kiss, and every murmur from my lips. Time, we only need more time, then I can give her everything.

Chapter Review

Jewel

S TRETCHING OUT MY ARMS, I'm surprised to find the bed cold. I slowly open my eyes and smile when I see a rose and a note on the pillow where Blake's head should be.

> *Good morning, beautiful. I got called into the office to deal with an emergency. I'll be home in plenty of time for our date.*
> *Love,*
> *Your husband.*

We've been man and wife for a month now. Thirty wonderful days and thirty even better nights. No matter how many times we make love, I can never get enough of Blake, a man who suddenly entered and took over my life.

He's so different from the man I met months ago, but I still see traces of the person I made the original deal with, especially when we're in the bedroom. The man's insatiable, but since being with him, I've discovered I am too.

No matter how many times I lie in his arms, and no matter how many ways we make love, each and every time is as exciting as the last. It's the one place Blake lets down his guard.

He's incredibly good to me, and he's even better with Justin, but parts of him are still held back, pieces of his soul he refuses to share. Maybe because he doesn't fully trust me, or he isn't capable of loving another human after what he went through with his parents.

Either way, I'm blissfully happy but, at the same time, almost unbearably sad. I'm in love with Blake, in love with this hard man who has such a beautiful soft side, a *hidden* soft side, and the thing that frightens me the most is realizing that he might never be able to return my feelings.

I try not to think about it too much, because if I do, I might not be able to honor our wedding vows into eternity. And that's what I want more than anything else. I desperately want to speak to Blake about having children, but he never mentions if he's at all interested in becoming a father. Instead, when the subject of fathers and fatherhood comes up, a shutter closes over his eyes, and he changes the conversation.

He's so good with Justin, but Justin is ten, almost eleven. Many men, and many women for that matter, don't want to have their own families, but I'm not one of them. Love and children have never been a condition of my marriage to Blake, and possibly never will be. This doesn't alter my love for my husband, though.

As hard as I try not to let the doubt creep into my thoughts of happiness, I can't help but worry. I want a family, a *real* family, one in which everyone loves each other equally. I want babies I can watch grow, and I want Blake's brothers to be our children's uncles in every sense of the word. I want noisy holiday dinners and lazy summer days at the lake. I want it all. Is that too much to ask for?

For a month, I pushed aside my worries and tried instead to focus on the good. But recently, even when asleep in his arms, I feel pain, my dreams filled with visions of Blake running off with someone else, abandoning Justin and me, and starting a new life with a woman he can love.

"Good morning, Jewel."

I startle when I step into the kitchen and see McKenzie sitting at the table, clutching some papers in her hands and looking forlorn. She waits for me to pour a cup of coffee so I can have a proper conversation. It's not looking like it will be pleasant.

"Hi, McKenzie. I normally love to see you, but when you're wearing that expression before I've had coffee, I tend to worry," I say with a brittle laugh before I sit down, gripping my cup tightly.

I don't ask how she got into the house, but McKenzie shares anyway. "Elsa let me in an hour ago. I've been waiting for you to wake."

"I love the days Elsa works," I say. "Breakfast is so much better than the bowl of cereal I usually grab out of haste and laziness." But why are we making small talk, I wonder, when it's more than obvious that McKenzie has something important to say?

"I . . . I don't know how to talk to you about this, Jewel," she says, pausing and starting again as she looks down at the table. "I . . . crap, this is complicated." This is a first. McKenzie's never been afraid to meet my eyes.

"You know what they say about bad news, McKenzie — it's better to spit it out and get it over with," I tell her while gulping down coffee. From the way McKenzie's acting, I have a feeling I'm going to need a lot more to get through whatever this is.

"Jewel, you know I care about you, don't you?" McKenzie begins, and my stomach clenches.

"Blake wants a divorce, right?" I say, a false bravery in my tone.

"No, nothing like that," McKenzie assures me.

"I'm not a fool, McKenzie. I've known all along this isn't going to last forever. And you've been honest with me so far. That's not always pleasant, but I know I can count on you to tell me the truth."

"I promise you, Jewel, it's not that," McKenzie says again.

"Please just tell me, McKenzie. Your hemming and hawing around is only making whatever this is, worse." I get a second cup of coffee for myself and refill McKenzie's cup as well.

Maybe the nightmares I'm having are coming true. Maybe a person like me isn't allowed to be too happy. I know Blake has been holding something back from me, so having McKenzie confirm my suspicions shouldn't be so devastating, but as I wait for her to speak, I can't breathe. No matter which way this goes, I'm going to suffer.

"It's not about Blake wanting to leave you. That's the last thing he'll want to do. It's just that . . ." McKenzie stops and looks at her hands again before she looks back up, sympathy in her eyes. "It's time I tell you the truth . . . he . . . uh . . . he did something you won't like . . ."

Chapter Review

Jewel

I BLINDLY WALK ALONG the sidewalk, tears streaming down my cheeks. McKenzie had apologized profusely for not telling me sooner, then apologized again for telling me now. She told me it might be better not to know the truth. She told me it really doesn't matter. But it does matter . . . It matters a lot.

It's about my brother — my brother and Blake. Now I know why he waited a month to come back to me. He planned on getting me one way or the other . . . and he wasn't going to stop until he got what he wanted. Why, though? Why me? Does he have to possess me no matter what it takes, by any means necessary, fair or unfair?

He went behind my back . . . and he's now Justin's legal . . . what? Legal father? He officially adopted him. He lied to me. I thought I still had a chance of gaining full control of my brother. But Blake used Justin so he could own me . . . and now I've lost my little brother to the man I can no longer give the benefit of the doubt to. This is my breaking point.

Has his deceit only been about great sex? Does he really want to possess me so badly that he's willing to take away anything that matters to me in order to keep me? Doesn't he know that all he had to do was offer me his love instead, and I'd be willing to stay forever?

Because Blake is Justin's adoptive father, he's the one with all the power. I have none. Even though Justin's my brother, even though I love him more than any other person, I've lost all rights to him. The hardest part is knowing that Justin will live a much better life with Blake than with me. Blake can give him the world . . . and I can barely give him a roof over his head.

How have I been foolish enough to fall in love with Blake? I never really knew the man at all. Was anything he told me true? I doubt it. I don't know anything anymore — except that I'm lost and feel more alone than ever before.

I've lost my brother, and it appears as if I've lost Blake too. I've lost him because this proves he'll always do whatever it takes to win no matter who he hurts. Except that he's never really been mine, so how can I lose what I never had?

He's never really been mine, so how can I lose what I never had?

I was his from almost the first day. Despair flows through me, and as I make my way back to the house I share with Blake and Justin, I have no idea what I'm going to do next.

I've been fighting for so long, but in the end, I have nothing to show for this fight. I can't stay with Blake. It will kill me. When I arrive at Blake's house — I no longer feel that it's mine — I open the door and look inside. None of this is mine. I didn't pick the house, didn't buy the furniture, and I didn't make it a home. No, I'm nothing more than a guest here.

When Blake comes around the corner, he has a smile on his lips, but it quickly vanishes when he sees my expression. I decide to push against my heartache and face him. There's no point in dragging this out, in prolonging my agony. Neither one of us need an emotional meltdown.

"I was worried when I came home and you weren't here," he says as he wraps his arms around me and bends down to kiss me. When I don't respond, he draws back, worry etched on his brow. He's a fantastic actor.

I haven't rehearsed what I'm going to say, so when the words come out, I'm as surprised as he is. "Why didn't you tell me?" My voice is flat and distant. I watch his eyes as I say the words.

Something flashes in his gaze that tells me he knows exactly what I'm talking about. His confusion turns to realization . . . and then pride. And now, I know our marriage, which barely began, is over. I can't believe my pain can get worse. It's worse. I refuse to respond to my hurt though.

My brother legally belongs with him. No one can love Justin more than I do, but that doesn't matter. I fought the courts . . . and I lost. The system just doesn't care. Blake's the one with money, and therefore he has all of the power, and he can provide a better life for Justin than I can. It's very black and white, isn't it?

I need to escape before I fall apart. I can't do anything that will prevent me from getting visitation with my brother. I'll have to go through Blake from here on out, and I'm not sure he'll have mercy on me once I walk away from him. I thought I could do anything to keep Justin, but I have a breaking point. I can't kill myself, and staying with a man who can't love me will slowly kill me. I thought I could do it . . . I was wrong.

"Jewel, we need to talk. Let's go into the living room and I'll explain," Blake says, reaching for me. He stops when I flinch. I can't tolerate his touch right now.

"There's nothing to say, Blake. You knew the only thing I cared about in this world was getting my brother, so you swooped in and stole him from me — you did what you've done your entire life, took something that doesn't belong to you in order to win a game only you knew you were playing. You might be able to give him a more financially stable life than I can, but that doesn't make you a better parent. And it definitely doesn't make you a better person." I almost choke on these last words, having to stop for a moment and gain my composure.

"Things have changed Jewel . . ." He breaks off when I hold up my hand. I can't hear this, can't tolerate his lies. If he truly felt things have changed, he wouldn't still be lying, letting someone else tell me what he's doing to undermine me.

"It's over, Blake. You won my brother, but you don't get to win me."

I turn and walk out of the house. Nothing in it is mine — absolutely nothing. I don't know what I'm going to tell Justin, don't know how to explain any of this to him, but right now I'm not capable of telling him anything without falling apart.

My world has once again been flipped upside down . . . and again, I have zero solutions for how to fix it.

Chapter Review

Blake

D AMN!" TYLER SAYS, sitting back with a stunned look on his face. "You continually decide to screw up your life, don't you?"

"You're a moron, Blake. This is low, even for you . . ." Byron adds.

"I didn't tell you because . . . hell, even while I was doing it, I knew it was wrong. I started the process because I was pissed . . . then I continued because I wanted Jewel to stay. I *needed* a reason for her to stay."

I've never done something this big without speaking to my brothers. We don't get sentimental very often, but we discuss everything in business and our personal lives, and this is certainly something I should've shared with them.

Jewel has been gone for three days, and she refuses to talk to me. She calls and talks to Justin, and spends a couple of hours with him every day when she knows I'm not home, and her brother's none the wiser about what's going on. But we won't be able to keep it from him much longer. Justin's wondering why Jewel isn't home in the morning. They've been apart for too long already. I've told him she's working a lot. It seems Jewel might be right . . . I'm lying to everyone I care about to make it easier on myself.

"Maybe she's relieved," I tell my brothers. "She's felt so much pressure to take care of Justin, and maybe now that she knows his future is assured, she's ecstatic and wants to be free of the obligation." I just admitted my biggest fear.

"Probably," Byron grumbles, but even he doesn't look convinced.

"I don't think so," Tyler says. "She loves you, Blake, and she loves Justin. There's no way she'd walk away unless she thought there was no other choice."

"I don't know what else to think," I say with a heavy sigh.

Tyler starts to fire off questions. "What exactly did she say? How did she act? What have you done lately? Think deeper."

"What do you want me to say?" I thunder. "This isn't helping."

"There has to be more to this than finding out you stole her brother out from under her — though that's a big deal," Tyler says. "But if you're man and wife, it doesn't matter. Because even if you legally adopted him, he's still hers too. I've seen the way Jewel looks at you, and looks at her brother. She loves you both immeasurably. For her to walk away, there has to be something else going on."

"Maybe you broke her," Byron says with a sneer.

I stop and stare at my brother. "What?"

"Oh, hell, Blake, don't get melodramatic on me. I was just kidding," Byron says, and he tries to look as if he doesn't care.

But I know my brother cares. This thought somehow makes me stop again. I think back to the last few months, think of all of my times with Jewel, the good and the bad, the laughter and the tears, the desperation, and the peace.

"She does know that you love her, right?" Tyler asks.

"Of course she knows," I say, but the wheels of my brain start spinning faster.

Tyler pushes. "Because you've told her?"

I pause as I think back on our time together. Have I actually told her I love her? Of course I have. But as I wrack my mind, I can't think of a single instance I've actually said so. Crap!

"Not with words," I finally reply.

"You guys are ridiculous!" Byron thunders. "Are you listening to what you're saying? Do you want to be just like our father?"

Byron stands up, his chair flying out behind him, and both Tyler and I watch as he storms from the room. We sit for a few moments in stunned silence before Tyler speaks again.

"Don't let this woman get away from you, Blake, or you'll go back to feeling and acting like that," he says as he points toward the door.

"Byron's fine," I say. But I can't deny the words. I'm not at all like my father, but I *had* been like my brother, and not too long ago — not trusting anyone, lying as easily as I speak the truth, and treating women as nothing more than play toys whose only purpose in life is to please me. I don't want to be that man anymore. I want to be the man in love with Jewel. I *am* the man in love with Jewel.

"I haven't said the words, Tyler, but she has to know how much I love her."

"How can she know if you haven't told her?" Tyler asks.

"Because I show her every single day. We make love and it's burning in my eyes. We snuggle on the couch, and I *have* to touch her. With everything I do, every hour of every single day, I have her in mind. She's my world, she and Justin both, and I can't imagine living without them now. Is that romantic enough for you? Sensitive enough, little bro?"

"Why are you telling *me* this, and not *her*?" Tyler asks.

"I . . . I don't know." Am I the biggest of fools? It feels like it.

"Look, she's had a rough year, Blake, and even though you were an ass, she still managed to fall for you. So you get this great woman, and she has a brother she adores, a boy you've grown to love as well, and now you get him too, and then you don't tell her you've adopted him, *and* you don't tell her how much you love her. What do you think she's thinking right now?"

"I don't know!" I shout.

"She thinks she's disposable."

"How can she possibly think that?"

"If you ever figure out how a woman's mind works, please enlighten us all," Tyler says, attempting a joke. I'm not in the mood.

"I won't lose her, Tyler. I can't!"

"Then go and fight for her."

"How can I fight for her if she won't talk to me?" I ask, furious that I sound so weak right now.

"You have to prove to her that you love her," Tyler says. "And, Blake, it won't be easy, because now she has walls in place. So you'd better have one hell of a plan before you storm the fortress."

When I leave the office building, I have no idea what I'm going to do. But I plan to figure it out before I go after Jewel. I was foolish during our entire relationship. I'm done with being that thoughtless man. I'm going to be the person Jewel deserves.

If you ever figure out how a woman's mind works, please enlighten us all

Chapter Review

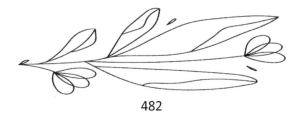

Blake

"BREATHE."

I stand outside Jewel's door and wonder how long I'll have to wait. I've knocked three times already and there's still no answer. I'll stay here all night if I have to.

Finally, the door opens, and she's standing before me. I inhale deeply when I see the way she looks, and guilt consumes me. I'm to blame for the circles beneath her puffy eyes, and for her ashen cheeks.

Even though she looks as if she's lost her entire world, she's still the most beautiful woman I've ever seen. It's because I have no doubt that she loves me and will be mine forever. I won't leave until she knows I love her. Then if I must, I'll give her space. I want her to have free will.

"Do you think I married you to gain control over you?" I ask, deciding it's best to get straight to the point.

"Yes, Blake, and I don't blame you for it. It's who you are. You've never tried to hide that from me." Her voice is flat, so sad, ripping me to my very soul.

"Would you still be with me if you didn't have to be?"

This makes her pause. She looks at me for several heartbeats, all sorts of emotions rushing through her eyes, but the final one to settle in her liquid depths is deep-seated sadness.

"It doesn't matter, does it, Blake? Because you *always* had control. You always had what you wanted, even if you wanted me for all of the wrong reasons."

How can I have broken this woman so thoroughly? I really have been a monster. I don't want to let her go. But I know I have to in order for her to know she has a choice. Before I can change my mind, before I can haul her into my arms and lose all focus of what I'm doing, I pull out the documents from my attorney. She doesn't take them from me; she looks at me with a trembling lip and glassy eyes.

"I'm handing over any and all legal rights to Justin," I tell her, holding the file in front of her. "With my influence, no judge will deny you. I'll make sure of it."

She looks from the document to me and then back at the documents again. In her confusion, the tears stop, but the despair on her face doesn't in any way disappear.

"I . . . I don't understand," she finally whispers.

"Jewel, I love you. Yes, I used to want to possess you. I used to want to own you, and I wasn't above using blackmail to do it. But that changed when I fell in love with you. I didn't know how to say the words. I thought I was telling you by showing you what I felt, and that's

484

been my downfall. You mesmerized me from the first moment our eyes met, and then something changed within me, something happened I never thought possible. The walls I'd built around my heart when I was a child suddenly began to crack, and one day I realized they were no longer there. You're the reason I wake up in the morning, the reason I can't wait to come home each evening. You've given me every ounce of happiness I have. I love you, Jewel. I love you so much that I can't imagine living one more moment without you." I want desperately to take her in my arms, but I need to hold back, to let her come to me.

I love you so much that I can't imagine living one more moment without you

"But . . . but our marriage isn't real. It's a business deal . . . and for Justin," she says, looking confused.

"The business deal doesn't matter, Jewel. We both know I'm not good at expressing my feelings. I wanted to marry you before I understood that it had nothing to do with my company. Maybe at first it was because I wanted you to be mine, because I couldn't let you get away, but I quickly realized it wasn't about possession. It was because my heart belongs to you. You're my everything. I apologize for the string of clichés, but you make me feel them. You make me a better man, and I need you to continue to have faith in me so we can be a family — I mean you, me, *and* Justin. I'll do anything to prove this to you."

When she pauses for another long moment, doubt begins to creep in. What if she's had too much? What if my confession is too little, too late? I can lose both her and Justin; I can't imagine how I'll survive it.

But if she needs me to walk away, I will. For her. All for her. I'll do anything for her.

To my surprise, her lips turn up a little, and I see hope return to her eyes. And she takes one tentative step toward me, and then another, and then she's wrapping her arms around me. And I realize we're going to be okay. I don't have the foggiest idea how long the two of us stand together, but when she finally pulls back, the love shining from her sparkling eyes is unmistakable.

"You hurt me so badly," she says.

"I know, Jewel. I also know I have a long way to go before I can redeem myself in your eyes, but I want you to give me the chance to do just that."

"I don't know how we can make this better," she says.

"Come home with me. Let me prove to you that I love you — that you're so much more than a possession."

"But so much has happened . . ." She stops speaking as sobs wrack her fragile frame.

"Do you love me, Jewel?"

I wait for her answer. If I'm wrong, if she doesn't love me, nothing else matters. She takes so long to answer, I almost give up.

"I love you so much," she says, "that I've spent the last few days wondering how I'm going to survive losing you. I told myself my feelings aren't real, but that isn't the truth. To live without you would be leaving a piece of my soul behind. I love you, Blake Astor. It's never been perfect, but you rescued me from a life of misery. And somehow in the middle of all of it, I fell for you, although I believe I was a fool to do so."

To live without you would be leaving a piece of my soul behind

"Yes, you were a fool to fall for me and for believing in me, but I'm damn grateful you did." I'm lost in her arms for several moments before I draw back again and gaze at her reverently. "I can't believe what an idiot I've been. Thank you for saving me, and for saving us."

"We've both been foolish, Blake, but it doesn't matter anymore. All that matters from this point forward is that we're always honest, and we continue to love each other through the good and the bad." She brushes a kiss across my jaw.

"I promise you, Jewel, I'll do my damnedest from here on out to make you know you're loved, worshipped, and appreciated. I want to make you the happiest woman alive."

She sighs. "That's a start."

I lean down and kiss her as the clock strikes midnight. I'm never going to lose this woman again, never going to treat her with anything but the upmost respect. She's a gift and I finally appreciate what I've been given.

"Let's go home," I say to my wife. And that's just what we do. Home, a concept that's been foreign to me for most of my life, but now has meaning. We walk into our new lives arm in arm, ready for whatever the world might throw at us next.

Chapter Review

McKenzie

I FLIP MY BLANKETS OFF with an angry shove, thrust my feet into my slippers, and blindly reach for my robe. Then I stomp through my house until I reach the front door. The loud pounding continues unabated. It's what woke me, and put me in my rotten mood.

"Go away!" I shout through the door. I don't give a damn who's making the infernal noise. It's two in the morning, and I'm not about to invite the ill-mannered person inside.

"I'm not leaving until we talk!" a man shouts right back at me. I freeze, suddenly overcome by fear. But no.

I'm McKenzie Beaumont, dammit, and I don't frighten easily.

"I'm calling the police," I say.

"Fine with me. The chief's a personal friend of mine," the man says with just enough arrogance that he might be telling the truth.

"And who are you?" I ask. Despite my bravado, the fear has returned in spades, and a shiver runs down my spine.

"Byron Astor!" he shouts back.

"Byron?" I open the small window that shows me who's standing on my doorstep. I'm shocked to see that it *is* Byron, Blake Astor's brother, standing in front of my door. "What in the world are you doing on my doorstep at this absurd hour?"

Then I start to panic. What if something happened to Blake? Or to Jewel? Without thinking, I unlock the door and thrust it open. "What's wrong? What's going on?"

Though I've only seen the man a few times, and though the only words we've spoken have been short and clipped, he moves forward, and walks inside.

"What's wrong?" I ask again.

"I have a question for you, Ms. Beaumont," he says, and that's when I smell the alcohol on his breath and notice his narrowed eyes. I never should've opened my door. I know Blake, but that doesn't mean I know this brother of his.

"Just ask your question and then get the hell out of my house," I say, thrusting my shoulders back as I get ready to do battle. I've been to hell and back more than once. There's no way this man's going to intimidate me.

"Just who do you think you are?" he menacingly asks.

"I'm sorry, Byron, but you're going to have to be a little more specific."

"You think you can mess with people's lives and get away with it. Well, I'm here to prove you wrong." I stumble back a step when he starts stalking me, and then I'm up against a wall with his arms caging me in.

"If you touch me, I'll press charges," I tell him.

"Oh, McKenzie, you'll soon learn I'm not one of the timid little men you're used to dealing with." And then he lowers his head to meet mine . . .

DOODLES

UPCOMING RELEASES

JANUARY

FEBRUARY

MARCH

APRIL

MAY

JUNE

JULY

AUGUST

SEPTEMBER

OCTOBER

NOVEMBER

DECEMBER

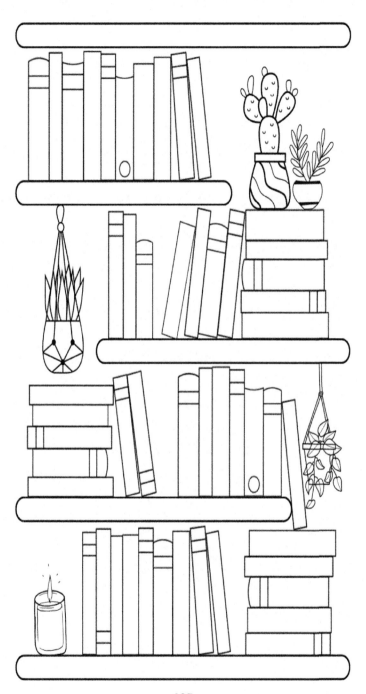

Looking for your next book?

I have series that are lighthearted,

dramatic, and in between. I have

brief comments about each of the

series listed below.

For a lighthearted feel, this series will go on and on starting with three brothers and the infamous Joseph Anderson who decides to play matchmaker. It then goes into his twin brother's children, and then they find a lost triplet that makes it super fun. Each story has a happily ever after, but characters will appear in the other stories.

The Andersons

Wins The Game

The Dance

The Fall

The Proposal

The Blackmail

The Runaway

The Final Stand

Unexpected Treasure

Hidden Treasure

Holiday Treasure

Priceless Treasure

The Ultimate Treasure

The Anderson Heirs came about, because it's time those in the stories above grow up. So these are the stories of their children all grown up and falling in love. These are all lighthearted and fun stories.

The Anderson Heirs

Book One: Sweet Noel
Book Two: Jacob's Challenge
Book Three: Jasmine's Homecoming

This series is super fun and full of action. I co-wrote it with a buddy of mine. The men in this series are based on real people he worked with while he was in the military or doing contractor work. Smoke is by far my favorite character of this series. You also see Jasmine growing up and having quite the attitude which leads to her own series listed below.

ANDERSON SPECIAL OPS

Shadows

Rising

Barriers

Shattered

Reborn

This is a spin-off branch of Andersons that are again a fun group of men in a new town. It's lighthearted and fun, and I really loved writing the series.

THE ANDERSON BILLIONAIRES

Finn

Noah

Brandon

Hudson

Crew

Now, we're coming to more of my dramatic writing. I LOVE, LOVE, LOVE this series. This story came about while I was driving with my husband to a camping spot. We were talking about what would make someone get married multiple times and we came up with this series together. I completely lived vicariously through Charlie (different from Derek and Emmy's Charlie) and all of the adventures she takes in this series. I love how it all comes around, and I personally love how it ends. The adventures she goes on in the middle, though, are so much fun. Please let me know what you think of this series because it's one of my favorites I've ever written.

TWELVE HORIZONS OF CHARLIE

Diamond

Sapphire

Opal

Emerald

This is certainly my most erotic series. But I'm well-known for my "clean" sex scenes. They are descriptive, they are sexy, and some of them are long, but I don't use crude language in my scenes. I use words like steel, core, heat. I personally get grossed out when crude words are used so I get creative in my writing. My hubby might have blushed a bit though when he read one of my books for the first time. He certainly was ready to try out some of the scenes he read. He doesn't mind helping with my research . . . not at all. I love this series, though. It's sexy, but of course it has siblings because family means the world to me, and I can't write anything without family. I love the bond between the siblings and parents. I love how sexy it is, and I love the three storylines. I hope you do as well.

SURRENDER SERIES

Surrender

Seduced

Scorched

Saved

And we're back to contemporary romance. This is another Anderson-type series with brothers and is fun and lighthearted with alpha men and sexy, confident women. Each story finishes but you'll want to read the entire series because you'll love all of the brothers.

UNDERCOVER BILLIONAIRES

Kian

Arden

Owen

Declan

This is another series I love. It's different from my other works and again co-written with my friend. This isn't romance, though there is romance in it. It's about Jasmine Anderson and the adventures she takes away from home. You'll see some of your favorite characters in it and meet some new people. This is more high adrenaline and crime fighting and it was super fun to write.

TRUTH IN LIES

One too Many
Two Secrets Kept
Three Outs
Four Seconds Gone
Five Goodbye's

I love this series because I have a total thing for pilots. There's just something hot about a man who can control a plane. I worked for the airlines for about 10 years and it was one of my favorite jobs. These are 4 brothers that are fun, sexy, and each story is unique. Ace is my fav, because he's such an ass for so long . . . but we all know how fun it is to take these kinds of men down to their knees.

BILLIONAIRE AVIATORS

Turbulent Intentions – Book One (Cooper)

Turbulent Desires – Book Two (Maverick)

Turbulent Waters – Book Three (Nick)

Turbulent Intrigue – Book Four (Ace)

I love this series too. It's again contemporary romance with alpha men and the women they think they deserve. This time it's cousins. It's one of my early series and it's lighthearted fun reading. They are certainly alpha but none of my men cross the line into irredeemable.

The Titans

The Tycoon's Revenge

The Tycoon's Vacation

The Tycoon's Proposal

The Tycoon's Secret

The Lost Tycoon

Rescue Me

This was my first series that was sold in stores and I was like a child at Christmas when I walked into the bookstore to see a book on the shelf with MY NAME on it. What a thrill for a girl who was raised in low-income housing and a single-wide trailer. I will never forget the thrill of that moment. I will never forget seeing it in People Magazine. I love this series. It's fun, lighthearted, and of course, Joseph Anderson comes and visits. If you want a great beach read, this is the series for you.

HEROES SERIES

Safe in his arms – Novella
Baby it's Cold Outside
Her Unexpected Hero – Book One
Who I am with you – Book Two – Novella
Her Hometown Hero – Book Three
Following Her – Book Four – Novella
Her Forever Hero – Book Five
Her Found Hero – Book Six

Okay, so this series came about at a romance conference where Jan, Ruth, and I were drinking WAY WAY WAY too much. We started chatting and decided billionaires were far too overdone. We were sitting there with a crew from Amazon and started talking about kings that had to kill the woman if she didn't fall in love. We thought it was hilarious. Alcohol might have fueled this. Then one of the reps said, "and then he kills her." We were drunk, but not stupid. We had to explain to the Amazon rep that we can't *actually* kill a heroine in a romance book. He told us then people will know how the story will end. By the end of the night we'd come up with Taken by the Trillionaire. We each wrote a novella, and we loved it! So we had to do a second set of princes because why the heck not? Next, we're going to have to do a third set, maybe set in America. A fun, silly night turned into some super fun stories. I love these two authors who will be lifelong friends. Here are our brilliant minds (fueled by a lot of free alcohol) in a series that will make you laugh and sigh.

TAKEN BY THE TRILLIONAIRE

#1 Xander – Ruth Cardello

#2 Bryan – J.S. Scott

#3 Chris – Melody Anne

#4 Virgin for the Trillionaire – Ruth Cardello

#5 Virgin for the Prince – J.S. Scott

#6 Virgin to Conquer – Melody Anne

Ahhh, I don't know what to say about this series. It's soul wrenching, and there were times I was writing it that I cried, laughed, yelled, and everything in between. This is my first women's fiction series. There is a romance in each book, but there's a story within too that might be hard for some to read. The first book deals with child sex trafficking. It's in no way glorified. I went through some things in my childhood, and thought it was time to write something with more depth. I hope you love the adventures these couples go through and show the world that our pasts don't define who we are today.

FIRST SERIES

He Saw Me First

She Saw Me First

At First Sight

With Lots of Love,

Melody Anne

VISIT MY WEBSITE HERE
WWW.MELODYANNE.COM

Printed in Great Britain
by Amazon

37427436R00284